Henry Chettle's Careers
A Study of an Elizabethan Printer, Pamphleteer, Playwright

Henry Chettle's Careers
A Study of an Elizabethan Printer, Pamphleteer, Playwright

Marie Honda

EIHŌSHA

Henry Chettle's Careers
A Study of an Elizabethan Printer, Pamphleteer, Playwright

First published in 2015
by EIHŌSHA
Daiichi-inokuchi Building
2-2-7 Iwamotocho, Chiyodaku, Tokyo
101-0032, Japan

Information of this title: www.eihosha.co.jp

All rights reserved
© Marie Honda 2015

Printed in Japan

Acknowledgements

I am most deeply indebted to Professor Anthony Martin of Waseda University, my supervisor and committee chair for my PhD dissertation, on which this book is based. It was he that first suggested I develop my master's thesis on Chettle into a PhD, and he has always been generous with his time. The scope of his knowledge, his profound insight, and his useful advice was invaluable to me in the completion of the dissertation. I would also like to thank my examiners. I am especially indebted to Professor Hiromi Fuyuki. As my vice-supervisor, she constantly gave me helpful suggestions and encouraged me with her kind words. I am grateful to Associate Professor Tetsuhito Motoyama for his proofreading, good advice and help, and witty jokes. I have benefited from the kind answers Professor Chiaki Hanabusa of Keio University has given to my questions, as well as his astute observations and suggestion for further readings. I am thankful to Professor Norimasa Morita for his useful comments and advice.

I wish to acknowledge Professor Emeritus Kunio Oi, who retired from Waseda University in 2002. He had supervised my undergraduate and master's theses. He mentioned Chettle when I was working on my master's thesis, which examined soliloquies in revenge tragedies, including *Hamlet*, *Antonio's Revenge*, and *Hoffman*. His passion for Shakespeare and his contemporaries inspired me so strongly that I continued onto postgraduate studies.

So many people in the Shakespeare Society of Japan, at the Shakespeare Institute, where I did a second master's degree, at Toyo University, my current workplace, as well as at Waseda University helped and supported me. Sadly, I cannot list all their names here, but among them, I particularly wish to thank Professor Haruo Nakano of Gakushuin University for allowing me to attend his research seminar and giving me insight into Elizabethan plays and society. I also owe thanks to Associate Professor Naoko Komachiya Ishikawa of Keio University for giving me beneficial advice and information. Professor John Jowett of the Shakespeare Institute kindly answered my questions on Chettle and sent me a related document by email when I had just started this study. I deeply admired his professionalism, which raised my motivation, and have always felt grateful for his support. I am indebted to Professor Hirohisa Igarashi of Toyo University, Dr. Ayako Yoshino, and Professor Masami Nakabayashi of Sagami Women's University for making helpful suggestions during the process of getting this work published, and also thank Mr. Masao Uji for his editorial work.

I am also grateful to my friends, Fumiaki Konno, Kenichiro Watanabe, Shinichi Suzuki, Yuzu Uchida, Yuto Koizumi, Yujing Ma, and Tomohiro Shimahara for their feedback, friendship, and encouragement. My gratitude also goes to my parents, Shigeki and Yoshiko, for their support.

This study was funded by Grant-in-Aid for JSPS fellows (KAKENHI, 19-55591). The publication was funded by Grant-in-Aid for Publication of Scientific Research Results (KAKENHI, 265042) and also by the Inoue Enryo Memorial Foundation for Promoting Sciences. I really appreciate these research grants.

An early version of Chapter 2 was published as a Japanese article titled "Sinsetsu-Hanuki no Mita Yume ni Miru Taishu Bunka [Popular Culture in *Kind-Heart's Dream*]" in *Shakespeare no Hirogaru Sekai [The Text Made Visible]* (Tokyo: Sairyu-sha , 2011), 91-114. Chapter 4, "(i) Rebellion," is a reworking of a Japanese article, "Ryuketsu Bamen no Daigomi [Relic of Bloody Scenes]," *Eibungaku* 89 (Tokyo: Waseda-Daigaku Eibungakukai, 2005): 15-26, and Chapter 4, "(ii) Downfall" and "(iii) Succession," of "Downfall and Usurpation in *The Tragedy of Hoffman*," *Eibungaku* 90 (Tokyo: Waseda-Daigaku Eibungakukai, 2005): 1-20. Chapter 5 is based on "Politics and Religion in Henry Chettle's Prisons: *The Downfall and Death of Robert, Earl*

Acknowledgements

of Huntingdon and *Sir Thomas Wyatt*," *Engeki Hakubutsukan Global COE Kiyo: Engeki-Eizogaku 2008*, vol. 4 (Tokyo: Waseda-Daigaku Engeki-Hakubutsukan, 2009): 23-50. Chapter 6 was first published as "*The Tragedy of Hoffman* and Elizabethan Military Affairs," *Engeki Kenkyu Center Kiyo* 6 (Tokyo: Waseda-Daigaku Engeki-Hakubutsukan, 2006): 197-207. Chapter 7, "(ii) *Patient Grissil*" develops a Japanese paper, "*The Pleasant Comedy of Patient Grissil* ni okeru Kekkon, Tomi, Toshi no Mondai [The Issues of Marriage, Wealth, and City in *The Pleasant Comedy of Patient Grissil*]," *Shakespeare News* 52.2 (Tokyo: The Shakespeare Society of Japan, 2013): 26-41. I wish to thank all the editorial board members and reviewers for their beneficial comments and support.

Abbreviations

Blind Beggar	Blind Beggar of Bethnal Green
Death	The Death of Robert, Earl of Huntington
Downfall	The Downfall of Robert, Earl of Huntington
DNB	Oxford Dictionary of National Biography
EEBO	Early English Books Online <http://eebo.chadwyck.com/home>
ESTC	English Short Title Catalogue <http://estc.bl.uk/F/?func=file&file_name=login-bl-estc>
ELH	English Literary History
Groatsworh	Greene's Groatsworth of Wit
Hoffman	The Tragedy of Hoffman
LION	Literature Online <http://lion.chadwyck.co.uk/>
MLN	Modern Language Notes
NQ	Notes and Queries
OED	Oxford English Dictionary
Orlando Furioso	The History of Orlando Furioso
Patient Grissil	The Pleasant Comedy of Patient Grissil
PBSA	The Papers of Bibliographical Society of America
Pierce Penniless	Pierce Penniless His Supplication to the Devil
Piers Plainness	Piers Plainness' Seven Years' Prenticeship
PMLA	Publications of the Modern Language Association of America
PQ	Philological Quarterly
RES	Review of English Studies
RQ	Renaissance Quarterly
RS	Renaissance Studies: Journal of the Society for Renaissance Studies
SEL	Studies in English Literature, 1500-1900
SP	Studies in Philology
SQ	Shakespeare Quarterly

Acknowledgements

SS	*Shakespeare Survey*
STC	*A Short-Title Catalogue of Books Printed in England, Scotland, & Ireland and of English Books Printed Abroad 1475-1640*, edited by W. Alfred Pollard and G. R. Redgrave, revised by W. A Jackson, F. S. Ferguson, and Katherine F. Pantzer (2nd ed.)
UMI	University Microfilms International
Wing	*Short-Title Catalogue of Books Printed in England, Scotland, Ireland, Wales, and British America, and of English Books Printed in Other Countries, 1641-1700*, edited by Donald Wing (2nd ed.)

Contents

Acknowledgements.......................................v
Abbreviations..viii

Introduction: Chettle's Life and Works 3

Part I Chettle and Print Culture 15

1 Chettle as Printer............................... 15

(i) Chettle and Thomas East: Burgeoning of Literary Interest and Expansion of Personal Relationships in Printing Industry......... 15
   (a) East's Publications between 1577 and 1590........................15
   (b) Literary Influence from East's Publications between 1577 and 1590 31
   (c) Chettle's Relationships with Authors, Printers, and Publishers in His Apprentice and Post-Apprentice Days......................39
   (d) Three Works by "H. C."..43

(ii) Chettle and John Danter: Professional Printer and Path to Authorship..52
   (a) Chettle's Relationship with Danter 52
   (b) Danter's Publications between 1591 and 1598 57
   (c) Literary Influence from Danter's Publications between 1591 and 1598 ...67
   (d) Chettle's Relationships with Authors, Printers, and Publishers at Danter's Press...77

(iii) Chettle and Publications by Printers Other Than East and Danter... 83
   (a) Personal Connections with Other Printers........................83
   (b) Literary Influence from Publications by Printers Other Than East and Danter..86

2 Chettle as Pamphleteer 98
    (i) Danter's Press and *Greene's Groatsworth of Wit*: Complicity among Editor, Printer, and Bookseller in the Early Modern Book Trade . . 98

    (ii) *Kind-Heart's Dream*: Rival Prints, Celebrity, Advertisement 111

3 Chettle as Dramatic Repairman. 120
    (i) *John of Bordeaux, or The Second Part of Friar Bacon* 120
        (a) Chettle's Hand in *John of Bordeaux* 120
        (b) Thematic Influence of *John of Bordeaux* on Chettle's Works........... 122

    (ii) *Sir Thomas More*.. 125
        (a) Chettle's Hand in *Sir Thomas More* 125
        (b) Thematic Influence of *Sir Thomas More* on Chettle's Works........... 128

    (iii) *Romeo and Juliet* (Q1) 130
        (a) Chettle's Hand in *Romeo and Juliet* (Q1) 130
        (b) Thematic Influence of *Romeo and Juliet* on Chettle's Works........... 135

Part II Politics and Religion 139

4 Power Struggles in *The Tragedy of Hoffman* and Elizabethan Social Upheavals: Rebellion, Downfall, Succession 139
    (i) Rebellion... 139
        (a) Hoffman's Motives for Revenge............................... 139
        (b) Revenge as Rebellion 146
        (c) *Hoffman* and Censorship 149

    (ii) Downfall.. 152
        (a) *Hoffman* and the Socio-Political Situation in the Late-Tudor Period 152
        (b) The Theme of Downfall in Chettle's Works 154
        (c) Allusion to Essex... 158

    (iii) Succession.. 161
        (a) Chettle's Ideas on the Succession............................. 161
        (b) *Hoffman* and the Stuart Succession 163

5 Catholic Rulers and Downfallen Protestant Prisoner.... 172

(i) Background of the Early Modern Prison...................... 172

(ii) *The Downfall and Death of Robert, Earl of Huntingdon*.............. 177
    (a) Robin Hood and King John.................................. 177
    (b) Martyrdom of Noble Prisoners: Lady Bruce, Her Son, and Matilda ... 179
    (c) Evils of Roman Catholics..................................... 183
    (d) Religious Conflicts and the Stuart Succession 185

(iii) *Sir Thomas Wyatt* 189
    (a) Wyatt, Jane, and Guilford as Protestant Martyrs in Their
        Imprisonment and Execution................................. 189
    (b) Criticism against Catholics and Spain: Evils of Mary Tudor
        and Winchester... 194
    (c) *Sir Thomas Wyatt* and the Stuart Succession 196

Part III Society: Soldiers, Pirates, Beggars 203

6 *Hoffman* and Elizabethan Military Culture............ 203

(i) Elizabethan Military Background 203

(ii) Problems of Soldiers....................................... 208
    (a) Captain's Exploitation and Poverty of Common Soldiers............ 208
    (b) Veterans in Chettle's Works 213

(iii) Chettle's Political Views on Peace/War Debate................ 218

(iv) Pirates in *Hoffman* and Elizabethan Government............. 220

7 Beggars in *The Pleasant Comedy of Patient Grissil* and *The Blind Beggar of Bethnal Green*, and the Elizabethan Money Based Economy 231

(i) Background of Elizabethan Poverty......................... 231

(ii) *Patient Grissil* 234

      (a) Representation of Beggars in *Patient Grissil*........................234
      (b) Conflicts between the Rich and Poor............................237
      (c) Different Values in *Patient Grissil* and the Elizabethan Money
          Based Economy 243

(iii) *Blind Beggar* 248
      (a) Representation of Beggars in *Blind Beggar* 248
      (b) Conflicts between the Rich and Poor............................258
      (c) Different Values in *Blind Beggars* and the Elizabethan Money
          Based Economy 264

Conclusion 271
Appendices..275
Bibliography...300

Henry Chettle's Careers
A Study of an Elizabethan Printer, Pamphleteer, Playwright

Introduction: Chettle's Life and Works

Henry Chettle (c.1560-c.1607), poet, stationer, pamphleteer, but known best as a playwright, has long been neglected by many critics. Although today he is less famous than other contemporary playwrights including Thomas Kyd, Christopher Marlowe, William Shakespeare, and Ben Jonson, in the Elizabethan period, he was famous enough to be recognized as one of the "best poets for comedy" (283) by Francis Meres in his *Palladis Tamia* (1598; STC 17834).

Chettle has been judged a hack, and his works are considered trivial by most critics, perhaps because of his link with Philip Henslowe, an impresario of the popular theater, the Rose, though this could also be because of the awkwardness and roughness of his style. Nevertheless, further analysis of his works in the context of the late Elizabethan social background may enhance their literary value. Chettle is worth studying not only because of his relationships with such literary figures as Robert Greene, Thomas Nashe, Anthony Munday, and Shakespeare, but also for his works, which, with markedly different characteristics from those of Shakespeare and Jonson, may help modern critics understand Elizabethan popular culture and also contemporary issues in politics, religion, and society more widely and deeply.

This book will investigate the socio-political aspects of Chettle's prose and dramatic works, as well as analyzing his role as a Jack of all trades with careers ranging from printer to dramatic repairman, which will show him to be a significant figure of Elizabethan literature – a totally different image from the minor writer he is generally considered to be. In particular, analyses will be made of such prose works as *Greene's Groatsworth of Wit* (1592; STC 12245), *Kind-Heart's Dream* (1593; STC 5123), and such dramatic works as *John of Bordeaux*, *Sir Thomas More*, *The Downfall of Robert, Earl of Huntington* (1598; pub. 1601; STC 18271), *The Death of Robert, Earl of Huntington* (1598; pub. 1601; 18269), *The Pleasant Comedy of Patient Grissil* (1599; pub. 1603; STC 6518), *The Blind Beggar of Bethnal Green* (1600; pub. 1659; Wing, D464), *Sir Thomas Wyatt* (1602; pub. 1607; STC 6537), and *The Tragedy of Hoffman* (c.1602; pub. 1631; STC 5125).[1]

Chettle was born in London circa 1560, as the son of a dyer. He was apprenticed to a printer, publisher, and bookseller, Thomas East, between 1577 and 1584 and became a member of the Stationers' Company in 1584 (Arber 2: 81; 693). As will be discussed below, Chettle probably wrote three works as "H. C." during his apprentice period. In 1591, he set up a partnership with two printers, William Hoskins and John Danter (Greg and Boswell, eds., *Records* 38); however, the partnership ended by the end of the year when Danter set up his press at Duck Lane (Jenkins 7).[2] After the separation, Chettle took to literary work. Chettle's first major work was editing *Groatsworth* in 1592, issued by Danter after Greene's death. Its authorship is problematic, and some critics attribute it to Chettle, as will be discussed in Chapter 2, "(i) Danter's Press and *Greene's Groatsworth of Wit*." Having written two prose works *Kind-Heart's Dream* and *Piers Plainness' Seven Years' Prenticeship* (1595; STC 5124), Chettle still remained in association with Danter; Chettle printed some of Nashe's works, such as *Strange News* (1592), issued by Danter, and he continued to work as a printer until at least around 1596. Chettle is named as a "compositor" in Nashe's *Have with You to Saffron Walden* and as a "printer" in the epistle for Munday, the translator, in *The Second Book of Primaleon of Greece*, both printed in 1596, as will be discussed in Chapter 1, "Chettle as Printer."

Chettle started to devote himself to writing plays in 1598, though he still refers to himself as "I henry [sic] Chettle of London Stationer" to pledge a debt to Henslowe on 22 October 1598.[3] Between 1598 and 1603, Chettle wrote forty-two plays for the Admiral's Men, and five plays for Worcester's Men, according to *Henslowe's Diary*.[4] Of these, he wrote fourteen exclusively by himself, the only one extant being *Hoffman*, and thirty-three plays, excluding such fragments as *Sir Thomas More*, in collaboration with Munday, Thomas Dekker, Michael Drayton, John Day, and Thomas Heywood among others.

As is often the case with such Elizabethan writers as Greene, Nashe, and Dekker, Chettle suffered from poverty, and he was frequently imprisoned for debt in Marshalsea Prison in 1599 (Henslowe 103, 119; Jenkins 24-25). Like Dekker, his experience in prison seems to have influenced the theme of prisoners in such works as *Death* and *Sir Thomas Wyatt*, as will be analyzed in Chapter 5.

Chettle's last works were two pamphlets, *England's Mourning Garment* and *A True Bill of the Whole Number That Hath Died*, both published in 1603. The former is a funeral elegy for Queen Elizabeth including accounts of some of the religious and political incidents of her reign, a record of her funeral procession, and praise for the new king James I. The first edition was printed by Valentine Simmes for Thomas Millington (STC 5121). It was popular enough that a piratical edition was issued by Mathewe Lawe, who paid a fine on 7 June 1603 for piracy. As Harold Jenkins suggests, a second authorized edition with an addition of twelve Barons in "the order of the funeral" was issued in the same year by E. Short for Millington (STC 5120; Arber 2: 836; Jenkins 48-49). This elegy is very important in illustrating Chettle's relations with contemporary writers, such as Shakespeare and Jonson as well as Dekker and Drayton, as is *Kind-Heart's Dream* whose preface mentions Shakespeare.

A True Bill of the Whole Number That Hath Died (STC 16743.2) is a short record on the number of the deaths due to the plague in 1603 with a brief world history of the plague from A.D. 81 to 1602. This work is merely a news report of the plague, and such plague reports were popular in that year; Dekker's *The Wonderful Year* (1603; STC 6535) was printed by Thomas

Creede for Nicholas Ling, John Smethwick, and John Browne; François Vallériole's *A Treatise of the Plague* (1603; STC 16676) was translated by Thomas Lodge, and it was printed by Creede and Simmes for Edward White and Ling.

Chettle is believed to have died before 1607 when Dekker's *A Knight's Conjuring* was published; Chettle is mentioned in this work to have newly arrived in the Elysian Fields: "*Chettle* sweating and blowing, by reason of his fatnes, to welcome whom, because hee was of olde acquaintance, all rose vp, and fell presentlie on their knees, to drinck a health to all the *Louers* of *Helicon*" (STC 6508; L1v).

In the history of literary criticism, there are few discussions of Chettle. Harold Jenkins' *The Life and Work of Henry Chettle* (1934) is the first published biography and the first published criticism of the complete works with priority given to textual criticism. It may not be too much to say that without this study, we would hardly know about Chettle and his ability as a writer. Seventeen years later, Jenkins edited *Hoffman*, which is still now the most authoritative text. F. L. Jones's "Henry Chettle: A Study of His Life and Works" (1925), an unpublished doctoral dissertation, also discusses Chettle's biography and complete works, but Jenkins's study is more significant and influential. More recently, John Jowett has played a leading role in Chettle studies; in 1983 he edited *Hoffman*, as his doctoral dissertation and, thus, produced the first modernized edition with simple notes. Subsequently, Jowett has produced many papers on Chettle, particularly in terms of textual criticism, including "Johannes Factotum: Henry Chettle and *Greene's Groatsworth of Wit*" in *PBSA* 87 (1993) and "Henry Chettle" in the *DLB* 136 (1994) among others. Emma Smith wrote the entry on Chettle for the *DNB* (2004), but she has not discussed Chettle elsewhere, aside from a conference paper she gave on *Hoffman*, which included details about its performance at Magdalen College, Oxford (2010), and also a brief introduction to her edition of *Hoffman* (2012). Chettle has, thus, seemingly become better known than before, but he is still neglected compared to many other Renaissance writers.

There have been a small number of individual studies. For the prose works, Warren B. Austin and Jowett have discussed Chettle's editorial work on *Groatsworth*, some parts of which offended Shakespeare, according to Chettle's apology as an editor in the preface to *Kind-Heart's Dream*. The analysis of this work up to now has not gone beyond the question of authorship. *Kind-Heart's Dream* was analyzed as a news pamphlet and satire by Alexandra Halasz and Arul Kumaran, but it has been generally considered in relation to *Groatsworth*. Chettle's *Piers Plainness* has been less discussed than the other two pamphlets. It has been considered in relation to the works of Greene and Nashe, but Mark Thornton Burnett more interestingly has pointed out its socio-economical and political nature in dealing with problems, such as famine, riot and the plight of apprentices. *England's Mourning Garment* has attracted critical attention in terms of Chettle's allusions to contemporary poets, such as Shakespeare, Drayton, Jonson, Dekker, and others. However, the rest of the work has been neglected; for example, Jenkins simply claims that this work was written in haste for profit and popularity, though it is not without merit (27). On the other hand, Jones regards its style highly, but focuses on Chettle's allusion to the contemporary poets only (330). *A True Bill of the Whole Number That Hath Died* has not been discussed at all. Even Jowett does not mention it, though he includes it in the list of Chettle's works in the *DLB*.

Chettle's plays have been discussed more than his prose, though they are still seen as inferior to plays by other dramatists. Collier first mentioned *Hoffman* in *The History of English Dramatic Poetry* (1819); he regarded the play as "a revolting mass of blood and murder, in which it must have been the author's object to concentrate all the horrors he could multiply" (51). After that, this idea became popular among critics; E. E. Stoll, A. H. Thorndike, and Fredson Bowers among others considered it as a hackwork or simply one example of numerous revenge tragedies. In this period, it was never individually studied. Jenkins examined such aspects of *Hoffman* as its production, genre, style, and imagery, and later edited the work. Jones claimed "*Hoffman* is a fine play. It has an excellent plot, well-delineated characters, impressive scenes, much beautiful verse and a variety of pleasing sentiments and motifs" (299). Despite the contribution of Jenkins and Jones, this play was considered a revenge tragedy until the 1980s. At the beginning of that decade, Jowett edited *Hoffman*, and M. A. Saunders analyzed the work as an example of the revenge tragedy in her doctoral dissertation. The critical reception of the play began to change slightly under the influence of New Historicism, and some individual studies were dedicated to *Hoffman*. In 1999, Richard Brucher discussed such social conditions as piracy, class consciousness, and rebellion in the Elizabethan Age; in 2001, S. J. Glady took a moralistic approach to the play. A more recent study is Paul Browne's paper on its source, pointing out the similarities of the execution of Hoffman's father and that of a Hungarian historical figure, György Dózsa, though the source still remains uncertain. Thus, with the exception of Brucher's study, the socio-political aspects of this play have not been fully discussed yet.

With regard to his plays written in collaboration with Munday, there have been even fewer studies than in the case of *Hoffman*. The plays, *Downfall* and *Death*, have received attention from M. St. C. Byrne only for being a collaboration; Jenkins, J. C. Meagher, Yoshiko Ueno, M. A. Nelson, Paul Dean, Jeffrey L. Singman, and Liz Oakley-Brown have shown interest in the play only for its Robin Hood theme with its unique protagonist, the Earl. Although the political issues such as Prince John's usurpation in the plays were indeed mentioned in some of these studies, they have not been discussed sufficiently.

Patient Grissil has been considered by Jenkins, G. R. Price and Harry Keyshian in the literary tradition of Griselda, dating back to the last tale in Boccaccio's *The Decameron*, while the play's collaborative authorship with Dekker and William Haughton has been considered by W. L. Halstead and D. M. Greene. More recently, there have been some New Historical and

Introduction: Chettle's Life and Works

Feminist approaches; Viviana Comensoli and Judith Bronfman discussed the sovereignty of marriage in the play; Helen Fulton analyzed its hierarchical problems; Felicity Dunworth investigated the maternity of Griselda and its association with Queen Elizabeth.

Blind Beggar is the least studied of the collaborative plays. Almost nobody has analyzed the work except Jenkins and Jones, who discussed its source, collaborative authorship, and plots. There are only three published editions; A. H. Bullen (1881), Willy Bang (1902), and J. S. Farmer's Tudor facsimile (1914). Recently, Will Sharpe worked on a critical edition, which became an unpublished doctoral thesis (2009).

Chettle's life and works, whether pamphlets or plays, have been for the most part dismissed by most critics. He is precisely a minor "hack" and, in a sense, a trivial writer. Nevertheless, Chettle should be re-considered to understand Elizabethan popular culture, politics, religions, and social issues better; he was central to this culture and had wide personal connections with such printers and publishers as East, Danter, John Charlewood, Edward Allde, William Wright, and Cuthbert Burby, such authors as Greene, Nashe, Munday, George Peele, Lodge, Robert Wilson, and Shakespeare, and also Henslowe among others. Working as a printer, pamphleteer, and playwright, Chettle expanded his personal relationships in the printing and theatrical worlds. In short, Chettle's wide activities represent Elizabethan popular culture itself.

Chettle's career illuminates various aspects of his life and times. Through these personal relationships, Chettle could obtain not only jobs, but also the opportunity to read the publications of East, Danter, and other printers including Henry Bynneman, Abel Jeffes, Peter Short, and Creede, Chettle's senior apprentice. The writers of these books range from Edmund Spenser, John Lyly, Greene, Nashe, Peele, Lodge, and Shakespeare to Raphael Holinsed and John Stow. Sourcebooks of Elizabethan authors have been generally researched, but it seems to remain obscure how the authors obtained and read books. Studying Chettle's early career may elucidate the process of book circulation, and also the close relationships between printing and the theater.

Similarly, Chettle's religious and political ideology as an anti-Catholic and objector to Spain seems to have been formed through reading Protestant works, issued by East and Danter, that included writings by John Bale, Jean Calvin, Heinrich Bullinger, Philip Melanchthon, and Henry Smith, as well as Nashe, Munday, and Peele, who supported Protestantism in their works. These books had a great effect on Chettle's plays, particularly, *Downfall*, *Death*, and *Sir Thomas Wyatt*.

Chettle gave voice to various aspects of Elizabethan culture: political, religious, and social opinions; harsh satire; depictions of violence, deprivation and injustice. These points are not so directly seen in the more famous plays of Shakespeare and Jonson, though found in Nashe, Munday, Peele, Dekker, and Heywood. However, interestingly, his attitude is not always consistent. Chettle's *Hoffman* explicitly denounces the arbitrary rule and injustice of the upper class and problematizes succession issues in the Elizabethan political context, though its frame is reminiscent of *Hamlet*. Such Elizabethan social issues as wounded soldiers, pirates, and beggars, and political and economical contexts are described in *Hoffman*, *Patient Grissil*, and *Blind Beggar*. On the other hand, *Downfall* and *Death* and *Sir Thomas Wyatt* stridently criticize Catholicism and also Spain, and make claims for the importance of Protestantism and an anti-Spanish policy with descriptions of noble prisoners including Lady Bruce, Matilda, Lady Jane, Guilford Dudley, and Sir Thomas Wyatt.

Chettle criticizes such capricious and evil rulers as the Dukes of Luningberg and Prussia in *Hoffman*, Gwalter, the Marquess of Saluzzo, in *Patient Grissil*, Sir Robert Westford and Young Playnsey in *Blind Beggar*, and as far as these plays are considered, he seems to be a dissident, who complains against society. However, he supports Elizabethan Protestantism, and goes so far as to uphold England's nationalism in *Downfall*, *Death*, and *Sir Thomas Wyatt*. Furthermore, Chettle shows another contradiction. He shows his

Introduction: Chettle's Life and Works

sympathy for the downfall of such innocent gentle people as Hoffman's father in *Hoffman*, Momford in *Blind Beggar*, and also Lady Bruce and Matilda in *Death*, and also such poor people as Grissil's family in *Patient Grissil*. These contradictions were probably needed to appeal to the audience. They certainly had complaints against the hierarchical society and social injustice, but at the same time, they admired such heroes as Sir Francis Drake and Robert Devereux, the second Earl of Essex. Drake was a commoner, but for his honorable activities the Queen made him a Knight. They may have criticized noble and rich people, but also they must have dreamed of receiving such promotion. Chettle seems to have been generally interested in social mobility from promotions to downfalls, and the dilemma between obedience and disobedience to the authorities, as much as any of his contemporary playwrights. Chettle was highly conscious of people in destitution and felt the social injustice of class distinction, possibly due to his own personal experience of being in debt and imprisoned, and also attacked a society dominated by money. However, at the same time, he is dictated by commercialism, which should be his enemy, and his opinions depend on the demand of audiences.

Further research on Chettle also has implications for Shakespeare studies. Chettle was Shakespeare's rival or hack counterpart; Chettle's revenge tragedy *Hoffman* resembles *Hamlet* so much that it has been considered a parody, as will be discussed in Chapter 4. Chettle wrote stage directions and added a couple of passages to the first quarto of *Romeo and Juliet* published by Danter. Moreover, both dramatists worked on the additions to *Sir Thomas More*, and most remarkably Chettle implicitly referred to Shakespeare in *Kind-Heart's Dream*, *England's Mourning Garment*, and probably called the younger playwright "an upstart Crow" (84) in *Groatsworth*.[5] These remarks suggest Chettle's strong consciousness of Shakespeare. The paths of the two playwrights, thus, crossed on several occasions.

This book is is composed of three parts thematically: Part I (Chapters 1, 2, and 3) will discuss Chettle and print culture, focusing on his careers as an apprentice, printer, pamphleteer, and dramatic repairman; Part II (Chapters 4 and 5) will discuss politics and religion in Chettle's plays and society; Part III (Chapters 6 and 7) will discuss such social problems as veteran soldiers, pirates, and beggars in his plays and society. In Part I, Chapter 1 will investigate Chettle's printing career biographically from his apprenticeship to when his becoming a freeman, through an analysis of the publications of East, Chettle's printing master, and Danter, Chettle's partner, in order to explore literary influences Chettle received from those books and the development of his personal relations with printers and writers. Chettle may also have read publications by printers other than East and Danter, such as Bynneman and Jeffes. I will also discuss Chettle's authorship of three poems by "H. C." to show his literary interest during this period. Chapter 2 will examine *Groatsworth* and *Kind-Heart's Dream* in the context of the Elizabethan popular culture which involves printing presses, interest in celebrities, and the theater; the first section will discuss Chettle's forgery in and publication process for *Groatsworth*, and explain his relationship with the printer and stationer; the second section will analyze *Kind-Heart's Dream* to explore the significance of the printing industry and the contemporary obsession with celebrities for the work. Chapter 3 will analyze Chettle's small contributions to the plays, *John of Bordeaux*, *Sir Thomas More*, and also the first or "bad" quarto of *Romeo and Juliet* and consider their literary influence on him. In Part II, Chapter 4 will discuss power struggles, focusing on *Hoffman* in terms of rebellion as revenge, downfall, and succession. Also, I will associate these problems with Elizabethan politics to investigate Chettle's political consciousness. Chapter 5 will discuss religious issues such as criticism against Catholicism and Spain through the descriptions of poor prisoners and evil authorities in *Downfall*, *Death*, and *Sir Thomas Wyatt*. Moreover, I will indicate Chettle's fear of James VI, King of Scotland, the most likely candidate to succeed Elizabeth at that time. In Part III, Chapter 6 will examine the representation of soldiers, including pirates, in *Hoffman* and *Blind Beggar*, and analyze the Elizabethan problems of veterans and the

Introduction: Chettle's Life and Works

peace/war debate. Chapter 7 will discuss the representation of beggars, juxtaposed with the rich, in *Patient Grissil* and *Blind Beggar* in the context of poverty, the rising money based economy, and the clash of different values.

This is the first historical study of Chettle's works in the twenty-first century. The book investigates Chettle's roles and personal relationships in the printing and theatrical worlds, and also his socio-political concerns in his works. The results of this study will be of use for scholars who study Shakespeare and other contemporary poets and playwrights, for Chettle's connections with and allusions to the contemporaries illuminate the Elizabethan popular culture; also, it will give some illumination to those who are interested in the relationships between printers, playwrights, and texts, as well as the connections between plays and the society of Renaissance England.

Notes

[1] All titles of Renaissance works in this book are modernized. I have modernized titles, following the STC usage, except for cases where the original spelling is in standard use. All quotations follow the original orthography. All composition dates of plays in this book follow Harbage, ed., *Annals of English Drama 975-1700*, rev. ed. (1964).

[2] For Danter's career, see Chiaki Hanabusa's unpublished PhD diss., "John Danter's Play-Quartos" 17-44 and also an article written in Japanese, "Insatsu-Gyosha" 26-43.

[3] See *Henslowe's Diary*, ed. by R. A. Foakes (2nd ed.), 119. All the quotations from the *Diary* follow this edition.

[4] Tables 1 and 2 in Appendix I list Chettle's plays including lost plays. For the Admiral's Company, see Chambers 2: 134-92 and also Gurr, *Shakespeare's Opposites*.

[5] All citations from *Groatsworth* are from D. Allen Carroll's edition. In the preface to *Kind-Heart's Dream*, Chettle apologizes to two playwrights for offending them in the letter section of *Groatsworth*, which Chettle edited after Greene's death, as will be further discussed in Chapter 2 "Chettle as Pamphleteer." Most critics have identified the playwrights as Shakespeare and Marlowe, and suppose Shakespeare reacted angrily at being called an "upstart crow." See Schoenbaum 117-18; Carroll's edition 131-45. However, Shoichiro Kawai provides an alternative idea: the "upstart crow" does not refer to Shakespeare, but to Edward Alleyn, the great actor of the Admiral's Men, and the two playwrights were Marlowe and Peele. See Kawai 165-214.

Part I Chettle and Print Culture

1 Chettle as Printer

(i) Chettle and Thomas East: Burgeoning of Literary Interest and Expansion of Personal Relationships in Printing Industry

(a) East's Publications between 1577 and 1590

Chettle started his career in printing before writing prose works and plays. His early life is obscure, but records in the Stationers' Register give some clues. On 29 September 1577, a record states that "Henrie Chettell sonne of ROBERT CHETTELL late of LONDON Dier Deceased hathe put himself apprentice to Thomas Easte Cytezen and stationer of London for viij yeres begynnynge at michelmas laste paste" (Arber 2: 81). Furthermore, on 6 October 1584, "Henry Chettell Sworne and admitted A freeman of this company" (Arber 2: 693). These records show Chettle was apprenticed to East, the printer, publisher, and bookseller, from 1577 to 1584, and he was probably born around 1560, considering the fact that apprentices usually started their service at the age of fifteen. His knowledge of Latin and mythology probably came from the Merchant Taylors' school, though there is no definite evidence for his education, according to Jones (1).

Chettle, thus, became a member of the Stationers' Company, but his printing career between October 1584 and 1590 is obscure due to a lack of records. The only extant item is the six shillings, "paid to Henrye Chettle to beare his charges to Cambridge aboute the Cumpanyes affaires" between December 1587 and February 1588 (Arber 1: 528). Critics have been puzzled by what "the Cumpanyes affaires" mean, but it remains uncertain.

Jenkins conjectures that there was some trouble between the Stationers' Company and the University of Cambridge press (5).

In 1591, Chettle set up partnership with Hoskins and Danter, a relationship that will be detailed in this chapter, "(ii) Chettle and John Danter," "(a) Chettle's Relationship with Danter;" however, Chettle registered only one book: "The bayting of *DYOGENES*," which is identified as Lodge's *Catharos* (STC 16654). This book was entered in Chettle's name on 17 September 1591, but its title page omits his name and gives the names of Hoskins and Danter (Arber 2: 595).

During this obscure period, 1585-1590, Chettle possibly continued to work for East, as such was a common practice at this time. D. F. McKenzie states that "many apprentices after their terms had expired were possibly content to stay on with their masters or even to work as booksellers in the provinces without taking up their freedom" (293). Moreover, as Majorie Plant points out, the apprenticeship normally spend some years as a journeyman, because the government drastically limited the number of master printers, and also even though they could become a publisher, they had little chance of success because the printer usually acted as publishers.[1] Therefore, there were numerous journeymen; for them it was difficult to obtain employment of any kind, and the Stationers' Company frequently received petitions regarding their poor status (Plant 137, 153).

Fortunately, Chettle obtained jobs in the printing industry and stage world. In his early career between 1585 and 1590, Chettle not only learned how to produce and sell books, but also developed his personal relationships to find a way to survive in the printing world. More remarkably, he had an opportunity to read a variety of books including those on medicine, the military, navigation, and literature at East's press, and these books possibly had a great influence on Chettle. In other words, analyses of East's book catalogue reveal Chettle's relationships with printers, booksellers, and authors, as well as the possibility that some of these books affected him when he wrote pamphlets and plays afterwards.

1 Chettle as Printer

The two tables in Appendix II are lists of the publications of East, in which Chettle may have taken part.[2] East is famous for printing music by William Byrd, John Dowland, Thomas Morley, and Thomas Weelkes, though in his early career, 1567-1572, he published medical and theological books in partnership with Henry Middleton.[3] East also inherited many texts from John Day, the printer. There is no record of his apprenticeship in *A Dictionary of Printers and Booksellers*, edited by Ronald B. McKerrow et al. (95). Besides Chettle, Thomas Scarlet was his apprentice from 25 March 1577 to 12 October 1586, and the relation between Chettle and Scarlet apparently still continued when Danter printed Henry Smith's *Thirteen Sermons upon Several Texts of Scripture* in 1592 and Greene's *The History of Orlando Furioso* in collaboration with Scarlet in 1594 (Arber 2: 75, 699).

According to STC, in Chettle's apprenticeship period, 1577-1584, East published seventy-eight items including reprints and excluding entries, which may be roughly categorized as follows: literature (27), religion (22), medicine (4), military (4), history (3), navigation (3), law (3), ethics (3), and others. Two prominent genres are literature (35% of all) and religion (28%).

In the Elizabethan period, the demand for books increased constantly. According to H. S. Bennett, "while the years 1558-79 saw the publication of some 2760 titles, this number was increased to 4370 between 1580 and 1603," though many of them include reprints. This suggests the growing demand of readers and the ability of the book trade to meet it. Chettle's apprenticeship period was exactly in the middle of the printing age. For the genre of these publications, Bennett states that religious literature made up 40% of all works published; literature (25%); politics and law (10%); scientific and quasi-scientific works (8%); others include commerce, economics, education, guides to conduct (5%) (Bennett 269-70).

East's publications between 1577 and 1584 do not contain religious works so much, and literary tracts exceed religious ones. However, before 1577, East's publications had a different trend. Soon after East became a freeman in 1565, East set up a partnership with Middleton, and this continued till 1572. During this period, East published some medical books, such as Thomas Phaire or Phaer's *The Regiment of Life* (1567), Giovanni da Vigo's *The Whole Work of That Famous Surgeon* (1571), John Jone's *The Baths of Bath's Aid* (1572) and *The Benefit of the Ancient Baths of Buxton* (1572). Vigo's whole works was first printed in 1543, and East reprinted this in 1571 and 1586. Also, he printed Sir John Mandeville's *The Voyage and Travel of Sir John Mandeville*, which had ten editions between 1496 and 1639, according to STC.[4] East printed this work on his own in 1568 and 1582. Moreover, East printed a manner book for servants and children, T*he Book of Nurture* in 1568, while printing such Protestant books as Lucas Harrison's *Calvin's Commentaries on the Psalms* in 1571 and Bullinger's *Common Places of Christian Religion* in 1572. After their partnership ended in 1572, East printed another medical book, Andrew Borde's *Breviary of Health* in 1575, 1582, and 1598. Thus, before Chettle apprenticed himself, East printed medical books, and hardly published any literature. With the shifting general trend in the printing industry, East published more and more literary books around this later period, though still continuously issuing medical books.

Among the literary works published in Chettle's apprentice period, the following books had some reprints, which suggest their popularity; Sir Thomas Malory's *Le Morte d'Arthur*; *Arthur of Little Britain*; Diego Ortúñez de Calahorra's Spanish romance, *The Mirror of Princely Deeds and Knighthood* (Parts 1, 2, 3, 4, and 5); Lyly's *Eupheus: The Anatomy of Wit* and *Eupheus and His England*; Spenser's *The Shepheardes Calender*.

Le Morte d'Arthur was first printed by William Caxton in 1485, and reprinted in 1498, 1529, 1557, 1578, and 1634. East printed it in 1578 only, according to STC. *Arthur of Little Britain* was printed by William Copland in 1560. There are two editions by Copland in 1560, and East reprinted it in 1582. The Arthurian stories were popular among Elizabethans and had an influence on such chivalric romances of Spenser and Sir Philip Sidney.

Calahorra's *The Mirror of Princely Deeds and Knighthood* has nine parts, and was translated from Spanish by Margaret Tyler. East printed the first five

1 Chettle as Printer

parts of this book and afterwards Chettle's acquaintances, such as Burby, Thomas Purfoot, and Edward Allde were involved in the publication of the series.[5] East printed the first part in 1578, 1580, and 1599, the second in 1582, 1585, and 1599, the third in 1586 and 1588-1589, and the fourth and fifth in 1583 and 1598. The sixth part was printed by Allde for Burby in 1598. The seventh part was printed by Purfoot for Burby in 1598. The eighth part was printed by Creede for Burby in 1599. The ninth part was printed by Simon Stafford for Burby in 1602.

The *Eupheus* series was popular. *The Anatomy of Wit* has nineteen editions in total. East printed the first edition and reprinted it in 1578, 1579, 1580, 1581, and 1587. *Eupheus and His England* has sixteen editions: East printed the first edition in 1580 and reprinted it in 1581, 1582, 1584, 1586, and 1588.

The Shepherdes Calender has seven editions between 1579 and 1617. Hugh Singleton printed the first edition in 1579. East printed the second in 1580, and the third with John Wolfe in 1586. This work is dedicated to Sidney. Spenser was a member of the Areopagus, an informal literary circle of Sidney, and other members included Fulke Greville and Gabriel Harvey among others.

These literary works are mainly chivalric and pastoral romances, and particularly the domestic writers, Lyly and Spenser, were popular, and had an influence on their contemporaries including Chettle, and such University Wits as Greene, Nashe, Lodge, Peele, and others. As will be discussed in the next section, Chettle's prose works *Piers Plainness* (1595) and *England's Mourning Garment* (1603) obviously follow *Euphues* and *The Shepheardes Calender*. Likewise, *Euphues* influenced Greene's *Mamillia*, *Gwydonius*, and *Menaphon*, Nashe's *The Anatomy of Absurdity*, and Lodge's *Rosalind* and *Euphues Shadow*. On the other hand, *The Shepheardes Calender*, particularly its "May eclogue" had great influence on Peele's *An Eclogue...to...Robert Earl of Essex* (1589; STC 19534), as Charles Whitworth notes (168), and this influence will be discussed below as well.

Among the other literary works, Greene's *Gwydonius* and Lodge's *An Alarum against Usurers*, which is dedicated to Sidney, are important because of the writers' later relationship with Chettle as well as in its literary influence on Chettle. Jean de Cartigny's French romance, *The Voyage of the Wandering Knight*, is interesting because its editor Robert Norman dedicated it to Sir Francis Drake (1581; STC 4700; A2r-3r). Norman was a hydrographer and wrote a pamphlet called *The New Attractive* issued by East in 1585. Similarly, Fernam Lopes de Castanheda's *The First Book of the History of the Discovery and Conquest of the East Indies* (1582) is dedicated to Drake by its translator, Nicholas Lichefield. Drake's popularity, particularly, among seamen, and also East's and the people's interest in navigation are, thus, seen in these pamphlets. Furthermore, East printed another navigational book, William Bourne's *A Regiment for the Sea* in 1580, and this book had eleven editions in total from 1574 to 1631. East printed five editions in 1580, 1584, 1587, 1592, and 1596. Bourne was a mathematician and former Royal Navy gunner.

Religious tracts published in this period are various: theology; sermons; commentaries on the Bible; catechism.[6] East printed such religious works by domestic writers as *Examples Drawn out of Holy Scripture* (1582) by John Merbecke, and *A Godly, Zealous, and Profitable Sermon* (1582) and *A Sermon on the Parable of the Sowers* (1582) by George Gifford. Merbecke was a Calvinist, theologist, and musician. Gifford, a Puritan preacher, is famous for *A Dialogue between a Papist and a Protestant* (1582; STC 11849), and two works on witchcraft; *A Discourse of the Subtle Practices of Devils by Witches and Sorcerers* (1587; STC 11852) and *A Dialogue Concerning Witches and Witchcrafts* (1593; STC 11850). Moreover, he is well-known for having attended to Sidney at his deathbed as a chaplain. However, more significantly, East printed works by famous reformers from the Continent; *A Learned and Fruitful Commentary* (1577) and *The Epistle of the Blessed Apostle* (1580; 1581) by Niels Hemmingsen, a Danish Lutheran theologian; *Of the Wonderful Popish Monsters* (1579) by Phillip Melanchthon, a German reformer and erudite successor of Martin Luther; *The Christian Disputations* (1579) by Pierre Viret, a Swiss reformer; *The Images of Both Churches* (1580) by Bale; *The Commentary* (1580) by Jean

Calvin; *A Treatise* (1583) by Antoine de la Roche Chandieu, a French Huguenot and Calvinist; *Pasquine in a Trance* (1584) by Caelius Secundus Curio, an Italian Protestant; *A Very Profitable and Necessary Discourse* (1584) by Zacharias Ursinus, a German reformer and theologian.[7] The focus of the works around 1579 and 1583 has much to do with the negotiation of a French Catholic, the Duke of Anjou, for Elizabeth's hand in marriage in 1579 and the Throckmorton Plot in 1583. What the marriage would bring to the two countries was peace, but most Elizabethans including Francis Walsingham and the Earl of Leicester opposed this match for "Anjou's religion and uncertainty of his motives," as Penry Williams suggests (*The Later Tudors* 281). The Throckmorton Plot was an attempt to assassinate Elizabeth and replace her with Mary Stuart by English Roman Catholics, that included the key conspirator, Francis Throckmorton. The Protestant works that East printed around this time were response to these religious events.

John Brooke was a translator of an anonymous pamphlet dealing with the Wars of the Huguenots, *A Christian Discourse* (1578), Melanchthon's *Of the Wonderful Popish Monsters* (1579), and Viret's *The Christian Disputation* (1579). Kathleen E. Kennedy remarks in the *DNB*:

> Between 1577 and 1582 six translations by Brooke were printed; printers specializing in ephemera, Thomas East and John Charlewood produced two-thirds of these titles…Nearly all Brooke's pieces were didactic Calvinist or Huguenot tracts…. (907)

Thus, most of the religious publications East printed in this period were Protestant, but it does not mean that East himself was an ardent Protestant, for he had relations with the Catholic musician, Byrd, after 1588, which will be discussed below. East was just "specializing in ephemera," and was concerned about sales rather than religious and political ideology.

England lagged behind in medical studies at this time, and Henry VIII and Elizabeth depended on Italian doctors; however, the spread of the plague drew people's attention to medicine. As more and more vernacular medical texts appeared, the number of unauthorized medical practitioners increased, as Margaret Pelling and Charles Webster discuss (228).[8] East continuously and frequently printed the medical books, and four items appeared in this period. A Church of England clergyman Thomas Brasbridge studied both divinity and medicine at Oxford, and wrote *The Poor Man's Jewel* (1578, 1580). This treatise on plagues was popular, and was published five times between 1578 and 1598. Other books include Guy de Chauliac's *Guydos Questions* (1579) and Fioravanti Leonardo's *A Short Discourse of the Excellent Doctor and Knight* (1580). Chauliac, a fourteenth-century French famous surgeon, was influenced by Galen, a prominent Roman physician. Following Galen, Chauliac insisted on the importance of surgery in his *Chirugia Magna*, which was extremely popular and translated into English, French, Hebrew, Dutch, Italian, and Provençal. *Guydos Questions* was composed of selections from *Chirurgia Magna*, and also Galen's book four of *De Methodo Medendi* and the epitome of the third book of *De Compositione Medicamentorum per Genera*. Leonardo was an Italian surgeon in the sixteenth century and made innovations in many fields of medicine, such as prevention of diseases, pharmacology, and therapy. *A Short Discourse of the Excellent Doctor and Knight* discusses surgery.

Elizabethan military books were originally based on the Roman and Greek classics, and written by veterans who had served on the Continent, to offer instruction on the art of battle (Webb 4). The large number of such titles recorded in Maurice J. D. Cockle's *A Bibliography of Military Books up to 1642* suggests how conscious Elizabethan people were of war issues. Henry Webb analyses the military books and Elizabethan wars, and interestingly he regards the three books that East printed between 1577 and 1590 as important and popular; Niccolò Machiavelli's *The Art of War*, Caius Julius Caesar's *The Eight Books*, and Thomas Styward's *The Pathway to Martial Discipline* (Webb 7-10; 13-16).

Between 1577 and 1584, East printed *The Pathway to Martial Discipline* and a Spanish captain, Luis Gutierrez de la Vega's *A Compendious Treatise*

1 Chettle as Printer

Entitled, De Re Militari (1582), translated by Lichefield. *A Compendious Treatise* was also issued as the second part of *The Pathway to Martial Discipline*, printed in 1582 (STC 23414). *The Pathway to Martial Discipline* was very popular in this period and appeared twice in 1581 and once in 1582, all printed by East. *A Compendious Treatise* is dedicated to Sidney by Lichefield. These books are practical guides for upper-ranking soldiers, namely generals and captains, and discuss how to train soldiers and fight effectively with interesting tables of strategic formation at battles and camps. In 1580, Elizabeth's greatest enemy, the Catholic Spanish king, Philip II annexed Portugal to Spain, ascended to the throne of Portugal, and established full control over the country. Elizabethans were alarmed by the expansion of the Spanish and Catholic power in Europe, and considered preparing for war. This background encouraged the publishing of these military books.

Among the other books from East's press, *The First Book of the History of the Discovery and Conquest of the East Indies* (1582) is interesting for being dedicated to Drake by its translator, Lichefield.

During Chettle's obscure period, namely 1585 to 1590, East published about fifty items excluding entries; music (13), literature (10), medicine (8), religion (5), military (4), history (3), navigation (3), Christian life (2), and others. In the period from 1588 to 1590, East devoted much of his time to printing music books, including reprints. The music prints occupy 25% of all; literature accounts for 20%, medicine 16%; religion 10%. These figures differ from the general tendency which Bennett suggests (269-70).

Plant lists hunting, hawking, archery, gardening, musical playing, playgoing, and card-playing as counter-attractions to reading (46). East's publications in this period seems to satisfy the demand of those who were attracted by these sorts of pastimes with Christopher Clifford's *The School of Horsemanship* (1585), and Leonard Mascall's *A Book of the Art and Manner* (1590), and numerous music books, written by Byrd, Nicholas Yonge, and Thomas Watson, and issued between 1588 and 1590. In particular, from East's press, numerous manuals on the military, navigation, domestic affairs, medicine, and gardening were issued, which suggests more ordinary people had access to the books more easily than before.

Clifford was a soldier and served in the Low Countries and other parts. *The School of Horsemanship* is dedicated to Sidney, who appointed Clifford to the service of Duke Cassemerus in 1579, according to Victor Skretkowicz, Jr. (408). Clifford's knowledge of horses was probably obtained in battle, according to Henry R. Plomer ("Thomas East" 308). This book mainly notes how to handle and take care of horses.

Mascall's book, which deals with gardening, particularly planting and grafting, was partly a translation of Davy Brossard's *L'Art et Maniere de Semer*, and partly a combination of works by other authors. Its number of reprints suggests its popularity. It had eight editions between 1569 and 1599, including a pirated edition by Simmes in 1596. Bynneman first printed it for John Wight in 1569. East printed it for Wight in 1590, 1592, and 1599. Mascall was a translator and author, and also, Clerk of Works at Christ Church, Oxford, Hampton Court Palace, and other buildings of Henry VIII, according to the *DNB* (138).[9]

As Jeremy L. Smith points out, East had not shown any interest in the music trade from 1565 to 1588 (15). However, in 1588 East became the assignee of Byrd, and he devoted himself to music prints till his death in 1608. In this field, composers wrote texts and often published them, and consumers were musician, generally amateur performers or collectors (J. Smith 16). More importantly, in Elizabethan England, music printing was regulated by "three competing monopolistic forces," which were "two patents granted by the queen—one for psalms with music and the other for general music—and a set of Stationers' Company privileges," and only patent holders or their assignees could legally print music (J. Smith 70).[10] Day was granted the patent in 1599, and he was the most prominent music printer in the period before East was involved in the field. On Day's death in 1584, the patent for metrical psalter transferred to his son Richard Day and was administered by his assignees, who were members of the Stationers' Company. Byrd held the Royal Patent for music publishing from 1575, jointly with Thomas Tallis until 1585, and then on his own until 1596, when the patent expired. After Thomas Tallis died in 1585, Byrd continued holding the patent, producing works with his assignee, East.

Music books seemingly have nothing to do with politics and religion; however, East was much involved in these issues, publishing Masses by a Catholic, Byrd, and also Dowland's *Second Book of Songs* (1600; STC 7095), which alludes to Essex's relation with the Queen, though East was neither a Catholic recusant nor Essex's supporter (J. Smith 96-110). In 1563, around the age of twenty, Byrd became an organist and master of choristers at the cathedral chapter in Lincoln. In 1572, he accepted a position as an organist of the Chapel Royal, where he met another Catholic organist, Tallis. Three years later, they were granted the patent for music printing by the Queen. However, Byrd moved to the village of Harlington about 1577 because his wife was listed as a Catholic recusant. Byrd himself appears in the recusancy lists from 1584. Nevertheless, he retained his post at the Chapel Royal.[11]

Smith observes that Byrd's Latin-texted musical works including *Cantiones Sacrae I* (1589) were issued for the specific interest of the Catholic community in England; also *Psalms, Sonnets, and Songs* (1588, 1599) contains a poem attributed to the Jesuit martyr, Henry Walpole. More interestingly, Smith points out the fact that Edward Forset, a Catholic recusant, was called to East's workplace to read and discuss a letter by Robert Persons that concerned the succession at five o'clock on the morning of 23 April 1600, according to the records of the State Papers (J. Smith 103). Furthermore, following Lilian Ruff and Arnold Wilson, Smith notes the relation between East's music printing, Dowland's *Second Book of Songs* (1600), and Essex. According to Ruff and Wilson, to support anti-Spanish Catholics in England, Essex, who officially was a champion of the Protestants, encouraged the new art-form of Italian madrigals composed in English. Most of the composers of the madrigals were Catholic ("The Madrigal" 3-51; "Allusion" 31-36).[12] Thus, Essex had great influence on music trade. In fact,

Thomas Watson's *Superius*, printed by East in 1590, was dedicated to Essex. Smith claims that the *Second Book of Songs* echoed Essex's letter to the Queen, in which he pleaded for her forgiveness, and sees this as a counterpart of *Richard II*, which implies his threatening Elizabeth with military power (J. Smith 108). Moreover, Smith remarks the possibility that East's residence was chosen for the house arrest of Lord Cromwell, one of Essex's conspirators (J. Smith 110-11).

These events are interesting, but lack firm evidence. However, it is certain that East was placed in the middle of political and religious turmoil, and Chettle probably witnessed these events. East was the assignee of Byrd, but issued his works not for religious reasons, but for money. In fact, he printed such Protestant writers as Bale, Calvin, and Melanchthon before 1585; he printed Bullinger, a Swiss Calvinist, Thomas Rogers, a Church of England clergyman, and some sermons and homilies in 1587, while publishing Pope's medical work in 1585, a Spanish doctor, Franciscus Arcaeus's medical book in 1588, and Byrd's music tracts from 1588. His concern was profit rather than political and religious ideology.

For literary books published in this period, with the exception of Publius Trentius's *Andria*, translated by M. Kyffin and published for Thomas Woodcock in 1588, there is little that is remarkable in them. Literary works are dominant in the list of what was published at East's press in this period as well, but most are reprints of such writers as Spenser, Lyly, and Ortúñez de Calahorra. These facts suggest that these works were so popular for such a long period.

East's interest in medical books continued from his early to late career, though two of his six medical items are reprints of popular books. One is Giovanni da Vigo's *The Whole Work of that Famous Surgeon*, an enlarged edition of *The Most Excellent Works of Surgery*, which E. Whytchurch first published in 1543. East reprinted it in 1571 and 1586. Vigo was an Italian surgeon in the early sixteenth century, and the two works are English translations of his book on surgery called *Practica Copiosa in Arte Chirurgia*.

1 Chettle as Printer

The other is Borde's *Breviary of Health*, which had seven editions between 1547 and 1598. The first edition was issued by William Middleton. East reprinted it in 1575, 1582, and 1598. Borde was an English physician and travelled around Europe in the sixteenth century. This is a self-help book of remedies and preventives he learnt from his travels; for example, it suggests the use of the oil of radish for ringing in the ears, green ginger for indigestion, and garlic for worms.

Among the other medical books, the most noteworthy is Galen's *Certain Works of Galen* (1586), a translation of books three to six of *Methodus Medendi* by Thomas Gale. Galen, the Greek physician, was the most influential medical authority in Elizabethan medicine.[13] More significantly, his theory on surgery influenced Elizabethan surgeons, such as Gale and George Baker. Moreover, in the same year, Gale compiled Galen's works into *Certain Works of Surgery*, and dedicated it to Lord Robert Dudley, Earl of Leicester.

In 1585, East printed two works; *A Brief and Necessary Treatise* by William Clowes, who was Gale's fellow physician and serving at St Bartholomew's hospital and in the Navy; and a medical handbook discussing herbal therapy, *The Treasury of Health* by Pope John XXI, also a medieval scientist. In 1588, East published two more medical books; *A Most Excellent and Compendious Method of Curing Wounds* written by the Spanish surgeon, Franciscus Arcaeus; *Libros Aliquot Pauli Aeginetæ* by George Edrichus or Etherege, an English physician and classical scholar. He was among the few Oxford physicians to publish a textbook of medicine and pharmacology, and this book was written specifically for the training of medical students.

East, thus, issued a large number of famous and popular medical books from Galen to Borde. In Renaissance England, research in the medical field, especially on surgery and the plague, developed, and many of the works written for medical practitioners in Latin and French were translated into English, while the number of self-help medical books increased; they were written for ordinary people such as those by Pope John XXI and Borde.

In this period, East printed four military books; John Polemon's *The*

Second Part of the Book of Battles Fought in Our Age (1587); Girolamo Cataneo's *Most Brief Tables* (1588); Machiavelli's *The Art of War* (1588); Caesar's *The Eight Books* (1590), translated by Arthur Golding. Compared with the earlier military books printed by East, the number of foreign writers increased in this period, and this obviously reflects the immediacy of warfare in Elizabethan England.

Polemon's *The Second Part of the Book of Battles Fought in Our Age* is distinguished from the other books discussing the art of war and military science. Poleman's book is literary and historical. The identity of Polemon remains a mystery, as even the *DNB* does not contain his name, and ESTC notes "the name may be a pseudonym." The first part was printed by Bynneman and Francis Coldock in 1577 (STC 20089). *The Second Part of the Book of Battles Fought in Our Age* describes twelve battles actually fought, particularly on the Continent. Among them, the most interesting battles are "The Battaile of Pescherias," or Lepanto in 1572 (STC 20090; K3r-R3r) and "The Battaile of Alcazar" in 1578 (R3r-Y3r). According to Warner G. Rice, Peele used the work as a source of *The Battle of Alcazar* (pub. 1594) as well as Johan Thomas Freigius' *Historia de Bello Africano* (428-31).[14] Rice points out such parallels between Polemon and Peele as Mohamet's dark complexion, and the names of characters. As I will further discuss in the next section, "(b) Literary Influence from East's Publication between 1577 and 1590," Peele had definitely met Chettle before Peele was mentioned in *Groatsworth* (1592), and read East's publications including *The Shepheardes Calender* and Henry Roberts's *A Most Friendly Farewell... to the Right Worshipful Sir Francis Drake* (1585). These books certainly influenced Peele's *A Farewell...to...Sir J. Norris and Sir F. Drake*, printed by Charlewood in 1589 (STC 19537), and also *An Eclogue to...Robert Earl of Essex*, printed by John Windet in 1589.

Renaissance Europe saw a large amount of warfare, which became more complex than before, and the art of war changed in strategy, weapon, fortification, training, and other aspects. This is the so-called "military revolution."[15] While some people persisted in holding to the classical idea of war, as depicted by the ancient Romans Vegitius and Caesar, others proposed more scientific and practical military strategies. Cataneo's *Most Brief Tables* is an example of the latter. Cataneo was an Italian mathematician who insisted on the significance of mathematics in the art of war including fortification, like English astronomer and mathematician Leonard and Thomas Digges' *Stratioticos* (1579; STC 6848), which was printed by Bynneman.[16]

By contrast, Machiavelli's *The Art of War* and Caesar's *The Eight Books* were popular classical military books, as Webb claims (7-10; 13-16). *The Art of War* was the first translation of Machiavelli in England; it preceded the translation of *The Prince*, first published in 1640, though the Italian original *Il Principe* was first printed by Wolfe in England in 1584. *The Art of War*, a translation of *Libro dell'Arte della Guerra*, was issued three times in total. While the original was first printed by Wolfe in England in 1587, the translation was first printed by John Kingston in 1562; the second by W. Williamson in 1573; the third by East in 1588. *The Art of War* is largely adapted from the classic writings of Vegetius, Frontinus, and Polybius, as Sydney Anglo remarks (522).

Caesar's *The Eight Books* was first printed by William Seres in 1565, and the second edition was by East in 1590. Anglo states that "one of the most popular literary-military genres of the Renaissance was the commentary upon some classical authority" including "Caesar, Aelian, Onosander, Polyarenus," and these books aimed "both to reconstruct the ancient military arts and relate them to the exigencies of modern warfare" (523).

All of the four military books were printed around 1588, the year of the Armada, and this suggests people's concern about military campaigns and practical military strategies to defend England from Spain, which continuously threatened England even after the Armada in the 1590s.

Between 1585 and 1590, East published only five religious tracts including homilies, which is very strange, judging from Bennett's statistics; Bullinger's *Fifty Godly and Learned Sermons* (1587); the anonymous *Certain Sermons* (1587); the anonymous *The Second Tome of Homilies* (1587); Thomas Rogers's the second part of *The English Creed* (1587); Laurence Chaderton's *A Fruitful Sermon* (1589). Moreover, in the earlier period, East concentrated on issuing Protestant works. Sermons and homilies had been used for spreading the doctrine of the Anglican Church; according to Christopher Baker, this was the suggestion of an English reformer and Bishop of Canterbury, Thomas Cranmer in the early sixteenth century (40-42). Rogers was a Church of England clergyman and wrote controversial works. Chaderton was an English Puritan divine. His *Fruitful Sermon* appeared five times between 1584 and 1618, which suggests its popularity. The reason for the publication of these books can probably be explained by the execution of Mary Stuart in 1587, when Catholics had more hostility against Protestants.

The general characteristic of the publications at East's press between 1577 and 1590 is the dominance of literary works including those by Lyly, Spenser, Malory, Greene, and Lodge among others; these include reprints, especially in the later period. Religious works are the second most prominent. The number of the writings of Protestant reformers, such as Melanchthon and Hemmingsen increased, particularly around the time when such religious events as Anjou's marital negotiation with Elizabeth, the Throckmorton Plot, and the execution of Mary occurred. Military books are as noteworthy as religious books, though the number of publications is smaller than works on music and medicine. Military issues were as important as religious ones, because they related to religion as well as politics. Elizabethan England's wars with Spain were ultimately a religious struggle between Protestants and Catholics, and also a political battle for naval supremacy. Elizabethan religion and politics were thus closely linked, and the publications of military books depended on such events as Philip II's annexation of Portugal and the Armada.

Books concerning navigation, horsemanship, and music, as well as literature, were frequently dedicated to such military heroes as Drake, Sidney, and Essex.[17] These heroes bore a strong influence on the printing industry. They were popular heroes in print as well as in society. Authors dedicated their works to the heroes, and wrote about them. Thus, though the printing industry published these works for profit, they were ultimately appropriated into the political and religious propaganda of those who were anti-Spanish and anti-Catholic. At first glance, music prints may appear to have nothing to do with religion and politics, but as Smith suggests, Byrd's works were produced with Catholics and Essex in mind.

It is uncertain whether or not Chettle read all of the works that East printed in this period, but he certainly read some or many literary books, such as those by Lyly, Spenser, Greene, and Lodge among others. Chettle's interest in literature was definitely formed during this period. On the other hand, his religious and political ideology was also obviously formed by reading some of the many books East published during this period, which were probably such Protestant works by Calvin, Melanchthon, Bullinger, and others, and also such military books as Styward, Polemon, and Machiavelli; Chettle's ideology as a militant Protestant is frequently seen in his plays, as will be discussed in Part II, "Politics and Religion" and Part III, "Society."

(b) Literary Influence from East's Publications between 1577 and 1590

The literary works printed by East were mainly chivalric romances in both periods concerned, such as editions of Malory's Arthurian stories, and thus his output seems to reflect the popular tastes of the time. Chettle also dealt with such themes, especially in his early works, such as in *Piers Plainness*. In Chettle's apprentice days, Lyly's first publications of the *Euphues* series, *The Anatomy of Wit* (1578) and *Euphues and His England* (1580), were one of the two major English literary works printed out of East's press. Another work was Spenser's early work *The Shepheardes Calender* (1581). Chettle possibly read these books as a form of literary apprenticeship, since he followed the Euphuistic style particularly in *Piers Plainness*, as Jenkins and Jowett note (Jenkins 44; Jowett, "Notes" 384). *Piers Plainness* begins with these passages:

Henry Chettle's Careers: A Study of an Elizabethan Printer, Pamphleteer, Playwright

> The Sunne no sooner entred Gemini, but Natures plentie and Earths pride, gave the husbandman hope of gainefull Harvest, and the shepheard assurance of happie increase; the first cherished with the lively Spring of his deade sowne seede: The seconde cheared by the living presence of his late yeaned lambes. (122)

The brief quotation appears to be an epitome of the elaborate Euphuistic style with alliteration, metaphors, and antitheses, but it comes to differ from Lyly's original style, or rather it seems a little ridiculed by a cynical Chettle, who adds to the chivalric romance realistic criticism against brokers and courtiers. Euphuism was fashionable in the 1580s, but it had become obsolete by the mid 1590s when *Piers Plainness* was written. Falstaff evidently parodies it in *1 Henry IV* as David Bevington and others point out: "though the camomile, the more it is trodden on, the faster it grows, yet youth, the more it is wasted, the sooner it wears" (2.4.403-05) (Bevington, ed., *1 Henry IV*, 196).[18] Lyly's original is "though the Camomill, the more it is trodden and pressed downe, the more it spreadeth, yet the violet the oftner it his [sic] handled and touched, the sooner it withereth and decayeth" (*The Anatomy of Wit* 8; STC 17051).

The influence of *The Shepheardes Calender* on Chettle is to be found in *England's Mourning Garment* (1603), a pastoral elegy for Elizabeth. Both in motif and style Chettle evidently follows Spenser, particularly his November eclogue, which laments the death of Dido, modeled on a poem about the death of Queen Loys written by the French poet, Clément Marot. The November eclogue begins with dialogues between Thenot and Colin, a typical shepherd's name used by Virgil, Marot, and John Skelton:

> THENOT. Colin my deare, when shall it please thee sing,
> As thou were wont songs of some jouisaunce?
> Thy Muse to long slombreth in sorrowing,
> Lulléd a sleep through kives misgovernaunce.[19]

England's Mourning Garment also begins with dialogues between Thenot and

1 Chettle as Printer

Collin:

> THENOT. *COllin*, thou look'st as lagging as the day
> When the Sun setting toward his westerne bed,
> Shews, that like him, all glory must decay,
> And frolicke life with murkie clowds o're-spred,
> Shall leaue all earthly beautie mongst the dead....[20]

In the November eclogue, a shepherd Collin laments the death of Dido. Some critics have associated Dido with Elizabeth (Parmenter 190-217; McLane 47-60), and most interestingly, Helen Cooper argued that this was the first pastoral elegy for Elizabeth, which Chettle composed when Elizabeth really died (108).

In *England's Mourning Garment*, Chettle identifies Spenser with Collin, and admires him, by remarking, "the excellent and cunning *Collin* indeed; (for alas, I confesse my selfe too too rude,)" (97), as Jones points out (338-39). Moreover, Chettle also praises, "warlike Poet *Philesides*" (87), or Sidney, and complains that poets flattered him when he was alive, but they forgot him after his death (97).

Furthermore, it is worth noticing that *The Shepheardes Calender* was dedicated to Sidney by Spenser. On the other hand, Peele's *An Eclogue to...Robert Earl of Essex* (1589), which is influenced by Spenser's poem, and particularly the May eclogue, is dedicated to Essex. Significantly, Peele praises not only Essex, but also Sidney, "*Philisides*" (A3v). "*Philisides*" reminds us of "warlike Poet *Philesides*" in *England's Mourning Garment*, and this suggests the possibility that Chettle read *An Eclogue* as well as *The Shepheardes Calender*.

Peele probably read *The Shepheardes Calender*, Roberts's *A Most Friendly Farewell... to the Right Worshipful Sir Francis Drake*, and Polemon's *The Second Part of the Book of Battles Fought in Our Age*, all of which were issued by East, as mentioned in the previous section, "(a) East's Publications between 1577 and 1590." These works must have influenced Peele's *A Farewell to...Sir John Norris and Sir Francis Drake* and *An Eclogue to...Robert Earl of Essex*.

Before Peele was mentioned in *Groatsworth*, Chettle obviously had met him, but how they met is uncertain. Peele met Lyly and Lodge at Oxford, while Chettle may have met the two at East's press when their books were published. Chettle certainly read those works of Peele, and *An Eclogue* especially had an influence on Chettle's *England's Mourning Garment*. As Peele admires Essex as a shepherd and Elizabeth as a shepherdess, Chettle praised Elizabeth as a shepherdess. In other words, *England's Mourning Garment* is an expansion of *An Eclogue*, which recounts Elizabethan military events concerning Essex, Sidney, and Drake, while *England's Mourning Garment* covers a more comprehensive and detailed history of Tudor England. Likewise, Peele's *The Battle of Alcazar* may have influenced a lost play, *King Sebastian of Portugal*, written by Chettle and Dekker in 1601. It is very interesting that the books which Chettle may have been involved in printing at East's press influenced Peele, and some years later Chettle produced works, influenced by Peele.

This is an example of how poets, playwrights, printers, and publishers had close relationships each other, and the authors could read publications printed by printers they knew well, while printers and publishers could read their books in return. The printers possibly helped the authors who would write for them, as East did for Peele, by showing them some books that they could use as sources. *The Battle of Alcazar* was printed by Edward Allde, not by East in 1594; however, Allde, a son of John Allde, Munday's printing master, was probably a friend of Chettle; Allde printed the first quarto of *Romeo and Juliet* with Danter in 1596. This work is generally called a "bad" quarto, and more significantly, some critics claim that Chettle added some lines and stage directions in preparing it for publication, as will be discussed in Chapter 3 "Chettle as Dramatic Repairman," "(iii) *Romeo and Juliet* (Q1)." Also, none of Peele's works were issued at East's press, but two works came from Danter's press, for which Chettle worked as a printer and author after 1590: *Titus Andronicus* (1594) and *The Old Wife's Tale* (1595).[21] Chettle criticized brokers in *Piers Plainness* (1595) and *Kind-Heart's Dream* (1593), but ironically, he himself was a broker who approached poets, play-

1 Chettle as Printer

wrights, printers, and publishers both for friendship and profit.

Lodge's *An Alarum against Usurers* was dedicated to Sidney, and it is generally considered as an autobiographical pamphlet. This tract greatly influenced Chettle's *Piers Plainness*. Jenkins remarks, "His [Chettle's] satiric portraits of the broker and the usurer owe something to Lodge's *An Alarum against Usurers*, and suggestions may also have come from *The Defense of Cony-Catching*" (44). The form of *Piers Plainness* itself is based on an anonymous Spanish novel *The Pleasant History of Lazarillo de Tormes*. In *Lazarillo de Tormes*, the servant-hero, Lazarillo suffers under seven mean masters. Likewise, Chettle's hero, Piers serves seven penurious masters as an apprentice. However, the ending is very different; Lazarillo becomes a corrupt official, while Piers turns his back on the court and lives a happy life as a shepherd serving Menalcas. Furthermore, as Burnett points out, Chettle's story refers to problems that preoccupied the Elizabethans, such as usury, brokerage, usurpation, and others ("Henry Chettle's *Piers Plainness*" 170-71). Political intrigues appear in the sub-plot among the King and Princes of Thrace, and the Queen of Crete. This sub-plot parallels with the main plot of Piers' services to a jester, a broker, a usurer, and others until Piers starts serving a usurping prince.

Just as Lodge criticizes brokers in *An Alarum against Usurers*, Chettle cynically states that those involved in brokerage form a mystery because "[t]hey cover their craft with charitie, pietie, pitie, neighborhood, friendship, equitie, and what not that good is" (144). Furthermore, Ulpian, the usurer, is described as a stingy master who gives little food to Piers, but he is accused of "clipping of gold, which according to the law of Thrace hie treason" (159-60). Ulpian is soon executed, and Chettle comments, "Here ends the tragedie of true Avarice" (160). It seems that nobody has yet connected Piers and Chettle, who apprenticed himself to East, but Piers' episodes may be a reflection of Chettle's personal experience to some extent like *An Alarum against Usurers* and Greene's autobiographical pamphlets. Perhaps, Ulpian's perniciousness is based on Chettle's own experience.

As discussed above, East printed numerous religious books including those by Bale, Calvin, Melanchthon, Viret, Bullinger, and others; significantly, all are Protestants. East published these Protestant books while printing the composition of Byrd, the Catholic composer. Nevertheless, East does not seem to have been interested in religious and political issues. His concern was selling books. On the other hand, Chettle was obviously influenced by these works, as can be seen in his later career as a playwright. Like his contemporaries, Dekker and Heywood, Chettle clearly favors Protestantism in his plays including *Downfall, Death, Sir Thomas Wyatt*, as I will analyze in Chapter 5 "Catholic Rulers and Downfallen Protestant Prisoners." In these works, Chettle bitterly criticizes Roman Catholics and also Spanish people as evil. Moreover, in *England's Mourning Garment*, Chettle strongly opposes Roman Catholics and insists on the supremacy of the Anglican Church, as will also be discussed in Chapter 5. Although it remains uncertain which book Chettle read, his religious and political ideology must have been established through such Protestant works during this period.

Medical books are also prominent in East's press, as shown in the previous section. According to Paul Slack, one hundred and fifty-three English medical titles were printed between 1483 and 1604, many of which were reprinted repeatedly, and also nearly one third of all the medical texts discussed simple remedies, though most of East's publications seem rather difficult and theoretical, usually based on Galen (239).[22] Moreover, some unlicensed doctors deceived ignorant people by selling false drugs or erroneous cures.

Chettle addresses this medical situation in *Kind-Heart's Dream*, through the voice of the ghost of Dr. Burcot (Burchard Kranich), a London physician originally from South Germany who had died in 1578. Chettle's Burcot complains about "*the impudent discreditors of Phisickes Art*" (23), exemplifying some cases of quackery.[23] According to this character, the spread of English vernacular medical writings could "make Phisick, among common people, esteemed common" (23); therefore, "if any can (in naturall sence)

1 Chettle as Printer

giue ease, they must be Artistes, that are able to search the cause, resist the disease, by prouiding remedies" (24).

The character Burcot compares such false cures as "cuttings, drawings, corrosiuings, borings, butcherings" to "tortures" (25). These surgical methods originally came from the writings of Galen, Chauliac, and Vigo, and Chettle probably read these books. However, some quacks wrongly interpreted and employed the methods, according to Burcot. Also, Burcot attacks a "wise woman" selling a spoonful of "strong water" as a cure, though it was "fountaine water," for forty shillings, and also an apothecary who misused an authorized prescription by a physician and killed his patient (26-27). Edward F. Rimbault, an editor of the work, comments "Chettle seems to have had good reason for his complaint" and points out "[i]n 1584, Christopher Langhton published 'A Letter, sent by a learned Phisitian to his friend, wherein are detected the manifold errors vsed hetherto of the Apothecaries…'" (Rimbault, ed., *Kind Heart's Dream* 74).

Chettle possibly became interested in these medical problems through his printing work and reading some medical pamphlets at East's press, though these do not seem to discuss quackery as does *Kind-Heart's Dream*. The figure of a doctor is also seen in *Hoffman*. Between Act III Scene ii and Act IV Scene i, Lorrique, Hoffman's tool, disguises himself as a French doctor, prepares poisoned wines, and deceives the Duke of Prussia and his idiot prince, Jerome, into drinking it. This is a bloody scene, but the chorus among Hoffman (disguised as Otho), Jerome's servant, Stilt, and the Duke includes a kind of medical joke:

> HOFFMAN.[24] Physitians for the Duke, my vncle faints,
> STILT. Surgeons for the Prince, my master falls.
> FERDINAND. Call no Phisitians, for I feel't too late,
>   The subtill poyson mingled with my blood…. (4.1.1579-82)[25]

The villainous Frenchman was a frequent literary figure around 1600. Jeremy Lopez claims that such heavily accented Frenchmen, as seen in Lodge's

The Wound's of Civil War, "will come at the turn of the century to signal a common foppish parody of the court intriguer," counting Lorrique as an example (310). It is uncertain how much Chettle knew directly of the medical field, but obviously he was keen on medicine as a literary trope.

Military books also had great influence on Chettle, since like other contemporary playwrights, he must have paid attention to this politically important issue of the period. East published several military books including such translations as Machiavelli's *The Art of War* and Caesar's *The Eight Books*, and also such popular vernacular books as Styward's *The Pathway to Military Discipline* and Polemon's *The Second Part of the Book of Battles* during Chettle's apprenticeship and unknown period, among which the most important was Polemon's *The Second Part*. As mentioned in the previous section, this book is noteworthy as the source of Peele's *The Battle of Alcazar*, but more significantly, Chettle read this book and obtained some knowledge of the battle of Lepanto. Chettle's first published piece of writing is probably *Pope's Pitiful Lamentation* (1579), as will be discussed in the next section; this work is an elegy for John of Austria, who brought victory to the Pope's army at the battle of Lepanto. Moreover, *England's Mourning Garment* refers to the "memorable battell of *Lepanto*," together with John of Austria (90). Furthermore, John of Austria is employed as a name of a character "John, Duke of Austria" in *Hoffman*.

The military is thematically a subject in *Piers Plainness*, *Downfall*, *Death*, *Blind Beggar*, and *Hoffman*, as will be discussed in Part II "Politics and Religion" and Part III "Society," but in particular, Chapter 6 "*Hoffman* and Elizabethan Military Culture" in Part II. While Shakespeare in describing battle scenes, especially in the theoretical confrontation between Fluellen and Macmorris in *Henry V* seems to have shown his knowledge of the art of war, matters which were frequently discussed in military books, Chettle seems to have approached the question of war more roughly and abstractly. Unlike other contemporary dramatists, Chettle does not describe details, but focuses on such political issues as rebellion and *coup d'état* and also on the relation of soldierly characters. All of the above plays deal with rebellion, which usually occurs for an unjust reason, while the banished are often valiant soldiers, such as Hoffman's father and Momford in *Blind Beggar*.

For other genres printed by East, navigation perhaps inspired Chettle in writing about piracy in *Hoffman*, but most of them have nothing to do with Chettle's works. Books on literature, medicine, and military thus had a large influence on Chettle's prose and dramatic works, and also Protestant works encouraged him to establish a religious and political ideology. His attitude of anti-Catholicism and anti-Spain were fundamental in his tracts including *Downfall*, *Death*, and *Sir Thomas Wyatt* among others.

(c) Chettle's Relationships with Authors, Printers, and Publishers in His Apprentice and Post-Apprentice Days

The catalogue of East's publications illustrates the range of Chettle's relationships with writers, particularly the University Wits, printers, and publishers, as well as his literary influences. The most remarkable of these relationships was his connection with Greene. As mentioned in the introduction, in *A Knight's Conjuring* (1607), Dekker depicts Chettle joining a company of dead poets including Marlowe, Peele, Greene and Nashe in the Elysian Fields (L1r-v). This suggests these writers were Chettle's friends.

Many critics have paid attention to the authorship of Greene's posthumous pamphlet *Groatsworth* (1592). The Stationers' Register records on 20 September 1592: ""William Wrighte / Entred for his copie, vnder master watkins hande / vppon the perill of Henrye Chettle / a booke intituled / GREENES *Groatsworth of wyt bought with a million of Repentance*" (Arber 2: 620). The words "vpon the peril of Henrye Chettle" and also Chettle's own reference to this book in the preface to *Kind-Heart's Dream* suggest the possibility that Chettle edited this for his close friend Greene. Moreover, some critics using computer analysis, suspect Chettle wrote some parts, as will be discussed in Chapter 2, "(i) Danter's Press and *Greene's Groatsworth of Wit*;" however, the question of how and when Chettle and Greene knew each other has received little or no analysis.

Chettle and Greene possibly met in 1584 when East printed Greene's *Gwydonius* for the bookseller William Ponsonby, who also published Sidney's *Arcadia* and Spenser's *Faerie Queene, Amoretti,* and *Colin Clout* as well as Greene's first book, *Mamillia*. Although Chettle became a freeman of the company on 6 October 1584, the book was entered on 4 November 1583, and it is, thus, probable that Chettle was involved in the work as a printer.

Danter printed *Groatsworth* and *The Repentance of Robert Greene* in 1592, but prior to these publications Danter had already met Greene when he transferred his apprenticehip from Day, who died in 1584, to Robert Robinson, a piratical printer. In 1589 Robinson printed Greene's *Ciceronis Amor* for Thomas Newman. Danter issued numerous literary works by Greene, Nashe, Peele, Lodge, and Shakespeare. Chettle obviously met these writers, probably except Shakespeare, at Danter's press, but he had already known them before starting to work there.

Lodge had been acquainted with Chettle, at least, by 1584, when *An Alarum against Usurers* was issued by East for Sampson Clarke. The Stationers' Register's entry is dated 11 April 1584, a time when Chettle was still East's apprentice. Whether or not it is coincidental that Greene and Lodge wrote books published by East in the same year, Greene, Lodge, and Chettle certainly were closely tied to each other in print culture. It is uncertain how Greene and Lodge met each other, but both of them were granted M.A.s from Oxford, though Greene took his B.A. and M.A. at Cambridge. They produced a play in collaboration: *A Looking Glass for London and England*, printed by Creede for William Barley in 1594.

Chettle, on the other hand, entered "The bayting of *DIOGENES*," namely Lodge's *Catharos*, which was printed by Hoskins and Danter for John Busby in 1591. Moreover, Lodge's *The Wounds of Civil War* was printed by Danter in 1594, and Chettle may also have been involved in this work, since, though Chettle's partnership with Danter was dissolved in 1591, Chettle still worked for him as a printer, as will be discussed in the

1 Chettle as Printer

next chapter. Furthermore, Chettle alludes to Lodge as "delicious sportiue Musidore" and encourages him to write an elegy for Elizabeth in *England's Mourning Garment* (98), which implies their constant and close relation.

Nashe, who was mentioned by Dekker in the work, met Chettle through Greene probably before 1591, when he started working at Danter's press. Nashe stayed at Cambridge between 1581 or 1582 and 1588, while Greene lived there between 1575 and 1583. Nashe wrote an epistle for Greene's *Menaphon*, printed by Thomas Orwin for Clarke in 1589. Clarke published Lodge's *Alarum against Usurers* in 1584 and must have known Chettle. Therefore, there is another possibility that Chettle met Nashe through Clarke as well as Greene before 1591. However, Chettle may have first met Nashe at Danter's press.[26]

Peele, who is also mentioned by Dekker, probably came to know Chettle at Danter's press when his collaboration with Shakespeare, *Titus Andronicus* (1594), and also *The Old Wife's Tale* (1595) were published there. However, they may have met earlier, at least, before 1592, since there is an allusion to Peele in *Groatsworth*, which Chettle edited and probably wrote partly. Moreover, as I discussed above, Peele definitely read Polemon's *The Second Part of the Book of Battle*, issued by East in 1587, and employed it as a source for *The Battle of Alcazar*, which was probably performed in the late 1580s around the Armada. Furthermore, Peele clearly read East's other publications, Roberts's *A Most Friendly Farewell… to the Right Worshipful Sir Francis Drake* and also *The Shepheardes Calender*. These works obviously influenced Peele's *A Farewell to…Sir John Norris and Sir Francis Drake* (1589) and *An Eclogue to…Robert Earl of Essex* (1589). Therefore, by 1592, Chettle had probably known Peele through Greene or Nashe or Allde (the printer of Peele's *The Arraignment of Paris*, 1585) or Charlewood (the printer of *A Farewell*, 1589) or Wright (the publisher of *A Farewell*).

Marlowe is also mentioned in Dekker's work and *Groatsworth*, but there are no clues to help elucidate the details of the relationship between Marlowe and Chettle. Probably, through Greene and Nashe, Chettle became an acquaintance of Marlowe. Thus, their relationship cannot be clearly traced, but it is certain that Chettle was greatly influenced by Marlowe's plays, such as *The Jew of Malta* and *The Massacre at Paris*.[27]

Another noticeable point in Chettle's early career is the relation with Munday. Chettle wrote some plays including *Sir Thomas More*, *Downfall*, and *Death* in collaboration with Munday, and also Chettle wrote an epistle to the annnonymous Spanish novel, *2 Primaleon of Greece*, translated by Munday: "To his good Friend M. Anthony Mundy" (STC 20366a; A3r). This book was printed by Danter for Burby in 1596. C. T. Wright suggests their friendship started in their youth, that is, Chettle's apprenticeship period ("Young Anthony Munday" 152-53). East did not print Munday's books, but in 1579 he issued works for George Baker (a translation of Chauliac's *Guydos Questions*) and Lyly (*The Anatomy of Wit*), both of whom worked for Edward de Vere, Earl of Oxford, respectively as a physician and a secretary; Munday was Oxford's servant and dedicated his early works, *The Mirror of Mutability* (1579; STC 18276) and *Zelauto* (1580; STC 18283), to him, as Wright remarks (153). Also, in 1580 East printed texts for Thomas Newton who had written some complimentary verses for Munday, and in 1582 East printed sermons by Puritan preacher, George Gifford, to whom Munday had made a dedication (Wright 153). Furthermore, in 1582, East printed Styward's popular book, *The Pathway to Martial Discipline*, with Charlewood. Likewise, in 1587, East printed a sermon with Charlewood. Charlewood printed dozens of Munday's books from 1577 to his death in 1593, and also printed *The Pope's Pitiful Lamentation*, translated by "H. C.," possibly Chettle, in 1578. Thus, it is likely that East had become acquainted with Charlewood by 1582. Moreover, Charlewood printed Greene's *Morando* (STC 12276) in 1584, and Nashe's first work, *The Anatomy of Absurdity* (STC 18364), in 1589, among others.

At East's press, Chettle, thus, expanded his personal connections with printers and publishers as well as authors. Chettle must have met such frequent partners of East as Gabriel Cawood, Ponsonby, John Harrison, the younger, Thomas Cadman, Wight, and others. Thomas Man and Thomas Gosson worked both with East and Danter, and particularly Gosson is significant for publishing Chettle's *Piers Plainness* (1595) and H. C., or probably Chettle's *A Doleful Ditty, or Sorrowful Sonnet of the Lord Dar[n]ly* (1579).

Creede, Chettle's senior apprentice, became a freeman in 1578, and he spent one year with Chettle at East's press (Arber 2: 679). Creede, however, remained a journeyman for a decade and a half, according to Akihiro Yamada ("Thomas Creede" 65). This suggests that Creede may have stayed longer at East's press with Chettle. Creede printed several works of Shakespeare including the second, third, fourth, and fifth quartos of *Richard III* (1598; STC 22315; 1602; STC 22316; 1605; STC 22317; 1612; STC 22318) and the second quarto of *Romeo and Juliet* (1599; STC 22323), and also issued the second edition of Greene's *2 Mamillia* (1593; STC 12270), the second edition of *Groatsworth* (1596; STC 12246), Lodge's *A Treatise of the Plague*, which is mentioned in the introduction, and Greene and Lodge's *A Looking Glass for London and England* (1594; STC 16679; 1598; STC 16680), and also Greene's *Pandosto* (1614; STC 12289) and *The Scottish History of James the Fourth* (1598; STC 12308).

As discussed above, Scarlet was Chettle's fellow apprentice. Scarlet became East's apprentice on 25 March 1577 and became free on 12 October 1586 (Arber 2: 698-99). On the other hand, Chettle began his apprenticeship on 29 September 1577 and became a freeman on 6 October 1584 (Arber 2: 81; 693). As Chettle stayed at East's press even after finishing his apprenticeship period, they spent such a long time together there, and their relationship must have continued longer. As Chiaki Hanabusa notes, Scarlet worked with Danter frequently, and they met probably through Chettle ("Insatsu-Gyosha" 39-41).

(d) Three Works by "H. C."

Kind-Hearts Dream (1593) has been widely accepted as being Chettle's first literary product, but there seems still to be room for debate concerning the three works by "H. C.:" *The Pope's Pitiful Lamentation, for the Death of His Dear Darling Don Joan of Austria: and Death's Answer to the Same…Translated after the French Printed Copy* (composed in 1578 and published in 1579; STC 12355); *A Doleful Ditty, or Sorrowful Sonnet of the Lord Dar[n]ly, Sometime King of Scots* (1579; STC 4270.5); *The Forest of Fancy* (1579; STC 4271). Critics have frequently identified these to be by Chettle or the contemporary poet, Henry Constable. Joseph Ritson attributed the three works to Chettle, but Jenkins, following William Hazlitt and Bullen, denied this, claiming that Chettle was an apprentice, probably in his late-teens, and too young to write them (Ritson 169; Hazlitt 212; Bullen 210; Jenkins 30-31).

On the other hand, C. T. Wright argued that the age of the writer does not matter and attributed the texts to Chettle, using external evidence, as discussed below. Certainly, Munday at around the same age as Chettle wrote many pamphlets between 1579 and 1582, as is also detailed below. Moreover, apprentices, usually from their late-teens to the early twenties, generally could read and enjoy "jest-books, ballads, didactic tracts, satirical pamphlets and plays" (Burnett, "Apprentice Literature" 27). Likewise, as an apprentice, Chettle was familiar with such pamphlets, made the most of the advantages of his apprenticeship at East's press, and probably dreamed of being a writer. His apprenticeship days seem to be reflected in *Piers Plainness*. Therefore, it is not too farfetched to speculate Chettle could have engaged in writing activities during this period.

Ritson attributed all three works to Chettle, while other critics have partly found Chettle's authorship; for *The Pope's Pitiful Lamentation*, editors of *Downfall* and *Death*, J. P. Collier and Egerton Brydges hesitated between Chettle and Constable (Collier 4; Brydges 6-7). Richard Ackermann, an editor of *Hoffman*, and Edward F. Rimbault, an editor of *Kind-Heart's Dream*, saw Constable as a more probable author for *A Doleful Ditty* (Ackermann xi; Rimbault xi). Warton hesitated between Chettle and Constable for *Forest of Fancy*, though Edmund Malone attributed it to Henry Cheke, an Elizabethan translator (Warton 386; Ault 78).

1 Chettle as Printer

More recently, Jowett supported Wright with two pieces of additional evidence in an article, as detailed below, and attributed the three works to Chettle in the *DLB*. However, there is no firm evidence for Chettle's authorship, as Emma Smith says in the latest *DNB*. Although nowadays computer analysis helps resolve authorship problems, no critic has seriously tackled this case with a statistical examination. There are only a few works that Chettle wrote on his own, and most of them except *Hoffman* are written in prose unlike the three tracts. Another problem is that his style possibly changed as he matured. Therefore, these authorship issues are impossible to resolve; however, I would like to add some points concerning both internal and external approaches to support the attribution to Chettle.

As Jowett notes, the three works were produced around the same time when *Euphues* was first published in 1578 ("Notes" 384). The euphuistic style can be seen in each tract, which may imply Chettle's hand, since he must have read *Euphues*. *The Pope's Pitiful Lamentation* (eight page-octavo) was entered on 24 March 1579 by Charlewood, though the final leaf notes "The fyrst of October," the date of John of Austria's death (Arber 2: 349). This is a small tract in verse in which Pope Gregory XII laments the death of John of Austria. Jowett associates John of Austria with Chettle's writing: first, he points out the two characters called John in *Hoffman*, namely John, the Duke of Saxony, and John, the Duke of Austria, both of whom are killed in the play; second, he shows bibliographical evidence from Chettle's epistle to *2 Primaleon of Greece* (1596); Chettle complains about the printer's errors and takes the example of "Ione for Iohn" (A3v) with which Jowett links "Ioan" on the title-page of *The Pope's Pitiful Lamentation* ("Notes" 384-85). The latter points seem less persuasive, but the first is a good point, to which could be added the mention of John of Austria in *England's Mourning Garment*. The title-page suggests the original was French, but *A Dictionary of Anonymous and Pseudonymous Publications* (3rd ed.) notes: "The 'French [printed] coppy' is untraced, and may be fictitious" (P184). If Chettle was certainly involved in this tract, his tendency to forgery, which is found in

Groatsworth and elsewhere, would have already started at this early point.

A Doleful Ditty is a broadside sheet entered by Gosson on 24 March 1579, coincidently the same date as *The Pope's Pitiful Lamentation* (Arber 2: 349). This ballad depicts in verse the murder of Henry Stewart, the Duke of Albany, known as Lord Darnley, on 9 February 1567. An earlier ballad "The Murder of the King of Scots" was probably printed soon after Mary's escape into England in 1568 (Percy 54-55). The violent tone is similar to that of *The Pope's Pitiful Lamentation* with a great deal of exclamation and alliteration. Chettle dealt with Scottish history in the lost play *Robert II, or The Scot's Tragedy* with Dekker, Jonson, and John Marston in 1599, and his concern about the country may have been already suggested twenty years before.

The Forest of Fancy has no entry record on the Stationers' Register; according to the title-page, it was printed by Purfoot in 1579. Two quarto editions were issued in the same year; the first edition contains fifty-eight leaves while the second has eighty. This work is printed in black letter, occasionally illegibly, and is composed of many short poems and a few long stories in verse. Mary Augusta Scott found the prose work based on Giovanni Boccaccio's *Decameron* (36-37). In 1569, Purfoot published a translation of Boccaccio's *A Notable History of Nastagio and Trauersari* (STC 3184), and it is highly likely that the author of *The Forest of Fancy* had read this before writing his work. The poems are miscellaneous: love letters; morals; merry songs and sonnets. Some verses refer to mythological persons such as Oedipus and Jocasta (B4r), with whom Chettle overlaps Hoffman and Martha in *Hoffman*, and also Medea and Jason (D2r), who are mentioned in the same play. Griselda, whom Chettle later used as a motif in his drama, is also mentioned in a letter from the author to his mistress (F4r); however, Elizabethan authors were usually familiar with Italian stories and Greek myths, and these are not sufficient to prove Chettle's authorship.

These internal approaches have limits because Chettle's extant single writings are only small in number, and there is no authorized transcription and edition for the three works; however, external approaches might be

1 Chettle as Printer

useful to trace Chettle's hand. The publication lists of the publishers for the three works possibly serve to show the relations between author and printer. C. T. Wright conjectured that Charlewood urged Chettle to write and publish *The Pope's Pitiful Lamentation* ("Young Anthony Munday" 152). This is only a conjecture, but it is likely that Charlewood knew Chettle and printed for the young apprentice, because Charlewood printed many works by Chettle's friends including Munday, Greene, and Nashe.

Charlewood was a prolific but notorious printer. There is hardly any record of his apprenticeship period, but the titles he entered are seen in the Stationers' Register from 1562. Between 1578 and 1580 he was fined for unlicensed printing, and between 1582 and 1583, he set up a partnership with William Wright and Wolfe, both of whom were involved in publishing *Kind-Heart's Dream* with Danter, as will be discussed in the following chapter. Among Charlewood's publications, the most notable are the Protestant writings of Bullinger, Calvin, and Henry Smith, though Charlewood is suspected to have been a Catholic by some critics (Wright, "Young Authony Munday" 158; T. Hill 48). Interestingly, Charlewood printed the afore mentioned Protestant works: the anonymous *Certain Sermons*, the anonymous *The Second Tome of Homilies*, and also Styward's military book *The Pathway to Martial Discipline* with East. However, more important are Charlewood's literary productions, which may indicate relationships between him, and Munday, Greene, and Nashe. Charlewood printed Munday's early works: *The Mirror of Mutability, Zelauto, A View of Sundry Examples* (1580; STC 18281), *A Brief Discourse of the Taking of Edmund Campion* (1581; STC 18261), *A Discovery of Edmund Campion and His Confederates* (1582; STC 18270), *The English Roman Life* (1582; STC 18272), *A Watch-Word to England to Beware of Traytors* (1582; STC 18282) among others, and some of them were published by Wright. Furthermore, Charlewood printed Greene's *Morando* (1584; STC 12276), *Gwydonius* (1587; STC 12262.5), and *Arbasto* (1589; STC 12217) as well as Nashe's *The Anatomy of Absurdity* (1589; STC 18364) and *Pierce Penniless His Supplication to the Devil* (1592; STC 18371). The 1587 *Gwydonius* is the second edition, the first having been by East in 1584, and as Charlewood and East published the anonymous *Certain Sermons* and *The Second Tome of Homilies* together in 1587, the two printers must have already established a close relation by that time. Nashe's *Pierce Penniless* was definitely read by Chettle, who referred to it in the passage concerning Gabriel Harvey in *Kind-Heart's Dream* and also copied the title in *Piers Plainness*.

Although Charlewood printed a miscellany of sonnets, *Diana*, written by another candidate for the "H. C." works, Constable, in 1592, it seems unlikely that Constable wrote *The Pope's Pitiful Lamentation* at the age of sixteen when he was enrolled in St. John's College, Cambridge, as discussed above. Neither does Cheke seem to be a possible candidate; he translated only an Italian tragedy, *A Certain Tragedy* and never worked with Charlewood. Furthermore, around 1 October 1578, the date on the last sheet of the work, Cheke was in France on business. Charlewood's connection with East, Munday, Greene, and Nashe seems to indicate that Chettle is more likely to be the author than Constable or Cheke.

C. T. Wright attributed *A Doleful Ditty* to Chettle as well, noting the relation between Chettle and his publisher, Gosson, for whom Danter later printed *Piers Plainness* in 1595 ("Young Anthony Munday" 152). Gosson apprenticed himself to Purfoot and became a member of the Stationers' Company on 4 February 1577. Gosson made his first entry into the Stationers' Register with "a ballad *concerninge the murder of the late kinge of Scottes*," or *A Doleful Ditty* on 24 March 1579. Curiously, on that same day Charlewood entered *The Pope's Pitiful Lamentation* as "*the Lamentacon of the pope for the Deathe of DON JHON [of Austria]*." Also, on the same day East entered "A *booke of ij wonderfull monsters*," though this work was neither published nor is extant (Arber 2: 349). This may just be meaningless coincidence, but it certainly shows what a closely knit community the printing industry was, because all three were related to Chettle. Afterwards, Henry Carr entered on 15 August 1586 "*A Dittie of the lord DAR[N]LEY somtyme Kinge of Scottes*," another work which is not extant (Arber 2: 454). Jenkins claims this may have

1 Chettle as Printer

been a reprint or another ballad dealing with the same theme (32, n.2).

Gosson did not publish many books from 1579 to 1596 (his birth and death dates are unknown). Six of them including *Piers Plainness* were printed by Danter, while one of them was a morality printed by East in 1580, when Chettle was his apprentice. Most of Gosson's publications were religious writings, which included texts by Henry Smith; one such was his brother Stephen Gosson's anti-theatrical pamphlet against Lodge, *Plays of a Good Name*. A few of them were anonymous news pamphlets of foreign battles, and the only literary productions were *A Doleful Ditty* and *Piers Plainness*, though these have characteristics of news pamphlets since the former deals with religious, historical, and political subjects and the latter socio-political. The strong connection Chettle had with Gosson and Danter as well as the ironical and political content of the ballad may detract from the possibility of Constable or Cheke being the author.

Furthermore, Chettle seems to have been interested in ballad culture. In *Kind-Heart's Dream* Chettle criticizes ballad mongers through the voice of Anthony Now Now. At that time, there were so many ballad mongers on the street, and there were attempts by the authorities to forbid the selling of ballads. Chettle seems to agree with the official perspective, but he shows sympathy for young apprentices, who were urged by their masters to engage in "singing brokerie," namely writing, selling and singing ballads instead of learning their trade.

> I haue heard say taken to be apprentices by a worthlesse companion (if it proue true that is of him reported) being of a worshipfull trade, and yet no Stationer, who after a little bringing them vppe to singing brokerie, takes into his shop some fresh men, and trusts his olde searuantes of a two months standing with a dossen groates worth of ballads. (19)

As Chettle's partner Hoskins was imprisoned and fined ten shillings in 1582 for having kept an apprentice for seven years without the instruction of printing, there seem to have been some bad masters in the industry (Arber 2: 583). Such neglected apprentices eventually became vagrants without obtaining a "Pattent" (21) and thus came to sing ballads like aged and disabled people:

> ...if there be any songes suffered in such publike sorte to be soong, beseech that they may either be such as your selues, that after seauen yeares or more seruice, haue no other liuinge lefte you out of Pattent, but that poore base life, of it selfe too badde, yet made more beggarly, by increase of nomber: or at least if any if besides you be therto admitted, thã it may be none other but aged and impotent persons.... (20-21)

Chettle only refers to apprenticeships in the printing industry here, but apprentices in other guilds were also so young and weak that their masters often exploited them. Consequently, their resentments against their masters exploded in violence. Particularly, in the mid-1590s the number of violent incidents increased due to famine and distress; for example, in 1592 a feltmaker's apprentice was imprisoned for debt in Marshalsea prison, and his fellow apprentices planned to rescue him, thus rioting—an episode which is alluded to in *Sir Thomas More*, according to Peter W. M. Blayney and Burnett (Blayney 189; Burnett, "Apprentice Literature" 36-37).

The plight of apprentices is described in *Plainness*, as well. The narrator-protagonist Piers is an apprentice serving seven different masters from a broker to a courtier, and he is poor and starving for lack of money, while his masters are wealthy.

These two works, more or less, reflect Chettle's experience as an apprentice. Jenkins, while denying the possibility that Chettle is the author of the three works in question, suggests Chettle may have written ballads and small literary works at his leisure (34); *A Doleful Ditty* might be one of them.

The Forest of Fancy was printed by Purfoot in 1579, according to the title page, but the Stationers' Register has no entry for this tract. This work seems to be linked with *The Pope's Pitiful Lamentation* and also *A Doleful Ditty*.

1 Chettle as Printer

As Jenkins points out, *The Forest of Fancy* and *The Pope's Pitiful Lamentation* share the explicit "L'acquis Abonde," French words which mean "abundant knowledge" at the end of each work, and this implies the two works were written by the same author (34).[28] Furthermore, Purfoot's former apprentice, Gosson's is the publisher of *A Doleful Ditty*, and "H. C." is probably someone whom both of them knew.

Purfoot was involved in publishing many books: religious writings; some statutes; a few literary works by such as Boccaccio and Henry Petowe. *The Forest of Fancy* includes some stories from Boccaccio, as Scott suggests (471-73). Although in the early Stuart period, his son, Thomas Purfoot, printed or reprinted some works of Greene and such Chettle collaborators as Heywood and Samuel Rowley, the older Purfoot does not seem to have published for Chettle's acquaintances except Petowe; Purfoot printed Petowe's *2 Hero and Leander* in 1598, and Petowe's *Philochasander and Elanira* in 1599. Petowe ("*Musæus*") is urged by Chettle to write an elegy for Elizabeth in *England's Mourning Garment* (98), and Petowe responded to him, promptly writing *Elizabetha Quasi Vivens, Eliza's Funeral* (1603; STC 19803.5).

The epistle to *The Forest of Fancy* provides a useful clue to its authorship. The author apologizes for his literary immaturity to the readers:

> ...though my yong yeares and small experience, will not permit me to wryghte so pithily as some haue done heretofore, whose worthy works are extant, and in great estimation, yet considering that I haue not done it either for gaine or glory, but partly to make my selfe more apte in other matters of more importaunce wherein I maye happen hereafter to be imployed, and partly to procure thy pleasure and profite.... (A4v-B1r)

The author observes that he is young and immature; therefore, if the words are true, he is not likely to be Cheke, who was thirty-one when the work was published, while Constable was seventeen, and Chettle was probably nineteen. The author underestimates the tract, but paradoxically he has confidence enough to say, "thy pleasure and profite (which may easilye be obtained)." The meanings of "other matters of more importaunce wherein I maye happen hereafter to be imployed" is not clear, but it probably suggests the author sought literary patronage. If this "H. C." is Chettle, it can be inferred that he intended to be an author in his youth, perhaps even before beginning to work as a printer, stationer and editor.

(ii) Chettle and John Danter: Professional Printer and Path to Authorship

(a) Chettle's Relationship with Danter

After becoming a freeman, Chettle settled on a partnership with Hoskins and Danter on 3 August 1591, according to the *Records of the Court of the Stationers' Company 1576 to 1602*, edited by W. W. Greg and Eleanore Boswell:

> Yt is thought good that will hoskins maye accept to be pten's wth him in printing henry Chettell and Iohn Danter pvidd always that there shalbe not alienacōn or transportinge made by hym to them or either of them or to any other of his Rowm or place of A mayster printer wthout consent of the mr. wardens and Assistente for the tyme beinge. (38)

The statement suggests Hoskins, the oldest partner, was the leader. Hoskins was admitted as a freeman on 15 May 1571 after being apprenticed to Richard Tottel (Arber 1: 146, 147). Danter apprenticed himself to Day and Robinson, and became a freeman on 31 September 1589. The three worked at Hoskins's press in Fetter Lane until Danter opened his shop on Duck Lane at the end of the year (McKerrow et al., eds., *A Dictionary of Printers* 84). How the three met is unknown, as there are few records about Hoskins and his publications, but Chettle and Danter seem to have known each other probably through Greene. As discussed in the previous section, Chettle possibly met Greene when East published his *Gwydonius* in 1584, while Danter's master, Robinson, printed Greene's *Ciceronis Amor* in 1589. Partnership in printing and publishing was common at that time, as Ben-

1 Chettle as Printer

nett remarks; printers and publishers needed partnerships for various reasons; for "lack of cash, lack of printing materials, or unwillingness to take a hundred per cent risk" (274).

At Hoskins's press, Chettle worked mainly as a printer.[29] On 17 September 1591, Chettle "Entred his copie by warrant from master Watkins The bayting of *DYOGENES*" with six pence (Arber 2: 595). This is his first and last entry in the Staioners' Register. The title-page omits Chettle's name, but he was probably engaged in the project. On the other hand, Chettle, with Hoskins and Danter, printed two books by Henry Smith in 1591. *A Fruitful Sermon* was entered on 18 August 1591. The only bibliographical information on the title-page is "Printed for Nicholas Ling. 1591," but the colophon reads: "Imprinted At London, by William Hoskins, Henrie Chettle, and Iohn Danter, for Nicholas Ling: & are to be sold at his shop at the West end of Paules. 1591." The title-page of a variant issue prints "the widdowe Broome" instead of Ling. The other book is *The Affinity of the Faithful*, which was entered to Ling on 12 September 1591. There are two variant issues of this book, too. One title-page prints, "Printed by William | Hoskins and Henrie Chettle, for | *Nicholas Ling*, and *Iohn* | *Busbie*. 1591," while the other has "Printed by William | Hoskins and Iohn Danter, for | *Nicholas Ling*, and *Iohn* | *Busbie*. 1591" (Jenkins 7).

After Danter set up his press and the partnership dissolved, Chettle became unemployed without his own shop (Jowett, "*Henry Chettle*" 145). This plight of the printer reminds us of the poor apprentice writing and selling ballads described in *Kind-Heart's Dream*. However, from this time, Chettle's concern slowly shifted from printing to writing; he became an editor, a pamphleteer, and a dramatist, who continuously worked with Danter.

The reason why the three separated is uncertain, but it could have been money trouble. An order of the Court of the Stationers' Company on 5 March 1593 suggests there was a dispute between Chettle and Danter, for which Thomas Dawson and Orwin were summoned:

> The matter in controu'sie betwene them is referred to Tho Dason and Tho orwin They to heare and determine the same yf they can: [*or els to certifie the court*]. and the said pties to enter into bond in vli a pece to stand to thward of the seid Comittees.... (46)

The cause of the controversy is unknown, though Sidney Thomas associates this issue with the publications of *Groatsworth* and/or *Kind-Heart's Dream* ("The Printing" 197). This case was eventually peacefully resolved, as their later business partnership shows (Jenkins 7-8; Jowett, "*Henry Chettle*" 145). Interestingly, on the same day, Danter was put on another "lyke sort" of trial for his conflict with Burby, who became independent from Wright on 13 January of 1592 and frequently worked with Danter.[30] Dawson and Orwin were again referred to: "And in lyke sort the controu'sie betwene Danter and Cutb. burby is referred to be ended by the seid Tho dason & Tho orwin" (46). Similarly, the business relation between Danter and Burby still continued after this trial occurred in 1593, so they reconciled peacefully.

As Jenkins and Jowett point out, Chettle's continuous partnership with Danter has been inferred both from an epistle to Etienne de Maisonneuve's Spanish novel *2 Primaleon of Greece* translated by Munday and from his letter to Nashe in *Have with You to Saffron Walden* (Jenkins 14-18; Jowett, "*Henry Chettle*" 155-58). *2 Primaleon of Greece*, for which Chettle wrote an epistle "To his good Friend M. *Anthony Mundy*," was printed by Danter for Burby in 1596. Chettle signed this epistle, "Your old Well-willer: *H.C. Printer*" (A3v). This suggests Chettle worked for Danter as a printer in 1596 after having written *Kind-Heart's Dream* and *Piers Plainness*, both of which were printed by Danter. On the other hand, Nashe's *Have with You to Saffron Walden*, printed by Danter in 1596, contains Chettle's letter with the signature "Your old compositor, *Henry Chettle*" (131), which suggests Chettle worked as a compositor for Danter.[31] Danter printed Nashe's *Strange News* (1592, 1593), *The Apology of Pierce Penniless* (1593), *The Terrors of the Night* (1594), and *The Unfortunate Traveler* (1594), and Chettle was involved in some or all of them.

1 Chettle as Printer

By 1596 Chettle was an author, printer, and compositor. Jowett claims that neither authorship nor editing existed as concepts at the time, but that the people apparently admitted the different roles of author and printer within the production of printed books ("*Henry Chettle*" 142-44; 160-61). Chettle seems to have used this notion; when he wrote as a printer, he insisted on his identity as a printer, occasionally escaping issues in question. In a letter to Nashe in *Have with You to Saffron Walden*, "Your old compositor, *Henry Chettle*" remarks:

> I Hold it no good manners (M. Nashe), being but an Artificer, to giue D. Haruey *the ly, though he haue deseru'd it by publishing in Print you haue done mee wrong…your booke being readie for the Presse, Ile square & set it out in Pages, that shall page and lackey his infamie after him (at least) while he liues, if no longer.* (131)

Nashe quotes this letter with the intention to show his support and attack Gabriel Harvey, but the cautious Chettle seems to avoid getting involved, insisting on referring to his identity as a printer and his business with the technical terms "*publishing in Print,*" "*Presse,*" "*square & set it out in Pages.*" In particular, "Artificer" denotes an artisan and is clearly distinguished from an author.

Before entering into playwriting, or at least around 1593, Chettle was probably regarded as a printer rather than an author. Even as a writer Chettle held on to his identity as a printer. In the preface to *Kind-Heart's Dream* Chettle observes, "*How I haue all the time of my conuersing in printing hindred the bitter inueying against schollers, it hath been uery well knowne, and how in that I dealt I can sufficiently prooue*" (6). This passage suggests Chettle had been engaged in printing for a long time, and admitted a difference between being a printer and a scholar; he is a less educated printer and different from a well-educated author. However, more remarkably, he refrains from "*inueying against*" the scholars. This suggests a printer could change the words without the permission of the author if necessary. In other words, Chettle was a corrector of press or a proofreader for Danter, as Jowett claims ("*Henry*

Chettle" 143). Chettle prefers this title, as it allows him to deny responsibility for the faults, but he unintentionally alerts the reader to the possibility of his hand in writing. Furthermore, using many technical terms, Chettle explains the publication process of *Groatsworth*; Greene left "*many papers in sundry Book sellers*," one of which was "*a letter written to diuers play-makers*" in *Groatsworth*, and "*I had onely in the copy this share, it was il written, as sometime Greenes hand was none of the best, lisensd it must be, ere it could bee printed which could neuer be if it might not be read*" (5-6). As seen in *Have with You to Saffron Walden*, Chettle uses printing terms and shows his knowledge of this area to emphasize he is a printer. In the early to mid 1590s, Chettle thus claimed his identity as a less educated printer even when he was an author.

In *Henslowe's Diary*, Chettle's name first appears on 25 February 1598 for *Death* (87), and Meres counted him as one of the "best poets for comedy" in *Palladis Tamia*, published by Short for Burby in the same year (283). After this, Chettle's name is frequently seen in the *Diary*, which suggests he devoted himself to writing plays; however, he still calls himself "I henry [sic] Chettle of London Stationer" to pledge his debt to Henslowe on 22 October 1598 (Henslowe 119).

Likewise, as Judith K. Rogers notes, Danter shows his professionalism in the dedications to the readers of Richard Barnfield's *Greene's Funerals* (1594; STC 1480), and Christopher Middleton's *The Famous History of Chinon of England* (1597; STC 17866): "Although a printer who wrote dedications during this period is not that unusual, Danter's rhetorical flourishes are unusual, and his repeated references to himself as a printer convey a sense of pride in his trade" (Rogers 76). Moreover, Danter appears on stage as a printer in *The Return from Parnassus*, an anonymous play printed in 1606 (STC 19309). Act I Scene iii begins with the stage direction, "*Enter Danter the printer*" (B3r). At first, Danter complains to a writer that he lost money on the last printing of the writer's work, but he starts new negotiations about another book by the author. These points suggest Elizabethan printers could occasionally be an author, and also become well-known in

1 Chettle as Printer

the stage world. In other words, the printing industry and theatrical world were closely linked to each other, and some printers including Danter and Chettle were famous, like authors and actors were. Through their writings in the epistles and dedications, Danter and Chettle appealed as printers to the readers, while Nashe mentioned them and made them known in *Have with You to Saffron Walden*.

(b) Danter's Publications between 1591 and 1598

Without opening a press and shop, Chettle probably decided to engage in whatever jobs were available in the production of books including compositing, editing, writing pamphlets, epistles, and parts of plays; in the process his interests may have shifted from printing to writing books. However, it is also possible that he desired to be a successful author from his apprentice days, as the author of *The Forest of Fancy* observed. Chettle possibly obtained jobs through his friends and acquaintances, no matter what kind of work they were. He continually cultivated a wide range of connections in the literary world. As Appendices III and IV show, Danter published eighty-one items, including reprints and excluding entries, between 1591 and 1598, the year before he died.[32] These items may be roughly categorized as follows: literature (44), religion (19), news (5), medicine (3), natural history (2), music (2), domestic science (2), and others. The most prominent genre is literature, accounting for 54%, and the second is religion, 23%. Unlike the average tendency of most printers described by Bennett, East printed a large number of literary works that surpassed that of religious books, as did Danter (269-70).

The authors of the literary works are Nashe (9), Greene (4), Chettle (3), Munday (2), Shakespeare (2), Peele (2), Lodge (2), Robert Wilson (2), Barnfield (2), Thomas Harman (2), Sidney (1), Ovid (1), and others.

The most prominent authors are Nashe and Greene. Danter issues Nashe's *Strange News* (1592, 1593), *Apology of Pierce Penniless* (1593), *The Unfortunate Traveler* (1594), *The Terrors of the Night*, and *Have with You to Saffron Walden* (1596). Among them, the first three books were reprinted, which suggests their popularity. *Strange News* was first printed in 1592, and reprinted once in the same year and twice in the following year, and all of them were issued by Danter. *Apology of Pierce Penniless* was printed by Danter twice in 1593. *Unfortunate Traveler* was first printed by Scarlet in 1594, and the second edition was jointly reprinted by Scarlet and Danter in the same year. Moreover, Nashe wrote a preface to Sidney's *Astrophil and Stella*, first printed by Charlewood and reprinted by Danter in 1591. Charlewood printed Nashe's first work, *The Anatomy of Absurdity* in 1589, and probably asked him to write the preface to *Astrophil and Stella*.

Danter printed Greene's three pamphlets around the author's death on 3 September 1592: *The Black Book's Messenger*, *Groatsworth*, and *The Repentance of Robert Greene*. *Groatsworth* was the most popular with six editions (1592, 1596, 1617, 1621, 1629, 1637), and this work was edited and probably partly written by Chettle, as I will discuss in Chapter 2, "(i) Danter's Press and *Greene's Groatsworth of Wit*." Danter also printed Greene's play *Orlando Furioso* in 1594.

Moreover, Danter printed Chettle's two pamphlets: *Kind-Heart's Dream* (1592) and *Piers Plainness* (1595). Interestingly, both *Groatsworth* and *Kind-Heart's Dream* were issued by Wolfe and Danter for Wright, and Chettle's reference to *Groatsworth* in *Kind-Heart's Dream* suggests the close relationship between the two works. Moreover, Chettle's first romance *Piers Plainness* is obviously inspired by Nashe's *Pierce Penniless*, first printed by Charlewood in 1592. The publishing process of these pamphlets and the relationships among Chettle, Danter, and Nashe will be further discussed in Chapter 2.

Danter also printed Munday's translations: the first two parts of *Primaleon of Greece* (1595, 1596) and *Axiochus* (1592). *Primaleon of Greece* is an anonymous Spanish romance, and the third part, also translated by Munday, was issued by Thomas Snodham together with the previous two parts in 1619. Significantly, the second part contains Chettle's epistle, "To his good Friend M. *Anthony Mundy*." The full title of a philosophical translation, *Axiochus*, printed by Charlewood and Danter for Burby, suggests the

1 Chettle as Printer

author is Plato, and also the translator is "Edw. Spenser:" "A most Excellent Dialogue, written in Greeke by *Plato*...Translated out of Greeke by *Edw. Spenser*." The identity of "Edw. Spenser" has been discussed; some critics have attributed it to Edmund Spenser, while others have assigned it to Munday. The argument remains unresolved. Frederick Padelford, who discovered this long missing-book and edited it, asserts the authorship of Spenser in the introduction of his edition. Rudolf Gottfried and Harold L. Weatherby supported Padelford and provided more internal evidence. On the other hand, Bernard Freyd, Marshall W. S. Swan, and C. T. Wright insisted on Munday's authorship based on the external evidence; Freyd pointed out the relation between the Earl of Oxford, whose name ("Earle of Oxenforde") appears on the title-page and Munday; Swan suggested a conspiracy among Charlewood, Munday, and Burby, and also the misuse of Spenser's popularity; Wright developed Swan's argument and suggested that "Munday may have translated the *Axiochus*, with Spenserian touches, or dug up a youthful version" ("'Edward' Spenser" 35). Significantly, Wright associated the misuse of Spenser's popularity with that of Nashe. In the preface to Munday's translation, *2 Gerileon* (1592), issued by Scarlet, "T. N." was mistakenly signed, according to Chettle's preface to *Kind-Heart's Dream*: "by the workemans error T. N. were set to the end...I confesse to be mine, and repent it not" (7). For the initials, Jenkins believed it was forged "because of the advertising power of Nashe's signature" (12), and Wright shared the opinion (35). Whether the translator was Spenser or Munday or someone else is unknown, but importance of the forgery for sales seems to hold for the publication of *Groatsworth*, as will be discussed in Chapter 2, "(i) Danter's Press and *Greene's Groatsworth of Wit*."

Danter issued Shakespeare's *Titus Andronicus* in 1594, and *Romeo and Juliet* in 1597. *Titus Andronicus* is now widely accepted as collaboration with Peele. Both plays were very popular. Danter printed only these first editions of the two plays. *Titus Andronicus* was reprinted in 1600 and 1602. *Romeo and Juliet* was reprinted in 1597, 1599, 1607, 1622, 1635, and Danter's edition is the so-called "bad" quarto, as will be discussed in Chapter 3, "(iii) *Romeo and Juliet* (Q1)."

Peele's *The Old Wife's Tale* (pub. 1595) was performed by the Queen's Men, according to the title-page. Compared with *Titus Andronicus* and *Romeo and Juliet*, this play was less popular and was not reprinted.

Lodge's moralistic prose work *Catharos* is significant because it was entered in Stationers' Resister under Chettle's name on 17 September 1591. *The Wounds of Civil War* was first printed by Danter in 1594, and reprinted by Simon Stafford in 1594. This play was performed by the Admiral's Men, according to the title-page. The stage-setting is ancient republican Rome, and the main theme is the conflicts between a General and politician, Gaius Marius, and the dictator, Lucius Cornelius Sulla.

Wilson's *The Three Ladies of London*, first issued by Roger Ward, was printed in 1584, and reprinted by Danter in 1592. Moreover, Danter issued Wilson's *The Cobbler's Prophecy* in 1594, and this was not reprinted. Both works deal with Elizabethan issues, such as economics, politics, and wars through such mythical characters as Mars and Venus, and also such allegorical characters as Contempt, Courtier, Love, Conscience, Lucre, Usury, Simony, Fraud, and others.

Greene's Funerals written by "R. B. Gent." is generally attributed to Barnfield. Also, Danter issued Barnfield's scandalous homoerotic poem, *The Affectionate Shepherd*. Both of them were printed in 1594. *Greene's Funerals* is a set of sonnets, of which the most interesting is Sonnet X. This sonnet has "[a] catalogue of certain of his [Greene's] books" including *Mamillia, Gwydonius, Ciceronis Amor, Menaphon, Orpharion, A Disputation, Arbasto*, and others, and R. B., or Richard Barnfield praises Greene's works and wit. In the preface to this work, Danter states that the verses were published without the author's knowledge: "*Greenes Funeralls*. Which contrarie to the Authours expectation I haue nowe published, for it was his priuate study at idle times" (A3r). Jowett suggests that Danter had some unfinished pieces that Barnfield never intended for publication, and that Chettle may have completed Barn-

1 Chettle as Printer

field's unfinished pieces as in the cases of *Groatsworth* and *Romeo and Juliet* ("Notes" 386). If so, Chettle's commendation of Barnfield in *Piers Plainness* may make sense. In this tract, the narrator and shepherd, Piers recounts to his new master, Menalcus, his careers and plight as an apprentice. Piers served such various masters as a broker, a usurer, a usurping Prince among others, and finally decided to live as a shepherd. At the end of this work, Menalcus says, "After long troubles I like thy desire of rest: for in a shepherds life is both repose and recreation," and goes on to say, "Young Daphnis hath given his verdict of *The Shepheards Content*: duely praising it, as it meriteth" (174). As Leo Daugherty points out, "Young Daphnis" alludes to Barnfield, who calls himself "*DAPHNIS*" (A2r) in his dedication to Lady Penelope Rich in *The Affectionate Shepherd*, and "*The Shepheards Content*" suggests a part of the tract "The Shepherds Content" (E1v-F4v) (Daugherty 58).

The Affectionate Shepherd was as scandalous as *Groatsworth*. The dedicatee, Penelope, and her lover, Charles Blount, accused Barnfield of using them as models for Queen Guendolena and Ganymede in the first part, "Tears of an affectionate Shepherd sicke for Loue" (A3r-E1r), according to Sonia Massai (1). In this homoerotic story, Daphnis (Barnfield) falls in love with Ganymede (Blount), but Ganymede and Guendolena (Penelope) love each other. This is obviously a parody of *Astrophil and Stella*, printed by Danter in 1591, and indeed "The Shepherds Content" mentions "sweet *Astrophel*" (F3r). Sidney's sonnet beautifully describes the love of Astrophil, who is modeled on Sidney, for Stella, who is modeled on Penelope. Knowing these troubles, Chettle dared to praise this work probably for three reasons. One reason is that in Danter's place, Chettle wanted to appease Barnfield for publishing *Greene's Funerals* without permission. Another reason is that Chettle intended to publicize Danter's press. Chettle advertised *Groatsworth*, *Strange News*, and other works issued by Danter.[33] A further reason is that Chettle just referred to the problematic tract as a joke, particularly as a form of a private gossip among Barnfield, Nashe, and other people surrounding Danter. They knew well of *Astrophil and Stella*, and Nashe even wrote the epistle; therefore, they enjoyed Barnfield's parody all the more. Barnfield was apparently involved in Danter's family.

Harman's *The Groundwork of Cony-Catching* is worth noticing for its popularity. This is a revised edition of the work partly published in 1566 or 1567 as *A Caveat* (STC 993).[34] It appeared in 1568, 1573, and 1592, and Danter issued it twice in 1592. The first two editions were issued by William Griffith in 1567. This had a long popularity, and a particularly great influence on Elizabethan cony-catching pamphlets including Greene's *The Black Book's Messenger* (1592) and the anonymous *Mihil Mumchance* (1597), both of which were issued by Danter. As will be discussed in the next section, "(c) Literary Influence from Danter's Publications between 1591 and 1598," Chettle's *Blind Beggar* is certainly influenced by these works on Elizabethan underground.

Ovid's *Metamorphoses* was more popular than Harman, and greatly influential on Elizabethan playwrights. The first edition was printed by William Seres in 1567, and it was reprinted six times between 1575 and 1612. Danter issued it in 1593 only. Furthermore, Baptista Mantuanus's *The Eclogues of the Poet B. Mantuanus Carmelitanus* (1594) had a great effect on Elizabethan literature. As H. R. D. Andes points out, in Shakespeare's *Love's Labor's Lost*, "good old Mantuan" is mentioned by Holofernes as his favorite author in Act IV Scene ii. According to Andes, the original version appeared twenty-three times between 1523 and 1638, and this was commonly used as a school textbook for Latin in England and the Continent (20). The translation was first issued by Bynneman in 1567, and it was reprinted by him in 1572, and by Danter in 1594.

Two anonymous plays, *Fair Em*, printed in 1591, and *The Life and Death of Jack Straw*, printed between 1593 and 1594, are also important.[35] Danter printed the first but undated edition of *Fair Em*, and it was reprinted in 1631. Greene attacked the author of *Fair Em* and parodied two lines from the closing scene in the preface to *Farewell to Folly* (STC 12241), printed by Scarlet in 1591. Moreover, the plot of *Fair Em* resembles that of Greene's

1 Chettle as Printer

Friar Bacon and Friar Bungay, performed around 1589. Critics, therefore, generally believe *Fair Em* was produced around 1589 and 1591, and that the text was published in 1591 (Chambers 4: 12). The play was probably performed by Strange's Men. The authorship has been attributed to Shakespeare, Greene, Wilson, and Munday, but it remains anonymous, according to an editor of the play, Standish Henning (51-80). Interestingly, all of the proposed authors were connected to Danter's publications, but more significant is the commitment of Scarlet, Chettle's fellow apprentice. Although Greene ridicules the author of the play, this may have been to promote the publication of *Fair Em* and its author.

The Life and Death of Jack Straw was first issued by Danter and reprinted by William Jaggard in 1604. The play has frequently been attributed to Peele, but the author remains uncertain (Logan and Smith 252-53). This play has four acts only.

Among religious books, Danter printed Henry Smith most, eight items including reprints, between 1591 and 1598. Smith was a Church of England clergyman and beloved by people as "Siluer tongu'd *Smith*," as Nashe notes in *Pierce Pennilesse* (192).[36] Smith was so popular as the Puritan preacher that his works were frequently printed by such contemporary printers as Charlewood, Wolfe, Scarlet, Orwin, Edward Allde as well. In particular, the number of the publications rapidly increased around 1591, the year of his death, which Nashe laments in the above work, and this holds for Danter's press. *The Affinity of Faithfull* has three editions, two of which were issued by Danter in 1591. Similarly, *A Fruitful Sermon* has two editions, both of which were printed by Danter in 1591. However, *God's Arrow against Atheists* was more popular and issued twelve times between 1593 and 1637, though Danter printed the first edition (1593) only.

For the other religious books, Danter printed sermons by such English clergymen as Bartimaeus Andrewes, Richard Greenham, Thomas Playfere, and also a Church of England Bishop, John Charldon, all printed in 1595, while he published Calvin's sermons in 1592. Among these, Playfere is worth mentioning because his *A Most Excellent and Heavenly Sermon* was popular enough to be issued eight times between 1595 and 1616. John Orwin first printed it in 1595, and Danter reprinted it in the same year. Moreover, Nashe praises "Mellifluous PLAYFERE," remarking, "Seldome haue I beheld so pregnant a pleasaunt wit coupled with a memorie of such huge incomprehensible receipt, deepe reading and delight better mixt than in his Sermons" (*Strange News* 314). Smith and Playfere were, thus, especially popular preachers at that time, and Nashe showed his Protestantism by praising them.

Danter was, thus, involved in issuing Protestant books; however, interestingly, he also printed Catholic works including Juvenall Borget's *The Devil's Legend* (1595), Nicholas Breton's *Mary Magdalene's Love* (1595), and the anonymous *Jesus Psalter* (1596). Among these books, *Jesus Psalter* was the most popular and problematic. The work is sometimes attributed to Richard Whitford, the Brigittine Monk, and it was translated by George Flinton. The work appeared ten times between 1529 and 1604, though Danter printed this edition only. In 1596 Danter had his press seized for printing this Catholic book (Plomer, "Bishop Bancroft" 170). Juvenall Borget is a pseudonym according to STC, and the full title of *The Devil's Legend* summarizes its content:

> the confession of the leaguers fayth: doctour Pantaloun, and Zanie his pupill, doo teach that all hope ought to be grounded on the puissant King Phillip of Spaine, and vpon all the happie apostles of the holy league, and that they ought not to doo as the Brytans, English-men, and Protestants doo.

This book insists on the unity of the Catholic leagues led by Spain, and it deals with both religious and political matters, which would have drawn the attention of Chettle and his contemporaries. Breton's treatise on Roman Catholicism, *Mary Magdalene's Love*, praises the Virgin and his references to Mary Magdalene have suggested that he was a Catholic, though his prose works show that he was an ardent Protestant. The appearance of

1 Chettle as Printer

these Catholic books around 1595 probably related to French King Henri IV's declaration of war on Spain in January 1595. Henri declared war on Spain, in order to show Catholics, that Spain was using religion as a cover for an attack on the French state, and to show Protestants, that he had not become "a puppet of Spain" through his conversion, but that he hoped to take the war to Spain and make territorial gain, according to Robert J. Knecht (272).

Unlike East, Danter printed news pamphlets about witches (1593), monsters (1594), a murder (1595), Italian cities (1595), and England (1595). The pamphlet on witches, *The Most Strange and Admirable Discovery of Three Witches of Warboys*, sold considerably well, being issued twice; Danter first printed it, and Widow Orwin reprinted it in the same year. News of murders, monsters, and witchcraft were popular, as M. A. Shaaber notes (141-44; 151-59). In this sense, Danter's publications appealed to the ordinary people.

Similarly, Danter's choices were different from East's in medical books. Danter printed less of them, printing three items including reprints. These are a learned physician's *Present Remedies against the Plague* and Nicholas Gyer's *The English Phlebotomy*. Who the learned physician and Nicholas Gyer were remains uncertain. Gyer does not appear in the *DNB*. Books on the treatment for plague were popular when it frequently spread, as mentioned above. *Present Remedies* was issued four times between 1592 and 1603. Charlewood first printed it in 1592, and Danter reprinted it in the same year and also in 1594. Similarly, medical books on blood-letting based on Galen's methods were common. Danter published books on domestic science, the education of women, and etiquette, the so-called how-to books, though they are few in number. Juan Luis Vives' educational book for women, *The Instruction of a Christian Woman*, was translated from Latin by Richard Hyrde. Vives, the Spanish humanist, was invited to England by Henry VIII and became a tutor of Princess Mary, or Mary Tudor. The original, *De Institutione Feminae Christianae* was written in 1523 and dedicated to Catherine of Aragon for the instruction of her daughter, Mary. The translations appeared nine times between 1529 and 1592, and Danter printed the last edition only.

William Fiston's translation of an anonymous French book called *The School of Good Manners* were issued three times in 1595, 1609, and 1618. This book instructs readers on how to treat children and others.

John Partridge's *The Treasury of Hidden Secrets* was printed twelve times between 1573 and 1637. This book on domestic science was very popular. The first edition called *The Treasury of Commodious Conceits and Hidden Secrets* was issued by Richard Jones in 1573, and Danter printed the enlarged edition in 1596. Similarly, Giovanni Battista Giotti's *A Book of Curious and Strange Inventions, Called the First Part of Needleworks* deals with domestic science. This was printed in 1596 only.

Richard Johnson's *The Pilgrimage of Man*, which is described in ESTC as a book on "conduct of life," appeared five times between 1598 and 1635. Danter printed the first edition only. Thomas Johnson's *Cornucopiae, or Divers Secrets* has two editions, and both were issued by Danter in 1595 and 1596.

Danter issued two music printings; *A New Book of Tablature*, which is a tutor for the lute and related instruments, and *The Pathway to Music*, which discusses music theory. Both works were issued for Barley in 1596, the year when the music patent expired.

Danter's publications, thus, center on literature and religion. Most interesting is that Danter issued such contemporary prose and dramatic works as those by Greene, Nashe, Munday, Shakespeare, Peele, Lodge, and Chettle, while also printing Harman, Ovid, and Mantuanus. East, in contrast, never printed any contemporary plays. Furthermore, it is significant that Nashe and Chettle occasionally supported Danter by writing epistles. Similarly, their friends including Munday, Lodge, Peele, and Wilson perhaps helped Danter by asking to print their works. Not only Nashe and Chettle, but also Munday, Lodge, and Peele wrote some prose works and were familiar with the printing industry. In return, they may have been given the chance to read Danter's publications or been allowed similar privileges.

1 Chettle as Printer

Among the religious books, Danter printed Smith and Playfere, and Nashe mentioned them in his works. If Nashe had known about their publication before writing his books, he could have been advertising for Danter's press. However, a more interesting point about religious books is that Danter issued both Protestant and Catholic books. This recalls East's case. East printed Protestant books while publishing for Byrd. As with East who seems to actually have had no religious reason for doing so, Danter probably was not interested in religious faith, but in money. As I discussed in the section of East's publications, Catholic books sold well. In fact, the problematic *Jesus Psalter* was issued ten times between 1529 and 1604.

For other books, the number of books on medicine and music is smaller for Danter than for East. Also, Danter did not issue any books concerning navigation and the military as East had done. On the other hand, Danter printed news pamphlets of a type that East never issued. The different tendency of the two printers arises from a shift in the printing industry as well as from difference in the printers themselves. After the Martin Marprelate controversy, prose works seem to have taken up personal attacks and gossip instead of pastoral and chivalric romances. Moreover, the 1590s saw the rise of plays, that is, the enlargement of the theaters and theater companies, and authors began to write plays. The publications of Danter closely reflect such contemporary social trends.

(c) Literary Influence from Danter's Publications between 1591 and 1598

Danter's literary publications, particularly the writings of Greene, Nashe, Lodge, Peele, and Shakespeare had a great effect on Chettle's works. Danter printed such sonnets as *Astrophil and Stella* and *The Affectionate Shepherd*, but the former tract does not seem to have influenced Chettle. The latter work, especially the part called "The Shepherds Content" had an influence on *Piers Plainness*, which alludes to the sonnets. The contention of "The Shepherds Content," "Who would not then a simple Shepheard bee,

/ Rather than be a mightie Monarch made?" is exactly reflected in Piers's preference to being a shepherd rather than a courtier (F4v).

Among the prose works that Danter issued, the most popular was Harman's *The Groundwork of Cony-Catching*, a revision of a popular pamphlet called *A Caveat*. This work describes life in the Elizabethan underworld, involving beggary, prostitution, fraud and others, and including a glossary of jargon. This tract influenced Greene's cony-catching pamphlets. Chettle clearly read Harman and Greene, and applied these rogueries to his works. *Kind-Heart's Dream*, printed by Danter, depicts contemporary life and culture in London with a juggler called William Cuckoe, who defends cony-catchers, while also seeing lawyers, gentlemen, and people of all trades as a juggler or a sort of cony-catcher (54-55).

Furthermore, *Kind-Heart's Dream* refers to "Mort," a female beggar, and this suggests Chettle's further familiarity with the underworld. In fact, "Mort" appears in *The Groundwork of Cony-Catching* (G4v-F3r), and this suggests Chettle's knowledge of the work. Similarly, *Piers Plainness*, also printed by Danter, mentions the "Ruffler," a beggar, who pretends to be a wounded soldier, and this is also described in *The Groundwork* (B1r-2r). *Piers Plainness* is set in Greece, but it occasionally describes Elizabethan society and attacks usurers and brokers because of their cheating. There is an episode in which Piers's master Ulpian, the usurer, is deceived by a rogue, and Piers calls him "Rufflar" (145), though he does not pretend to be a soldier. Also, Chettle's collaborative play, *Blind Beggar*, depicts contemporary London. The main plot is the banishment of a General called Momford. He is trapped by his brother and banished from England; however, he stays there by disguising himself as a blind beggar to watch his daughter. His patched gown is the typical costume of a beggar. In the sub-plot, two cony-catchers, Canby and Hadland, practice fraud on Tom Strowd, the yeoman, and others through disguises and tricks.

Ovid's *Metamorphoses* also had a great influence on Chettle as well as on such contemporaries as Shakespeare and Greene. Specifically, the story

1 Chettle as Printer

of Tereus's rape of Philomela (Book 6) drew Chettle's attention. In *Piers Plainness*, the King of Thrace notes, when he is about to be banished by his treacherous son: "In this wood Tereus ravisht and wrongd Philomele" (130). In *Hoffman*, the episode is mentioned by Hoffman's accomplice, Lorrique. He suggests Hoffman rape Martha, the chaste widow of the Duke of Prussia: "Shut her perpetuall prisoner in that den; Make her a Philomel, proue Tereus" (5.2.2387-88). In *Blind Beggar*, a villainous gentleman called Young Playnsey forcefully courts a beautiful girl Bess, as will be discussed in Chapter 7, "(iii) *Blind Beggar*," and this vividly recalls Lavinia's rape in *Titus Andronicus* as well as the story in *Metamorphoses*.

Furthermore, other characters in *Metamorphoses* are employed by Chettle as well. *Piers Plainness* refers to such magicians as Medea and Circe, and also Apollo (133). Media appears in Book 7, Circes appears in Book 14, and Apollo appears in Book 1 of *Metamorphoses*.

Danter issued nine plays including works by Wilson, Greene, Lodge, Shakespeare, and Peele, and some of these certainly influenced Chettle. Wilson's *Three Ladies of London* and *The Cobbler's Prophecy*, which criticize the evil of money and Roman Catholicism, had the most important effect on Chettle's prose works and plays. Wilson is generally accepted as being an actor-playwright like Shakespeare and Munday, as Scott McMillin and Sally-Beth MacLean, and also Lloyd Edward Kermode, the latest editor of *The Three Ladies of London* suggest (McMillin and MacLean 4-5; Kermode 28-29). In fact, in Meres's *Palladis Tamia*, Wilson is listed before Chettle among the "best poets for comedy" (284), and being second only to Richard Tarlton, Wilson is praised for his "learning and extemporall witte… at the Swanne," a theater built around 1595 in London (286). Wilson and Chettle wrote some plays for Henslowe in collaboration with Munday, Drayton, and Dekker, in the late 1590s, though unfortunately, all of them are lost. Wilson was a veteran in the theatrical world, though the dates of his birth and death are uncertain, and Chettle must have been influenced by him in writing plays.

The Three Ladies of London was probably first performed by Leicester's Men, to which Wilson belonged, and then revived by the Queen's Men, which was formed as the best acting company in 1583, and Wilson was selected to join them, according to McMillin and MacLean (16-17). The play criticizes contemporary London, where money increasingly dominates, through allegorical figures as found in medieval morality plays. The story centers on the tension among three ladies called Lady Lucre, Lady Love, and Lady Conscience; Lucre attempts to control Love and Conscience, aided by Dissimulation, Fraud, Simony, and Usury; eventually, Love and Conscience succumb to Lucre, but all of them are punished by a judge called Nicholas Nemo who restores the social order.

Chettle must have known this play, which seems to have strongly influenced his works. The vice of usury in the play influenced Chettle's description of usurers in *Kind-Heart's Dream* and *Piers Plainness* as well as Lodge's *An Alarum against Usurers*. Moreover, the description of three beggars in *The Three Ladies of London* must have influenced *Patient Grissil* and *Blind Beggar* to some extent. For example, a sturdy beggar called Tom pretends to be lame and blind to earn money from Fraud, but fails. Similarly, beggars in *Patient Grissil* are minor characters and invited to a feast. In *Blind Beggar*, Momford, a banished gentleman, pretends to be a blind beggar to remain in England. Also, both plays denounce rich people and money as evil as in *The Three Ladies of London*, as will be discussed in Chapter 7.

Furthermore, the anti-Catholicism of Wilson's play influenced Chettle's plays even more, particularly, *Death*, the second part of the Robin Hood plays, and *Sir Thomas Wyatt*. *The Three Ladies* shows Simony's connection with his birthplace Rome, "that ancient religious city" (Sc. 2: 228), and also the Pope.[37] Simony recounts: "On a time, the monks and friars made a banquet, whereunto they invited me, / With certain other English merchants, which belike were of their familiarity" (229-30). This suggests the corruption of Roman Catholic clergymen. Moreover, Simony goes on to say, "when I was at Rome, and dwelt in the Friary, / They would talk how

England yearly sent over a great mass of money, / And that this little island was more worth to the Pope" (269-71). Simony suggests England paid the tithe "in Queen Mary's time" (276), and that the Pope was very pleased with it.

Similarly, *Death* shows the strong connection between the Prior of York and Rome, when he kills Robert, or Robin, by a poison sent from Rome. Moreover, King John orders the monk and abbess to persuade Matilda, or Marian, to sleep with him, by promising he will give a large amount of money to their abbey every year, and they accept his offer. *Sir Thomas Wyatt* more directly criticizes Catholics such as Mary Tudor and Spanish Philip II. Wyatt opposes their marriage and rebels, but he fails. However, his rising and execution is sympathetically described.[38] Simony's reference to Mary seems to express Wilson's strong criticism against her.

Wilson's *The Cobbler's Prophecy* was possibly performed by the Queen's Men (McMillin and MacLean 102). This play questions such Elizabethan social issues as money, corruption of the ruling class, and wars through the mythological and allegorical figures as well as human characters. In the opening scene, Jupiter summons gods to restore the corrupted Boeotia, in which Security, a nurse of sin, has bred Contempt. Mercury, the messenger of the gods, charms Raph, the cobbler, and gives him the prophecy that Venus, with Contempt, has a hidden child, who will ruin the state. Raph reveals this to Mars, who is infatuated with Venus, who has a husband, Vulcan, and Mars becomes furious. Eventually, the child is born, and Mercury delivers the message from Jupiter that Venus has been stripped of her title and banished out of heaven, and also Boeotia is invaded by foes, but it will not win until the barn of Contempt has been burnt. War breaks out soon after. Contempt forsakes Venus, and his barn is burnt. Eventually, Sateros, a great soldier, brings victory to Boeotia, assisted by Mars.

The main theme of this play seems to be the peace and war debate, which was topical in the late Elizabethan period. In peaceful Boeotia, Mars is corrupt and infatuated with Venus. On the other hand, Sateros has fought against Persian, Asian, and Moorish powers for his monarch, but he is disgraced now. Also, Porter, the old soldier, at Mars's court complains to Raph that he has become lame by war, while his armors have rusty by peace after the war. The Duke concludes the play, stating that the state should be supported both Arts and Armes, or scholars and soldiers.

The problems of ill-treated veterans like Wilson's Sateros are discussed in *Hoffman*. Hoffman's father used to serve the Dukes of Luningberg and Prussia as a great solder, but he is dismissed and banished by them for a reason. A veteran, Old Stilt, has served Hoffman's father, but now he lives a poor life in peacetime.[39] The importance of wars that *The Cobbler's Prophecy* discusses has, thus, a great influence on Chettle.

Moreover, *The Cobbler's Prophecy* condemns the corruption of the ruling class. Charon, the ferryman of hell, says to Raph that the number of the Popes, prelates, princes, and judges increases, and currently there is no room in hell. According to Charon, these people bring money to hell. Also, the ghost of a friar calls Charon for a boat. He is so troubled because of nuns, and he is in a hurry. What the trouble is remains unknown, but it is probably sexual. Like *The Three Ladies of London*, the corruption of Roman Catholic churchmen provoked Chettle to criticize them in his plays, particularly *Death*, and the corrupted rich people are described in *Hoffman*, *Patient Grissil*, and *Blind Beggar* among others.

Lodge's *The Wounds of Civil War*, performed by the Admiral's Men, is also significant for Chettle's works. This play describes the ancient Roman conflict between Marius and Sulla, both of whom die in the end. The source is Appian's *Roman History*, which was translated by "W. B." and first printed by Bynneman in 1578 (STC 712.5). Lodge altered the source in some ways, and in particular gave significance to a minor character, Junius Brutus. Andrew Hadfield believes the first performance took place in 1586, the year before Mary Stuart's execution, and claims that the play attacks "tyranny and the violence it produces" and insists on the superiority of "reasoned argument and the preservation of political institutions to suc-

1 Chettle as Printer

cess by militarism" (99). However, more significantly, Hadfield regards this play as a "response to the fear of religious war breaking out in England if the succession question was not resolved in a sensible way" (99). Moreover, Hadfield goes on to say that Lodge as a Catholic warns Elizabethans against civil war, which could break out on the succession of James, the son of Mary Stuart (99). This is a very interesting argument because *Hoffman* deals with exactly the same topic in a scene of common people rebelling over the legitimacy of a succession, though *Hoffman*, performed around 1602, seems to describe the succession issue more directly and urgently, as I will discuss in Chapter 4, "(iii) Succession." Lodge's play, thus, may have inspired Chettle's concern about the succession and religious issues.

Furhermore, as mentioned above, Lopez refers to a Frenchman called Pedro in *The Wound's of Civil War* along with Lorrique's disguise as a French doctor in *Hoffman* as examples of court-intriguing Frenchmen with heavy accents (310). However, Lodge's Frenchman is so nice that he refuses to kill Marius for "forty crowns" (3.2.994).[40]

Titus Andronicus, as a sensational and bloody revenge tragedy, had a great influence on Chettle's *Hoffman*. The two plays hardly have anything in common in their plots. In *Titus Andronicus*, a father takes revenge for his daughter, while in *Hoffman* a son avenges his father, but both protagonists kill a number of their enemies without the hesitation that Hamlet shows. In particular, Lavinia's rape influences Hoffman's scheme to rape a widowed Duchess, Martha, and also Young Playnsey in *Blind Beggar*, though these are perhaps affected by Shakespeare's source, Ovid's *Metamorphoses* (Book 6) as well.

Similarly, two anonymous plays had a large effect on Chettle's plays. *Fair Em* is a chivalric romance with two plots. The main plot describes the love of William the Conqueror for Mariana, a Swedish Princess held in the Danish court, and Blanch, the daughter to the King of Denmark. William falls in love an image of Blanch on the shield that the Marquess of Lubeck carries in a tournament. William, disguised as Sir Robert of Windsor, travels to Denmark to see Blanch, but falls in love with Mariana, who loves

Lubeck. Through a plot by the ladies, William finally accepts Blanch as his wife. In the sub-plot, Em, the beautiful daughter of the miller of Manchester, is wooed by three courtiers, Valingford, Mountney, and Manvile. Em chooses Manvile, and pretends to Valingford that she is blind and to Mountney that she is deaf to avoid them. However, Valingford knows the fact that Manvile has been betrothed to Elner living in Westchester, and exposes this to Em. In the end, the two plots are united. At court, Manvile loses the both women in front of the King. Also, Em's true identity is revealed; she is actually a gentlewoman, the daughter of Sir Thomas Goddars, who has been wrongly banished by William and disguised as a miller. Finally, Valingford marries Em.

These plots, particularly the subplot, are similar to *Blind Beggar*. The disguise of Goddars as a miller recalls Momford's disguise as a blind beggar in *Blind Beggar*, and also Em's pretending to be blind recalls Momford. Moreover, other characters occasionally disguise themselves as well in *Fair Em* and in *Blind Beggar*. Furthermore, the two plays share the restoration of the status of the fathers (Goddars and Momford) by the Kings (William and Henry VI) and the marriage of the daughters (Em and Bess) in the final scene. Moreover, Manvile's inconstancy resembles Young Playnsey, who courts Bess, though he has a wife in *Blind Beggar*. *Blind Beggar* contains more historical and political issues in its multiple plots, but *Fair Em* certainly influenced *Blind Beggar*, and partly *Patient Grissil*, in which a poor but fair daughter marries a rich man.

Another anonymous play, *Jack Straw*, describes the Peasants' Revolt led by Wat Tyler in 1381. In the opening scene, Straw kills the Collector, and this encourages Parson Ball to suggest a rebellion to Straw, Wat Tyler, Tom Miller, and Nobs. They march from Kent to London, but their rebellion fails; Straw is killed by the Lord Mayor of London, and Ball and Tylor are sentenced to death, while the other rebels are pardoned by King Richard II.

Chettle frequently describes rebellions in his works, and particularly *Hoffman* and *Sir Thomas Wyatt* are influenced by this play. The activity of

1 Chettle as Printer

Hoffman, an outlaw, getting revenge by killing numerous upper-class people is itself a rebellion. At first, Hoffman kills others for revenge, but gradually he desires to usurp their positions. Disguised as Otho, the Prince of Luningberg, Hoffman becomes the heir of the Duke of Prussia, Otho's uncle, because the Duke has favored his nephew and disinherited his foolish son, Jerome, in Act II Scene i. On the other hand, Jerome becomes furious and rebels against his father with his common soldiers, who oppose the foreign Prince Otho (Hoffman) in Act III Scene i. Jerome's comical rebel may be a parody of *Jack Straw*, and the rebellion fails in the end, but its cause, the legitimacy of succession, is very important, as will be discussed in Chapter 4, "(iii) Succession."

Sir Thomas Wyatt describes another historical rebellion led by Sir Thomas Wyatt in 1554. Curiously, the three historical rebellions of Tyler, Jack Cade, and Wyatt occur in Kent, and all of them were dramatized. Wyatt's rebellion is much closer to Jack Straw's than Jerome's, though Wyatt is a gentleman. Wyatt rebels against Mary Tudor's marriage to Philip of Spain, but fails, and he is finally executed. For *Jack Straw*, Stephen Schillinger remarks, "the rebellion is largely positioned sympathetically" (94). Similarly, Wyatt's rebellion is described sympathetically, as I will further discuss in Chapter 5, "(iii) *Sir Thomas Wyatt*." However, Wyatt's rising lacks the utopianism that Parson Ball and Jack Cade in Shakespeare's *2 Henry VI* suggest, and instead focuses on evading Spanish power and elevating nationalism.

Moreover, the leveling sentiments and hostility toward rich people that Parson Ball and others held inspired Chettle very much. There are many characters who criticize rich people in his works. Hoffman mocks the ruling classes who enjoy tilts and has strong antagonism against them. As Chapter 7 "Beggars in *The Pleasant Comedy of Patient Grissil* and *The Blind Beggar of Bethnal Green*, and the Elizabethan Money Based Economy" will show, *Patient Grissil* and *Blind Beggar* problematize the social inequality between the poor and rich people. Both plays criticize mercenary and self-interested rich people, while praising honest and virtuous poor people.

Romeo and Juliet had some effect on Chettle. In *Downfall* and *Death*, Robert (Robin) and Matilda (Marian) love each other, but Robert is poisoned, while Matilda commits suicide to escape the lustful King John. Moreover, *Hoffman* similarly describes star-crossed lovers, Lodowick and Lucibella. Lodowick is killed by Hoffman, and Lucibella goes mad. The 1597 edition of *Romeo and Juliet*, printed by Danter and Edward Allde, is the so-called "bad" quarto, and some critics claim that Chettle wrote the stage directions and some parts of the play.[41]

As in the case of East's publications, religious books had an effect on Chettle. Smith and Playfere, whom Nashe mentioned in his works, were influential on Chettle's Protestantism. On the other hand, he may also have read such Catholic works as *Jesus Psalter* in order to attack Catholics.

Chettle, thus, seems to have been influenced by Danter's publications, specifically such literary works as *The Groundwork of Cony-Catching*, *Metamorphoses*, *Three Ladies of London*, *The Cobbler's Prophecy*, *The Wounds of Civil War*, *Titus Andronicus*, *Fair Em*, and *Jack Straw*. *The Groundwork of Cony-Catching* along with Greene's cony-catching pamphlets may have influenced Chettle's *Kind-Heart's Dream*, *Piers Plainness*, and *Blind Beggar*.

Unlike East, Danter did not issue military books, but Chettle must have read or seen battle scenes in *The Cobbler's Prophecy*, *The Wounds of Civil War*, *Titus Andronicus*, and *Jack Straw*, and the warning against civil war in *The Wounds of Civil War* seems to be reflected in *Hoffman*. The anti-Catholicism in *The Three Ladies of London* and *The Cobbler's Prophecy* is definitely echoed in *Death* and *Sir Thomas Wyatt*, though Smith and Playfere's sermons also influenced him.[42] Similarly, the evils of rich people in Wilson's plays influenced *Hoffman*, *Patient Grissil* and *Blind Beggar*.

On the other hand, the Tereus episode in *Piers Plainness* and *Hoffman* certainly comes from *Metamorphoses* and *Titus Andronicus*. Riot scenes in *Hoffman* and *Sir Thomas Wyatt* draw on *Jack Straw*. Also, there seems to be a strong connection between *Fair Em* and *Blind Beggar* in the plots of Em and Bess, both of whom regain their status and marry good gentlemen in the end.

1 Chettle as Printer

Chettle, thus, was influenced by these literary works published by Danter, and he was probably encouraged to edit *Groatsworth* and write *Kind-Heart's Dream* and *Piers Plainness*, not only by Danter, but also by such booksellers as Wright and Gosson, and others with whom he was intimate, such as Nashe, Munday, Lodge, and Peele. Moreover, Chettle's experience of reading the play-books must have helped him become a prolific playwright in the end.

(d) Chettle's Relationships with Authors, Printers, and Publishers at Danter's Press

As discussed above, Chettle was certainly involved as a printer in Nashe's works, and in *2 Primaleon of Greece*, translated by Munday. Chettle had close relations with Nashe and Munday as well as Greene. How and when Chettle met Nashe is uncertain, but it may have been through Greene or Clarke or Danter.[43] In any case, Chettle was regarded as part of a group with Greene and Nashe, as such contemporary writers as Nashe and Dekker related. Nashe included Chettle as one of "my frends" along with as "*Marloe, Greene*" in *Have with You to Saffron Warden*, published by Danter (131). Also, Dekker describes Chettle joining a company of dead poets including Marlowe, Peele, Greene, and Nashe in the Elysian Fields in *A Knight's Conjuring* (L1r-v). At Danter's press, Chettle nurtured his friendships with Nashe and Munday. Chettle may have read their works issued by printers other than Danter.

At Danter's press, Chettle apparently developed his literary network, particularly in connection with playwrights, while reading their works and learning how to write pamphlets and plays himself. With regard to Lodge and Peele, Chettle probably met them at East's press.[44] Their works published by Danter influenced Chettle, but Chettle may have read their other works issued by another printer.

Chettle wrote several plays for Henslowe in collaboration with Wilson as well as Munday, as Appendix I, Table 1 shows. Chettle probably first met Wilson at Danter's press through the publication of his plays. In *Kind-Heart's Dream*, Chettle attacks the contemporary theatrical world through the voice of Tarlton's ghost, and Nashe also mentions Tarlton in *Pierce Penniless* (215). Tarlton died in 1588, and he was a fellow actor of Wilson. Chettle and Nashe may have heard Tarlton's anecdotes from Wilson.

Chettle mentions Shakespeare in *Kind-Heart's Dream*, as will be further discussed in Chapter 2 "Chettle as Pamphleteer," and worked with him in the writing of *Sir Thomas More*, along with Munday, Dekker, and Heywood. Chettle was certainly influenced by Shakespeare, but their relation is obscure. Unlike such playwrights as Munday, Peele, Lodge, and Dekker, Shakespeare was probably not familiar with the printing industry; he was an actor-playwright like Munday, and he did not know printers and booksellers very well, though he did know Richard Field.

Even before working with Danter, Chettle must have already known numerous printers and publishers, but his personal connection was probably further expanded more at Danter's press. As Appendices III and IV show, Danter worked with such printers as Wolfe, Charlewood, Scarlet, Edward Allde, and also with such booksellers as Thomas Newman, Nicholas Ling, Busby, Wright, Burby, Barley, Thomas Millington, Gosson, Thomas Gubbin, and Richard Jones.

Of these printers and publishers, Wolfe, Charlewood, Allde, Wright, Gosson, Scarlet, Ling, Burby, and Millington were especially significant to Chettle. Wolfe and Wright were involved in the publication of *Groatsworth* and *Kind-Heart's Dream*. Charlewood frequently worked with East, worked once with Danter for *Axiochus*, and issued H. C.'s *The Pope's Pitiful Lamentation*.

Chettle frequently worked with Allde, the son of John Allde, whom Munday served in his short apprentice period. *Romeo and Juliet* (1597) was printed by Danter in collaboration with Allde, and Chettle probably helped Danter with the publication of the first quarto, as discussed in Chapter 3, "(iii) *Romeo and Juliet* (Q1)." Chettle may have written a couple of passages and stage directions. Afterwards, Allde issued Chettle's plays written in collabo-

1 Chettle as Printer

ration with other writers, *Patient Grissil* (1603) and *Sir Thomas Wyatt* (1607).

Gosson published *Piers Plainness* in 1595 and also H. C.'s *A Doleful Ditty, or Sorrowful Sonnet of the Lord Dar[n]ly* in 1579, and he was an apprentice to Purfoot, who issued H. C.'s *The Forest of Fancy* in 1579. The "H. C." of all these works probably suggests Henry Chettle.[45] When taking this into consideration, it can be speculated that Chettle knew Charlewood and Gosson before working at Danter's press.

Scarlet was Chettle's fellow apprentice and collaborated with Danter in printing some works. As Hanabusa discusses in "Insatsu-Gyosha," particularly in 1594, Scarlet's press was in financial straits, and Danter may have helped him by asking Scarlet to print parts of *Orlando Furioso* and *Cobbler's Prophecy* (40-41).[46]

Burby had apprenticed himself to Wright for eight years from the end of 1583 and became a freeman in 1592 (Arber 2: 712, 872). *Axiochus* was his first entry, and after that he published numerous literary works with Danter: Greene's *The Repentance of Robert Greene* and *Orlando Furioso*, Nashe's *Unfortunate Traveler*, Wilson's *The Cobbler's Prophecy*, Munday's translations, *1 and 2 Primaleon of Greece*. Moreover, Burby published another translation by Munday, *2 Gerileon of England* (1592), for which Chettle wrote an epistle pretending to be "T. N. [Thomas Nashe]," and also Meres's *Palladis Tamia*, printed by Short in 1598. Furthermore, Burby entered *Patient Grissil* in March 1600, and this was printed by Allde for Henry Rocket in 1603 (Arber 3: 158). Burby, thus, was a significant bookseller for Chettle as well as for Danter.

Ling apprenticed himself to Bynneman for eight years from 1570 and took up his freedom in 1579 (Arber 2: 679). Ling was "an early neighbor of Chettle" because East's press was close to Bynneman's in 1579, according to C. T. Wright ("Young Anthony Munday" 153). Ling published Smith's sermons in 1591; by then he should have known Chettle, and their relationship was long-lasting. Ling edited *England's Helicon* (1600) including Chettle's poems, one of which came from *Piers Plainness*, as Wright points out (153).

Similarly, Millington was significant to Chettle. He published only *Titus Andronicus* with Danter, but he is important for publishing *England's Mounrning Garment* with a printer, Simmes, in 1603. Chettle probably met Millington at Danter's press.

Interestingly, these printers and publishers issued the literary works of authors including Greene, Nashe, Munday, and Lodge at other presses as well. For example, of Greene's works, which may have not actually been written by Greene, Wolfe issued *Greene's Mourning Garment* for Newman (1590; STC 12251) and *The Second Part of Cony-Catching* for Wright (1591; STC 12281; 1592; STC 12282). Scarlet issued *Greene's Farewell to Folly* for Gubbin and Newman (1591; STC 12241), and also *The Third and Last Part of Cony-Catching* (1592; STC 12283 and 12283.5) for Burby. Allde printed *Greene's Vision* (1592; STC 12261). Charlewood issued *Morando* (1584; STC 12276) with John Kingston for White.

Among Nashe's works, Charlewood issued his first work *The Anatomy of Absurdity* (1589; STC 18364) for Thomas Hacket, and also the first edition of *Pierce Pennliess* (1592; STC 18371) for Jones. *Pierce Pennliess* was reprinted by Jeffes for Busby three times in 1592 (STC 18371, 18372, and 18373) and once in 1593 (STC 18374), and also reprinted by Creede, Chettle's senior apprentice, for Ling in 1595 (STC 18375).

Also, with regard to Munday, Charledwood issued a large number of his works; he issued *A Brief and True Report* (1582; STC 18261) and *A Brief Discourse of the Taking of Edmund Campion* (1581; STC 18264) for Wright, and *The English Roman Life* (1582; STC 18272; 1590; STC 18273) for Ling.

In the case of Lodge, Scarlet issued *Prosopopeia* (1596; STC 16662a) for White. Orwin issued the first edition of *Rosalind* for Gubbin (1590; STC 16664), and also *Robert Second Duke of Normandy* for Ling and Busby (1591; STC 16657) among others. Jeffes issued *Euphues Shadow* (1592; STC 16656) and *A Margarite of America* (1596; STC 16660) for Busby. Creede issued Greene and Lodge's *A Looking Glass for London and England* (1594; STC 1598) for Barley.

1 Chettle as Printer

In Peele's case, Allde published *The Device of the Pageant* (1585; STC 19533), and also *The Battle of Alcazar* (1594; STC 19531) for Richard Bankworth. Charlewood issued *A Farewell… to…Sir J. Norris and Sir F. Drake* (1589) for Wright. Scarlet printed *Descensus Astrææ* (1591; STC 19532) for Wright.

Furthermore, Dekker may have had little to do with Danter at that time because he started writing at the end of the 1590s, but he was important for mentioning Chettle along with Greene, Nashe, Marlowe, and Peele in *A Knight's Conjuring*, which was printed by Creede for Barley in 1607. As Creede printed some of Dekker's works, Allde issued his tracts including *Patient Grissil* (1603; STC 6518) and *Satiro-Mastix* (1602; STC 6520.7) among others.

These facts reveal that there were certain kind of circles among some authors, printers, and publishers in the Elizabethan period. Such authors as Nashe, Munday, Lodge, Peele were not only closely linked to one anoter, but also friendly with certain printers and publishers including Charlewood, Wolfe, Scarlet, Allde, Creede, Burby, Ling, Millington, Busby, and Jeffes. For example, Charlewood was a "fatherly printer" for Munday and Chettle and encouraged young Munday and Chettle to write literary works, according to C. T. Wright ("Young Anthony Munday" 152). Charlewood issued numerous works of Munday for William Wright, Ling and others. Similarly, he seems to have been a father-like figure for Nashe when printing his first work *The Anatomy of Absurdity*. Wolfe issued dozens of Greene's works including *A Quip for an Upstart* (1592; STC 12301). Jeffes issued Nashe and Lodge's well-known works for Busby, though Chettle attacked Jeffes as a ballad-seller in a French romance, *2 Gerileon of England*, translated by Munday and printed by Scarlet for Burby, as will be discussed below. Scarlet issued Nashe's *Unfortunate Traveler* with Danter and Greene's cony-catching work for Burby.

These close relationships between the authors, printers, and publishers suggest that the literary publications were collaborative, and frequently a result of personal friendships. As the example of *The Return from Parnassus* shows, authors and printers like Danter had direct dealings with each other when publishing books. They worked together for their mutual profit. As the production of Elizabethan plays was collaborative among playwrights and theater companies, the publication of books was collaborative among authors, printers, and booksellers. The authors offered their books to printers and publishers for publication, but also printers and publishers like Charlewood encouraged the authors to write some works in hope that it would serve as publicity for themselves.

Without a printing-house, Chettle worked with Danter as a journeyman printer at least till 1596, and in the process, began to write pamphlets and fragments of plays. He expanded his relations with literary persons, though he may have been waiting for such an opportunity since his apprenticeship days.[47] In other words, Chettle obtained work through his connections with Danter, Nashe, and Munday among others. As a compositor, he was involved in the publications of Nashe's works including *Strange News* among others. On the other hand, Chettle edited *Groatsworth*, and wrote *Kind-Heart's Dream* and *Piers Plainness* as an author, as will be discussed in Chapter 2, "(i) Danter's Press and *Greene's Groatsworth of Wit*." Chettle was probably encouraged to do these works not only by Danter, but also by such booksellers as Wright and Gosson, and such his friends as Nashe, Munday, Lodge, and Peele.

Furthermore, Chettle built his connections to the theater by working at Danter's press. It was perhaps in the early 1590s that Chettle largely participated in the writing of *Sir Thomas More* to help the main author, Munday, as will be discussed in Chapter 3, "(ii) *Sir Thomas More*." It was their first and last time to create a play in collaboration with Shakespeare. At this time, Chettle would have known the other collaborators, Dekker and Heywood as well.

Afterwards, between 1590 and 1602, Chettle and Munday wrote several plays in collaboration including *Downfall* and *Death, Chance Medley, 2 Cardinal Wolsey*, as Appendix I shows. Wilson also frequently co-authored plays with Chettle. They wrote in collaboration *1, 2 Earl Goodwin and His Three Sons, Pierce of Exton, 1, 2 Black Bateman of the North, The Funeral of Richard Coeur de Lion, Chance Medley, Castiline's Conspiracy*. During this period Chettle also wrote many plays in collaboration with such other playwrights as Dekker, Heywood, and Drayton. As he worked in the printing industry, using his connections, he approached Henslowe, and also playwrights and actors in the theater.

(iii) Chettle and Publications by Printers Other Than East and Danter

(a) Personal Connections with Other Printers

At East and Danter's presses, Chettle thus expanded his personal relationships with authors, printers, and publishers. In addition to these two printers, Chettle also made the acquaintance of such printers and publishers as Creede, Bynneman, Jeffes, Orwin, Dawson, Simmes, and Short.

Creede was an apprentice to East and must have met Chettle in 1577. As mentioned above, Creede issued Shakespeare's plays including the second, third, fourth, and fifth quartos of *Richard III* (1598; 1602; 1605; 1612) and the second quarto of *Romeo and Juliet* (1599). He also printed such works by Greene including reprints, *A Looking Glass for London and England* (1594), *Groatsworth* (1596), *Gwydonius* (1593), *2 Mamillia* (1593), *Pandosto* (1614), and *The Scottish History of James the Fourth* (1598). Like Chettle, Creede probably met Greene at East's press. Creede was also interested in Chettle's other fellow writers. Creede issued Wilson's *The Pedler's Prophecy* (1595; STC 25783), Lodge's *A Treatise of the Plague* with Simmes in 1603, and also Dekker's *The Wonderful Year*, a work dealing with the plague as well (1603), *Magnificent Entertainment Given to King James* (1604; STC 6510), and *A Knight's Counjuring* (1607).

Bynneman, who is known for printing Holinshed's *Chronicles* (1577), was a neighbor of East in 1579 when Chettle was working for East (C. Wright

"Young Anthony Munday" 153). Naturally, Bynneman's apprentices, Ling and Jeffes stayed there. Chettle would have known Bynneman, Ling, and Jeffes. To East, however, Bynneman was not only a neighbor, as Jeremy L. Smith notes: "Bynneman owned many lucrative patents...East obtained convenient trade work and perhaps an overflow of copies from Bynneman's business" (17). Indeed, East issued Bourne's *A Regiment for the Sea* in 1580, 1584, 1587, 1592, and 1596, while the first edition was printed by Bynneman in 1574. Also, East printed Polemon's *The Second Part of the Book of Battles Fought in Our Age*, while the first part was printed by Bynneman and Francis Coldock in 1577. Moreover, East issued Mascall's *A Book of the Art and Manner* in 1590 and 1592. This was first printed by Bynneman in 1569. Furthermore, Danter issued Mantuanus's *The Eclogues* in 1594 after Bynneman's death in 1583. This was first issued by Bynneman in 1567, and reprinted by Bynneman in 1572. Bynneman's copies were, thus, transferred to East, and also occasionally to Danter.

Jeffes is alluded to by Chettle in the epistle to *2 Gerileon of England*, translated by Munday and printed by Scarlet for Burby in 1592. Chettle is offended that Jeffes has issued a rival translation of *Gerileon*, while also printing lascivious ballads. Indeed, Jeffes was a notorious printer, according to *A Dictionary of Printers and Booksellers*, edited by McKerrow et al.:

> On December 3rd, 1595, his press and letters were seized for printing *The Most Strange Prophecie of Doctor Cipriano* "and diverse other lewde ballades and things very offensive," and for this and resisting the searchers he was committed to prison until he made submission. (156)

Chettle's accusation of Jeffes was apparently true, though what "*The Most Strange Prophecie of Doctor Cipriano*" was is unknown. Moreover, Nashe complains that Jeffes printed the second edition of *Piers Plainness* in a hurry, and Nashe could not insert the stories about Greene's ghost and others.[48] As Jeffes printed works by Nashe and Lodge, he must have also been Chettle's

1 Chettle as Printer

close acquaintance.

Orwin and Dawson, mentioned above, had not worked with Danter, but they were acquaintances of Danter, Chettle, and Burby. An order of the Court of the Stationers' Company on 5 March 1593 notes a dispute between Chettle and Danter, for which Orwin and Dawson were summoned (46). Also, on the same day, Danter was tried for another controversy with Burby, and Dawson and Orwin were again summoned for this (46). Moreover, Orwin was an apprentice to Purfoot, who was the master of Gosson and issued H. C.'s *The Forest of Fancy*. Also, Orwin was involved in the publication of the Martin Marprelate tracts, and also issued a number of Greene's works; *Pandosto* (1588; STC 12285); *Menaphon* (1589; STC 12272); *Greene's Never Too Late* (1590; STC 12253). Dawson issued *1 Mamillia* (1583; STC 12269). Thus, Orwin and Dawson must have known Danter, Chettle, and Burby very well.

Simmes had not worked with Danter either, and apprenticed himself to Henry Sutton between 1576 and 1585; at the same time, he served Bynneman as well, according to W. Craig Ferguson (244). Simmes issued Chettle's *England's Mounrning Garment* for Millington in 1603, but before then, he may have met Chettle around Bynneman's press which was close to East's. Simmes printed numerous literary works. For example, he issued Shakespeare's quartos, including these of *Richard II* (1597; STC 22307), *Richard III* (1597; STC 22314), and *Hamlet* (1603; STC 22275); *Nashe's Lenten Stuff* (1599; STC 18370), Dekker's *The Shoemaker's Holiday* (1600; STC 6523), and Munday's collaboration, *1 Sir John Oldcastle* (1600; STC 18795); he also reprinted Lodge's *Rosalind* (1598; STC 16667), Greene's *Menaphon* (1599; STC 12273), and *Greene's Never Too Late* (1602; STC 12254.5; 1607; STC 12255).

Similarly, Short had not jointly printed works with Danter, but he frequently worked with Burby, Jones, Millington, East, Jeffes, Allde, and Simmes among others, according to Yamada ("Peter Short" 240-41). Chettle probably knew of Short through these printers and booksellers. Short issued Meres's *Palladis Tamia*, but also he is known for issuing Shakespeare's works including an abridged and corrupt text of *3 Henry VI* (1595; STC 21006), the second edition of *The Rape of Lucrece* (1598; STC 22346), and a corrupted *The Taming of a Shrew* (1594; STC 23667; 1596; STC 23668) as well as music scores by such as Dowland and Morley.

Outside East and Danter's presses, Chettle seems to have extended his personal relationships with these printers and publishers, and interestingly, also with fellow writers, such as Nashe, Lodge, and Dekker among others. The printing industry was such a small world, and authors, printers, and publishers worked together for mutual benefit. Printers and publishers jointly worked to avoid risks, while they had dealings with their resources, or authors. One partnership led to another partnership, and their personal relationships became eventually expanded.

However, as far as East and Danter's presses are concerned, there seem to have been very little interaction between the two. East and Danter never printed in collaboration, though Charlewood worked with both of them. In particular, Danter produced some works by Chettle and his friends, Greene, Nashe, Munday, Peele, and Lodge. On the other hand, though Danter issued *Titus Andronicus* and *Romeo and Juliet*, they were probably piratical; he had very little dealings with Shakespeare. Munday and Chettle wrote *Sir Thomas More*, and Peele created *Titus Andronicus*. Indeed, the Admiral's Men, for which Chettle and his friends wrote, and the Lord Chamberlain's Men, for which Shakespeare wrote, were the two greatest theater companies, and they competed with each other at the time. Moreover, Shakespeare did not write pamphlets, and he was not familiar with the publishing world. By contrast, Chettle and his friends, particularly Nashe, were deeply involved with publishing, and their literary activities elucidate the closeness of the printing, theatrical, and literary circles to us.

(b) Literary Influence from Publications by Printers Other Than East and Danter

Working both for East and Danter, Chettle, thus, expanded his rela-

1 Chettle as Printer

tionships with authors, printers, and booksellers. As I have shown with the example of Peele, authors could probably read books which their printers or publishers produced.[49] Printers like Charlewood occasionally encouraged authors to write and publish their works, probably lending such useful books as Polemon's *The Second Part of the Book of Battles Fought in Our Age* (1587), and in return, the printers gained some profit through these works.

Chettle clearly took advantage of his position and read the books issued by East and Danter, but also he probably could obtain copies printed by other printers or booksellers he knew, including Creede, Bynneman, Jeffes, Orwin, Simmes, and Short, as well as manuscripts written by his fellow writers including Nashe and Peele. For plays, Chettle could have sought inspiration from the stage, but reading plays would cost less and be more useful for him to use as sources of his works.

Nashe's *Pierce Penniless* was first issued by Charlewood in 1592 without his permission, and reprinted by Jeffes in 1592 and 1593. Chettle had obviously read this work before mentioning "Pierce" in *Kind-Heart's Dream*, and writing *Piers Plainness*. Chettle probably obtained the manuscript from Nashe. Nashe's style of bitter criticism in this work partly influenced Chettle's these style in pamphlets. However, more importantly, its religious and political ideologies, Protestantism and the rejection of Spain, and also its antagonism toward the rich must have stimulated Chettle's work such as *England's Mourning Garment*, *Death*, *Sir Thomas Wyatt*, *Patient Grissil*, and *Blind Beggar*, in which Catholics, Spaniards, and rich people are ill described. For instance, as Nashe bitterly accuses "Philip [II] of Spain as great an enemy to mankind as the diuell" (184) of waging wars for his profit in *Piers Plainness*, Chettle criticizes him as Elizabeth's "open and professed enemie" (90) in *England's Mourning Garment*.[50]

Munday wrote numerous pamphlets from anti-Catholic tracts to translations of continental chivalric romance. Munday also worked for the state as a writer and intelligence agent. He wrote such anti-Catholic pamphlets as *A Brief Discourse of the Taking of Edmund Campion* (1581; STC 18264), *A*

Discovery of Edmund Campion and His Confederates (1582; STC 18270), and *A Watch-Word to England* (1584; STC 18282). Moreover, Munday tracked down priests and other recusants, working for such government agents as Richard Topcliffe and Sir Thomas Heneage.[51] Chettle's anti-Catholicism was obviously influenced by Munday's tracts and activities. On the other hand, Munday's translations of chivalric romances also influenced Chettle, particularly *Palmerin d'Oliva*, printed by Charlewood for Wright in 1588 (STC 19157), and dedicated to the Earl of Oxford. As F. L. Jones suggests, the idea of killing people with a burning crown in *Hoffman* was probably taken from *Palmerin d'Oliva*, and the use of a burning crown was common in French and German chronicles (301). However, the burning crown came from Seneca's *Medea* as well.

Furthermore, the Martin Marprelate controversy may have influenced Chettle's religious ideology and his style in writing pamphlets. Between 1588 and 1589, a series of Puritan tracts appeared under the alias Martin Marprelate, attacking Anglican-Churche. Such writers as Lyly, Nashe, and Munday were requested by the Archbishop of Canterbury, John Whitgift, to write against Martin pseudonymously.[52] *Pap with an Hatchet*, printed by Orwin in 1589 (STC 17463), has been attributed to Lyly, and *An Almond for a Parrot* (1589; STC 534) is now widely accepted as Nashe's work, though McKerrow, the editor of *The Works of Thomas Nashe*, included it among Nashe's apocrypha, according to Charles Nicholl (McKerrow 5: 59-63; Nicholl, "Thomas Nashe" 238-39). It is uncertain which works Munday wrote, but as David M. Burgeron claims, *The Just Censure and Reproof of Martin Junior* (1589; STC 17458) attacks Munday (740). Chettle was apparently not drawn into this controversy, but he probably read the Martin and anti-Martin pamphlets, and learned how to criticize people.

Peele probably gave Chettle his manuscript of *An Eclogue...to...Robert Earl of Essex*. *England's Mourning Garment* is strongly influenced by *The Shepheardes Calender* and also by *An Eclogue*. *An Eclogue* is also influenced by *The Shepheardes Calender*, but depicts Elizabethan politics more directly in connection to Essex and Sidney. As Frank Ardolino claims, Peele clearly praises English Protestantism under Elizabeth in this work, as well as *The Arraignment of Paris*, *The Tale of Troy*, *Descensus Astrææ*, *A Farewell…to…Sir J. Norris and Sir F. Drake*, *Edward I*, and *The Battle of Alcazar* among others (147-49). Chettle probably read these works, and *England's Mourning Garment* seems to adopt Peele's political ideology and praises Elizabeth with reference to the Armada and her speech at Tilbury (105).

Edward I, dealing with Robin Hood, criticizes the Spanish and Catholic Queen Elinor of Castile, and the attack on Catholics recalls Chettle and Munday's Robin Hood plays, *Downfall* and *Death*. In these plays, another Eleanor, John's mother, appears, but she is also described as a lustful and vicious queen, and the Catholics are bitterly criticized.

The Battle of Alcazar, printed by Edward Allde in 1594, may have had an influience on Chettle and Dekker's lost play, *King Sebastian of Portugal*, performed in 1598. Peele's play describes the Battle of Alcazar in 1578. King Sebastian was believed to have died in the battle, but "a man appeared in Italy claiming to be Dom Sebastian in 1598," according to David M. Bergeron (742). Munday translated a pamphlet depicting the story, *The Strange Adventure*, written by José Teixeira in 1601 (STC 23864).

How close Chettle and Marlowe were remains uncertain, but Chettle was strongly affected by Marlowe's plays. *The Jew of Malta* was entered by Ling and Millington on 17 May 1594, but the only extant edition is that of 1633 (Arber 2: 649; STC 17412). On the day before, Danter issued a ballad called *"the murtherous life and terrible death of the riche Jew of Malta"* (Arber 2: 650). The connection between the two works remains unknown. The villainous revenger, Barabas, resembles Hoffman, and his shocking death recalls that of Hoffman in the final scene. On the other hand, *The Massacre at Paris*, printed by Allde in 1594, must have inspired Chettle as well as Dekker (STC 17423). *Hoffman* is a play warning against civil wars, which could break out because of the Stuart succession issues; similarly, Dekker depicts people's fear of civil wars after Elizabeth died in 1603 in *The Wonderful*

Year.[53] Chettle and Dekker certainly knew of the French civil wars through Marlowe's play.

Drayton's *The Legend of Matilda* was printed by John Roberts for Ling and Busby in 1594 (STC 7205). This work of poetry describes the tragedy of Matilda, who has been pursued by King John and prefers death to a dishonorable life. The plot of Matilda in *Death* is certainly influenced by Drayton's work, and her tragedy underscores the evils of John and the Roman Catholics in the play. Chettle and Munday wrote some works in collaboration with Drayton after 1598, and by then, they may have known each other. If not, Chettle and Munday could have obtained the book through Ling or Busby, and read it.

The anonymous *The Defense of Cony-Catching* defends cony-catching. Greene's cony-catching pamphlets were criticized by Harvey in *Four Letters*, and "Cuthbert Cony-catcher" mounts a defense of cony-catchers in the pamphlet according to Kumaran ("Print" 133-34). Kumaran attributes the pamphlet to Greene and Nashe ("Robert Greene" 261). As Kumaran points out, a juggler William Cukoe's defense of cony-catchers follows that of Cuthbert. Both of them regard the upper-class, who deceive people for their own profits, as cony-catchers, and defend cony-catching ("Print"134-36). Jenkins sees the pamphlet as influencing the description of brokerage and usury in *Piers Plainness*, but without detailed evidence (44). Chettle must have read this work, probably written by Greene and Nashe, and made use of it when writing his works.

Chettle, thus, had access to the books written by his fellow writers, but also read some tracts written by others and printed or edited by his acquaintances. *Piers Plainness* clearly draws on anonymous *The Pleasant History of Lazarillo de Tormes*. In *Lazarillo de Tormes*, the servant-hero, Lazarillo, suffers under seven mean masters. Similarly, in Chettle's work, the apprentice-hero Piers serves seven penurious masters. The Spanish picaresque, which has been attributed to Diego Hurtado de Mendoza, was translated by David Rowland and printed by Jeffes in 1586 (STC 15336). This translation was reprinted by Jeffes in 1596 (STC 15337), whereas Creede issued the second part in 1596 (STC 15340). Chettle probably asked Jeffes to show him a copy. As *The Unfortunate Traveler* is also influenced by *Lazarillo de Tormes*, Nashe may have also asked the same thing of his printer.

Chettle's plays frequently deal with English history and are probably based on Holinshed's *Chronicles* and Stow's *Chronicles* among others. The episode of Lady Bruce in *Death* must have been derived from Holinshed. The sad story of Jane and Guilford in *Sir Thomas Wyatt* seems to have been based on John Foxe's *Acts and Monuments*, better known as *The Book of Martyrs*. The antagonism between the Duke of Gloucester and the Bishop of Winchester, Cardinal Bewford, over their love for Eleanor in *Blind Beggar* probably drew on Holinshed and Stow.

Bynneman issued Holinshed's *Chronicles* in 1577 and Stow's *Chronicles* in 1580. Around this time, Chettle could read the books easily at Bynneman's, which was in his neighborhood. Short printed the fifth edition of *The Acts and Monuments* in 1596 (STC 11226). Short had worked with Burby, Richard Jones, Millington, East, Jeffes, Allde, Simmes, when he issuing *Palladis Tamia* mentioning Chettle. Chettle was probably acquainted with Short, and obtained this book.

Chettle's plays seem to draw on Seneca as well. Seneca's *Ten Tragedies* was edited by Thomas Newton and printed by Thomas Marsh in 1581 (STC 22221). Whether or not Chettle met Marsh is uncertain, but he must have met Newton at East's press for the publication of *A View of Valyaunce* in 1580, and would have been able to read his edition of Seneca. Hoffman declares his tragedy "[s]hall passe those of Thyestes, Tereus, / Iocasta, or Duke Iasons iealous wife" (1.3.407-10). These are characters in Seneca's tragedies. Indeed, Chettle is very conscious of Seneca; Hoffman as Otho attempts to marry Otho's mother as Oedipus did with his mother, and also rape her as Tereus did Philomela. Chettle's lost play, *Agamemnon*, written with Dekker and performed in 1598, was perhaps based on Seneca's *Agamemnon*.

Chettle was also much influenced by Shakespeare, though there is nothing definite to link the two directly. As they were playwrights for rivaling theater companies, they would not have shared their manuscripts. However, Chettle seems to have occasionally imitated Shakespeare's works. He certainly read *Titus Andronicus* and *Romeo and Juliet*, printed by Danter, and probably read *3 Henry VI*, *Richard III*, *The Taming of Shrew*, and *The Rape of Lucrece*. The villainous and ambitious figure of Hoffman is reminiscent of Richard in *3 Henry VI* and *Richard III*. The sub-plot of Gwenthyan and Sir Owen in *Patient Grissil* is a parody of Petruchio and Kate; Sir Owen struggles with Gwenthyan, the shrew, and finally succeeds in taming her like Petruchio. Fuethermore, *The Rape of Lucrece* is wittily mentioned when "*Melicert*," or Shakespeare, is blamed by Chettle for not writing an elegy for the deceased Elizabeth in *England's Mourning Garment*: "Nor doth the siluer tonged *Melicert*, / Drop from his honied muse one sable tears ... Shepheard [Shakespeare], remember our *Elizabeth*, / And sing her Rape, done by that *Tarquin*, Death" (98).

Chettle probably acquired these books from his fellow printers and booksellers. Short issued an abridged and corrupt text of *3 Henry VI* for Millington in 1595, and also a corrupt text of *The Taming of a Shrew* in 1594 and 1595. Simmes and Short printed *Richard III* in 1597, and Creede reprinted it in 1598, 1602, 1605, and 1612. Field issued *The Rape of Lucrece* for John Harrison, the younger in 1594, and Short reprinted it for Harrison in 1598. Harrison frequently worked with East, and published *The Shepheardes Calender* and religious tracts including those by Calvin.

Chettle could read the publications issued by East and Danter, but also read the works written by his friends, Nashe and Munday and the other literary works printed by Bynneman, Jeffes, Short, and Simmes among others. How Elizabethan authors obtained and read their sourcebooks has been obscure, but the example of Chettle who was acquainted with the printing industry and the theater could be a clue to solving this enigma.

*

1 Chettle as Printer

This chapter has explored Chettle's involvement in the printing industry, the source of his literary interest, and also his personal relationships. As an apprentice and journeyman, Chettle served East and had opportunity to read East's publications including works by Lyly, Spenser, Greene, and Lodge. Also, he might have composed three published works of poetry at this early stage in his career. After setting up a partnership with Danter, Chettle worked as a pamphleteer as well as a printer. Making the most of his status, Chettle read what Danter printed, such as works by Greene, Nashe, Shakespeare, Peele, Lodge, Wilson, and Munday. Furthermore, Chettle cultivated friendships with such printers and booksellers as Danter, Scarlet, Allde, Wright, Burby, Ling, and Millington, as well as such authors as Nashe, Munday, Peele, Lodge, and Wilson. At the same time, Chettle extended his personal relationships with such printers and publishers as Bynemann, Jeffes, Orwin, Dawson, Simmes, and Short, some of whom issued Chettle's books later; he also probably obtained same books from them and read such books as *Chronicles* by Holinshed and Stow, and also *Lazarillo de Tormes*.

This analysis of Chettle's careers, personal relationships, and reading has illuminated numerous issues. His involvement in printing and writing pamphlets had much to do with his personal connections with authors, printers, and publishers. In particular, Chettle's relationships with actor-playwrights, Munday and Wilson, and also Danter's appearance in *The Return from Parnassus* suggest the printing industry and theatrical world were close to each other. Moreover, sourcebooks are frequently discussed, but how authors acquired and read has not been sufficiently explained. The case of Chettle makes clearer how books may have been circulated, and how writers were able to have access to them. Furthermore, as the examples of *The Return from Parnassus* and also Charlewood have shown, the publication of books was a collaborative effort among authors, printers, and publishers, just as theatrical productions were a collaborative effort among playwrights and theater companies. The best example of this is the publication of *Groatsworth* and *Kind-Heart's Dream*. Chettle was involved in both works probably with Nashe, and they were jointly printed by Wolfe and Danter for Wright, as Chapter 2 will explain.

Notes

1. A journeyman printer was one who had finished his apprenticeship, but who was not in partnership or a permanent position; instead he worked on a wage basis.
2. These tables are based on STC (2nd ed.). For STC numbers of the books discussed here, see the tables. As the items listed in Appendix II are so large in number, only the most important ones are included in the Works Cited.
3. For East's publications, see Plomer, "Thomas East, Printer" and J. Smith.
4. Richard Powlter's *The Fountain of Flowing Felicity* should be located in Lambeth Palace, but it is missing according to STC, and what the book is remains uncertain. All the number of editions concerning East, Danter and other contemporary printers are from STC.
5. For Burby's relation with Chettle, see Chapter 1, "(ii) Professional Printer and Path to Authorship" and Chapter 2 "(i) Danter's Press and *Greene's Groatsworth of Wit*." For Purfoot, see Chapter 1, "(i) Chettle and Thomas East," "(c) Three Works by 'H. C.'." For Allde, see Chapter 2, particularly "(i) Danter's Press."
6. For Elizabethan religious publishing, see Collinson, Hunt, and Walsham 29-93.
7. Hemmingsen and Ursinus studied under Melanchthon.
8. For the background of Elizabethan medical books, see Bennett 179-89.
9. Mascall wrote on other interesting subjects; in 1581, he produced a book on agriculture called, *The Husbandly Ordering and Government of Poultry*, while publishing a manual to remove stains, *A Profitable Book Declaring Dyers' Approved Remedies* in 1583, which was reprinted in 1588, 1596, and 1605. His manuals thus generally treated subjects from leisure to domestic affairs.
10. For the background of music printing, see J. Smith 19-22.
11. See Monson 326. For further analysis of Byrd's life and music prints, see Fellowes; Brett; Harley.
12. For Essex's secret relation with Catholics in England, see Hammer, *Polarisation* 174-78.
13. Galen connoted that each living thing was created with four humors, namely, phlegm, blood, black bile, and yellow bile, though this idea originated from Hippocrates, the ancient Greek physician.
14. This idea is now widely accepted. See Edelman 196-97.

1 Chettle as Printer

[15] For the military revolution, see Duffy; Parker; Eltis; Anglo 564-72.
[16] The third part of *Most Brief Tables* is largely based on Machiavelli's *The Art of War*, which relies on the classical military method.
[17] According to Alistair Fox, Essex (sixty-six dedications) received the most dedications in books published between 1590 and 1600, even more than Elizabeth (fifty-six). See Fox 231; 245-48.
[18] All citations of Shakespeare except *Romeo and Juliet* are from *William Shakespeare: The Complete Works*, 2nd ed. (Oxford: Oxford UP, 2005).
[19] The quotation is from Hugh Maclean's edition (455).
[20] C. M. Ingleby, ed., *Shakespeare Allusion-Books*, Part I, 6. Subsequent quotations from *England's Mourning Garment* are based on this edition.
[21] Recent scholars have suggested that *Titus Andronicus* was written by Shakespeare in collaboration with Peele, and particularly Act I has been attributed to Peele, as Stanley Wells, the editor of the play in the Oxford Complete Works of Shakespeare (2nd ed., 2005), claims (155). This edition assigns the work to "William Shakespeare with George Peele." Also, see Merriam, "Influence," Vickers, Bate, and Motoyama.
[22] See also Halasz 126.
[23] All quotations from *Kind-Heart's Dream* follow G. B. Harrison's edition (1966).
[24] The original speech-prefix is Sarlois due to the confusion between Hoffman and Sarlois in the latter part of the play, but here I have changed it to Hoffman for convenience. See Jenkins, ed., *Hoffman* vii-viii.
[25] All citations from *Hoffman* are from Jenkins's edition.
[26] For further discussion on Chettle and Nashe, see Chapter 2, "(i) Danter's Press and *Greene's Groatsworth of Wit*."
[27] See Chapter 1, "(iii) Chettle and Publications by Printers Other Than East and Danter," "(b) Literary Influence from Publications by Printers Other Than East and Danter."
[28] STC 4271 Reel number 238:12 contains this explicit together with "Finis. *H. C.*" while reel number 952:01 misses U4r-v including these words.
[29] See Appendix III.
[30] The relations among Danter, Burby, Wright, and Chettle will be discussed further in Chapter 2, "(i) Danter's Press and *Greene's Groatsworth of Wit*."
[31] All the quotations from *Have with You to Saffron Walden* follow McKerrow's edition, *The Works of Thomas Nashe*, vol. 3.
[32] The tables in Appendices III and IV are mainly based on STC (2nd ed.). For STC numbers of the books discussed here, see the tables. As the items listed in Appendices III and IV are so large in number, only the most important ones are included in the Works Cited. I counted Calvin's *Sermon of Master John Calvin*, printed in 1592 (STC 4440),

– 95 –

and Nashe's *Unfortunate Traveler*, printed in 1594 (STC 18381) as Danter's publications, following Hanabusa's unpublished doctoral dissertation, "John Danter's Play-Quarto" 34, and Appendices 3 and 4b. Also, for *Unfortunate Traveler*, see his more recent article, "Notes on the Second Edition" 556-59.

33 See Chapter 2, "(ii) *Kind-Heart's Dream*: Rival Prints, Celebrity, Advertisement."

34 For the details of the first edition, see Edward Viles and F. J. Furnivall, eds., *The Rogues and Vagabonds* iv-vi, and also Kinney 296.

35 The title page of *Jack Straw* notes 1593 (A2r), while the colophon mentions 1594 (F3v).

36 All the quotations from *Pierce Penniless* are from McKerrow's edition, *The Works of Thomas Nashe*, vol. 1.

37 All quotations from this play follow Kermode's edition.

38 For the anti-Catholicism in Chettle's plays, see Chapter 5 "Catholic Rulers and Downfallen Protestant Prisoners."

39 For further discussion, see Chapter 6, "(ii) Problems of Soldiers," "(b) Veterans in Chettle's Works," and also "(iii) Chettle's Political Views on Peace/War Debate."

40 The quotation follows John Dover Wilson's edition.

41 For further discussion of Chettle's commitment to the play and literary influence of the play on his works, see Chapter 3, "(iii) *Romeo and Juliet* (Q1)."

42 Frank Ardolino claims that *The Old Wife's Tale* celebrates Elizabeth and Protestantism, but the argument is not persuasive, though Peele's other works did praise Protestantism.

43 For Greene and Clarke, see Chapter 1, "(i) Chettle and Thomas East," "(c) Chettle's Relationships with Authors, Printers, and Publishers." Nashe lodged with Danter. For details on the relation between Nashe and Danter and Nashe's role as a literary adviser for Danter, see Nicholl, *A Cup of News* 224-25.

44 See Chapter 1, "(i) Chettle and Thomas East," "(c) Chettle's Relationships with Authors, Printers, and Publishers."

45 See Chapter 1, "(i) Chettle and Thomas East," "(d) Three Works by 'H. C.'."

46 For the share-printing of *Orlando Furioso*, see Hanabusa's "The Printer of Sheet G" 145-50. For *The Cobbler's Prophecy*, see Hanabusa's "Shared Printing" 333-49.

47 Chettle signed for his debt to Henslowe as a "London Stationer" on 22 October 1598; as F. L. Jones observes, once having become a member of a guild, he had remained a stationer, as Munday remained a draper (Henslowe 119; F. Jones 6).

48 For further discussion of Jeffes, see Chapter 2, "(i) Danter's Press and *Greene's Groatsworth of Wit*," and also "(ii) *Kind-Heart's Dream*: Rival Prints, Celebrity, Advertisement."

49 See Chapter 1, "(i) Chettle and Thomas East," "(b) Literary Influence from East's

1 Chettle as Printer

Publications between 1577 and 1590."
[50] For further discussion of Chettle's anti-Catholic and anti-Spanish attitudes, see Chapter 5 "Catholic Rulers and Downfallen Protestant Prisoners." For his criticism of wealthy people, see Chapter 7 "Beggars in *The Pleasant Comedy of Patient Grissil* and *The Blind Beggar of Bethnal Green*, and the Elizabethan Money Based Economy."
[51] See Bergeron 740. For Munday's anti-Catholicism, see Chapter 5, "(ii) *The Downfall and Death of Robert, Earl of Huntingdon*," "(d) Religious Conflicts and the Stuart Succession."
[52] For more details of the Martin Marprelate controversy, see McKerrow, ed., *The Works of Thomas Nashe*, vol. 5, 34-65. A recent critic Kumaran suggests Greene's involvement in the anti-Martin pamphlets throughout his article "Robert Greene's Martinist."
[53] For further discussion, see Chapter 4, "(iii) Succession."

2 Chettle as Pamphleteer

(i) Danter's Press and *Greene's Groatsworth of Wit*: Complicity among Editor, Printer, and Bookseller in the Early Modern Book Trade

Pamphlet physically meant "a short quarto" according to Joad Raymond, and it became a popular medium for delivering news as well as ballads and broadsides from the early sixteenth century in England (Raymond 2; Shaaber 1). The news may be roughly categorized into two types: on one hand, religious and political propaganda from battles to royal family, and on the other, sensational news of earthquakes, monsters, witchcraft, and others (Clarke 13-14).[1] Print culture had originally developed for the religious purpose of spreading the Bible, but the purpose gradually became secular and commercial, particularly after the 1580s. At that time, the pamphlet became widespread, and the term became accepted by the public with frequent use: "it came to refer to a short, vernacular work, generally printed in quarto format, costing more than a few pennies, of topical interest or engaged with social, political or ecclesial issues" (Raymond 8). Its popularization was due to an increase in literacy and conflicts between Catholics and Protestants after the Reformation; particularly, the Martin Marprelate controversy contributed to its expansion (Raymond 11-12).

By the 1590s the term pamphlet was used widely as a noun, verb and adjective. Nashe contemptuously used it as a verb in the preface to *Pierce Penniless* reprinted in 1592: "what a coyle there is with pamphleting on him after his [Greene's] death" (153). Nashe ridicules the literary conditions in which many pamphlets on Greene including *Groatsworth* were issued subsequent to his death, as discussed below. It is slightly ironical that the great pamphleteer Nashe scorns his profession, but the terms concerning pamphlets were, indeed, pejoratively used, because such texts were considered to be unreliable (Raymond 8). In short, for the Elizabethan commoners, pamphlets were cheap and easy to obtain and read, but at the same time, tended to be worthless fabrications.

However, the pamphlet played an important role in Elizabethan culture. Today there is no media similar to the pamphlet. The pamphlet was such an ambiguous media combined with true and fictional news, literature, textbooks, and criticism of politics, religion and society among other things that it could not be clearly categorized by genre. One example is "rogue literature" or "cony-catching pamphlets," written by Harman and Greene. Rogue literature describes London's underworld both factually and fictionally from the viewpoint of an honest man who comments on and moralizes about the social situation, and this tradition was followed by later writers, such as Dekker and Middleton.[2] This genre is, in a sense, a forerunner of journalism, but at the same time it is fictional literature. Greene's autobiographical pamphlets that were issued after cony-catching pamphlets generally follow this line. *Groatsworth* is itself a banal pamphlet, describing Greene's life in destitution, but it is most notable and problematic for its allusion to contemporary dramatists, and also because of its authorship and publication process.

Danter printed Greene's three pamphlets around the time of the author's death on 3 September 1592: *The Black Book's Messenger* was entered by Wright on 21 August 1592 (Arber 2: 619), and issued by Danter in the same year; *Groatsworth* was entered on 20 September 1592 (Arber 2: 620); *The Repentance of Robert Greene* was entered on 6 October 1592 (Arber 2: 621). Among them *Groatsworth* was the most popular with six editions (1592, 1596, 1617, 1621, 1629, 1637). Danter printed the first edition only. Interestingly, the second edition was issued by Creede, Chettle's senior apprentice at East's press, and this suggests the close relationship between Creede's press and Danter's.

Henry Chettle's Careers: A Study of an Elizabethan Printer, Pamphleteer, Playwright

As Chettle observes in the preface to *Kind-Heart's Dream*, many papers were left to various booksellers after Greene's death, and the above three were given to Danter. Among them, *Groatsworth* became the object of attention due to questions about its authorship soon after it was published. Chettle and Nashe were apparently suspected at the time, but both of them denied it, as will be discussed below. In the early twentieth century, C. E. Sanders reignited this authorship issue. Sanders claimed the Robert story was written by Greene before his illness began, but that the concluding part written in the first person was Chettle's forgery. In 1969, Austin found Chettle's hand in the work through computer aided stylistic analysis, though this claim became controversial. R. L. Widmann and T. R. Waldo rejected it mainly because the number of Austin's samples was small. Recent scholars still argue over the authorship question without definite evidence. Charles Crupi and Kumaran attribute the work to Greene, while such scholars as D. Allen Carroll, who edited the latest critical edition, and Jowett attribute it to Greene and Chettle, a view with which Katherine Duncan-Jones concurs (Crupi 32; Kumaran, "Print" 48, n.1; Carroll 1-31; Jowett, "Johannes Factotum" 455-86; Duncan-Jones 449-52). However, more recent scholars argue against these theories. Richard Westley claims Austin's analysis is not enough, and that Greene wrote the work on his own. Through the lexical and orthographical evidence from LION, Westley has "found forty-one words that appear throughout *Groatsworth* and Greene's other prose writings and not at all in Chettle" (374). On the other hand, Donna Murphy proposes that Gabriel Harvey wrote it. Murphy believes Austin's analysis is doubtful, and using a more extensive corpus, found fifty-eight words in *Groatsworth* which were not located in Greene's other works. Moreover, she remarks, "[a]s *Groatsworth* accused Marlowe and Greene of atheism, Gabriel charged Nashe with atheism in *Pierce's Supererogation*" (252), and suspects Chettle had met Greene and known his hand. However, she keeps silent about the relationship between Gabriel and Peele, who is also alluded to in the tract.

These critics have tackled the authorship problem with computer analysis, following Austin. However, the lexical approach does not produce a definite conclusion because there is the possibility that someone else imitated Greene's hand and claimed his own work to be Greene's, whether entirely or partly. Murphy states that "[c]ertain vocabulary indicates that the author of *Groatsworth* used words and themes from some of Greene's works to make it appear that Greene wrote it" (250). Moreover, she points out that Nashe added two of the fifty-eight words which appears in *Groatsworth*, but not elsewhere, to the preface to Greene's *Menaphon* (1589), and claims that similarities between Nashe's preface and *Groatsworth* may have urged people to accuse Nashe of writing *Groatsworth* (250).[3]

In an influential article, "Johannes Factotum," Jowett approaches the authorship issue by analyzing the external evidence, focusing on Chettle's relations with Danter, as well as by reviewing the internal evidence of Austin's analysis. Jowett concludes that *Groatsworth* is a combination of Greene's writing with Chettle's fabrications, and he describes Chettle as "an upstart Johannes factotum." Moreover, most recently Steve Mentz believes "Greene wrote at least some of the text," but he "cannot determine exactly what" (117). Mentz analyzes Greene's prose works by genre without the aid of computer analysis, and points out the parallels between the structure of *Groatsworth* and Greene's career in prose including "Lylian romance," "Novella collections," "Greek Romances," "Farewell to Folly," "Cony-Catching," "Repentance Tract," and "Satire/Invective" (124-29). According to Mentz, each section of *Groatsworth* corresponds to one of these categories; for example, the letter section beginning with "*To those Gentlemen,*" which alludes to Marlowe, Nashe, Peele, and Shakespeare, is categorized as "Satire/Invective."[4] Mentz, thus, pays attention to the role of Greene, "a marketable commodity" (116), in the late Elizabethan printing industry, and concludes:

> The *Groatsworth* finally suggests that collaboration, which is fast becoming a nor-

mative idea in discussions of early modern dramatic authorship, may not be limited to fraught or friendly relations between playwrights: dead writers, deceptive stationers, forgers, and other figures of murky motives and unknown tendencies may contribute materially to collaborations as well. (130)

Mentz's argument is interesting and persuasive, and I agree with his idea that the work is a collaboration. However, he does not fully discuss the personal relationships between Greene, Nashe, Chettle, Marlowe, Shakespeare, and the publisher, Wright, though he mentions "fraught or friendly relations between playwrights." Also, Mentz does not even mention Peele and the printers, Danter and Wolfe, who are important in considering the production of *Groatsworth*, though he discussed Greene's significance in the printing world.

Such external evidence of the authorship issue, which Jowett and Mentz propose, could be extended more, considering the relationships of people in Danter's press, that is, Chettle, Nashe, Wright, and also Wolfe along with such playwrights as Marlowe, Peele, and Shakespeare. Through an analysis of these personal relationships, I will suggest that Greene wrote some parts of the work, but at the same time, Chettle and possibly Nashe were brought into the production process, at least in the latter part which includes allusions to Marlowe, Nashe, Peele, and Shakespeare.

The Stationers' Register records on 20 September 1592, soon after Greene's death: "William Wrighte / Entred for his copie, vnder master watkins hande / vppon the perill of Henrye Chettle / a booke intituled / GREENES *Groatsworth of wyt bought with a million of Repentance*" (Arber 2: 620). "Vppon the perill" are enigmatic words, but it probably means under the responsibility; therefore, Chettle was evidently engaged in the production, though he later became desperate to avoid such assertions of responsibility.

In the preface to *Kind-Heart's Dream*, Chettle explains the printing process after Greene's death, as discussed above, and apologizes to "*one or two of*"

2 Chettle as Pamphleteer

"*diuers play-makers*" who were offended by a letter to them in *Groatsworth* "*as if the originall fault had beene my fault*" (6-7); Chettle acknowledges their suspicion of his authorship, stating "*because on the dead they cannot be auenged, they wilfully forge in their conceites a liuing Author: and after tossing it two and fro, no remedy, but it must light on me*" (5-6); Chettle, then, repeatedly denies his authorship as well as Nashe's, attributing it to Greene: "*I protest it was all Greenes, not mine nor Maister Nashes, as some vniustly haue affirmed*" (6-7); "*Thus Gentlemen, hauing noted the priuate causes, that made me nominate my selfe in print; being aswell to purge Master Nashe of that he did not, as to iustifie what I did, and withall to confirme what M. Greene did*" (7).

As discussed in Chapter 1 "Chettle as Printer," Chettle consistently claims his identity as a printer and attempts to deny his authorship in *Groatsworth*, remarking, "*How I haue all the time of my conuersing in printing hindred the bitter inueying against schollers*" (6). Moreover, he uses many technical terms for printing, such as "*print*" (5, 7), "*papers*" (5), "*Booke sellers hand*" (5), "*publish*" (6), "*copy*" (6), and "*licensd*" (6) among others, though he is an author of this work, as his signature shows at the end of the preface. Furthermore, he emphasizes he was urged to write this pamphlet: "*To come in print is not to seeke praise, but to craue pardon*" (5); in other words, he had "*the priuate causes, that made me nominate my selfe in print*" (7). Unconsciously or intentionally, he employs the term "print" instead of "write." *Kind-Heart's Dream* attacks ballad sellers, the spread of the medical texts and quacksalvers, actors, and Harvey through the voices of such ghosts as those of Greene and Tarlton, and Chettle was afraid that some readers would be offended; therefore, to avoid the risk, he deployed numerous excuses. As Chettle goes on to say, "*Had not the former reasons been, it had come forth without a father: and then should I haue had no cause to fear offending, or reason to sue for fauour*," he would have published *Kind-Heart's Dream* anonymously without the authorship issues of *Groatsworth* (Kumaran, "Print" 112). Indeed, many of his works were published anonymously, such as *Hoffman*, or with the initials "H. C." (the three early works and *Piers Plainness*), and in *England's Mourning Garment* his name "*Hen: Chettle*" appears in the middle, at the end of the funeral record with "To the Reader" (112). His reluctance to claim authorship, perhaps to avoid offense, can be seen elsewhere.

Although, thus, denying his and Nashe's authorship of *Groatsworth*, Chettle implies their commitment to the work and the printing industry. In the preface to *Kind-Heart's Dream*, Chettle also briefly denies Nashe's hand in the epistle to *2 Gerileon of England* (1592), translated by Munday and issued by Scarlet, "*though by the workemans error T. N. were set to the end: that I confesse to be mine, and repent it not*" (7). For the initials, Jenkins sees it as a forgery, and states that it was "because of the advertising power of Nashe's signature" (12). Similarly, as mentioned in Chapter 1, "(ii) Chettle and John Danter," "(b) Danter's Publications between 1591 and 1598," C. T. Wright states that it was misleadingly signed "to trade on the popularity of Thomas Nashe" ("'Edward' Spenser" 35). Significantly, Wright associated this episode with the translator of the Plato's *Axiochus* (1592). The title-page notes the translator is "*Edw. Spenser*," and such critics as Padelford, the editor of the work, and Weatherby attribute it to Spenser, while such scholars as Freyd, Swan, and Wright assigne it to Munday. Wright suggests "Munday, Burby, and their helpers were capable of misusing Spenser's name," and also Munday may have translated it with "Spenserian touches" ("'Edward' Spenser" 35). If Chettle lied about the authorship of *Groatsworth*, and also the translator was Munday, curiously, the forgeries of *Groatsworth*, *2 Gerileon*, and *Axiochus* would have happened in Chettle's circle in the same year. As the example of the Martin Marpelate controversy shows, the lies about the authorships spread in the Elizabethan literature, or at least among Chettle's friends, including the anti-Martins, Nashe and Munday. This kind of forgery was needed for sales, and Chettle, Danter, and their friends attached to Greene's name value in the publication of *Groatsworth*. T. N.'s passages in the preface to *Kind-Heart's Dream* seem to be an abrupt digression, and what exactly Chettle intended to say is uncertain, but he probably had in mind forgery, print, and Nashe in connection to *Groatsworth*.

2 Chettle as Pamphleteer

Nashe himself denies his hand in *Groatsworth* in the epistle to *Pierce Penniless His Supplication to the Devil*, which was entered under Richard Jones's name on 22 August 1592 and printed by Jeffes; Charlewood had printed it without Nashe's permission earlier the same year, and Nashe complains about it in the epistle to Jeffes. Curiously, it was the same date as the entry of *2 Gerileon of England*. According to Nashe, if Jeffes had not republished it immediately, he would have inserted epistles "to the Ghost of *Macheuill*, of *Tully*, of *Ouid*, or *Roscius*, of *Pace* the Duke of Norfolks Iester; and lastly, to the Ghost of *Robert Greene*, telling him, what a coyle there is with pamphleting on him after his death" (153). Jowett claims the "coyle" might include *Kind-Heart's Dream*, but in particular suggests suspicions of Nashe's co-authorship in *Groatsworth* ("Johannes Factotum" 474). However, this can be seen as an advertisement for *Kind-Heart's Dream*, which was entered under Wright's name on 8 December and printed by Danter and Wolfe, and *Groatsworth*, also entered under Wright and printed by Danter and Wolfe. These were the only works that Danter and Wolfe printed in collaboration (Thomas, "The Printing" 196-97; Jowett, "Johannes Factotum" 467; Jowett, "Credulous to False Printers" 99-102). Therefore, the two works must have been closely related. Chettle and people surrounding him, such as Danter and Wright possibly intended to publish *Kind-Heart's Dream* as a sister pamphlet when producing *Groatsworth*, and Nashe had already known this when writing the epistle.

Nashe, however, in the preface to *Pierce Penniless*, denies his commitment to *Groatsworth*, scorning the work:

> Other news I am aduertised of, that a scald triuial lying pamphlet, cald Greenes groats-worth of wit, is giuen out to be my doing. God neuer haue care of my soule, but vtterly renou[n]ce me, if the least word or sillable in it proceeded from my pen, or if I were any way priuie to the writing or printing it. (154)

Noticeably, he denies his involvement as a printer or ghostwriter as well as an author. His relationship with Danter was possibly well-known. In *Have with You to Saffron Walden*, Nashe himself describes the situation of "*Danters* press," where Nashe is called "*Danters gentleman*, who is as good at all times as *Wolfes right worshipfull* Gabriel" (128). Nashe suggests his identity as a literary adviser for his landlord, Danter, can be compared to that of his rival author Gabriel Harvey, who was Wolfe's literary adviser (Jowett, "*Henry Chettle*" 142-43).

Both Chettle and Nashe deny their authorship of *Groatsworth*, while describing their connection to the printing industry. In *Kind-Heart's Dream* Chettle seemingly denies his and Nashe's commitment to *Groatsworth*, but paradoxically he reveals their close involvement with the printing industry and acts of forgery. Also, in the epistle to *Pierce Penniless*, Nashe denies his commitment to *Groatsworth*, but actually publicizes the work and also *Kind-Heart's Dream*, another pamphlet issued by Danter's press, and admits his close link with the industry. These denials, ironically, seem to expose their involvement in the work.

Since there were neither modern ideas of copyright nor of authorship at that time, the authorship question should not be restricted to the author, but printers and booksellers were also involved; in Danter's press the relationships seem to have been particularly close.[5] As seen above, Chettle and his friends Greene, Nashe, Munday published their works through Danter and worked together on some publications, whether as authors or printers. Furthermore, Chettle and Nashe were Danter's literary advisers who corrected sentences before publishing them, as Gabriel Harvey was Wolfe's adviser, according to Jowett ("*Henry Chettle*" 142-43). Such literary advisers were needed for the press because printers were usually "ill acquainted with Poetrie" and made errors, as Chettle observed in *England's Mourning Garment* (112).

The production of *Groatsworth* involved many people close to Danter: Greene as author, Chettle as editor and part-author, Danter and Wolfe as printers, though the title-page omits their names, Wright as stationer and

2 Chettle as Pamphleteer

publisher, and perhaps Nashe as Chettle's assistant. Wolfe printed sheets A-C, and Danter printed sheets D-F covering the problematic letters, which supports the attribution of that part to Chettle's authorship (Thomas, "The Printing" 196-97; Jowett, "Johannes Factotum" 467). Wright, whose name only appears on the title-page, holds a claim for the authorship of "W. W." in "The Printer to the Gentle Reader:" "nowe hath death given a period to his [Greene's] pen, onely this happened to my handes which I have published for your pleasures: Accept it favourably because it was his last birth and not least worth, in my opinion" (41). Thus, before Chettle attributed the pamphlet to Greene, Wright had already done so. As discussed above, Wright entered and published *Kind-Heart's Dream* shortly after this publication, and the two works share the same producers: author (Chettle), printers (Danter and Wolfe), and stationer (Wright).

Furthermore, *The Repentance of Robert Greene* is another pamphlet on Greene issued in the same year, 1592, by Danter for Burby, who became independent from Wright on 13 January of that year. Burby worked with Danter on many other works including Greene's *Orlando Furioso*, and Munday's two volumed of translations, *Primaleon of Greece*. The author of *The Repentance* has been generally accepted as Greene, and Chettle may possibly have edited it, as Jowett notes ("Johannes Factotum" 477-81). *Greene's Vision* also described Greene's ghost, and was issued by Edward Allde, whose father was Munday's printing master, for Thomas Newman, the publisher, soon after Greene's death. Newman remarks in the epistle "Manie haue published repentaunces vnder his name." Chettle was probably influenced by this in writing *Kind-Heart's Dream*, as Jowett remarks ("Johannes Factotum" 474, n.38). Stories on Greene's ghost were so popular that they appeared frequently in pamphlets, as Lawrence Manley points out (325).

Greene's works were printed by Danter after Greene's death, and involved a variety of people: Chettle, Wolfe, Wright, and Burby. Also, Nashe supported Chettle and publicized his *Kind-Heart's Dream*, by mentioning people's enthusiasm for "pamphleting" on Greene. The team may thus have planned the publication of serial pamphlets on Greene when Danter obtained Greene's manuscripts. Chettle's forgery in *Groatsworth*, particularly in its letter, was used to draw people's attention to Greene, and Chettle himself and Nashe publicized the succeeding pamphlets on Greene by Danter's press, while denying their authorship. Moreover, associating the Nashe-Harvey controversy with their printers Danter and Wolfe, the two printers perhaps made a secret commercial treaty. Wolfe worked for both parties, for he had already become established as a frequent printer of Greene (Jowett, "Credulous to False Prints" 98). In other words, the two printers urged the authors to write pamphlets one after another in order to generate sales, or the two authors may have had an arrangement as well. After Greene died, Harvey turned on his friend Nashe, who had already been familiar with quarrels after his experience of the Martin Marprelate controversy, and attacked him.[6] In *Kind-Heart's Dream*, the ghost of Greene encourages Pierce Penniless, namely Nashe, to take revenge on Harvey. Jowett sees this as publicity for Nashe's *Strange News* ("Johannes Factotum" 467). As in the case of this controversy, Danter and Wolfe may have incited Chettle to write about Shakespeare to evoke controversy.

Apart from the commercial interests of the printers, the reason why Chettle attacked Shakespeare is mysterious. It was probably because he used Shakespeare's reputation to draw attention. However, it may have come from jealousy rather than hate because Chettle and the four years younger Shakespeare came from the same social background, as Jowett suggests; their fathers were craftsmen, and they did not go to university ("Johannes Factotum" 483-84). Apparently, Shakespeare and also Jonson were outside of the Greene-Nashe-Chettle group, and they seem to have been regarded with suspicion or hostility according to *England's Mourning Garment*. In the tract, Chettle urges Shakespeare, "the siluer tonged *Melicert*," to "mourne her [Elizabeth's] death that graced his desert," while criticizing Jonson, "English *Horace*," remarking, "Of her he seems to haue no memorie" (98). By contrast, Chettle chides his "three deers," Dekker ("*Antihorace*"), Marston ("*Mœlibee*"), and Petowe ("*Musæus*") to write an elegy for Elizabeth, noting, "All such whose vertues highly I commend" (98).[7]

Moreover, what has not been previously discussed on this issue is that Chettle's *Hoffman* seems to owe much to Shakespeare's *3 Henry VI*. Famously, *Groatsworth* parodies "Tygers hart wrapt in a Players hyde" (48) from the line of the Duke of York "O tiger's heart wrapped in a woman's hide !" (1.4.137) in *3 Henry VI*, while Nashe mentions Talbot of *1 Henry VI* in *Pierce Penniless*. These references show Chettle and Nashe's awareness of Shakespeare as well as the popularity of the series. Chettle's *Hoffman* has been frequently discussed by N. Delius and others in terms of an imitation of another revenge tragedy, *Hamlet*, as well as being under the the influence of *Richard III* by C. V. Boyer. However, its relation with *3 Henry VI* has never been discussed. As shown in Chapter 1, "(iii) Chettle and Publications by Printers Other Than East and Danter," Short issued an abridged and corrupt text of *3 Henry VI* (1595) for Millington. Chettle probably obtained it through the two, who were his acquaintances. *3 Henry VI* and *Hoffman* share a similar plot; at first, Richard/Hoffman intend to revenge their father, but after having done so, they desire the crown. The crown is symbolically used in *Henry VI*, especially in the first part and *Hoffman*. Just as the crown made of paper, in *1 Henry VI*, in *Hoffman*, the burning crown used for torture seems to represent the vanity of power. Also, there are some parallels between *3 Henry VI* and *Hoffman*:

> a homely swain. (*3 Henry VI*, 2.5.22)
> homely curds…. (*3 Henry VI*, 2.5.47)
> the homely Cakes…. (*Hoffman*, 1.1.151)

> kindling coals that fires all my breast / And burns me up with flames that tears would quench. (*3 Henry VI*, 2.1.83-84)
> ther's another fire / Burnes in this liuer lust, and hot desire, / which you must quench; must? (*Hoffman*, 4.2.1909-11)

Like one that stands upon a promontory / And spies a far-off shore....
(*3 Henry VI*, 3.2.135-36)
Ile to yon promonts top, and their [sic] suruey.... (*Hoffman*, 1.1.26)

I can... set the murderous Machiavel to school. (*3 Henry VI*, 3.2.191-93)
ile seeke out my notes of Machiauel, they say hee's an odd politician.
(*Hoffman*, 2.1.510-11)

Chettle was an imitator after all, as Jowett claims ("Johannes Factotum" 485). In other words, the theft was by Chettle, not Shakespeare. Chettle wrote parts of *Sir Thomas More* around this period, the early 1590s, in collaboration with Shakespeare and others. According to the preface to *Kind-Heart's Dream*, Chettle knew Shakespeare after the publication of *Groatsworth* and admired his gentle manners. Remarkably, about five years later they became rival playwrights; Shakespeare for the Lord Chamberlain's Men and Chettle for the Admiral's Men. Moreover, with regard to Shakespeare's dramatic texts, Chettle has been connected to *Romeo and Juliet*, issued by Danter in 1597, as will be shown in Chapter 3, "(iii) *Romeo and Juliet* (Q1)." Danter also printed Shakespeare and Peele's *Titus Andronicus*. As discussed in Chapter 1, "(iii) Chettle and Publications by Printers Other Than East and Danter," Chettle was acquainted with the printers and publishers who issued Shakespeare's works, and he probably obtained some of them because his works, particularly *Hoffman*, seem to show Shakespeare's influence.

With the others referred to in *Groatsworth*, Marlowe, Nashe, and Peele, there seemed to have been no trouble. The three were all University Wits and Greene's friends. The relationship between Marlowe and Chettle is uncertain, but Dekker depicts Chettle joining a company of dead poets including Marlowe, Peele, Greene and Nashe in the Elysian Fields, and notes that they are friends in *A Knight's Conjuring* (L1r-v). Probably, through Greene and Nashe, Chettle became an acquaintance of Marlowe. By 1592, Chettle had probably known Peele through Greene or Nashe or Allde (a printer of Peele's *The Arraignment of Paris*, 1585) or Charlewood (a printer of *A Farewell*, 1589) or Wright (a publisher of *A Farewell*), and Danter printed *The Old Wife's Tale* in 1595.

Finally, I will suggest the possibility of a more radical idea that such offences might have never occured. In other words, this scandal might have been fabricated by Chettle, Nashe, Danter, and others. As far as contemporary writings are concerned, nobody else seems to mention *Groatsworth* but Chettle and Nashe. Their purpose is uncertain, but perhaps they just wanted to evoke a scandal against themselves to make their pamphlets known better in the literary world and also to promote larger sales of publications from Danter's press. In a sense, the allusions to their contemporary, or rather fellow playwrights, whether good or bad, might be helpful to make them celebrities because, as Oscar Wilde notes in *The Picture of Dorian Gray*, "There is only one thing in the world worse than being talked about, and that is not being talked about."[8] In this context, it can be said that these playwrights may have been also involved in the series of projects, or rather schemes of issuing *Groatsworth* and *Kind-Heart's Dream* from Danter's press.

(ii) *Kind-Heart's Dream*: Rival Prints, Celebrity, Advertisement

Kind-Heart's Dream (1593) is a text most famous for its preface apologizing to Shakespeare for the publication of *Groatsworth* (1592), which had criticized him as an "upstart crow," as discussed above. Leaving aside the preface and its relation to the earlier work, however, Chettle's *Kind-Heart's Dream* also contains other remarkable points in understanding Elizabethan popular culture, particularly in terms of celebrities and printing.

The text of *Kind-Heart's Dream* centers on the invocation of deceased and living celebrities in what might be described as sixteenth century show business, with figures including Munday, Greene, Nashe, and Tarlton. The story of Chettle's pamphlet is narrated by "Kind-heart," an aged toothdrawer. In a dream, Kind-heart meets in London, five visible apparitions including some deceased celebrities: the ghosts of Anthony Now Now, a fictional character, but certainly a parody of Chettle's close friend, Munday; Dr. Burcot, Burchard Kranich, a noted German physician and mining entrepreneur in London; Greene, the writer and playwright; Tarlton, an actor and clown; and William Cuckoe, a juggler. The characters evoked by Chettle make various admonitions: Anthony Now Now attacks ballad singers; Dr. Burcot complains about the spread of medical texts in vernacular English and the prevalence of quacks, though he himself was criticized as a "full and foule-mouthed physitian" by John Clarke, the apothecary, in *The Trumpet of Apollo* (1602; STC 5353; A4r); Greene urges Pierce Penniless (that is, Nashe) to revenge himself on Gabriel Harvey; Tarlton proclaims the importance of plays; and Cuckoe, who was a notable person, according to Chettle, but unidentifiable for later scholars, defends cony-catchers, while also describing lawyers, gentlemen, and people in all trades as a sort of cony-catcher (54-55).

Among the speakers, Tarlton, Greene, and Nashe were most frequently depicted as popular fictionalized characters, particularly as ghosts, in pamphlets printed between the 1570s and 1640s.[9] However, these pamphlets dealt with the figures individually, while *Kind-Heart's Dream* is remarkable as a collection of fictional and real stories on dead and living celebrities. This is a typical pamphlet of the time dealing satirically with such banal themes as ballad singers, medical practitioners, lawyers, usurers, and also plays and cony-catching (Clark 164-223). However, what makes this pamphlet stand out is that it refers to topical debates and gossip, particularly in the literary world, which it depicts as a kind of celebrity culture.

Anthony Now Now (Anthony Munday) criticizes ballad mongers for their idleness and printing illegally without a license, but this can be read in particular as Munday's inveighing against the piratical printer Jeffes. In the preface, which was usually the place for advertisements at that time,

2 Chettle as Pamphleteer

Chettle mentions a French romance, *2 Gerileon of England*, translated by Munday and published in 1592, a year before this pamphlet was issued. In addition to his denying Nashe's authorship of *Groatswortht*, Chettle claims the author of the epistle to *2 Gerileon of England* was not Nashe either; he notes "*though by the workemans error T. N. were set to the end*" and goes on to say, "*I confesse to be mine, and repent it not*" (7). As discussed above, Jenkins observes that the error was Chettle's forgery "because of the advertising power of Nashe's signature" (12), and C. T. Wright follows him ("'Edward' Spenser" 35). This work was published in 1592, nine years after the first part, and during that time a rival translation printed by Jeffes had appeared. In the epistle to *2 Gerileon of England* Chettle as T. N. criticizes Jeffes and allusively blames him for printing "such odious and lasciuious ribauldrie as *Watkins Ale*, *The Carmans Whistle*" and identifies him with "someone wainscot fac'd fellowe, that is abel to print no good thing" (A4r), as Wright and Jowett have observed (Wright, *Anthony Munday* 95-98; Jowett, "Henry Chettle" 152). Similarly, in *Kind-Hearts Dream* Chettle criticizes Jeffes through the voice of Anthony Now Now, mentioning the ballads "Watkins Ale" and "The Carmans Whistle" (17) (Jowett, "Notes" 388; "*Henry Chettle*" 152). Indeed, Jeffes was a notorious printer. As quoted above, *A Dictionary of Printers and Booksellers* states that "On December 3rd, 1595, his press and letters were seized for the printing of *The Most Strange Prophecie of Doctor Cipriano* 'and diverse other lewde ballades and things very offensive,' and for this and resisting the searchers he was committed to prison until he made submission" (156). Chettle's accusation of Jeffes was apparently true.

Jeffes, however, published important literary works, including Nashe's *Pierce Penniless* (1592; 1593), Kyd's *Spanish Tragedy* (1594), Lodge's *Rosalind* (1592; 1596) and *A Margarite of America* (1596). As discussed in Chapter 1, "(iii) Chettle and Publications by Printers Other Than East and Danter," Chettle and Jeffes were neighbors; the presses of theirs printing masters, East and Bynneman, were close. Chettle probably read the publications of Jeffes, and among these, the most important is the anonymous *The Pleasant*

History of Lazarillo de Tormes, translated by Rowland and printed by Jeffes in 1586 and reprinted by him in 1596. This is the main source of *Piers Plainness*. Chettle obviously obtained this from Jeffes.

The allusion to Jeffes may have been understood only among people involved in the printing industry, and thus was a kind of private gossip or joke among Chettle's friends like Nashe and Munday. The exact relation between Chettle and Jeffes is unknown, but the bad reputation of Jeffes may have served to make his name prominent in a sense. Moreover, the conflict among Harvey, Greene, and Nashe alluded to the ghost of Greene in *Kind-Heart's Dream* may be read as a similarly private matter. In the section of Greene's supplication to "Pierce Pennilesse" (Nashe), Greene complains about Harvey's inveighing against Greene's works, poverty, life and death, and urges Nashe to reply. Sandra Clark claims the three were public persons with their private lives and scandals exposed, and that they were similar in status to media stars today (32). More recently and significantly, Bryan Reynolds and Henry S. Turner states that "the primary point of contention among writers such as Harvey, Greene, and Nashe was an emerging notion of *celebrity*," though scholars have usually seen them as the university wits, who abandoned a career in the university or church and lived in London's literary market place (74-75). As far as their writings are concerned, they seem to have been popular stars, or celebrities at the time, but their popularity, or rather notoriety seems to have been created by their individual voices. Although Greene and Nashe were counted as "best poets for comedy" along with Chettle by Meres, their good repute amongst contemporary writers are not to be found elsewhere, and their bad reputation is only seen in Harvey's writings. This fact suggests that the serial controversy was distorted and exaggerated by the writers themselves and also by the printers Danter and Wolfe, as a means for making themselves widely-known. The critique of Greene is, thus, composed of private issues in the literary world, parodying the form of Nashe's work, *Pierce Penniless*, and also to an extent revenge tragedy, in the line, "Awake (secure boy)

2 Chettle as Pamphleteer

reuenge thy wrongs, remember mine" (37).

On the other hand, in the case of Tarlton, the critique would have drawn the more general reader's attention. Such readers could so easily imagine the figure of Tarlton, the popular entertainer, that writers frequently used. Chettle introduced Tarlton in his work and had him defend plays and players with allusion to Nashe who also defended them in *Pierce Penniless*. The debate about the theater was topical; Puritans such as Stephen Gosson criticized plays as vicious and immoral, while Sidney and Lodge wrote defenses.

At the time, the visual images of writers were not so important as for actors, though in the following period, authors like Jonson and John Donne had their portraits on the title-page; nevertheless, writers could be famous, at least in the literary world, by creating their own images through such anecdotes as Greene's autobiographical pamphlets. Tarlton became a legend through anecdotes written by other persons after his death, though such titles as *Tarlton's News out of Purgatory* (1590; STC 4579) and *Tarlton's Jests* (1613; STC 23683.3) suggest his authorship, and his image had probably remained the same as that during his lifetime. Writers, however, did not show their faces to the public, and people could imagine them only through their printed texts, whether such depictions were real or fictional. These images survived after their deaths, and later pamphleteers described their ghosts in *Greene's News Both from Heaven and Hell* by Barnaby Riche (1593; STC 2259), *Greene's Ghost in Haunting Cony-Catchers* by Samuel Rowlands (1602; STC 12243), *Tom Nash His Ghost* by John Taylor (1643; Wing, T518A) among others.

General Elizabethan readers were likely to have been interested in the conflicts between or gossip of celebrities from royal families and entertainers just as common readers are in our time. From the beginning, the pamphlet reported on the private lives of royalty as public news. In 1508, Henry VII's daughter, twelve year-old Mary, was married to the eight-year-old Prince Charles of Austria, and this news was the subject of a newsbook, written by Henry's Latin secretary, and printed the following year. Subsequently, the details of the marriage between Henry VIII and Anne Boleyn were depicted in a pamphlet printed in 1533 (Stephens 92-93). In the period of the Martin Marprelate controversy (1588-89), the target of personal gossip and scandal shifted to the clergy, and in the 1590s such literary writers as Harvey, Greene, and Nashe denounced each other in print using detailed personal gossip.

With the growth of Elizabethan show business, the private lives and personal connections of writers seem to have drawn people's attention as the royal family had done previously. The literary world was so small that feuds and friendships among writers might be publicly known through the exposition of personalities, and readers could understand the allusions to literary figures as well as writers, as Clark suggests (31). Using such features of the celebrity or gossip culture, Chettle attempted to draw people's attention to his first major work as a writer, and also to establish his new position as an author familiar with the literary and entertainment world.

Another interesting aspect of this pamphlet is its status within the printing industry. When he wrote *Kind-Heart's Dream*, he was still working as a printer for Danter, who had set up a partnership with Chettle, though this was dissolved within a year. The pamphlet was entered by Wright and published by Danter and Wolfe. *Groatsworth* was also entered to Wright and also printed by Danter and Wolfe. These were the only works that Danter and Wolfe printed in collaboration (Thomas, "The Printing" 196-97; Jowett, "Johannes Factotum" 467, "Credulous to False Prints" 99-102); therefore, the two works must have been closely related. Chettle and the people surrounding him such as Danter and Wright may have intended to publish *Kind-Heart's Dream* as a sister pamphlet when producing *Groatsworth*. In other words, these two pamphlets were produced by the same team, and Chettle seems to be publicizing Danter's press throughout *Kind-Heart's Dream*. Pamphleteers had no patronage system, and personal connections to get jobs were important for them, as were sales.

2 Chettle as Pamphleteer

Nashe frequently praised his landlord Danter for having aided him in *Have with You to Saffron Walden*. On the other hand, Chettle seems to create publicity for Danter's publications rather than his personality, in criticizing rival printers in this pamphlet. Chettle had wide knowledge of printing and personal connections in the industry and seems to have thought of practical ways to help Danter.

In the preface to *Kind-Heart's Dream*, Chettle discusses *Groatsworth* with such intentions, though there was implicit. In the section on Greene, Chettle advertises works to be printed by Danter more explicitly. Chettle's Greene urges Nashe to reply to Harvey's "twofold Edition of Inuectives" (37), or *Four Letters*. Indeed, shortly after *Kind-Heart's Dream* was published, Nashe's reply *Strange News* was printed by Danter. Moreover, as shown in Chapter 1, "(ii) Chettle and John Danter," "(b) Danter's Publications between 1591 and 1598," Chettle alludes to Barnfield's *The Affectionate Shepherd*, printed by Danter, at the end of *Piers Plainness*, also issued by Danter. Chettle's allusion to another book issued by Danter seems to be an advertisement for Danter's press as well as for Barnfield. Furthermore, Cuckoe's defense of cony-catching can be seen as an advertisement of other cony-cathing pamphlets issued by Danter, namely Harman's revised *The Groundwork of Cony-Catching* and the anonymous *Mihil Mumchance*.

On the other hand, Chettle criticizes such rival publication genres as ballads, including those printed by Jeffes, and also medical texts. Nashe and Dekker similarly attacked ballad singers, perhaps since ballads were so popular and marketable in print. Every printed text was supposed to be entered by the Stationers' Company, but ballads slipped through the system, and were widely and cheaply published (Wurzbach; Kumaran, "Print" 117); thus, serious writers complained about the ballad printers and sellers partly from jealousy. Medical texts were also marketable. Paul Slack numbers one hundred and fifty-three English titles published between 1483 and 1603. Overall, in the sixteenth century, three hundred and ninety-two medical texts were published including reprints ("Mirrors of Health" 239).

Henry Chettle's Careers: A Study of an Elizabethan Printer, Pamphleteer, Playwright

Chettle, thus, attacked these rival prints to support Danter.

Chettle's first acknowledged entry into the world of print as an author connects him, and the group around him, with the inter-related worlds of print, stage, controversial literature, and celebrity culture. Although Chettle himself was, and has remained, a much less known figure than some of those he wrote for and against, the utilization of the pamphlet as a commercial and advertising medium can be seen in this early text.

*

This chapter has discussed Chettle's two famous, or rather notorious pamphlets. It might not have been accidental that Danter, Wolfe, Wright, Chettle, and probably Nashe were engaged in publishing them. Both pamphlets allude to actual persons, especially involved in the literary world; Shakespeare, Marlowe, Nashe, Peele in *Groatsworth*; Munday, Dr. Burcot, Nashe, Tarlton, Cuckoe in *Kind-Heart's Dream*. Some of these figures might have been already famous in the early 1590s, but it must have been a good way to make some of them, for example, Munday, Nashe, and Chettle, well-known to others. In other words, these pamphlets were produced by a team for their own profit, taking advantage of the public interest in celebrities or gossip. It may have, thus, been a windfall to Munday, while Danter, Wolfe, and Wright wanted to increase sales. Nashe, on the other hand, very probably desired to become more famous and took part in scandals to write and sell more books. Chettle himself perhaps hoped to have his name included in the list of the writers above, and dreamed of entering into the theatrical world.

Notes

[1] Danter printed several of these kinds of pamphlets; for example, *Strange Signs Seen in the Air*, *Strange Monsters* (1594), *A Most Horrible and Detestable Murder* (1595), *News from Rome, Venice, and Vienna* (1595).

[2] For the details of rogue literature, see Manley 341-55, Aydelotte, Fuller, Salgādo,

2 Chettle as Pamphleteer

Dionnne and Mentz. See also this book, Chapter 7, "(i) Background of Elizabethan Poverty."
3 I will discuss Nashe's involvement in the work below.
4 See *Groatsworth* 80-87.
5 For author-printer-publisher relationships and copyright in early modern England, see Plant 73-121. Also, see Gaskell 183-85.
6 For further discussion of the Greene-Nashe-Harvey controversy, see McKerrow's edition, *The Works of Thomas Nashe*, vol.5, 65-110.
7 Dekker and Petowe responded to Chettle, writing *The Wonderful Year* (1603) and *Elizabetha Quasi Vivens, Eliza's Funeral* (1603).
8 The quotation is from the edition of Penguin Books 8.
9 See Manley 325. Interestingly, Naoko Komachiya Ishikawa discusses Tarlton in print along with the Harvey-Nashe quarrel in her unpublished doctoral thesis, "The English Clown" 90-127.

3 Chettle as Dramatic Repairman

(i) *John of Bordeaux, or The Second Part of Friar Bacon*
(a) Chettle's Hand in *John of Bordeaux*

The extant manuscript of John of Bordeaux is MS. 507 in the Duke of Northumberland's Library at Alwick Castle in England, and there is no printed text, though we can read the text in a modern edition by William Lindsay Renwick in consultation with Greg as general editor.[1] As Renwick points out, there are two gaps followed by the speech-headings of John of Bordeaux on fol. 11r; one of them (ll.1090-1101) was filled by Chettle, which suggests his early dramatic activity (vi-vii).

For authorship, most critics attribute the play to Greene as it is a sequel to *Friar Bacon and Friar Bungay* (c.1589; pub. 1594; STC 12267), which was performed for the Queen's Men, according to the 1594 quarto (Renwick xi-xii; Thaiss and Day 1439; Ioppolo 120). Similarly, on the production date, there is no record of this play either in *Henslowe's Diary* or the Stationers' Register, and specifying a date is difficult, but critics generally accept 1590-94, following Renwick, who gives two pieces of evidence. Renwick first pays attention to an actor, John Holland who played Asteroth, a devil in the play, and whose name appears in marginal directions in the lines 466, 678-89, and 1159. Holland was a member of Strange's Men and perhaps of Pembroke's around 1590-93. Renwick also points out Henslowe's first entry of *Friar Bacon* performed by Strange's on 19 February 1592 and a second entry of the play by the Queen's and Sussex's on 1 April 1594. Renwick, thus, attributes the play to Strange's and also shows character-names shared with *Rosalind, Selimus, The Old Wife's Tale,* and *A Knack to Know an Honest Man,* all of which are believed to have been produced between 1590 and 1594 (viii-

3 Chettle as Dramatic Repairman

xi). Renwick named the play *John of Bordeaux* to distinguish it from *Friar Bacon*, but *The Second Part of Friar Bacon*, which Renwick alternatively suggests, seems possible, as Grace Ioppolo notes (120), though Friar Bungay does not appear, and the setting is moved from England to Germany.

The issue of the play's production history, however, has evoked controversy. Renwick believes the manuscript, which "would make some 1720 lines of print," is a shortened version of a longer text, and claims that it is a copy for "a company already familiar with the play," with the two missing scenes and two gaps (viii). Harry H. Hoppe suggests the extant text was a memorial reconstruction, or "a bad quarto that never reached print," showing evidence of irregular verse, length and repetition of words among others (119-32). Laurie E. Maguire refutes Hoppe's points one by one, and claims the play is not "bad;" she concludes that the play was written by two authors, probably Greene and Nashe, who composed the plot and committed it to a scribe, and that Chettle filled one gap, while the other one was tasked but not completed (124).

Such critics as Renwick and Ioppolo conjecture that Chettle was asked to fill the gap for a revival (Renwick xiii; Ioppolo 121). Ioppolo draws attention to the record which notes that Henslowe gave five shillings to Middleton on 14 December 1602 "a prologe & A epelope for the playe of bacon for the cort," and also his payment of five shillings to Chettle on 29 December 1602, "for a prologe & epyloge for the corte" (Henslowe 207). The entry for Chettle does not specify the play, but as Ioppolo remarks, it could be identical to "the playe of bacon," thus, probably *Friar Bacon* (Ioppolo 214, n.54). However, there is no definite evidence.

It is uncertain whether Chettle wrote this for the original or a revival, but his style suggests that it was written early in his career, probably soon after 1592, as Jenkins observes (57). According to Jenkins's conjecture, Chettle did not have any association with Strange's Men, who may have performed *John of Bordeaux*, as he implies he had lately known Shakespeare in *Kind-Heart's Dream*, published at the end of 1592. Jenkins thus sees the writing as Chettle's first dramatic work. Similarly, Sidney Thomas conjectures Chettle was employed to fill the gap in *John of Bordeaux* between 1590 and 1594, giving no additional evidence but following Renwick's suggestion on the date of the play ("Henry Chettle" 12). Even if Chettle was given the task by Henslowe in the late 1590s, his *Diary* should have noted additions to or the mending of the play in a similar way it does to Middleton's writing the prologue and epilogue for "the playe of bacon," but actually there is no such record. Therefore, it is possible that Chettle's addition occurred in the early 1590s.[2]

(b) Thematic Influence of *John of Bordeaux* on Chettle's Works

John of Bordeaux is the title character, a brave knight in a thirteenth century French epic (*chanson de geste*), in which he carries out great tasks with the support of the fairy King Oberon. A modernized translation, *The Ancient, Honorable, Famous, and Delightful History of Huon of Bordeaux*, was issued in 1601 by Purfoot, who had also published H. C.'s *A Doleful Ditty* in 1579. The play, however, seems to have been modeled on the figure of John in Lodge's *Rosalind*, first printed by Orwin (1590): "This hardie Knight thus enricht with Uertue and Honour, surnamed Sir Ihon of Bordeaux, hauing passed the prime of his youth in sundrie battailes against the Turkes, at last (as the date of the time hath his course) grew aged" (1; STC 16664). Greene, who may have been the author, and Chettle were familiar with Lodge, and they certainly read *Rosalind*.

The play *John of Bordeaux* mainly describes John's banishment, which was due to the scheming of Ferdinand, the son of Emperor, Frederick. John is a commander of Ferdinand's army which is fighting against the Turks, but the villainous Ferdinand hates him because he lusts for John's wife, Rosaline, who is also exiled and becomes a beggar. An English magician, Friar Bacon, aids John and overthrows Vandermast, Ferdinand's magician. John of Bordeaux's soliloquy, written by Chettle, occurs after a dialogue between two shepherds, who pity Rosaline's banishment:

3 Chettle as Dramatic Repairman

> My Rosaline condemnd for Burdeaux cause
> proud [yong] fferdinand the fo vnto her life
> Courage assume vnto thee, triple force
> And in the justice of her innocence
> attempt to free her from deaths violence
> But Iohn thou art an exile, and descride
> the law layes hold on thee releeues not her :
> But a disguise shall maske me from their hate
> to free my Rosaline Ile tempt my fate
> But Burdeaux thou art poore, and pouertie
> can get no cloake, no couert, no disguise
> great harts in want may purpose not effect (1090-1101)[3]

The recurrent alliterations, apostrophes, rhymes, and antitheses that feature in this speech can be seen also in *Piers Plainnes*, though that is a prose work. Aemilius, Prince of Thrace, is undeservedly banished to sea by his wicked brother and lands in Crete. One night, in a soliloquy, he laments his "Outlawes day" and also shows his love for Aeliana, Queen of Crete, who has rescued him, hoping she will make his status higher:

> Poor Aemilius, exild from Thrace, in Crete captive, my brother forcing the one, beauty constraining the other…But some comfort were it knew I thou hadst assailed Aeliana so. Immortall powers why doate I so…But comfort thy selfe Aelimius, she hath vouchsafed to be thy Princely Mistris…I, that rises from hir Princely bounty to requite thy travel in hir rescue, no colour of hope that as a lover shee will regard thee: but as shee hath beautified thy poore estate with rich ornaments and Honorable tytles…. (150-51)

As well as the characteristics of verse, the awkward usages of "But" are shared with John of Bordeaux's speech. Similarly, in Chettle's later play, *Blind Beggar*, another unfairly exiled nobleman, Momford, laments in a soliloquy, as will be further discussed in Chapter 7 "Beggars in *The Pleasant Comedy of Patient Grissil* and *The Blind Beggar of Bethnal Green*, and the Elizabethan Money Based Economy." Unlike John, Momford can adopt a disguise, though as a beggar.

Jenkins explains that John's lines and Chettle's addition to *Sir Thomas More* suggest his earlier verse was much more regular than that in his later works (57). The date of *Sir Thomas More* is problematic, as discussed below, but Jenkins believes Chettle made his addition about 1594. His style in that play seems to support this idea. Chettle's writings are inserted where the sentenced More reveals his grief to his wife, philosophizing about the mortality of every human: "Now will I speak like More in melancholy; / For if grief's power could with her sharpest darts / Pierce my firm bosom...O, happy banishment from worldly pride, / When souls by private life are sanctified!" (Sc.13: 53-83). These alliterations and rhymes are typical of Chettle's early style.

The reason why Chettle was employed for this task also remains uncertain; he was a close friend of Greene, and may have read Greene's foul copy, or composed it together with him; however, the influence of this work on Chettle's plays, which will be analyzed in the following chapters, seems noteworthy. The name of "fferdinand," the son of the Emperor, seems to be used for Ferdinand, the Duke of Prussia, in *Hoffman*. Ferdinand mistreats Hoffman's father, the admiral, and banishes him for his debt and then executes him for piracy. Although this Ferdinand is old, his son Otho is young, arrogant, and ruthless, though not lustful. Chettle's interest in magic is not found in his other extant works, but John's unjust downfall is echoed by those of such great soldiers as Momford, Robert in *Downfall* and *Death*, and Hoffman's father in *Hoffman*. Rosaline's starvation and begging are reminiscent of Lady Bruce in *Death* and Momford. Moreover, the use of disguise, the evil of the court opposed to the simple shepherds, and the lascivious nobleman in *John of Bordeaux* are also characteristic of Chettle's plays as well as plays by his contemporaries.

I have discussed Chettle's involvement in *John of Bordeaux* and its influence on him. Christopher J. Thaiss and Frank Day claims this play "is more social than political," and that "[r]ather than supporting a particular view of a specific national situation, it attempts to move the audience to identify with the poor folk portrayed on stage," who are represented by the begging Rosalind and her children (1040). The play is set in Germany, but the people's way of life and the emphasis of Bacon's Englishness seem to reflect London in the Elizabethan period, and the issue of beggars was a socio-political rather than a social problem. The authorities feared social disorder and regulated vagrants under the Poor Law, as will be discussed in Chapter 7. The play, however, also describes the release of prisoners, who are thieves and rogues, through Bacon's magic. Even more remarkable, however, is the release of the evil prisoners; "the ar [sic] all theves this a Cupturs and this a hors steler the rest ar nimers and suck like" (1217-19). Similarly, in *Sir Thomas More*, the rebels release debtors, felons, and murders from prison. This episode perhaps alludes to the apprentices' prison-break in 1592; a feltmaker's apprentice, imprisoned for debt in Marshalsea prison, was rescued by his fellow apprentices, as Blayney and Burnett suggest (Blayney 189; Burnett, "Apprentice Literature" 36-37). Chettle's role is small in the writing of this play, but it had a great effect on Chettle's later descriptions of banishment, poverty, beggars, and topical political issues.

(ii) *Sir Thomas More*

(a) Chettle's Hand in *Sir Thomas More*

Sir Thomas More has been regarded as a masterpiece of a play, but its extant manuscript seems to be even more mysterious and interesting than the story itself. First and foremost, the background to the manuscript is obscure. The manuscript was included in the Harleian collection of the British Museum as MS. Harley 7368 in 1753 after being in the possession of the second Earl of Oxford, who had obtained it from his friend John Murray. Its prior history is unknown.[4]

From the penmanship, punctuation, and quality of ink and paper, Greg recognizes seven hands in the manuscript, excepting the vellum wrapper, and labels these hands S for "the Scribe of the original play" and A, B, C, D, E, T. He attributed Hand D to Shakespeare, E to Dekker, and T to Edmund Tilney, the Master of the Revels (vii-x). After Greg, analysis has further extended our knowledge of the play, and Jenkins summarizes the currently accepted theory in the supplement to Greg's edition, attributing S to Munday, A to Henry Chettle, B to Heywood, C to a playhouse bookkeeper, D to Shakespeare, E to Dekker (xxxiv). However, the authorship both of the original and of the additions remains problematic.

The process of producing dramatic texts in Renaissance England is now thought to have been frequently collaborative; an author wrote a play for a theatrical company, who rewrote it for the convenience of stage devices or for avoiding censorship, which had been operating since the early 1580s, implemented by the Master of Revels. There was no notion of copyright in England until the enactment of the Copyright Act in 1710, and the plays belonged to the acting company. *Henslowe's Diary* shows us that collaboration among several playwrights in writing plays was common, and that adding to and revising plays written by other playwrights was also frequently performed, as seen in Chettle's addition to *John of Bordeaux*. As Appendix V suggests, Chettle and Dekker frequently performed these kinds of jobs, though the most famous example is Jonson's additional material for *The Spanish Tragedy* in 1601, which had originally been written by Kyd around 1587. It is not known whether there was a sort of ranking of playwrights, but the table implies Chettle and Dekker were most frequently tasked, while Munday, who is sometimes called "Antony the poyet" by Henslowe in his *Diary*, did not undertake such jobs, and Jonson did this only once for the said play (Henslowe 203, 204, 205).

The attribution of the different hands, except for Tilney's, in the manuscript has been much discussed. There are two stages in the analysis, one relating to the original script and the other to the additional parts, which seems now less problematic. Regarding the additional parts, Hands A, C, and E are generally assigned to Chettle, a bookkeeper, and Dekker respectively (Mets 17-19).

With regard to the original manuscript, Munday has been thought undoubtedly to be the scribe, though some of the later revisers have been suggested as collaborators in the original composition. Greg doubts the handwriting to be that of Munday, observing the mistake of "fashis" for "fashion" (Sc.16: 117) and suggests the possibility of a collaboration. E. H. C. Oliphant remarks, "It would seem, then, that Munday, Henry Chettle, and B (Heywood?) first collaborated on the play; Dekker may also have come in later as a reviser." Oliphant also attributes Scenes 1-7 to Munday, Scene 8 to Dekker or Munday, Scene 9 to Heywood (?), Scenes 10-13 to Chettle, Scenes 15-17 to Heywood (?) (226-35). This opinion is endorsed by Jenkins and A. C. Partridge (Jenkins 59-71; Partridge Ch. 7). J. M. Nosworthy suggests Chettle and Dekker worked with Munday on the original work ("Shakespeare and *Sir Thomas More*" 12-25), and is defended by Gabrieli and Melchiori, who provide three reasons for their belief that the original was collaborative: collaboration was common in Renaissance plays; all extant and lost plays involving Munday for public theaters are collaborations; there are different types of styles in the original parts, which appear to be particularly those of Dekker and Chettle (13).

More recently and radically, Jowett has deepened and expanded Oliphant's analysis, with his attribution of Scenes 10-13 to Chettle, based on Chettle's favorite words, rhyming words, asseverations, errors of transcription, parallels with *Hoffman* and *Kind-Heart's Dream* among other factors. After these tests, Jowett states that Scenes 1, 6, 7, 8, 10, and 13 may be assigned to Chettle, though he hesitates to ascribe Scene 2 to him, and concludes that Chettle was responsible for "six perhaps seven scenes—at a minimum, over one-third of the original text" ("Original Text" 148). Gary Taylor, Brian Vickers, and Wells generally follow Jowett, and noticeably, Jowett acknowledges Munday and Chettle as authors of the work and goes on to note "with revision and additions by Dekker, William Shakespeare and Heywood" in his edition for the Oxford complete works of Shakespeare (2005) (Taylor, "The Date and Auspices" 115; Vickers 38; Wells 115). Jowett's suggestions seem to be persuasive. The external evidence that Munday and Chettle were old, close friends and wrote other plays in collaboration endorses this, as discussed elsewhere in this book. As internal evidence, according to Jowett, the insurrection scenes in *Sir Thomas More* seem to originate from Chettle, not from the Hand D Shakespeare (142), as the patriotic insurrection is closer to that of *Hoffman* rather than Jack Cade's. Rebellion is one of Chettle's favorite themes as with his contemporaries, as described in *Piers Plainnes*, *Downfall* and *Death*, and so are the themes of the downfall of noblemen, banishment, imprisonment, which can be seen in these works and others. In summary, concerning Chettle's commitment to *Sir Thomas More*, it is possible that Munday, "our best plotter," mainly composed its plots with the support of Chettle, and Chettle mainly wrote the stage directions and performed major revisions on the play.

(b) Thematic Influence of *Sir Thomas More* on Chettle's Works

Sir Thomas More describes the rise and downfall of Sir Thomas More, based on Holinshed's *Chronicles*, according to Tracey Hill (10). Munday and Chettle surely had opportunity to read the book, printed by Bynneman. The first half depicts riots of commoners against foreigners and More's promotion for suppressing them. The latter half deals with More's friendship with Erasmus, and also his downfall and execution. This play may not have had a major effect on Chettle, though it did perhaps influence Chettle's lost plays, *The Life of Cardinal Wolsey* and *The Rising of Cardinal Wolsey*. However, such certain points as riots, imprisonment, downfall, and execution may have affected Chettle to some extent.

The rising of ordinary people obviously shows Elizabethan xenophobia. This is shared with Nashe's *Pierce Penniless* and *Unfortunate Traveler*, but more significantly, it appears in *Hoffman* as well. This play describes a riot of commoners in Prussia, who oppose Prince Otho of Luningberg succeeding the King of Prussia. Prince Jerome of Prussia is an idiot, and his father the

3 Chettle as Dramatic Repairman

King of Prussia nominates his nephew as his successor. The commoners claim that a foreigner should not be their King, and the strong xenophobia is shown in a manner that echoes the urgent succession issues of the Elizabethan times.[5]

Furthermore, Doll, a London citizen, criticizes More as a cony-catcher, and this recalls *Kind-Heart's Dream* as well as *The Defense of Cony-Catching*. More reasons with the rebels and promises them that if they obey him, they will be pardoned. However, Doll is suspicious of him, remarking, "Keep thy promise now for the King's pardon, or, by the Lord, I'll call thee a plain cony-catcher" (Sc. 6: 188-90). The words turn to be true. A broker and leader of the rebels, John Lincoln, is executed on stage, though it happens because the Sherriff has killed him quickly before the King pardons the rebels. At the execution, Doll states that "Thou [Lincoln] lived'st a good fellow, and died'st an honest man" (Sc. 7: 70-71). The sympathetic descriptions of the rebels are reminiscent of those of *Jack Straw* and *Sir Thomas Wyatt*. More importantly, however, Doll's identification of More as a cony-catcher is shared with *The Defense of Cony-Catching* and *Kind-Heart's Dream*. In the both works, such upper-class people as lawyers and gentlemen are called cony-catchers who deceive other people.[6] This idea was probably common, but it is interesting More is accused of cony-catching.

The banishment and imprisonment of More also influenced Chettle's plays. More offends the King for refusing to sign a document, and eventually he is banished and executed. More's downfall is sympathetically described. The banishment of great men is one of Chettle's favorite themes, as with other contemporaries; there are Aemilius, Prince of Thrace, in *Piers Plainness*, Robert in *Downfall*, Hoffman's father in *Hoffman*, and Momford in *Blind Beggar*. On the other hand, prisoners frequently appear in Chettle's works. Just as with the case of banishment, innocent nobles are imprisoned by tyrannical rulers like More. Aemilius is undeservedly banished to sea by his wicked brother and lands in Crete. He falls in love with Aeliana, Queen of Crete, but he is caught and confined by her uncle Duke Rhegius, who loves her as well. In *Death*, a nobleman, Bruce, refuses to give his son to the tyrannical King John, and Lady Bruce and her son are imprisoned in a dungeon in Windsor Castle, where they starve to death.[7]

Also, More's choice to be banished is shared by Grissil's father, Janicola in *Patient Grissil*. More prefers being banished to staying at court and remarks: "O, happy banishment from worldly pride, / When souls by private life are sanctified!" (Sc.13: 82-83). Noticeably, these lines were probably written by Chettle, and this idea is echoed in *Patient Grissil* when Janicola is banished out of the court and pleasantly resumes his old lifestyle as a basket-maker in the country, as will be further discussed in Chapter 7, "(ii) *Patient Grissil*."

Moreover, in *John of Bordeaux*, Bacon releases prisoners, who are thieves and rogues, through his magic, as mentioned in the previous section. Similarly, in *Sir Thomas More*, the rebels release from prison debtors, felons, and murders. When the two plays were produced, and also which was earlier are uncertain, but the descriptions probably were based on the apprentices' prison-break in 1592, an event in which a feltmaker's apprentice was imprisoned for debt in Marshalsea prison, then rescued by his fellow apprentices.

Chettle wrote longer additional lines in *Sir Thomas More* than in *John of Bordeaux*, and probably helped Munday to write some original passages, as Jowett suggests. The play itself seems to have had hardly influenced Chettle's extant works, but some elements, such as xenophobia, risings, imprisonment, and banishment are echoed in *Piers Plainness, Downfall, Death, Hoffman, Blind Beggar*, and *Patient Grissil* among others. Chettle was interested in these topics and employed them in his works.

(iii) *Romeo and Juliet* (Q1)

(a) Chettle's Hand in *Romeo and Juliet* (Q1)

The third play that Chettle was possibly involved in is *Romeo and Juliet*,

3 Chettle as Dramatic Repairman

though simply as an annotator to help Danter prepare the publication of its first quarto in 1597.[8] The lack of records in the Stationers' Register suggests Danter may have issued this without a license. Among Shakespearean scholars, Danter is, thus, seen as a notorious piratical printer, but he also issued such plays as *Titus Andronicus, Orlando Furioso*, and *The Wounds of Civil War*, according to Lukas Erne, the latest editor of the first quarto of *Romeo and Juliet*, printed in 2007 (35).[9] The second quarto was printed by Creede for Burby in 1599, "*Newly corrected, augmented, and amended*," which suggests "the first edition had been a commercial success and sold out in two years," as Erne points out (42).[10]

Jenkins and F. L. Jones in their studies of Chettle never mentioned his involvement in the quarto, so this is quite a new fact to Chettle studies and worth investigating to consider his activities that brought together the page and stage. Among the New Bibliographers, this corrupt text was believed to have been produced through the "memorial reconstruction" by actor-reporters. Hoppe was the first to suggest this theory. Greg and such editors as Brian Gibbons followed Hoppe (Greg, *The Shakespeare* 62-64; Gibbons, ed., *Romeo and Juliet* 4-13). The play has been edited generally based on the second quarto, the "good" quarto, which is much longer in length and has regular versification, but with occasional use of Q1 to fill in the lines or scenes of Q2. Q3 is mainly based on Q2, and Q4 on Q3. Erne presents detailed comparisons between Q1 and Q2 and shows some differences, though the two versions are basically similar in describing the same characters and the same events in the same order; for example, Q2 is almost one third longer (700 lines) than Q1; the language of Q1 and Q2 differ very much except for the first seven scenes (2). However, significantly, Q1 includes three different, so-called "un-Shakespearean" passages, which are distinctly different from Shakespeare's style, and also longer, more detailed and numerous stage directions.

The first of these three passages is a dialogue between Romeo and the Friar, with Juliet joining them in the cell. Q1's length is a little shorter than

Q2's in general, but more importantly the language is totally different from Q2's; also, Q1's Juliet is more audacious than Q2's with a rather shocking stage direction (cf. Q2: STC 22322: F1v-2r):

> *Enter Romeo, Frier [sic].*
> ROMEO. Now Father Laurence, in thy holy grant
>   Consists the good of me and *Iuliet.*
> FRIER. Without more words I will doo all I may,
>   To makes you happie if in me it lye.
> ROMEO. This morning here she pointed we should meet,
>   And consummate those neuer parting bands,
>   And come she will.
> FRIER. I gesse she will indeed,
>   Youths loue is quicke, swifter than swiftest speed.
>   *Enter Iuliet somewhat fast, and embraceth ROMEOeo.*
>   See where see comes.
>   So light of foote nere hurts the trodden flower:
>   Of loue and ioy, see see the soueraign powee.
> IULIET. *Romeo.*
> ROMEO. My *Iuliet* welcome. As doo waking eyes
>   (Cloasd in Nights muysts) attend the frolicke Day,
>   So Romeo hath expected *Iuliet,*
>   And thou art come.
> IULIET. I am (if I be Day)
>   Come to my Sunne: shine foorth, and make me faire.
> ROMEO. All beauteous fairness dwelleth in thine eyes.
> IULIET. Romeo from thine all brightnes doth arise.
> FRIER. Come wantons, come, the stealing houres do passe
>   Defer imbracements till some fitrer time,
>   Part for a while, you shall not be alone,
>   This holy Church have ioynd ye both in one.
> ROMEO. Lead holy Father, all delay seemes long.
> IULIET. Make hast, make hast, this lingring doth vs wrong.
> FRIER. O, soft and faire makes sweetest worke they say.
>   Hast is a common hindrer in crosse way.   *Exeunt Omnes.*
> (Q1: STC 22322: E4r-v)

3 Chettle as Dramatic Repairman

Q1's stage direction "*Enter Iuliet somewhat fast, and embraceth Romeo*" (E4r) is replaced in Q2 by the more simple "Enter *Iuliet*" (F2r). Erne regards Q1's descriptive stage direction as "strange" and comments that the embracement seems to continue until Friar Laurence interrupts them (30).

The second non-Shakespearean passages of Q1 come when Juliet hears news brought by the Nurse and misunderstands Romeo is dead, not Tybalt:

> Ah Romeo, Romeo, what disaster hap
> Hath seuerd thee from thy true Juliet?
> Ah why shou'd Heauen so much conspire with Woe,
> Or Fate enuie our happie Marriage,
> So soone to sunder us by timelesse Death? (Q1: F3v)

Compared to its counterpart in Q2 (G2r), Q1's passage sounds more objective and simplistic.

The third non-Shakespearean passage of Q1 is Paris's short monologue at Juliet's tomb:

> Sweete Flower, with flowers I strew thy Bridale bed:
> Sweete Tombe that in thy circuite dost containe,
> The perfect modell of eternitie:
> Faire Iuliet that with Angells dost remaine,
> Accept this latest favour at my hands,
> That liuing honourd thee, and being dead
> With funerall praises doo adorne thy Tombe. (Q1: I4v)

Except for the first line, the language is completely different from Q2's speech, which forms a sestet rhyming ababcc (L1v-2r).

Chettle's involvement was first suggested by Hoppe, who believed Chettle to be a possible candidate for the reporter-versifier. Sidney Thomas analyzed the three un-Shakespearean passages, showing their parallels with Chettle's vocabulary, images, and "descriptive" stage directions in his works; he also provided the external evidence that Chettle worked with

Danter as late as 1596 when Chettle mentioned he had done all to further the edition of Munday's translation, *2 Primaleon of Greece*, printed by Danter. Thomas, in conclusion, assigned the un-Shakespearean passages to Chettle ("Henry Chettle" 8-16). In terms of bibliography, Jowett concentrated on stage directions and strengthened Thomas's theory. Jowett paid attention to Danter and Edward Allde, collaborating on the printing of Q1.[11] Erne points out Chettle's collaboration with Allde's printing house and states that Chettle's connection with Allde is not "well-documented" unlike his relations with Danter. However, Chettle may have already known Allde. He was the son of John Allde, to whom Munday apprenticed himself in the 1570s alongside Edward Allde, as Tracy Hill notes (32). After being made freeman in 1584, Edward Allde published a large number of books, including *Patient Grissil* (1603), *Sir Thomas Wyatt* (1607), and *Basilikon Doron*, piratically printed in 1603.

Danter printed sheets A-D and Allde worked on sheets E-K. Curiously, Allde's portion is set in a smaller type-pace and has more spaces and stage directions than Danter's. From these facts, Jowett deduced that Chettle, Danter's former partner and subsequent assistant, served as annotator and wrote stage directions to fill the gap; Jowett gives numerous parallels in stage directions with those in Chettle's works and also in such plays as *Orlando Furioso*, *Titus Andronicus*, and *The Old Wive's Tale*, issued by Danter between 1593 and 1595, which Chettle might have annotated. For the un-Shakespearean passages, Jowett accepts Thomas's argument to be persuasive and makes the new discovery that Q1 has the alternative reading "his [Romeo's] agill arme" (F2v), which is generally adopted by modern editors in place of Q2's "His aged arme" (G1r); noticeably "agill" never occurs in Shakespeare, while it appears in exactly the same spelling in *Hoffman* (Jowett, "*Romeo and Juliet*" 54-74). Although such critics as Jeffrey Kahan and Erne doubt the authorship of the non-Shakespearean lines, the arguments of Thomas and Jowett seem persuasive.

3 Chettle as Dramatic Repairman

(b) Thematic Influence of *Romeo and Juliet* on Chettle's Works

If Chettle wrote the un-Shakespearean parts, his style is slightly different from that in *John of Bordeaux* and *Sir Thomas More* and is closer to *Downfall, Death,* and *Hoffman*. The plot can be paralleled with that of *Death*; Robert (Robin) is poisoned to death, though by his uncle; his fiancé Matilda commits suicide in an abbey by taking poison; the villainous King John, who has pursued Matilda, visits her tomb like Paris in the final scene; the dead Matilda is crowned with flowers by Eleanor, John's mother. However, the role of the Friar is totally distinct from that in *Romeo and Juliet*. This play depicts a lustful friar or monk and abbess comically obsessed with money, as will be discussed later. Matilda escapes to the abbey to avoid John's wooing, but the clergy gladly receive money from John to persuade her to sleep with him and urge her on with obscene words. Considering the proximity in the date of the production of the two plays and the popularity of *Romeo and Juliet, Death* may have been written to rival, or perhaps even parody *Romeo and Juliet*; young love, banishment, and poison are common motifs, but *Death* portrays merry life as an outlaw in Sherwood, and criticizes Catholicism, mocking the poison sent from Rome and the immoral churchmen.

The tragic young couple of Lodowick, Prince of Saxony, and Lucibella, Princess of Austria, in *Hoffman* is also reminiscent of *Romeo and Juliet*. Lodowick and Lucibella love each other, but there is conflict between their fathers, the Dukes of Saxony and Austria. They fall into Hoffman's trap, and they are stabbed to death by Lodowick's younger brother, Mathias, who believes Lucibella has betrayed his and run away with a Greek. Their fathers become furious enough to attempt to kill each other. Hoffman, who disguises himself as Otho, pretends to reconcile them, and stabs the Duke of Austria. After that, Lucibella is revived and goes mad like Ophelia, who has lost her father and lover as well.

Some phrases in *Hoffman* recall *Rome and Juliet* as well. The third non-Shakespearean passage of Q1 *Rome and Juliet*, or Paris's short monologue at Juliet's tomb notes, "Sweete Flower, with flowers I strew thy Bridale bed"

(I4v); similarly, dying Lodowick believes Lucibella is dead, and remarks, "*Austria* your daughteris [sic] become a bride for death" (3.1.1004).

Moreover, after having revived, Lucibella goes insane and speaks as a lunatic:

> Oh a sword, I pray you kill me not,
> For I am going to the riuers side
> To fetch white lilies, and blew daffadils [sic]
> To sticke in *Lodowicks* bosome, where it bled,
> And in mine owne; my true loue is not dead.... (4.1.1432-36)

This is an obvious parody of mad Ophelia gathering flowers and Juliet stabbing herself. Chettle mocks *Hamlet* in *Hoffman*; in carrying out revenge, Hoffman is not melancholic but practical, though in the opening scene, he implies that he has been melancholy, saying, "HEnce Cloud of melancholy" (1.1.1); for Wittenberg, the idiot Prince Jerome asserts that "I am no foole, I haue bin at *Wittenberg*, where wit growes" (1.2.276-77). On the other hand, Lorrique, Hoffman's accomplice, when suggesting that Hoffman rape Martha, the chaste widow of the Duke of Prussia, recalls *Titus Andronicus* as well as *Metamorphoses*: "Shut her perpetuall prisoner in that den; Make her a Philomel, proue Tereus" (5.2.2387-88). Chettle, thus, mocks his rival Shakespeare throughout his play.

*

This chapter has looked at Chettle's minor dramatic activities: dozens of his lines in *John of Bordeaux*; about seventy lines in *Sir Thomas More*; stage directions and some forty lines in Q1 *Romeo and Juliet*. Unlike Munday, who appeared on stage as a boy actor, wrote an Italian play for the court as early as 1584, and received patronage from the Earl of Oxford, Chettle did not have much connection with the theatrical world probably till the early 1590s, and his name became slightly known around 1598, when Meres mentioned it. Consideration should be given to his relationship with

3 Chettle as Dramatic Repairman

Greene, Nashe, and Danter and also his self-consciousness or professionalism as a printer, which is suggested in his signature as "compositor" in Nashe's *Have with You to Saffron Walden* (1596), as "printer" in *2 Primaleon of Greece* (1596), and also his handwritten, "Chettle of London Stationer," in his written oath for Henslowe in Autumn 1598. As his printing career started in apprenticeship, so in a way did his dramatic career, writing small parts of the plays including stage directions. Even after his name begins to appear frequently in *Henslowe's Diary*, Chettle still did such small tasks as mending or adding passages for Henslowe, at least as late as 1602, as Appendix V shows. He was apparently a Jack of All Trades his whole life.

Notes

[1] According to Renwick, the manuscript is written on 14 leaves, 11 ¾×8 ¼ inches, without a title-page, and the last page is badly torn. See his edition, vi-vii.

[2] It seems closer in style to *Piers Plainness* and H. C.'s three works than to later plays like *Hoffman*.

[3] All quotations from *John of Bordeaux* are based on Renwick's edition for the Malone Society.

[4] According to Greg, whose edition for the Malone Society is still authoritative, this thin folio volume has approximately about 12 ½×8 ¼ inch-leaves, and twenty-two leaves survive, including the first two of the wrappers; fol. 3-5, 10, 11, 14, 15, 17-22 and some later insertions (v).

[5] For further discussion, see Chapter 4, "(iii) Succession."

[6] For further discussion of the works, see Chapter 1, "(iii) Chettle and Publications by Printers Other Than East and Danter."

[7] For further discussion of prisoners, see Chapter 5, "(ii) *The Downfall and Death of Robert, Earl of Huntingdon*," "(b) Martyrdom of Noble Prisoners."

[8] The full title of the first quarto is *An Excellent Conceited Tragedy of Romeo and Juliet*.

[9] The earlier editions of the play appeared in 1995 (ed. by Cedric Watts), and also in 2000 (ed. by Jill Levinson and Barry Gaines).

[10] The fill title of the second quarto is *The Most Excellent and Lamentable Tragedy of Romeo and Juliet*.

[11] For Allde's involvement, see Henning 363-34; also, the more convincing Hanabusa, "Edward Allde's Types" 423-28.

Part II Politics and Religion

4 Power Struggles in *The Tragedy of Hoffman* and Elizabethan Social Upheavals: Rebellion, Downfall, Succession

(i) Rebellion

(a) Hoffman's Motives for Revenge

Hoffman is believed to have been written in 1602, as revealed from the record of *Henslowe's Diary* on 29 December 1602: "Lent vnto Thomas downton...to geue vnto harey chettle in pte of payment for A tragedie called Hawghman" (207). The quarto of 1631 is the only extant text; its title-page records "it hath bin diuers times acted with great applause, at the *Phenix* in *Druery-lane*." From these two points, *Hoffman* may be thought to have been popular enough to have been repeatedly played from 1602 to at least 1631, a period when revenge tragedy was in vogue, though there is no actual performance record.

Revenge tragedy is defined by A. H. Thorndike, the first to name the genre and define it, as follows:

> The revenge tragedy, a distinct species of the tragedy of blood, may be defined as a tragedy whose leading motive is revenge and whose main action deals with the progress of this revenge, leading to the death of the murderers and often the death of revenger himself. (125)

In *Elizabethan Revenge Tragedy*, Bowers discusses representative revenge tragedies from the Elizabethan period to the Caroline period, such as *Spanish Tragedy*, *Titus Andronicus*, *The Jew of Malta*, *Antonio's Revenge*, *Hamlet*, *Hoffman*, *The Revenger's Tragedy* and *Women Beware Women* by Middleton, *The*

Henry Chettle's Careers: A Study of an Elizabethan Printer, Pamphleteer, Playwright

Atheist's Tragedy by Cyril Tourneur, *The Duchess of Malfi* by John Webster, and *The Cardinal* by James Shirley among others. Of these plays, *The Jew of Malta*, *Titus Andronicus*, and *Hamlet* seem to have particularly influenced *Hoffman*. Chettle probably read or saw *The Jew of Malta* and *Titus Andronicus*, as discussed in Chapter 1, "(i) Chettle and Thomas East," "(c) Chettle's Relationships with Authors, Printers, and Publishers in His Apprentice and Post-Apprentice Days." The villainous revenger Barabas resembles Hoffman, and his shocking death recalls that of Hoffman in the final scene. Also, the character of Hoffman seems to resemble Richard in *3 Henry VI* and *Richard III*, as shown in Chapter 2, "(i) Danter's Press and *Greene's Groatsworth of Wit*." Chettle probably read or saw these plays through Short, Millington, or Simmes, as discussed in Chapter 1, "(iii) Chettle and Publications by Printers Other Than East and Danter," "(b) Literary Influence from Publications by Printers Other Than East and Danter."

Lorrique, Hoffman's accomplice, suggests a plan for Hoffman to rape Martha, the widow Duchess of Luningberg; this associates her with Philomel, and is reminiscent of Lavinia's rape in *Titus Andronicus*. As the discussed in Chapter 3, "(iii) *Romeo and Juliet* (Q1)," the main plot of *Hoffman* is revenge for the father, and it is shared with *Hamlet*. The madness of the Princess of Austria Lucibella resembles that of Ophelia; both of them go insane through having lost their fathers and lovers. However, *Hoffman* seems to parody *Hamlet* as well as Shakespeare's other plays.

Revenge tragedy flourished most in the late Elizabethan to early Jacobean period and plays of this genre were called "get-penny" by contemporary stage-managers (Simpson 126). Many critics have claimed that Chettle followed this trend and wrote the play for the popular audience (Thorndike 193; Jenkins 84-85; Saunders 106). Blood shedding scenes dominate the play so much that most critics have paid particular attention to them; Collier calls it "a revolting mass of blood and murder" (51); Boyer discusses it as "a tissue of improbabilities dependent for interest upon intrigue and violence" (143); Jowett, in the introduction of his edition, describes it as "a play which will excel all others in violence and horrific spectacle" (iii). *Hoffman* can be, thus, seen as popular entertainment or more specifically a crowd-pleasing thriller (Thorndike 193; Jenkins 84-85; Saunders 106).

However, *Hoffman* also questions political matters in a manner innate in the genre of revenge tragedy. Although earlier critics such as Thorndike and Bowers discussed revenge tragedy in terms of form and convention, others like L. G. Salingar and J. W. Lever discussed the general political aspects of the genre. More recent critics such as Jonathan Dollimore, Christopher Hill, and Wendy Griswold have discussed more specific political points. Dollimore and Hill argue that skepticism toward rulers was generally expressed in Elizabethan and Jacobean drama. Dollimore claims that most of these plays expose and attack rulers who have lost the people's trust, with descriptions of their corrupt courts (4). Hill supports this position, arguing these dramas express the situation in which "the powers and duties of monarchs are being questioned" (*Writing* 9). Moreover, Griswold comments on the relation between the foreign settings of revenge tragedy and Renaissance England. She claims that "the foreign horrors—dynastic struggles, intrigues, bloodshed at court" in revenge tragedy reminded the English audience of their problems of "order, stable central government, and peaceful succession;" playwrights could deal with their real concerns, the issues of a corrupt court and inept rulers while avoiding censorship with "the use of Continental settings" (74-75).

Hoffman undoubtedly problematizes such political aspects, particularly rebellion, the downfall of great men, and monarchical succession, issues which were especially topical in 1602. Chettle seems to have indirectly reflected on the three points, avoiding censorship by using the foreign setting of Danzig in Poland. Late-Tudor England was unstable because of the people's anxiety about poverty, Spanish wars, Irish and domestic rebellions, and the succession; the authorities, thus, censored plays more strictly through fear of social disorder. For example, *The Isle of Dogs* (1597) was banned, and its author Nashe and three actors, including Jonson, were imprisoned (Marcus 31).

The plot of *Hoffman* is summarized as follows: Hoffman's father has been executed for piracy before the play begins, and Hoffman decides to take revenge not only on the Dukes of Luningberg and Prussia, who ordered and watched his father's execution, but also on their innocent family members. After vowing his revenge in the opening scene, Hoffman kills one of his enemies, Otho, the son of the Duke of Luningberg, with "a burning crown," or hot iron (1.1). Disguising himself as his victim, Hoffman enters into the court of Prussia, where he becomes the heir of the Duke of Prussia, because the Duke, Otho's uncle, has favored his nephew and disinherited his foolish son, Jerome (2.1). Hoffman kills two enemies, disguised first as a hermit and then as Otho (3.1), while Jerome becomes furious and rebels against his father. Hoffman, as Otho, intervenes in this conflict and the Duke allows Jerome to stay in his court as his taster (3.2). Hoffman deceives Jerome into poisoning himself as well as his father, and becomes the new Duke of Prussia (4.1). His other principal foe, the Duke of Luningberg, suddenly dies of natural causes, and Hoffman attempts to kill his widow, Martha. Hoffman, however, falls in love with her, decides not to kill her, and attempts to obtain her by force (4.2). Meanwhile, Hoffman's pawn, Lorrique, reveals Hoffman's true identity to his enemies, and they plan to take revenge on the usurper. Hoffman is finally executed by them with the same burning crown he had previously used on Otho (5.3).

In the pioneer revenge tragedy, *The Spanish Tragedy*, for example, the protagonist Hieronimo delays his revenge; even though he knows the murderer of his son, he cannot believe it; again, he does not act after he is convinced of the identity of the criminal; instead, he hopes God and the law will punish the crime. The reasons for the delay can be understood in various ways, but the greatest reason lies in the prohibition against revenge in contemporary society.

In the Elizabethan period, private revenge was religiously and legally forbidden, as Bowers claims (3-40). People followed the Bible which read,

"Vengeance is mine, I will repay" (Rom.12: 19) and thought that revenge was supposed to be taken by God. Francis Bacon regarded revenge as "a kind of wild justice," and concluded that public revenge for Caesar and Henry III largely succeeded, but that private revenge bore no fruit (72-73).

On the other hand, *Hoffman* describes no psychological conflict within the protagonist: Hoffman repeatedly murders without hesitation. The reason for this lies in his villainous personality. In earlier revenge tragedies, Lorenzo in *The Spanish Tragedy*, Piero in *Antonio's Revenge*, and Claudius in *Hamlet* played the role of the villain, not the protagonist. With the villain hero, Chettle did not have them feel hesitation, and moved the accomplishment of the revenge from the final scene to the opening scene; he could devote himself to depicting plural acts of revenge. In other words, as Bowers observed, Chettle was "disdainful of earlier hero revengers with their hesitant action" (128). Thus, Chettle created a new type of revenge tragedy.

This play explores the conditions from which revenge derives, instead of the psychological conflicts and the delay for revenge. In revenge tragedy, motives for revenge, indeed, play an important part in the dynamics of the play. Hoffman can be thought to have two main motives for revenge: the grudge against the Dukes who executed Hoffman's father and their excessive means of execution.

Hoffman expresses his grudge against the Dukes of Luningberg and Prussia, before killing Otho, the son of Luningberg:

> What though your father with the powerfull state
> And your iust vncle duke of *Prusia*
> After my father had in thirty fights
> Fill'd all their treasures with fomens spoyles,
> And payd poore souldiors from his treasury
> What though for this his merits he was nam'd
> A prescript out law for a little debt,
> Compeld to flie into the Belgique sound
> And liue a pirate? (1.1. 156-64)

From these lines, the fate of Hoffman's father is revealed. He had served the two Dukes loyally and offered booty to them, while he gave money to poor soldiers out of good will and had thus run into debt; subsequently he was banished by the Dukes because of his debt and turned into a pirate; finally, he was executed for piracy.

Piracy was illegal and the elder Hoffman was, therefore, legally executed; however, for Hoffman, the son, the execution was unjust. He believes in the cause of his revenge, ascertaining "Where trueth leadeth, what coward would not fight? / Ill acts moue some, but myne's a cause that's right" (1.1.11-12).

Hoffman does not clearly show the reason for his grudge against the Dukes, but two reasons can be inferred from the episode about Hoffman's father, a story which is repeatedly related by Hoffman and other characters (1.1.103-07, 155-64; 4.2.1837-38; 5.1.1965-70): namely, the ingratitude of the Dukes and the excessive punishment for piracy.

Regarding the first reason, the ingratitude, the two Dukes reward Hoffman's father's loyalty first with banishment, then with execution. As Brucher pointed out, the Dukes are described as "arbitrary, expedient and/or incompetent" (210).

The Duke of Luningberg never appears on stage in the drama, but is only reported to have died naturally in the latter part. However, his son Otho is depicted as a cruel and insolent prince. Hoffman reports that Otho had "pleasure" (1.1.218) when he saw the execution of Hoffman's father, and in another scene, he says, "father this youth scorn'd / When he was set in an ascending throne, / To haue you stand by him" (1.3.400-2).

The Duke of Prussia, the uncle of Otho, often appears and behaves arrogantly. He disinherits his son because of his dullness (1.2), attempts to kill the son and others who rebel against him, as discussed above, and executes without evidence a servant of his son for treason (4.1). Prussia is a Machiavellian villain who kills his son in order to retain power. Hoffman is compelled to take revenge on these ruthless and ungrateful rulers, since they have forgotten their debt to his brave father.

For the second reason, the excessive punishment, the penalty for piracy was hanging in the Elizabethan period; nevertheless, Hoffman's father was tortured and executed with a hot iron crown. The hot iron crown was frequently employed in capital punishment for treason in early modern Europe and was widely known as a gruesome method of execution (Brucher 214). Moreover, this excessive penalty reminds us of Michel Foucault's theory that the purpose of execution was spectacle, as Brucher remarks (Foucault 47). In other words, the Dukes execute him for the purpose of demonstrating the state power to the people rather than simply punishing Hoffman's father. His skin is flayed from his body, and his bones on the gallows are left exposed as a warning to other commoners.

For these reasons, Hoffman believes in the rightness of his revenge, though the execution itself was legally justified. After killing Otho, Hoffman disguises himself as his victim and succeeds in entering into the aristocratic world, but later he sees Otho's mother Martha and reveals his identity. Martha is virtuous enough to have tearfully implored the Duke of Luningberg to free Hoffman from prison, when he had stolen the bones of his father from the gallows, and Hoffman has kind feelings for Martha. Martha, remembering the incident, asks, "Art thou the lucklesse son of that sad man / Lord of Burtholme some time Admirall?" (4.2.1837-38). As E. J. Shlochauer points out, the two terms "lucklesse son" and "sad man" suggest her pity for Hoffman, and particularly for his father who has fallen from admiral to pirate and has been executed (cxxii).

The Duke of Saxony, a relative of Martha, is asked by his brother, Rodrick, about the execution of Hoffman's father, and answers,

> I doe remember the Admirall
> *Hoffma*n, that kept the Iland of Burtholome
> Was by the Duke of *Prussia* adiudg'd

To haue his head sear'd witha [sic] burning crowne.... (5.1.1965-68)

The terms, "I doe remember" (1965), "Admirall" (1965), and "Burtholome" (1966), show that the execution of Hoffman's father is still vividly remembered and shocking some years after the incident. The Duke of Saxony does not express direct sympathy like Martha, but the downfall and execution of Hoffman's father must have deeply troubled him. Thus, the remarks of Martha and the Duke of Saxony as well as Hoffman indicate that this execution appeared outrageous to everyone.

As a result of analyzing Hoffman's motives of revenge to Hoffman, the abnormality of the execution and the oppression of the rulers emerge. Hoffman's father is, in a word, exploited and executed as a display of state power. The Hoffmans must have had complaints about the capricious Dukes, but they cannot directly challenge them, because they are subjects and inferiors who have to obey their superiors. Hoffman's revenge, thus, seems to be a kind of rebellion or subversion against the ruling class.

(b) Revenge as Rebellion

After murdering Otho in Act I Scene i, Hoffman disguises himself as Otho for the greater part of the play. As a means of approaching their opponents, Hieronimo and Hamlet use "madness," while Antonio employs the disguise of a fool and a mask. The disguise of a person in a higher position is, thus, exceptional. Hoffman kills his aristocrat enemies successively, though outwardly one nobleman murders another noble person, since he wears luxurious costumes and behaves as Otho. Nevertheless, a rogue of the lowest status, in fact, kills the aristocrats. As Andrew Gurr claims, most audience members were lower classes in those days (Gurr, *The Shakespearean Stage* 199); therefore, to them, this point may be thought to be more intriguing than thrilling.

In most revenge tragedies, the inferior takes revenge on the superior, as Wendy Griswold remarks (90). Indeed, Hoffman takes revenge on the whole family of the Dukes, Hieronimo on the prince, Antonio on the Duke, and Hamlet on the King. Katherine Eisaman Maus significantly notes the close relation between revenge tragedy and social status: "Elizabethan and Jacobean revenge tragedies explore the particular stresses and incongruities produced by the highly stratified society of late sixteenth- and early seventeenth-century England" (xi). Moreover, Maus exposes the socially inferior audience's psychology: "Renaissance revenge tragedy taps the repressed frustrations of such situations, presenting the delicious spectacle of subjects hoodwinking and finally annihilating their superiors" (xii).

The plot of *Hoffman* follows a typical pattern of revenge tragedy. It has revenge as its main theme and includes a number of conventions, such as the revenger's vow, disguising and death, though it has some formal differences from the norm such as plural revenges and a lack of hesitation on the part of the revenger. However, certain aspects, particularly Hoffman's rise to power and his motivation, reflect Chettle's political consciousness. Hoffman initially takes revenge for his deceased father, but after killing the first victim, Otho, he appears to begin to be fascinated by power.

Hoffman announces his intention of carrying out multiple acts of revenge with the assertion that Otho's death is "the prologue to the 'nsuing play" (1.1.237). He disguises himself as Otho and enters the court of Otho's uncle, the Duke of Prussia, where he becomes the heir of the Duke after the deposition of the true heir, Prince Jerome. Jerome has been disinherited by the Duke as "a witlesse and insufficient prince" (2.1.489), though Jerome asserts that "I am no foole, I haue bin at *Wittenberg*, where wit growes" (1.2.276-77), an obvious mocking of *Hamlet*. From this point Hoffman begins to seek power, as he soliloquizes:

I am suppos'd the heire of *Luningberg*,
By which I am of *Prussia* Prince elect.
Good: who is wrong'd by this? onely a foole:
And 'tis not fit that idiots should beare rule. (2.3.645-48)

As early as Act II, he thus begins to think of power. The word "foole" (647) indicates the deposed Jerome, and "idiots" (648) can be thought to imply all of his ruling class enemies, the Dukes and their heirs including Jerome. Hoffman thinks that he is a more suitable ruler than these aristocrats, especially Prussia and Luningberg, who viciously treated his brave father, and he bitterly criticizes their ability as governors.

In Act IV Scene i, Hoffman poisons Prussia and Jerome, and finally becomes the new Duke of Prussia. Hoffman has, thus, completely subverted the social order through revenge. Hoffman then identifies himself to Martha, Otho's mother, relating a fictional story about Otho's death, and becomes her heir, the Prince of Luningberg. Now, Hoffman attempts to incestuously marry her, and kill the rest of her relatives, namely the Duke of Saxony and his heir and younger son, Mathias, and thus gain all of their kingdoms. Hoffman professes his desires in a soliloquy: "Dukedomes I will haue them, my sword shall win, / If any interposer crosse my will" (4.2.1907-08). Hoffman here no longer appears to be preoccupied with revenge, but with lust for power, though soon after this scene his identity and wrongs are to be revealed and punished.

Hoffman's desire, thus, changes from revenge to power. His reason for gaining power seems to be from the arbitrariness of or skepticism toward the actual rulers. As discussed above, the downfall of Hoffman's father is repeatedly referred to by such characters as Martha and Saxony, as well as by Hoffman throughout the play, and it seems to play a key role in Chettle's criticism of the ruling class.

Hoffman's successive murder of the aristocrats must have appealed to the audience in a hierarchical society by "presenting the delicious spectacle," as Maus remarks, since Hoffman is an outlaw, who has been imprisoned for stealing the skeleton of his father from the gallows (xii). Unlike other stage revengers, he successively kills a large number of aristocrats. At a glance, a nobleman kills other nobles, but actually the murderer is a rogue. Thus, the blood shedding scenes are seen as subversive.

4 Power Struggles in *The Tragedy of Hoffman* and Elizabethan Social Upheavals: Rebellion, Downfall, Succession

When *Hoffman* was first performed around 1602, English society was unstable; the number of poor people had greatly increased due to serial bad harvests (1594-97) and the plague (1592), and consequently the gap between the rich and the poor had expanded. On the other hand, many incidents invoked people's anxiety such as wars against Spain and in Ireland, succession issues, increasing crime, and insurrection. Under these conditions, the general frustration must have become stronger; therefore, it is natural that many commoners in the audience felt pleasure at the socially inferior Hoffman's revenge on the socially superior. This is especially true since revenge tragedy was produced for public theatres, one of which, the Fortune, was possibly where the play was performed for the first time (Griswold 68).

The villain-hero Hoffman kills princes, who are infatuated with love and tilts, and eventually replaces one of the Dukes. As Ronald Broude claims, Hoffman has subverted the social order through revenge (55). In brief, Hoffman emphasizes the binary opposition between the ruler and the subject through the act of revenge. At least, some parts of the public theater audience may have enjoyed much of Hoffman's revenge, since the character in the lowest social position murders noble people one after another and finally becomes the ruler.

(c) *Hoffman* and Censorship

In the early 1580s, the Master of the Revels began to have the power to censor all scripts of plays before their performance, with regard to their treatment of politics, religion and foreign policy, and to eliminate or revise inappropriate parts. Many plays were forbidden to be played or published for this reason, and offenders were punished with fines or imprisonment, factors which made playwrights turn to self-censorship (P. Williams, *The Later Tudors* 411-14; Clare 24-27; Hadfield 1-3).

Taking into account this strict censorship, the question arises why *Hoffman* was performed without problems in spite of its subversive political content. It is possible to think that *Hoffman* is not a politically dangerous play, but merely an entertainment full of blood. However, a more likely explanation is that Chettle may have avoided censorship tactically through certain means.

One way of avoiding censorship in the Renaissance was to use a foreign setting. It was Poland in *Hoffman*. According to Griswold, revenge tragedies reflected people's contemporary concerns about politics and religion, but "the use of Continental settings allowed the dramatists to address problems such as court corruption or dynastic instability, problems of real concern to their audiences, without risking censorship or imprisonment" (74-75). In short, revenge tragedy generally deals with contemporary social issues, and playwrights locate the settings in foreign countries. Thus, in revenge tragedy, Italy is frequently employed as a setting in such plays as *Antonio's Revenge* and *The Revenger's Tragedy*, because the English people regarded Italy as both an attractive land, where Renaissance culture flourished, and as an evil Catholic country full of Machiavellian intrigues.

In the case of *Hoffman*, Danzig in Poland provides the setting, which is rare for a revenge tragedy, but it belongs to the same Baltic area as *Hamlet*. Bowers claimed that the Germans appeared to the English as vindictive revengers who watch vigilantly for a chance to engage in violence (Bowers 56). Chettle, thus, avoided censorship with the foreign setting despite his inclusion of subversive elements such as the murders of those in authority by the lower orders.

A second method of avoiding censorship may have been the inclusion of self-referentiality, which repeatedly appears in the text of *Hoffman*. Chettle employs the terms of theater to emphasize that this is a fictional play. For example, after killing his first victim Otho, Hoffman asserts, "This but the prologue to the 'nsuing play. / The first step to reuenge, this seane is donne" (1.1.237-78). Furthermore, he cuts off Otho's skin and hangs his bones on a tree next to those of Hoffman's father, soliloquizing:

> He was the prologue to the Tragedy
> That if my destinies deny me not,
> Shall passe those of Thyestes, Tereus,
> Iocasta, or Duke iasons iealous wife;
> So shut our stage vp, there is one act done
> Ended in *Othos* death; (1.3.407-12)

Hoffman here mentions Greek tragedies, and he consciously claims that he will write a more excellent scenario for his next revenge; thus, Hoffman frequently uses theatrical references.

According to A. A. Al-Ghamdi, the revenge tragedy is itself a play within a play; a protagonist conceives and writes a scenario, directs and plays a role. The genre thus emphasizes its theatricality and insists that the world in the revenge tragedy is very different from the real world (24). With such theatrical self-references, Elizabethan playwrights frequently emphasized the fictionality of the theatrical world and put some psychological distance between the stage and the audience. Chettle, therefore, could obscure the direct relation between his play and society, and avoid censorship and people's criticism by utilizing such theatrical self-references to emphasize the play's fictitiousness.

A third means of avoiding censorship lay in the creation of the protagonist as a villain hero. Hoffman deceives and kills aristocrats while bitterly criticizing them, but it is because Hoffman is a villain that he can say or do anything he wants. The Elizabethan audience would have known that Hoffman is a villain at the beginning of the play from the lines of Lorrique, "this is an excellent fellow / A true villaine fitter for me then better company" (1.1.101-02). After killing Otho, Hoffman disguises himself as his victim, successively kills the nobles, and obtains the dukedom, which results in the subversion of the social order. However, his true identity is exposed by his pawn, Lorrique, and in the final scene Hoffman is executed. The social order is, thus, restored; the revenge tragedy starting with the burning crown ends with the same crown.

The death of the revenger in the final scene is a major convention of the revenge tragedy. Since revenge was forbidden by God and the law, any good hero with right motives was to be punished and degraded as a villain, once he violated this code with an act of revenge. Therefore, in revenge tragedy, most protagonists die after completing their revenge: for example, Hieronimo and Bussy commit suicide; Barabas falls into the kettle of boiling water, and dies, cursing like Hoffman; Titus is killed by Saturninus, while Hamlet is killed by Laertes; the only survivor Antonio among the revengers retires from the world at the end of the play, which has frequently raised criticism.[1]

Following such practice, Chettle obeyed the moral code with the death of the protagonist, and *Hoffman* could be accepted by the public and the officials. Chettle may have realized in advance that as long as Hoffman died in the end, he could commit evil acts throughout the play. Chettle, thus, sets the play in what is today part of Germany, emphasizes its theatricality with self-referential lines, and makes the protagonist a villain so that he can present safely subversive issues, though on the surface the play appeared to be a sensationalist entertainment.

(ii) Downfall

(a) *Hoffman* and the Socio-Political Situation in the Late-Tudor Period

The previous section looked at Hoffman's revenge as rebellion as well as at the general political aspects of the play. Believing the innocence of his father, Hoffman first decides to take revenge, and kills his aristocratic enemies underhandedly to destroy the social order. The rulers want to hold on to political power and misuse it, but Hoffman also seeks power. In other words, the play seems to center on power struggles between the socially superior and inferior rather than the revenge plot. In the unstable society of the late Elizabethan period, several power struggles were seen, especially at the court. Elizabeth had many favorites, encouraged them to dispute, and controlled their fates capriciously. Among them, the Earl of Essex and Robert Cecil had the two largest factions, though Essex failed in his rebellion against Elizabeth.

In such prose works as *Kind-Heart's Dream*, *Piers Plainness*, and *England's Mourning Garment*, Chettle shows his concern about current social and political issues; ballad singers, the theater, usury, wars agaist Spain, and the Irish rebellions. Among them, the most serious issue is the succession. This had been a matter of dispute throughout the reign of Queen Elizabeth, who refused to declare her successor up to the last moment, and often experienced the danger of intrigues or assassination in such conspiracies as the Throckmorton Plot and the Babington Plot. Although the succession debate had been critical in the 1560s, when Elizabeth directly opposed Mary, Queen of Scotland, it became most urgent and serious in the last years of her reign, when *Hoffman* was written. James VI of Scotland was the most obvious potential candidate, but there were the two major problems: his mother, Mary, had been executed for treason, and he was a foreigner (P. Williams, *The Later Tudors* 384; Watkins 14).

At court, the Earl of Essex was in intense rivalry with Cecil, but this conflict ended with Essex's rising and execution in 1601. His tragic fate had so great an impact as to be frequently mentioned in works, such as Daniel's *Philotas* and others (Heinemann, "Political Drama" 188-89). This major incident, Essex's rebellion, must have been present in all audiences' minds when they saw *Hoffman* at the end of December, 1602, three months before Elizabeth died. As discussed above, Hoffman's father is banished to an island for his debt and executed for piracy before this play begins. This episode is repeatedly mentioned not only by Hoffman, but also by other characters, and it is so shocking that Chettle seems to emphasize it deliberately.

The fate of Hoffman's father is thus objectively terrible, and this kind of story, the destruction of great men by capricious rulers, frequently occurred in the real Elizabethan world. According to Brucher, "Hoffman insists on the state's capricious, ungrateful treatment of his father's good service, which was a familiar enough story in the late 1590s and early 1600s," and goes on to assert that there was little distinction between privateering and piracy, both means by which young enterprising men such as Drake could be easily enriched (212-13). These professions were attractive, but their situations largely depended on rulers; as Brucher illustrates, Captain John Smith complained that King James had outlawed privateering; he claimed the unemployed gentlemen could remain rich, but that the unemployed poor must turn to piracy (213). In conclusion, Brucher attributes piracy to the economic conditions *circa* 1600 in England (220). The economic conditions were indeed terrible in those days because of inflation, serial bad harvests and plague, and a general increase in poverty. If the economic situation had been better, Hoffman's father would have been richer and not have run into debt. He, in fact, was poor and his debt led to his execution.

(b) The Theme of Downfall in Chettle's Works

The downfall of Hoffman's father seems to reflect a general dramatic and literary interest in such matters. There is a similar story in *Downfall* and *Death*, the Robin Hood play.[2] Robin Hood, a legendary outlaw yeoman, appears in these works as a nobleman, Robert, the Earl of Huntington, which was probably Munday's original idea. Both plays are set in the time of King Richard I. In the first play, Richard leaves for the Holy Land and entrusts Ely with the reign of the land. The Earl is outlawed by his butler and uncle, the Prior of York, because he is in debt to his uncle, and flees to the forest with his betrothed, Matilda, called Marian, the daughter of Lord Fitzwater. The Earl is affected by the political conflicts which leads to usurpation by the ruling class; of this ruling class are his butler and uncle as well as Prince John, who usurps the throne during the absence of his brother Richard, but finally all of them are reconciled with each other. In the second play, the Earl is poisoned by his uncle, who desires his earldom (Sc. 5), Matilda is also poisoned by John, now king, who desires her; the play ends with John's repentance.

In Scene iii of the first part, the Earl suddenly rises from the banquet to celebrate his betrothal Matilda, realizing the plot conceived by their villainous guests to disturb the banquet and proclaim the Earl is an outlaw. The Earl explains to Matilda the reason why he laments:

> Thy <u>Robin</u> is an outlawe, <u>Marian</u>,
> His goods and landes must be extended on,
> Himselfe exilde from thee, thou kept from him,
>   <u>She</u> <u>sinks</u> <u>in</u> <u>his</u> <u>armes</u>.
> By the long distance of vnnumbred miles. (*Downfall*, Sc.3: 210-14)[3]

This exaggerated behavior, however, is actually intended to deceive and allow them to escape the guests. The Earl then explains to the noble guests the reason for his rising from the banquet, and particularly criticizes his steward, Warman, for the plot to disturb the betrothal, which involves Prince John loving Matilda and his mother Queen Eleanor loving the Earl:

> You that with ruthlesse eyes my sorrowes see,
> And came prepar'd to feast at my sad fall,
> Whose enuie, greedinesse, and iealousie
> Afforde mee sorrowe endlesse, comfort small,
> Knowe what you knewe before, what you ordaind
> To crosse the spousall banquet of my loue,
> That I am outlawed by the Prior of Yorke,
> My traiterous vncle, and your trothlesse friendss. (Sc.3: 323-30)

This complaint reminds us of Hoffman's speeches describing the achievement and downfall of his father "What though your father with the powerfull state … And liue a pirate?" (1.1.156-64). The theme of downfall also recurs in a minor character, Lord Fitzwater, Matilda's father. He is banished by Prince John, because he has opposed the match between John and

Matilda, and fought with him, calling him "a tyrant lord" (Sc.7: 1218). He laments his outlaw status:

> Fitzwater once had castles, townes, and towers,
> Faire gardens, orchards, and delightful bowers:
> But now nor garden, orchard, towne, nor tower
> Hath poore Fitzwater left within his power. (Sc.10: 1476-79)

Both the Earl and Fitzwalter used to be nobles, but the self-interested and lustful aristocrats trap them, turn then into outlaws, and exile them from England. After some political confusion, they regain their right and honour in the end with the return of King Richard I.

The theme of downfall is also seen in *Blind Beggar*.[4] The story occurs during the reign of King Henry VI (1421-71) and is partly historical and partly pseudo-historical. The protagonist General Momford is proclaimed an outlaw for treason through a trap conceived by his brother, Sir Robert Westford, and Young Playnsey. Momford disguises himself as a blind beggar to stay in England, and lives in Bethnal Green. Robert attempts to possess Momford's land, while Strowd, a Norfolk yeoman claims his right to the land which Momford mortgaged to him. They fight in a duel, and Robert is believed to be dead while Strowd is to be executed for murder; however, Robert revives and Strowd's life is saved. Furthermore, Playnsey attempts to seduce Momford's daughter Bess, but she is saved by Momford, who pretends to be Momford's brother in disguise, and Playnsey is beaten in the ensuing fight. Several fights follow and in the final scene three battles occur between Momford and Robert, Captain Westward, Momford's cousin, and Playnsey, Strowd and two rogues, Canby and Hadland. Momford, Westward, and Strowd win. Momford reveals his identity and regains his right and honour, as his innocence is proclaimed, while his cousin is married to his daughter. On the other hand, Robert and Playnsey are put on trial, and Canby and Hadland are exiled.

In the opening scene, Momford is proclaimed to be outlaw by Lord Cardinal:

> thou know'st by Law of Arms
> Thou merit'st death with more than common torture:
> But thy exceeding vallour often tride,
> Sets open Mercies gate, whose gentle hand
> Leads thee from death, but leaves thee banished
> From *England*, and the Realms and Provinces
> Under protection of the *English* King.... (1: 94-99)[5]

Momford is thus to be banished from England, though he is innocent and so noble that his cousin Captain Westford says, "there breaths not a more noble Spirit / In any Souldiers breast, than noble *Momfords*" (61-62).

The downfall of the Earl is similar to that of Hoffman's father with respect to their debts and banishment by villainous superiors who desire power, while the situation of Momford is similar to Hoffman's father in that they are great soldiers. From these examples, Chettle can be seen to have been very interested in this theme.

Chettle also deals with the motif of downfall in his political prose work, *Piers Plainness*. This work describes the citizen life of usury and brokerage, and court intrigues such as the usurpation of a vicious son, Celinus who deposes and banishes his father, the King of Thrace, with his twin brother, Aemilius, the next successor, and his younger sister, Rhodope, the second successor.

As a collaborative playwright, Chettle portrayed historical persons such as Sir Thomas More, Thomas Wolsey, Jane Grey, and Thomas Wyatt—all of whom were overthrown and executed— in *Sir Thomas More*, *The Life of Cardinal Wolsey*, *The Rising of Cardinal Wolsey*, and *Lady Jane*.[6]

Not only Chettle but also a number of his contemporaries seem to have been interested in the theme of downfall; for example, it is dealt with in Marlowe's *1, 2 Tamburlaine the Great*, Shakespeare's *Richard III*, *Richard II*,

Hamlet, Othello, Jonson's *Sejanus His Fall,* Daniel's *Philotas,* George Chapman's *Bussy D'Ambois,* and *The Conspiracy and the Tragedy of Charles Duke of Byron* among others.

The topic appears to have been much discussed in those days. For example, in *Blind Beggar,* Captain Westford comforts Momford, who is depressed because of his fall, with these philosophical words:

> If you be just, as I suppose you be,
> Know Innocence ends not in misery;
> Kings have had falls, great Souldiers overthrown,
> No riches in this earth is a mans own,
> He strives, he toyls, with many pains he takes it,
> In an age gets it, in one hour forsakes it. (1: 119-124)

The Captain states that downfall happens to great men like "Kings" (21) and "Souldiers" (21) including Momford, and that prosperity disappears in a moment, no matter how hard it has been to gain it. Considering the lists of the plays dealing with downfall, which I mentioned above, it is true that it happens to "Kings" like Richard III, Richard II, and "Soldiers" like Othello and Sejanus.

This kind of tragedy dealing with the downfall of mighty persons is called "De casibus" tragedy, the term deriving from *De Casibus Virorum Illustrium* by Boccacio (Doran 115-28). This book had great influence on Elizabethan histories and tragedies through its translation, *The Fall of Princes* by John Lydgate, and *The Mirror for Magistrates,* edited by William Baldwin.[7]

(c) Allusion to Essex

The theme of the downfall seems to be reflected in some of the plays which I mentioned above, particularly *Hoffman.* Considering the date of *Hoffman*'s production, 1602, the fall of Hoffman's father may be thought to be influenced by the current most sensational incident, namely the downfall and execution of Essex in 1601.[8]

Essex had many enemies in the court and in particular, Robert Cecil was his greatest opponent. They had competed for patronage and power, while they had disagreed over foreign policies such as the Spanish issue. Cecil advocated reconciliation with Spain, but Essex wanted to defeat it thoroughly. Essex had been more popular than Cecil among people as a handsome young military hero. Therefore, people's feelings about his execution were complex; he was officially condemned for atheism and treason, but he was privately regarded as a great man of tragic fate, misled by others such as his secretary, Henry Cuffe, and a victim of court intrigues.[9] After Essex's rising, Cecil became more influential until the Queen's death, and then under James I, won favour and kept power in the court. Nevertheless, Cecil's dominance at court was disliked by many people besides Essex's supporters, such as soldiers, other courtiers, and country gentlemen. The commoners never forgave Cecil, who implacably opposed their hero Essex. When Cecil died in 1612, few people mourned, while many people rejoiced (Bevan 128).

Their underlying sympathy with the fate of their hero seems to be reflected in literary works. Margot Heinemann argues that a good deal of early-Stuart drama alludes to tragic and political downfalls, for it was common in those days to write about a favored military leader who confronted a state heading toward absolutism, and was then destroyed by treason ("Political Drama" 188-89). Moreover, Ruff and Wilson suggest that Elizabethan lute song lyrics, including those by John Ramsey and Dowland, allude to his downfall ("Allusion" 31-36). There were so many pamphlets and plays exploring the causes of Essex's fall that the Privy Council immediately acted, for example, in the summoning of Daniel in 1605, as Hammer notes (*Polarisation* 959).

There are many politically risky works alluding to Essex's downfall, but perhaps the most famous is Daniel's tragedy, *Philotas* (1604). This story deals with the downfall of Philotas, the favourite general of Alexander the Great, who is arraigned for treason, because he does not impart his knowledge of a conspiracy against Alexander, and because of the intrigues of courtiers. As a result, he is tortured and executed. Daniel was summoned before the Privy Council in 1605, when the play was published, to explain the resemblance between the trial and execution of Philotas, and those of Essex. Daniel claimed that he had written the first three parts before Essex's insurrection and that he did not mean to allude to it. His excuse was accepted (Heinemann, *Puritanism and Theater* 41).

In the Jacobean age, the poet, John Davies, and the historian, William Camden, and in the Caroline age, a diplomat Henry Wotton also portrayed Essex as a tragic figure.[10] Moreover, continental writers produced fictional dramas about the fate of Essex; for example, Dutch plays include Antonio Coello's *Dar la Vida por su Dama* performed in the 1620s, and Gauthier de Costes de la Calprenède's *Le Comte d' Essex* in the 1630s (Hammer "Robert Devreux" 959).

The fate of Essex can be seen as resonant, too, in *Hoffman*. Hoffman's father is similar to Essex. Both of them were once favoured by their monarchs as brave men, but by degrees they lose favour, coming eventually to be executed. In short, their fate largely depends on their capricious rulers. Also, the debt of Hoffman's father may well have reminded the audience of that of the extravagant Essex. From an early age Essex was in debt: when he was nine, his father died and left him a good deal of debt.

Chettle was a friend of Peele, and he must have read Peele's *An Eclogue to…Earl of Essex* (1589), and other works, as shown in Chapter 1 "Chettle as Printer," particularly, "(i) Chettle and Thomas East," "(b) Literary Influence from East's Publication between 1577 and 1590." Chettle was anti-Catholic and anti-Spain like Nashe, Munday, and Peele, and this religious and political identity was formed through the publications of East, Danter, and others. Chettle perhaps admired Essex like Peele. As will be discussed in Chapter 5 "Catholic Rulers and Downfallen Protestant Prisoners," Chettle's works describe such Protestant heroes as Robert and Wyatt, and they seem to have Essex in mind. However, his direct reference to Essex is not seen, even in *England's Mourning Garment*, which depicts Elizabeth and the Tudor history. The tract illustrates the Irish rebellions, and praises Henry Sidney, Lord Deputy of Ireland, as well as his son, but it never mentions Essex. The tract appeared in 1603, and reference to Essex's fall was taboo. In the work, Chettle outwardly praises Elizabeth, but his true attitudes toward her are uncertain.

(iii) Succession

(a) Chettle's Ideas on the Succession

The concept of succession, or more precisely, usurping succession seems to appear to have close relations with that of downfall in Renaissance literature; take, for examples, the works mentioned in the previous section, the downfall of the King of Thrace occurs, together with the usurping succession of his son Celinus in *Piers Plainness*; the downfall of Hoffman's father occurs in turn with the usurping succession of Hoffman; the downfall of the Earl of Huntington occurs, as Prince John usurps the throne in the Robin Hood plays.

In a political romance, the prose *Piers Plainness*, Celinus, a vicious prince of Thrace, cooperates with Celydon, "a Protectour of a cheefest strength of Thrace" (126), who plans a *coup d'état* against the King of Thrace. Celinus has a twin brother and a younger sister, but because of his idleness, he is not considered for succession. Celinus is thus incited by Celydon to kill all his family members as well as Celinus, his twin brother:

> It is in vaine (saith he [Celydon]) to purpose the ruine of Celinus alone, sith your father ... hath absolutely dispossest you of all claime to the Kingdom, naming your sister next in succession if Aemilius die: if both he and she depart issulesse, he hath bequeathed the Kingdome to the election of the State. (126)

Celinus agrees with Celydon and becomes his pawn. When they capture the King, his son and daughter in the woods, Celydon commands the son and the daughter be suffocated; however, the King begs for mercy and suggests another plan, their exile:

> I sweare to thee by the immortal powers, and my children with like vow shall confirme my oath, if thou exile us together, or severall, so thou preserve our lives, we will obscure our States, and never returne to Thrace, except recalled by thee, Celinus, or both. (130)

Celydon accepts this and after appeasing the mutiny of the multitudes caused by the *coup d'état*, he becomes the governor of Thrace, though outwardly Celinus plays the role of king, and Celydon is his protector. The King and his children are banished by ship and land on islands separately, but eventually they meet again and restore the social order.

The themes of downfall and usurpation in *Hoffman* show the instability of society and the mobility of power in Germany, and this politically fluctuating situation can be thought to have reflected the Elizabethan society, especially with regard to the succession. While the succession issue causes Celinus to usurp his father's throne, it also causes Jerome to confront his usurper Hoffman. *Hoffman* is, as we have seen, a political drama as well as a revenge tragedy. Hoffman first kills his aristocratic enemies to revenge his father, but he starts to seek power, and eventually becomes the Duke of Prussia. Political instability is closely linked to succession issues and inappropriate rulers.

In Act III Scene i, Prince Jerome rebels against his father, the Duke of Prussia, because Prussia regards his son "A witlesse foole" (1.2.290) and proclaims that he will disinherit Jerome and adopt his favorite nephew, Otho (the disguised Hoffman), as his successor (2.1). Jerome soon vows "red reuenge" (2.1.508) and holds a grudge against his father and his usurper, Hoffman.

Jerome's insurrection and the civil war scene seem to reflect Elizabethan people's anxieties about the succession question. Hoffman (Otho) attempts to intervene between the Duke of Prussia and the civil soldiers supporting Jerome as "the true and lawfull Prince" (3.2.1338), but the commoners will not follow their "vn-lawfull" (1166-67) and "false Prince" (1206), that is, Hoffman. Jerome's servant, Stilt, and his father, a veteran captain, Old Stilt, challenge Prussia and Hoffman.

> STILT. We scorne pardons, Peace and pitty; wee'l
>   haue a Prince of our owne chusing, Prince *Ierom*.
> OLD STILT. I, I, Prince *Ierom* or no body; be not obstacle old
>   Duke, let not your owne flesh and blood bee inherited of
>   your Dukedome, and a stranger displac'd in his retority [sic].... (1214-18)

They are brave enough to criticize the Duke's arbitrary decision for having chosen "a stranger" (1218) as his successor, and Old Stilt emphasizes Hoffman's status as a foreigner.[11] This is a remarkable point, because the Elizabethans certainly abhorred foreigners, such as Spaniards, Jews, Moors, Turks as well as the Scottish and Irish, and there were some campaigns to exclude aliens.

When Hoffman tries to calm the still rebellious people, by saying, "Forbeare a little worthy Countrymen" (1237), young Stilt bitterly retorts, "Nay we deny that, we are none of your Countrymen; / you are an arrant arrant Alien" (1238-39). His foreignness is again emphasized here. The term "Countrymen" (1237) usually invokes patriotism, as Antony's famous speeches express in *Julius Caesar*; however, this offends young Stilt and others, and Hoffman becomes more isolated as a foreigner.

On the question of the legitimacy of the succession, the dukedom of Prussia is divided into two groups of opinions, the poor commoners and the rich ruling class, and this expresses the ideological split in the monarchy, which may well have reminded the audience of the situation in their own country.

(b) *Hoffman* and the Stuart Succession
   The dispute over the succession in the play seems to be conceived from

its real topical importance in the late Tudor period. The successor to the throne had been, in fact, problematic throughout the reign of Elizabeth, because she never married and only announced her successor shortly before her death. Her reign saw the productions of various plays, especially histories reflecting succession issues, particularly in the 1560s and 1600s. For example, *Gorboduc*, *The Tragedy of Locrine*, and *King Lear* deal with succession and the division of the kingdom. In the late 1590s, when Elizabeth was over sixty, this issue grew more urgent.

As mentioned in the previous section, King James VI of Scotland was the prime candidate to succeed to the throne, but he had two major problems: he was a foreigner and his mother had been a Catholic, executed for treason. Moreover, the Stuart line had low priority in the succession. According to the stipulations of Henry VIII's will, which debarred the Stuart line, after Elizabeth, the crown should pass first to Lady Frances Grey and her heirs, second, to her younger sister Lady Eleanor Clifford and her heirs, and thirdly, to the "next rightful heirs" (P. Williams, *The Later Tudors* 383). Although people recognized that James was unlike his mother and a Protestant, they must have been anxious about his religious views and governance.

Authorities were fearful of social disturbance and prohibited people to "discuss the succession question," according to Thomas Wilson, the keeper of the records and historian, but some writers secretly published pamphlets about the succession in other countries (2). In *The State of England Anno Dom. 1600*, Wilson listed twelve candidates for the succession including James Stuart, Lord Beauchamp, the son of Catherine Grey, Arbella Stuart, who had many Catholic supporters, the Earl of Derby, the Earl of Hertford, and Henry Seymour, with a defense of James. Robert Parsons, a Jesuit, wrote a disputatious pamphlet, *A Conference about the Next Succession to the Crown of England* (1594) under the name of D. Doleman and supported the Spanish Infanta, the daughter of Philip II. The pro-James faction, namely William Watson, Edmund Ashfield, Henry Hooke, and Edmund Pudsey disproved

4 Power Struggles in *The Tragedy of Hoffman* and Elizabethan Social Upheavals: Rebellion, Downfall, Succession

Parsons and blamed him for reopening "the war of the roses," as Marie Axton remarks (97). This pamphlet is interestingly dedicated to Essex, which suggests Parsons wanted his support, and that Essex may have had ties with the Catholic leagues.[12] On the other hand, Peter Wentworth, a Protestant and a member of parliament, was imprisoned for urging Elizabeth to settle her successor, supporting James in this.

Chettle also seems to have been interested in this subject and had an opinion of James. As mentioned above, Chettle reviews the reign of Elizabeth and praises her for three virtues, "faith" (87), "Hope" (91), "Charitie" (91), in *England's Mourning Garment*. As the full title expresses, this tract includes an entertainment for the new King, James.[13] Nevertheless, this portion of the work is very different from the previous parts. The praise for Elizabeth dominates almost all of the work and the entertainment for James covers only a few pages. He certainly mentions James in the last part of the section on Elizabeth, but his words for James are not favorable and can be read as a warning. For example, after praising Elizabeth's "Charitie," or "the thirde and principall diuine Grace to the eye of mortall" (91), Chettle demands the same of James:

> as I first noted touching her Charitie, which was still so tempered, notwithstanding her great charge in aiding her distressed neighbours, that she was ever truely liberall, and no way prodigall: as I trust his Royall Maiestie shall by the treasure finde. (102)

On sea battles, Chettle also wants James to follow her example. He praises her, and warns him:

> For such tenants made she many buildings, exceeding any Emperors Nauy in the earth, whose seruice I doubt not will be acceptable to her most worthy Successor, our dread Soueraigne Lord and King. (104)

Chettle does not directly express his disapproval of James, but implicitly this work is part of a general tendency to disapprove of James through an emphasis on Elizabeth's Golden Period (C. Hill, *Writing* 57; also, P. Williams, *The Later Tudors* 388). In addition, Chettle criticizes contemporary writers such as Shakespeare and Jonson for not writing elegies for Elizabeth: he suggests that they quickly began to seek the patronage of James, the new great patron.[14] In this work, Chettle, thus, casts a retrospective look on the glorious days of Elizabeth and hopes for such in the next age, though with some doubt. He is unquestionably a patriotic writer.

Most of his contemporaries are thought to have approved of James as the successor, but some disliked him for being a foreign king. Matthew Freeland, a yeoman of Esher, was accused of professing on 4 July 1599, "the kinge of Scotts was right heyre apparent to the Crowne of England" (*Calendar of Assize Records, Surrey Indictments, Elizabeth I* 496). On the other hand, Thomas Browne, a yeoman, and William Fletcher, a saddler, were accused of criticizing James as a foreign governor soon after his accession in 1603. Browne claimed on 31 March 1603 that "he" who "lived a Scot should not were the Crowne of England, and that althoughe all the men of England would joyne with the Kynge, yet he would be against him" (*Calendar of Assize Records, Hertfordshire Indictments James I* 4-5). Fletcher asserted on 25 March 1603, "we...ought not to rejoyce for that any forraine prynce should raigne over us" (*Calendar of Assize Records, Sussex Indictments, James I* 1). Browne and Fletcher emphasize the foreignness of James, and Fletcher's words, "forraign prynce" remind us of young Stilt's phrase, "you are an arrant arrant Alien" (3.2.239).

The London stage had negative feelings toward James and scorned him and Scottish people in the late-Tudor period, according to James Shapiro. For example, following Gary Taylor and Annabel Patterson, Shapiro observes that Shakespeare's 1600 Quarto of *Henry V* omits some parts concerning "the Scot," particularly King Henry's fear of the Scots (A3r-v) and the ridicule of Captain Jamy (3.3), as well as the allusion to Essex, included in the 1623 Folio (Taylor, ed., *Henry V* 3-9; Patterson 71-92; Shapiro 430-

33). Greene's *The Scottish History of James the Fourth* describes the marital life between James, the lustful Scottish King, and Dorithea, the virtuous daughter of the English King; in the opening scene, James falls in love with a daughter of a Scottish nobleman in the middle of his wedding and attempts to murder Dorithea; however, this intrigue fails, and Dorithea lives secretly; believing Dorithea is dead, the English King prepares to attack Scotland, but the two countries reconcile after James's apology to Dorithea. This play was first staged around 1590-91, entered in the Stationers' Register in 1594, and published in 1598. Shapiro states that "the publication a decade after its composition...was meant to capitalize on the increasing topicality of Stuart succession in 1598-1599" (430-32). Interestingly, Chettle himself also wrote a Scottish history play, *Robert II or The Scot's Tragedy*, with Jonson, Dekker and probably Marston, which was played in 1599 and never printed. Shapiro associates this play with the Stuart succession and the history of Robert, who was the first Stuart King, and who had trouble in choosing his heir among at least twenty-one children (428-29).

Jerome's rebellion in *Hoffman* seems to reflect the current political issues, and as Brucher notes, "the plot devices serve the play's critique of the ruling class and play directly on audience anxieties about orderly succession and the wounds of civil war" (215). The Duke is described as a selfish, vain, simple tyrant while Jerome is an extraordinary idiot. Their family discord over the succession develops into a civil war, a pattern which had frequently happened in English history and was felt to be possible at that time. Chettle certainly read *The Wounds of Civil War* by Lodge, and received inspiration from it. When *Hoffman* was first staged at the end of 1602, shortly before the Queen's death, the Elizabethans were intensely afraid of potential social disorder brought on by her death, as Dekker describes the situation immediately after her death:

> *Who did expect but ruine, blood, and death,*
> *To share our kingdome, and diuide our breath.*

Henry Chettle's Careers: A Study of an Elizabethan Printer, Pamphleteer, Playwright

> *Religions without religion,*
> *To let each other blood, confusion*
> *To be next Queene of England, and this yeere*
> *The ciuill warres of France to be plaid heere*
> *By English-men, ruffians, and pandering slaues,*
> *That faine would dig vp gowtie vsurers graue....*[15]

The Elizabethans were concerned about the possible outbreak of a civil war after the death of Elizabeth, especially with the memory of the French Wars of Religion. The civil wars between the Catholics and the Huguenots started in 1562 and ended in 1598 with the Edict of Nantes. The St. Bartholomew's Day Massacre (1572) most vividly represents the cruelty of the wars with 4,000 Huguenots killed by Catholics. This was so horrible an incident that the Elizabethans knew of it well, through pamphlets, rumors, and plays, such as Marlowe's *The Massacre at Paris* among other accounts.[16] Chettle probably read his friend, Marlowe's play, printed by his other friend, Edward Allde, in 1594, and knew of the French civil war.

Chettle, thus, indirectly described people's concerns about the succession and its possible consequence, civil war, in *Hoffman*. Three months after this play was written, James I peacefully succeeded to the throne, principally because there was no other strong candidate, not because all the people accepted his right to the throne (Axton 132). The early Stuart Age was seemingly peaceful, and no civil war occurred, as Dekker described, but by degrees, commoners came to complain about the absolutism of the Stuart monarchy, and directly about James and his son, Charles I; finally, civil war broke out in 1642, ending with the execution of Charles in 1649. Therefore, in the long run, the succession problem in *Hoffman* can be seen as an omen for the future of the nation.

*

This chapter has discussed Chettle's political consciousness, focusing on the issues of rebellion, downfall, and succession in *Hoffman*. Hoffman takes revenge on the ruling class that has executed his father. Hoffman's revenge seems to be a thrilling entertainment, but it is also seen as a kind of rebellion and is, thus, highly subversive. Whether or not the audience sympathized with the wicked Hoffman is uncertain, but the tensions of their hierarchical society may have been reflected in Hoffman's serial murders of aristocrats, who lived in ease and comfort, as Maus notes (xii).

Downfall is Chettle's favorite theme, as seen in *Hoffman*, *Piers Plainness*, *Downfall* and *Death*, and *Blind Beggar*. Among these works, the downfall of Hoffman's father seems to have had the greatest impact, and his misfortune is recounted by the characters including Hoffman. Considering the background when this play was written, there may be an allusion to the execution of Essex in that of Hoffman's father. Both men were brave soldiers, and their destiny of being misused and executed by the government seems to be very similar. Hoffman's father has been executed before the play starts, but instead, the execution of Otho and Hoffman occurs on stage. Although frequently describing the execution of noble characters, Chettle does not show such execution scenes on stage. He may also have intended to bring to mind Essex's execution through those of Otho and Hoffman as well as Hoffman's father. Perhaps, Chettle refrained from putting the execution of Hoffman's father on stage for fear of being condemned by the authorities, who might have associated the scene with Essex's execution.

Succession is also a favorite theme, as seen in *Hoffman* and *Piers Plainness*. Hoffman's accession to the dukedom of Prussia as Otho, and the commoner's uprising led by Prince Jerome seems to cynically reflect the Elizabethan succession issue, particularly the Stuart succession. The legitimacy of Hoffman's (Otho's) succession is in question, because he is a foreigner, as was the case of James VI. The common people insist that the idiot Jerome should be the true successor, while his father and others support Hoffman.

These political issues in *Hoffman*, thus, reflect the situation of late Elizabethan society. Chettle may well have known people's concerns through his involvement in printing and pamphlets, and he probably held his own personal views on these matters. He felt social injustice from the standpoint of the lower orders and criticized the arbitrary attitude of the ruling class. However, incoherently, as a nationalist, he did not wish for a foreign king. In this point he obeys the social norm.

Chettle's political views are complex. In *Hoffman*, Chettle seems to support an Essex-like character, Hoffman's father; in *Downfall* and *Sir Thomas Wyatt*, Chettle describes similar characters, Robert and Wyatt, as will be discussed in Chapter 5 "Catholic Rulers and Downfallen Protestant Prisoners." Chettle, thus, apparently shows his sympathy for Essex. In *England's Mourning Garment*, however, he praises Elizabeth. Perhaps, Chettle preferred Elizabeth to James, but he had ambiguous feelings for her. He may have used her to show his negative attitudes toward James.

Chettle's perspectives are, thus, vague, but it is certain that his primary concern was profit. He wrote plays to satisfy audiences' demands. In the preface to *England's Mourning Garment*, Chettle condemns those who do not lament the death of Elizabeth as "Time-pleasers" (80), but he seems to have been himself a time-pleaser.

Notes

[1] See Reavley Gair's edition, *Antonio's Revenge* 38-39.
[2] For more general information and religious aspects of these works, see Chapter 5 "Catholic Rulers and Downfallen Protestant Prisoners."
[3] All quotations from *Downfall* and *Death* follow J. C. Meagher's edition for Garland.
[4] For more information and social issues of this play, see Chapter 7 "Beggars in *The Pleasant Comedy of Patient Grissil* and *The Blind Beggar of Bethnal Green*, and the Elizabethan Money Based Economy."
[5] All citations from *Blind Beggar* follow Bang's edition. This edition does not divide scenes, and I indicate only the numbers of acts and lines.
[6] The *Cardinal Wolsey* plays and *Lady Jane* are lost. *Lady Jane* was written with Dekker, Heywood, Wentworth Smith, and John Webster and may be identified with the first part, the story about Lady Jane, of *Sir Thomas Wyatt*, whose title-page names Dekker and

4 Power Struggles in *The Tragedy of Hoffman* and Elizabethan Social Upheavals: Rebellion, Downfall, Succession

Webster as its authors.

[7] For their influence on Elizabethan playwrights like Marlowe and Shakespeare, see Farnham; Campbell; Budra.

[8] For the details of the downfall and execution of Essex, see Hammar, "Robert Debreux" 955-59.

[9] For the details see L. Smith 253, 273-74, Smuts 68.

[10] See Davies's *Scourge of Folly* (1611); Camden's *The History of the Most Renowned and Victorious Princess Elizabeth* (1635); Wotton's *A Parallel between Robert Late Earl of Essex and George Late Duke of Buckingham* (1641).

[11] Otho is the Prince of Luningberg, another country, though the Dukes of Prussia and Luningberg are relatives.

[12] For the dedication, see Hammer, *Polarisation* 177. For Essex's secret relation with Catholics in England, see Hammer, *Polarisation* 174-78.

[13] The full title is "Englandes Mourning Garment: Worne here by plaine Shepheardes; *in memorie of their sacred Mistresse*, ELIZABETH, Queene of Vertue while shee liued, and Theame of Sorrow, being dead. To which is added the true manner of her Emperiall Funerall. After which foloweth the Shepheards Spring-Song, for entertainement of King IAMES our most potent Soueraigne. Dedicated to all that loued the deceased Queene, and honor the liuing King."

[14] For the details of the patronage of James, see Honda 11-16.

[15] The quotation comes from G. B. Harrison, ed., *The Wonderful Year* 22.

[16] See Bennett, ed., *The Massacre at Paris* 176.

5 Catholic Rulers and Downfallen Protestant Prisoners

(i) Background of the Early Modern Prison

In the Elizabethan period crime became of increasing concern to the government with the spread of poverty, while religious or political offenders were regarded as more problematic and dangerous. Consequently, imprisonment was an effective means to regulate the people. In fact, confinement could occur to anybody, whether man or woman, for such offences as "[v]agrancy, petty theft, being out of a parish without lawful cause and with no visible means of support, slander, debt, assault, disorderly conduct, suspicion of witch craft," among which "debt and assault" were the two commonest causes (Salgado 164).

John Taylor, the water poet, briefly described the history and features of eighteen prisons in London in *The Praise and Virtue of a Jail and Jailors* (1623; STC 23785): The Tower, Gatehouse, Fleet, Newgate, Ludgate, Poultry Counter, Wood-street, Bridewell, White Lion, King's Bench, Marshalsea, Counter, Clink, The Hole at St. Katherine's, East Smithfield, New Prison, Lord Wentworth's, and Finsbury. Among these prisons Newgate was the principal prison for various offenses, such as petty treason, felony, misdemeanor, and was governed by the City of London. On the other hand, Marshalsea was the second prison under the direct jurisdiction of the Crown. Although any type of offenders could be held there, particularly religious offenders, namely Catholics, and pirates were imprisoned there in the Elizabethan reign (Dobb 88-89). However, the subject of prisons before the eighteenth century has been little discussed; many critics feel it is difficult and complex because of the lack of records and public debates on prisons, the difference in attitudes toward cruel punishments between

5 Catholic Rulers and Downfallen Protestant Prisoners

early modern society and today, so it is impossible to understand the early modern notion of prisons perfectly (J. Sharpe 18).

Punishments in Elizabethan society ranged from public execution, mutilation, bondage, imprisonment, labor, to banishment and other penalties. In this period, corporal punishment and public executions were dominant and significant in displaying the authority's power. In the last half of the eighteenth century, humanistic philosophers and lawyers started protesting against public execution, and prison became mainly a place for non-corporal punishment (Foucault 73-131). However, corporal punishments were beginning to be replaced by imprisonment and transportation, which first appeared around 1600, and Elizabethan literature often describes prisons (Spierenburg 46-47).

One characteristic of Elizabethan prisons seems to have been a kind of theatricality: punishment was public and required an audience (J. Sharpe 19). For Elizabethans, public execution was an entertainning show as well as a horrible lesson. It was a judicial and political ritual by which power was manifested (Foucault 47). Similarly, prison seems to have been seen not only as a horrible but also as a theatrical place. Although people could not peer inside, they could imagine scenes of punishment by seeing the buildings scattered throughout London and by reading chronicles, plays, and pamphlets depicting the confinement of famous people. More significantly, many political and religious offenders were imprisoned. The number of such prisons was uncomparably large, when politics and religion were unstable, and both issues were closely related (J. Thomas 11).

Elizabethan literature and drama frequently portray prisoners in their social context, though the theme of prison itself is a literary tradition in such romances as Sidney's *Arcadia*. In these works, offenders are frequently imprisoned for such political reasons as treason, rebellion, the monarch's displeasure, or for religious reasons rather than debt and felony. Moreover, many historical persons are represented: More in *Sir Thomas More*, Wyatt, Lady Jane, Guilford Dudley in *Sir Thomas Wyatt*, and Queen Elizabeth in

Heywood's *1 If You Know Not Me, You Know Nobody* among others.

In Elizabethan plays, the function of the prison is generally seen as metaphorical. E. D. Pendry pointed out how prisons functioned as schools, churches, hospitals, before Foucault's influential theory, as exemplified in Elizabethan plays and pamphlets (295-98). For example, *The Roaring Girl* describes explicitly the association between prison and school. In this play, Sir Davy attempts to imprison his prodigal son in the "Counter" (3.3.76, 77), but Sir Alexander objects to this proposal, because prisoners are so eloquent like university scholars that they could deceive keepers to get out of prison. Sir Alexander observes that the Counter is "an university! / Scholars learn first logic and rhetoric; / So does a prisoner" (3.3.93). The association of prison with school and hospital can be seen in Falstaff's words as well. In Act I Scene ii of *2 Henry IV*, the Lord Chief Justice comes to summon Falstaff for robbery, but Falstaff pretends not to hear him, remarking on irrelevant military issues to his servant. Falstaff explains his deafness, referring to "Galen" (116), and the Lord Justice says, "To punish you by the heels would amend the attention of your ears, and I care not if I do become your physician" (122-24). The analogy between medicine and imprisonment is completed by Falstaff:

> I am as poor as Job. Your lordship may minister the potion of imprisonment to me in respect of poverty; but how I should be your patient to follow your prescriptions, the wise may make some dram, of a scruple, or indeed a scruple itself. (125-30)

Chettle, however, does not give prison such metaphorical meanings, but depicts it as a symbol of political power, questioning the authority who imprisons the subject capriciously in such a way as Foucault suggests. Shakespeare generally presented prisons less politically, or rather ambiguously, but his prison in *Measure for Measure* is an exception. It shares the political aspects with Chettle's works, particularly *Death*, and both plays have similar plots. In *Measure for Measure*, a lustful ruler seeks to seduce a novitiate nun,

5 Catholic Rulers and Downfallen Protestant Prisoners

using his political and religious power, while in *Death*, a lustful king pursues a chaste girl with his power, though she escapes to an abbey and becomes a nun afterwards. However, *Measure for Measure* is more complicated involving a bed-trick and the disguise of the Duke, and treats politics, religion, and law in more complex and serious ways.

Chettle's prisoners are largely innocent and are imprisoned by tyrannical, sometimes lustful, monarchs for their self-interest or displeasure. The offences of the prisoners can be frequently attributed to the displeasure of rulers in Chettle's writings. The prisoners are mostly placed in dark dungeons and described so pathetically that other characters pity them, while the rulers are portrayed as tyrannical, ruthless, selfish, and occasionally lascivious.

The pathos of the prisoner is directly described in the prose romance *Piers Plainness*, where the lustful Duke Rhegius imprisons his enemy Aemilius, the banished prince of Thrace, who happens to land on Crete. The Duke loves his niece, the Queen of Crete, while she and Aemilius love each other. One night, the villainous Duke invites Aemilius for dinner to his castle to kill him, and his servant deceitfully takes Aemilius to "a deep dungeon," a horrible place, "where a day equalled the night in darkenes, only a small glimmering through a cranny in the wall descended" (172); therefore, "Aemilius that knew no reson for this wrong...could not but complaine in that disconsolate place" (172).

In *Hoffman*, the protagonist is villainous and certainly commits a crime, having stolen the skeleton of his father, "a bare anatomy...chain'd vnto the common gallowes" (1.1.174-75), but believing the innocence of his father and himself, he complains about the behavior of the ruling class and his miserable status in a dark dungeon: "My innocent youth as guilty of his sinne, / Was in a dungeon hidden from the sunne, / And there I was condemn'd to endlesse night" (178-80). The miserable conditions in the dungeon are portrayed pathetically, and the petition of the Duchess, Martha, reinforces the pity. Hoffman describes her petition, remarking, "She kneeld and wept for me...Beseeching from that vow I might be freed" (184-85). Consequently, he is set free under his oath that he will never steal again. Hoffman's imprisonment can be seen to suggest the absolute power of the upper class. The rulers can punish the offenders or pardon them at their will. The lives of the subjects depend on the whim of the monarch, and prison is ultimately a symbol of political power rather than a place for correction. Indeed, in spite of his oath, Hoffman steals the bones again, and he remains subversive within the nation.

The pathos of the prisoners described above seems to reflect the general concept of prisons in Elizabethan writings. Prison was thought to be equally miserable as other signs of death such as graves and hell. As John Earle observed in *Microcosmographie* (1628), the Elizabethan prison is:

> ...the grave of living, where they are shut up from the world and their friends; and the worms that gnaw upon them their own thoughts and the jailor. A house of meager looks and ill smells, for lice, drink, tobacco are the compound. Pluto's court was expressed from this fancy; and the persons are much about the same parity that is there (26).[1]

Geoffrey Mynshul follows the idea and categorizes it in *Essays and Characters* (1618; STC 18319): "A prison is a graue to bury men aliue, and a place wherein a man for halfe a yeares experience may learne more law, then hee can at *Westminster* for an hundred pound. It is a Microcosmus, a little world of woe, it is a map of misery...It is a place that hath more diseases predominant in it" (3). The Elizabethan prison was depicted as a much more physically horrible place than the modern prison.

Chettle's prisons are thus political and horrific, but his collaborative plays *Death* and *Sir Thomas Wyatt* are more remarkable in dealing with religious as well as political issues with regard to incarceration. Catholic churchmen and rulers imprison Protestant heroes, wrongly from the standpoint of Protestants. The two works obviously attack Roman Catholics. In short, the prisons in the works are political and religious symbols of the monarchical power. These criticisms against Catholics possibly come from Chettle's anti-Catholic and anti-Jamesian attitudes at a time the succession issue was urgent, and in France, the Huguenot war between Catholics and Protestants had just finished with the Catholic King Henri IV's 1598 Edict of Nantes.

(ii) *The Downfall and Death of Robert, Earl of Huntingdon*
(a) Robin Hood and King John

Chettle's collaborative play, *Death*, describes the fear of prison in the political and religious context. This play is a sequel to *Downfall*, and the two plays, identified as "Robyne Hoode," "Roben Hoode," or "Robert hoode" in *Henslowe's Diary*, were licensed by the Master of Revels in March 1598 (Henslowe 86-88). The title pages of the two plays suggest both of them were published in 1601 and acted by the Admiral's Men. Munday wrote the first play, and Chettle revised both plays for a court performance, while Munday wrote the latter in collaboration with Chettle. Chettle received sums of 10 shillings on 18 and 25 November for revising the two plays for the court performance, which suggests the popularity of the plays, as Jenkins notes (Henslowe 101-02; Jenkins 110). It remains uncertain which sections each writer wrote, though Jenkins confidently attributes the tragedy of Matilda in *Death* to Chettle (133).

Many critics point out that Chettle and Munday's plays were innovative in portraying Robin as an aristocratic, following Richard Grafton; he had been the yeoman in the previous literary tradition.[2] Robin Hood was depicted as a yeoman in the May games, in such earlier works as the fifteenth-century ballads *A Gest of Robin Hode* and *Robin Hood and the Monk*, and in such contemporary plays as Peele's *The Famous Chronicle of Edward I*, the anonymous *George a Greene*, and the lost *Pleasant Pastoral Commedy of Robin Hood and Little John*. In Chettle and Munday's version, Robert changes his name to Robin Hood after escaping to Sherwood while Matilda, the daughter of Lord Fitzwater, changes her name to Marian. This dramatized version had a great influence on later works in the seventeenth century, including Martin Parker's ballad *A True Tale of Robin Hood* and Robert Davenport's play *King John and Matilda*. Unlike the previous yeoman Robin, Chettle and Munday's Robert is conservative and weak rather than subversive and stout (Singman 69-74). Such characters as John and York plot hierarchical disorder, but ordinary people neither usurp political power nor start a riot.

The two plays are, thus, in the Robin Hood tradition, but also come from the legend of Matilda, as well as the history of King John, especially in *Death*, as Donna Hamilton points out (132).³ The plays are rather confusing with mixed elements, and critics have argued over the plays' genre. Richard Helgerson sees the plays as much based on chronicles like the history plays, while Liz Oakley-Brown regards them as tragedies and histories. From the point of views of historical accuracy and King John's major presence the two plays, the works could be called history plays. Moreover, as is often the case with history plays, these works obviously question political and religious injustice (Bevington 295); John's absolutism and tyranny are represented in his overthrowing the Prior of Ely, and the banishment and imprisonment of such innocent people as Robert, Matilda's father, Lord Fitzwater, Lady Bruce, and her youngest son. Similarly, Robert's steward Warman helps the Prior of York outlaw his nephew Robert and becomes the Sheriff of Nottingham as reward, though Warman is banished by John in a later scene. On the other hand, the corrupt monk and abbess try to incite Matilda into sleeping with John, who "will bestowe hundred markes a yeare" to their abbey (2266), though Matilda refuses this request, disparaging them as "false seeming Saints" (2556), as further discussed below.

King John is described as a lustful villain usurper in the plays, which seems to be derived from the widely-known legend of Matilda. This legend can be seen in a sixteenth-century manuscript of the chronicle of Dunmow and also Drayton's *The Legend of Matilda* (Jenkins 119-21). As discussed in Chapter 1, "(iii) Chettle and Publications by Printers Other Than East and

Danter," "(b) Literary Influence from Publications by Printers Other Than East and Danter," Chettle probably was enabled to read the book by the publishers, Nicholas Ling or Busby. On the other hand, Bale and Foxe depicted John as a patriotic Protestant martyr, and their work was followed by the anonymous *Troublesome Raigne of King John*, an undoubted work of propaganda of anti-Catholicism and anti-Spain in the aftermath of the Armada. Shakespeare's *King John* is religiously neutral and deals with succession issues as its central focus. More remarkably, unlike these preceding plays, Chettle and Munday's work neither describes John's conflict with the Pope and the barons, nor his death (Levin 261). Chettle and Munday focus on John after his failure rather than John's challenge and excommunication. In other words, they criticize John for being the pontiff's servant and having offered England and paid tithe every year to the Pope.

(b) Martyrdom of Noble Prisoners: Lady Bruce, Her Son, and Matilda

In *Downfall* and *Death*, John's absolutism and tyranny seem to take the form of his exiling and confining of innocent people, particularly Lady Bruce and her son, and Matilda. In *Downfall*, such ruling class figures as Ely and Warman are banished and imprisoned by John, but their imprisonment is not described, only mentioned. In *Death*, a nobleman, Bruce, refuses to give his son to John, and Lady Bruce and her son are imprisoned in a dungeon in Windsor Castle. When a servant Brand takes them to the dungeon, the lady entreats him, "helpe vs, assist vs Blunt, / We shall be murdred in a dungeon" (Sc.12: 1907-08), and this association of prison with death seems a common idea, as the above quotations of Earle and Mynshul suggest. The mother and son unfortunately starve to death in the dungeon. Young Bruce, the eldest son, fails to rescue them and creates a window in the wall to let people see their dead bodies and know of John's tyranny. A messenger relates this episode to the King:

> That euery one may see the rufull sight,
> In the thick wall he [Young Bruce] a wide windowe makes:
> And as he found them, so he lets them be
> A spectacle to euery commer by,
> That heauen and earth, your tyrant shame may see.
> All people cursing, crying fie vpon
> The tyrant mercilesse, inhumane Iohn. (Sc. 15: 2228-34)

This episode is recorded in Holinshed's *Chronicle*. This is probably the source, and Chettle had a chance to read it through his acquaintance with Bynneman, its printer, as discussed in Chapter 1, "(iii) Chettle and Publications by Printers Other Than East and Danter," "(b) Literary Influence from Publications by Printers Other Than East and Danter."

However, this scene shows John's tyranny more clearly and strongly. It is interesting that "people" recognize John's villainy through the grotesque "spectacle" of dead bodies, including that of a young child. This horrible description is reminiscent of bloody revenge tragedies like *Titus Andronicus*, *Antonio's Revenge*, and particularly *Hoffman*, in which the skeleton of Hoffman's father on the gallows suggests the absolute power of the ruling class demonstrated through public execution, as Foucault discusses. Young Bruce repeatedly relates the story of his mother and brother (Sc. 18: 2737-54; 2866-902). When he explains it to the noblemen on John's side, he ironically asks, "Shall I againe / Set open shop, shew my dead ware"? (2741-45), comparing the dead people to merchandise. Jenkins and Nora Johnson point out the horror of the scene, and Jenkins certainly attributes this scene and Matilda's tragedy to Chettle on the basis of the melodramatic strength of his *Hoffman* (Jenkins 133; Johnson 117).

Moreover, Young Bruce sees their death as martyrdom:

> Had I not reason, thinke you, to make wide
> The windowe that should let so much woe forth?
> Where sits my mother martyrede by her selfe,
> Hoping to saue her childe from martyrdome: (2866-70)

5 Catholic Rulers and Downfallen Protestant Prisoners

This passage indicates the starving mother ate and gave parts of her body to her son, but he would not eat it. Young Bruce goes on to describe their death and praises his younger brother for not having eaten his mother's body and having died "nobly" (2897). The term "martyrdome" (2869) seems to emphasize the innocence of the mother and son and also the injustice of the King, so much that the Elizabethan audience must have pitied them and recognized John's villainy.

As Johnson points out, this martyr plot should be seen as a parallel to Matilda's death (115). Pursued by John, Matilda escapes to an Abbey, where the vicious monk and abbess together with John's servant, Brand, urge her to sleep with him, but she refuses. By John's order, Brand gives Matilda poison, and she acceptingly drinks it and dies. Subsequently, John repents killing her and decides to visit "her tombe, a monthly pilgrimage" (3043), where a verse is engraved on her tomb: "Within this Marble monument, doth lye / Matilda martyrde, for her chastitie" (3047-48).

Matilda is not imprisoned like Lady Bruce and her son, but her escape to the nunnery can be interpreted as a kind of confinement because John's desire drives her there. In other words, she wants to be confined to preserve herself from John. At the time, as Pendry suggests, the church was considered a figurative prison, and possibly so were abbeys (295-98). Likewise, Foucault points out the analogy of the prison with the cloister. Foucault notes authoritative systems to control the subject's body which might be called "disciplines" and "[m]any disciplinary methods had long been in existence—in monasteries, armies, workshops" as well as in prison and school before the seventeenth century (137). With regard to surveillance, Nina Taunton states that panopticism "was already operating at major institutional levels in the literature on war in the 1590s," exemplifying the watchfulness apparent in the Elizabethan army and in *Henry V* (159). The idea of surveillance probably existed at that time, and Matilda's abbey also functions as a prison in which the monk and abbess watch her under the control of King John.

Matilda finds relief temporarily at Dunmow Abbey, but John knows where she is and buys out the monk and abbess with "a hundred markes a yeare" (2266). The monk accepts this offer immediately, counting Matilda as a "[d]eare ware" (2268) and the transaction as "a bargaine" (2269). Matilda and Lady Bruce and her son are depicted in a similar manner as commodities as well as martyrs. As mentioned above, when explaining the death of his mother and brother, Bruce describes them as "dead ware" (2742), using ironical marketplace language, while the monk regards Matilda as "[d]eare ware." However, the important difference is that the clergy are involved in this commercial transaction. They are, thus, closely bound to the King with money. The following tragic comic scene only exposes their corrupt morality, in mockery of the Roman Catholic church, as Carole Levine and Johnson among many other critics suggest (Levine 266; Johnson 117).

The clergy attempt to persuade Matilda in various ways, though in vain. The abbess fervently proclaims that Matilda's lying with John is a trifling matter, and the monk adds a shocking blow, "the sin is veniall: / Considering you yield for charitie, / And by your fall, the Nunnery shall rise" (2518-20). The term "veniall" obviously refers to the Roman Catholic notion of venial sin, and forms the peak of Chettle and Munday's mocking of Catholicism. As a result, Matilda recognizes the true identity of the two religious people and sees "Two damned spirits, in religious weedes, / Attempt to tempt my spotlesse chastitie" (2530-31). The phrases "in religious weedes" are formerly employed by the Prior of York when plotting to poison Robert: "Now for a face of pure hypocrisie: / Sweete murder, cloath thee in religious weedes" (Sc.3: 237-38). The monk, abbess, and Prior are thus described as the same type of Catholic villains in the same "religious weedes," in another condemnation of Catholicism.

Matilda, thus, voluntarily goes to the Abbey; however, it is not a refuge, but a prison where the churchmen work as jailors under the control of John.

In short, the King kills Lady Bruce, her son, and Matilda in prison, which serves as an institution to control and wield power, though he finally repents his wrongdoings that lead to Matilda's death. In the plays, prison is a political and religious symbol representing John's absolute power; even religious sanctuary is controlled by the King, and the clergy also are corrupted and villainous, as his mother Queen Eleanor admits: "Nor Church, nor chappell, Abbey, Nunry, / Are priuileg'd from his intemperance" (Sc.16: 2388-89).

(c) Evils of Roman Catholics

The heartbreaking descriptions of innocent prisoners serve to expose John's cruelty, tyranny, and unjust absolutism, and their deaths can be perceived as a form of martyrdom which reforms John. This martyrdom may be seen as an act of Protestantism since the criticism of Roman Catholicism is resonant everywhere in these plays. John is described by Chettle and Munday as a villain who allies himself with evil Catholic churchmen, though depicted as a patriotic Protestant hero and a victim of the Pope by Bale, Foxe, and the author of *The Troublesome Raigne of King John*. Moreover, Robert's uncle, the Prior of York, is depicted as a villain throughout the two plays. In *Downfall*, he is the mastermind of Robert's downfall plot. The Prior wants to exile Robert to deprive him of his property and outlaws him for debt. In *Death*, the Prior continues to hate Robert and poisons him. The Prior is, in brief, the precise embodiment of evil, and other clerical characters are also villains.

The word, "Rome," is mentioned twice in the plays, each with implications of evil. In *Downfall*, Prince John has two things he desires: usurpation and Matilda. While King Richard is absent on a crusade, the Bishop of Ely governs the state, but John usurps his position and imprisons him in Nottingham. Soon after this incident, John asks Lord Fitzwater to call back his daughter from Sherwood where she lives with Robert and give her to the prince. The Lord, however, asserts that Robert is "her true knight" (Sc. 7:

1172) and "my noble sonne" (1187). John becomes jealous of Robert and attempts to separate them:

> Liuing with him, she liues in vitious state,
> For Huntington is excommunicate:
> And till his debts be paid, by Romes decree,
> It is agreed, absolu'd he can not be:
> And that can neuer be. (1190-94)

The religious word "excommunicate" (1192) suggests that by deposing Ely, John is now at the head of the religious as well as the political world. Hamilton notes the solidarity between the Prior of York and Warman as suggesting the alliance between the church and the state against Robert (130); however, in my view, it is only foreshadowing John's usurpation and government as a religious and political leader. In fact, in the sequel, having legitimately become king, John bribes the monk and abbess, which indicates that he controls the sanctuary. Also, the word "excommunicate" carries a slight sense of irony in view of the historical excommunication of John by the Pope in 1209, something which is never mentioned in *Downfall* and *Death*. In these plays, Robert seems to be a substitute for a heroic Protestant John who opposed Roman Catholics, as seen in Bale and Foxe. Chettle and Munday's John is possibly the King after failing and becoming the Pope's servant.

"Romes decree" (1193) is another religious concept. Hamilton remarks, "A Protestant reading of these lines can again identify the Roman Church as the enemy" (131). These lines truly present Roman Catholicism as the enemy of Protestantism, but at the same time seem to show the close relation between the Roman Catholics and John as evil enemies of Robert.

In *Death*, the Prior of York gives Robert "a pretious drinke" (Sc. 3: 250) of poison to cheer him:

> Vnto your cheere, Ile adde a pretious drinke,

5 Catholic Rulers and Downfallen Protestant Prisoners

>   Of colour rich, and red, sent mee from Rome.
>   There's in it Moly, Syrian Balsamum,
>   Golds rich Elixer: O tis pretious! (250-53)

Regarding this passage, Tracey Hill states that the Prior "is subtly associated with the supposed deceits of Catholicism," and recognizes "[t]he play's casual anti-Catholicism" (60); however, in my opinion, it seems to show "obvious" anti-Catholicism rather than a "casual" prejudice. "Rome" reminds the audience of the intimate relation between the Prior and Roman Catholicism, and the poison sent from Rome significantly suggests that Robin dies as a Protestant martyr to a Catholic trick, as such Protestants as Wyatt, Jane, and Guilford die in *Sir Thomas Wyatt*.[4] Similarly, Queen Eleanor mentions "[t]he beautious garland, sent me out of Spaine" (2398) and offers it to Matilda in praise of her chastity. The relation between Eleanor and Spain is never referred to elsewhere, and it is reminiscent of the relation between English Queen Mary Tudor and the Spanish King Philip I in *Sir Thomas Wyatt*.

This corruption of Roman Catholic clergymen certainly comes from *The Three Ladies of London*, which influenced Chettle very much.[5] Like the Prior of York, a character called "Simony" is strongly tied with Rome, his birthplace, and talks about the corruption of the monks and friars, who are acquainted with English merchants (Sc. 2: 228-42). Moreover, Simony refers to the greediness of the Pope, who used to be pleased to receive the tithe from England during the reign of Mary Tudor (269-84). The play was first performed in the early 1580s and published in 1584 and 1592, but anti-Catholicism continued into the late 1590s, as *Downfall* and *Death* shows.

(d) Religious Conflicts and the Stuart Succession

In the Elizabethan period, such religious issues were critical. Elizabeth often experienced the danger of intrigues or assassinations in such Catholic conspiracies as the Throckmorton Plot and the Babington Plot. Catholics were banned from practicing their religion in England, and some Catholic recusants, such as Edmund Campion and Parsons secretly assembled to organize Jesuit missions, writing a number of pamphlets in defense of their religion for their companions inside and outside of England. The mainstream was, however, anti-Catholic in its views, and there were many anti-Catholic pamphlets including the anonymous *Tarlton's News out of Purgatory* (1590) and *Two Most Strange and Notable Examples* (1591; STC 15704) and Riche's *Greene's News both from Heaven and Hell* (1593), as Clark has discussed (189-90).

Furthermore, as mentioned in Chapter 1 "Chettle as Printer," Munday worked for the state as a writer and intelligence agent. He wrote such anti-Catholic Pamphlets as *A Brief Discourse of the Taking of Edmund Campion*, *A Discovery of Edmund Campion and His Confederates*, and *A Watch-Word to England*. Furthermore, Munday hunted down other priests and other recusants, while working as an intelligencer for Richard Topcliffe and Sir Thomas Heneage (Bergeron 740).[6]

Chettle was not such an active anti-Catholic campaigner, but he probably shared the same Protestant attitudes as his close friend Munday. In his elegy for Elizabeth, *England's Mourning Garment*, Chettle dedicates most of the work to praising the lately deceased Queen, while welcoming King James in only a few pages. To glorify Elizabeth, Chettle traces the beginning of the Tudor period and attacks Mary Tudor and other Catholics like Dr. William Parry, while insisting on the legitimacy of the Church of England. Jacobean writers would later criticize James by hailing Elizabeth, but Chettle had already done this at the point of the King's accession to the throne.[7] Moreover, before devoting himself to writing plays in 1598, Chettle worked for a notorious printer, Danter, as a compositor, while writing pamphlets and fragmentary plays, as discussed earlier. Danter entered two lost ballads *"the Deathe of Sir ROGER WILLIAMS"* on 22 December 1595 and *"England's resolution to beate back the Spaniardes"* (Arber 3: 56). Sir Roger

5 Catholic Rulers and Downfallen Protestant Prisoners

Williams was a Protestant soldier and a close comrade of the Earl of Essex, to whom he had dedicated his influential book on the arts of war, *A Brief Discourse of War* (1590; STC 25732; Hammer, *Polarisation* 51, 239). Danter's first master was Day, who had been imprisoned by Mary Tudor for his Protestantism, and who subsequently published Foxe's *The Book of Martyrs*. Danter also printed the works of the Protestant preacher, Smith, two of which were published while Chettle was Danter's partner. It is unknown whether Chettle was involved in printing the two ballads, but Chettle was certainly part of what might be considered to be a Protestant network of literary persons.

Noticeably, Bevington associates Chettle and Munday's Robert with the third Earl of Huntingdon, Henry Hastings, who received Protestant support as a candidate to become Elizabeth's successor during the 1560s: "the third earl of Huntingdon had been, as a candidate for succession to the throne during the 1560s, the hope of many ardent Protestants fearful of Elizabeth's untimely death" (295). In 1562, Elizabeth contracted smallpox, and Huntingdon became a potential candidate. He was of strong Protestant lineage; his father Francis Hastings supported his relative, Northumberland who promoted the accession of Lady Jane Grey, and like his relative was imprisoned by Queen Mary.[8]

The subject of succession is, indeed, not so central as in *Troublesome Raigne of King John* and Shakespeare's *King John*, but Chettle and Munday's plays depict a potential candidate who could succeed as the next King, Prince John's usurpation and temporary government, and also King John's tyrannical and embarrassing reign. The plays were written five years before James's accession, at which time he was seen as the most likely potential candidate to the throne (P. Williams, *The Later Tudors* 384; Watkins 14). In this political context, Chettle and Munday may have portrayed John as a political ruler, and in *Death*, as a religious ruler, with James in mind.[9] As the King of the Scotland, James claimed a divine right in *The True Law in Free Monarchy* (1598; STC 14409) and *Basilikon Doron* (1599; STC 14348). How much of this aspect of James was known in England is unclear, but the concept itself was most likely known through Jean Bodin's *De Republica* (1576), though an English translation of this work, *The Six Books of a Commonweale*, was not issued until 1606.

James was brought up as a Protestant, but people in England were worried that he would convert to Catholicism, as the French King Henri IV had done. Their anxiety, indeed, continued even after Elizabeth died. Dekker describes the situation immediately after her death during which people were terribly afraid that a similar situation to the French civil war, or the Huguenot war (1562-98) would happen in England (22). Furthermore, James's wife, Anne of Denmark, converted to Catholicism sometime in the 1590s, and this was used by James to obtain the support of the Catholics, while possibly reinforcing people's worries about his accession (Bingham 25, 54-57).

Munday and Chettle's bitter criticism against Roman Catholicism can be read as an implicit attack on James's relations with the Catholic league, whereas the legend of Robin Hood itself represents England's nationalism and patriotism.[10] Contemporary Robin Hood plays such as Peele's *Edward I* and *George a Greene* were patriotic as well, though the heroes were commoners (Knight 117-21). The words "England(s)" and "English" resound throughout the plays, occurring thirty-three times (eighteen in *Downfall* and fifteen in *Death*). More significantly, as John Skelton, who presents the prologue, remarks in the first scene, the plays form a play-within-a play; the plays are supposed to be written for Henry VIII (Hamilton 129). As the plays claim to be intended for court performance, the King could also by Skelton to be performed before "the king" (*Downfall*, Sc.1: 17), a figure accepted to be suggest Elizabeth. The Protestant monarchs loved Robin Hood. Henry VIII disguised himself as Robin Hood and went to the woods for May Day in 1510 and 1515 (Knight 109-10). Elizabeth also did so in 1557 (Ueno, *Robin Hood Monogatari* 74-75). On the other hand, the Catholic Mary Stuart of Scotland forbade the Robin Hood games on May Day. On

5 Catholic Rulers and Downfallen Protestant Prisoners

20 April 1562 at St Andrews, Queen Mary issued a proclamation warning against planning "May Games which: 'vnder colour of Robene Hudis play purpoissis to rais seditione and tumult within our said burgh,'" though the games did not disappear (Fisher 31). François Laroque remarks on the relationship between popular festivals, including May Day, and nationalism:

> Encouraging local festivals and rural traditions was a step toward strengthening national unity...A double reflex of insularity and xenophobia (rather anti-Catholicism) helped to rally the people to the policies of the sovereign and to arouse their animosity against the expansionist and subversive efforts of countries in the pay of the Pope.... (71)

Considering the popularity of Robin Hood and its festive origin, Chettle and Munday's plays express English nationalism, oppose foreign countries, such as France and Spain, mentioned a few times in the texts, and glorify England and the English monarchs, Henry VIII and Elizabeth.[11] *Downfall* and *Death* are, in short, national chronicle plays that aim to build an English identity at a time of crisis with the possibility of a foreign king governing Englishmen.

(iii) *Sir Thomas Wyatt*

(a) Wyatt, Jane, and Guilford as Protestant Martyrs in Their Imprisonment and Execution

Sir Thomas Wyatt was also a collaborative play. According to the title-page, it was acted by the Queen's Majesty's Servants, written by Dekker and Webster, and published in 1607 in a very bad quarto, probably based on memorial reconstruction. This printed text is usually identified with the two parts of *Lady Jane*, though it is presumably a shorter version of the play, produced around October 1602 by Chettle, Dekker, Heywood, and Wentworth Smith, according to *Henslowe's Diary*, though the individual writing parts remain unclear (Henslowe 218; Hoy 311-12; 317-18). The

Queen's Majesty's Servants was formerly Lord Worcester's Men, for whom Henslowe commissioned *Lady Jane*.

Sir Thomas Wyatt focuses on an English soldier Sir Thomas Wyatt and his rebellion against Mary Tudor's marriage with Philip of Spain in 1554, along with other historical events: the Nine Day Queen, Lady Jane Grey's accession and deposition, Mary Tudor's accession, and the execution of Wyatt, Lady Jane, and her husband Guilford Dudley. The play opens at the moment that the Duke of Northumberland has obtained the will of the dying Edward VI confirming the Duke of Suffolk's daughter Jane as his successor, and Lady Jane immediately accedes to the throne. However, the Council proclaims Mary Tudor as queen, as the legitimate heir, and Mary imprisons Jane and Guilford in the Tower. Supporting Jane, Wyatt opposes Queen Mary over her marriage with Philip of Spain, raises an army of Kentish men, and marches through London, but he is captured. The final scene is a series of executions of Wyatt, Jane, and Guilford. Their executions do not occur on stage, but the head of Jane is brought by "the Heades-man" onto stage immediately before Guilford's execution.

As Julia Gasper and Kathleen McLuskie claim, a strong Protestantism is seen in the play. The deaths of the three prisoners, Wyatt, Jane, and Guilford are read by many critics as martyrdoms of innocent Protestants, though the words "martyrdom" or "martyr" never appear in the texts (Bevington 293; Gasper 56). By contrast, Mary's imprisonment and execution of the three seem to emphasize her villainy and adherence to absolutism. At the time of the play's production she was in fact hated vehemently, particularly as Foxe had condemned her bloody persecutions of Protestants in *Acts and Monuments*, known also as *The Book of Martyrs* (Gasper 60). Wyatt's soliloquy in the Tower expounds on his innocence and pessimism, for which the audience would feel sympathy, as noted by McLuskie (40):

> The sad aspect, this prison doth affoord,
> Iumpes with the measure that my heart dooth keepe:

5 Catholic Rulers and Downfallen Protestant Prisoners

> And this inclosure here, of naught but stone,
> Yeildes far more comfort then the stony hearts
> Of them that wrong'd their country, and their friend.
> Heere is no periur'd Counsellors to sweare
> A sacred oath, and then forsweare the same,
> No innovators heere, doth harbor keepe,
> A stedfast silence, doth possesse the place,
> In this the Tower is noble being base. (5.2.1-10)[12]

The Elizabethans usually regarded prison as a horrible place like a grave, as discussed above, but Wyatt ironically finds it comfortable, though he is of course depressed. To him it is almost a refuge, without "the stony hearts / Of them that wrong'd their country, and their friend" (4-5) and "periur'd Counsellors" (6) and "innovators" (9).

Shortly after this, the Bishop of Winchester comes to the Tower to sentence Wyatt to execution by hanging and quartering. Until the end, Wyatt insists on his innocence, though Winchester calls him a traitor; Wyatt asserts "Traitor and *Wyats* name, / Differ as farre as *Winchester* and honor" (14-15) and also "I haue no Bishoppes Rochet to declare / My innocencie, this is my crosse, / That causelesse I must suffer my heads losse" (20-22). Significantly, in the historical sources, Wyatt makes these speeches to his captor, Sir Philip Denie, not Winchester, who was responsible for the deaths of numerous Protestants and is described as wicked in Jacobean history plays. This alteration seems to make the scene represent religious conflicts and underscores Wyatt's patriotism and martyrdom for his Protestant beliefs (Gasper 56). The Bishop of Winchester is portrayed as a merciless villain, who makes Wyatt's death "a sport" (27), or who enjoys his execution, and the description of him as the enemy of Protestantism reminds us of the Prior of York, and the monk and abbess in the Robin Hood plays.

Wyatt's final speeches in the play clearly show his anti-Spanish attitude as well as his anti-Catholicism:

Henry Chettle's Careers: A Study of an Elizabethan Printer, Pamphleteer, Playwright

> Then here's the end of *Wyats* rising vp,
> I to keepe Spaniards from the Land was sworne,
> Right willingly I yeelde my selfe to death,
> ………………………………………………..
> But now King *Phillip* enters through my blood. (32-37)

Wyatt is evidently depicted as a patriot, who dies to save England from Spain, his body being identified with England. The last line is particularly figurative, and it probably suggests England is dying through contamination by Spain.

Jane and Guilford's imprisonment scene is less overtly political and religious than Wyatt's, but shows the worries and sadness of the prisoners. Jane and Guilford are imprisoned separately, awaiting execution and are seen over the course of one morning. They care about their bodies and each other, and Jane deplores life in prison, "My lookes (my loue) is sorted with my heart, / The Sunne himselfe, doth scantly show his face, / Out of this firme grate" (3.2.9-11). This darkness was a typical image of prison, as Lady Bruce also expressed. Guilford gives voice to the fear of prisoners waiting for their death, which reminds us of Earle and Mynshul's description of prison as a grave:

> The nights are teadous, and the daies are sad,
> And see you how the people stand in heaps,
> Each man sad, looking on his aposed obiect,
> As if a generall passion possest them?
> Their eyes doe seeme, as dropping as the Moone,
> As if prepared for a Tragedie. (22-27)

Guilford thus sees other prisoners in a pitiable light, as he describes their suffering, whether their death sentences are just or not. Guilford repeats the meta-theatrical word, "Tragedie" (27), in a later scene, when he and Jane are executed. Guilford sarcastically welcomes Lord Arundell and asks if he has "come…now to see / The blacke conclusion of our Tragedie"

5 Catholic Rulers and Downfallen Protestant Prisoners

(5.2.55-56). These phrases seem to reinforce the central message of the story as well as the innocence of the couple, and the cruelty of Mary and the noblemen on her side.

Although Wyatt and Guilford's executions occur off stage, that of Jane is dramatized on stage; or more accurately, she exits for the execution itself, but her head is brought back onto the stage and shown to Guilford and the audience. Historically, Guilford was first beheaded, and Jane probably watched through the window, but in this play Jane's execution precedes that of Guilford so that Jane's death is pathetically described in her husband's passionate long speeches. If the order of the execution had been reversed, and Guilford's death came earlier than Jane's, the boy actor who played Jane could not speak such long lines and glorify Jane as a martyr. When Winchester executes Jane and maliciously says to Guilford, "Behold her head" (158), Guilford bewails her death, insisting on her innocence which is in contrast to the villainy and mercilessness of the lords:

> Looke *Norfolke*, *Arundell*, *Winchester*,
> Doe malefactors looke thus when they die?
> A ruddie lippe, a cleere reflecting eye,
> Cheekes purer then the Maiden oreant pearle,
> That sprinckles bashfulnes through the clowdes,
> Her innocence, has giuen her this looke: (162-67)

The merciless lords remind us of the noblemen of John's faction, to whom Young Bruce describes the death of his mother and young brother with the commercial metaphor in *Death* (2741-45). Likewise, Jane's pure cheeks which are compared to the "oreant pearle" correspond to Young Bruce's description of his young brother's teeth as "oriental pearle, or snowe-white yuory" (2867). The pearl is employed to represent the purity and innocence of both.

Guilford, thus, reinforces Jane's innocence, blames the lords for their wrongful acts, and asserts that they will meet again in heaven. The tragic love of a young couple like Romeo and Juliet is most resonant in Guilford's phrases: "Though on the earth we part, by aduerse fate, / Our soules shall knock together at heauens gate" (176-77).

The sad story of Jane and Guilford had been already known to the Elizabethan audience through such historical records as Foxe's *The Book of Martyrs*, Grafton's *Chronicle*, Stow's *Annals of England*, and Holinshed's *Chronicle*, and also through such poems as William Warner's *Albions England* and Drayton's *England's Heroical Epistles* (Hoy 312-13). As discussed in Chapter 1, "(iii) Chettle and Publications by Printers Other Than East and Danter," "(b) Literary Influence from Publications by Printers Other Than East and Danter," Chettle was given a chance to read Holinshed and Stow by their printer Bynneman, and also the *Book of Martyrs* by its printer Short. However, despite the historical fact that Wyatt died in the summer of 1553, while Guilford and Jane died in February 1554, the play dramatizes the death of the couple shortly after, or almost at the same time as that of Wyatt, though as already noted, Wyatt's death occurs off stage. This intentional alteration of history seems to link closely together and categorizes them as Protestant martyrs. The couple neither share a scene with Wyatt nor talk with him, and they have been distant from the common people, but the device makes it possible for them to appear sympathetic to the commoners and thus also to the audience. Wyatt's patriotic speech quoted above (5.2.32-37) must have continued to echo at the execution of Jane and Guilford, and highlighted their misfortune.

(b) Criticism against Catholics and Spain: Evils of Mary Tudor and Winchester

The imprisonment and execution of Wyatt, Jane, and Guilford are thus obviously described sympathetically, emphasizing their innocence, Protestantism, and patriotism, which by contrast reinforce the evil of Mary Tudor and the Bishop of Winchester. These two Catholics were particularly abhorred by the Elizabethans (Gasper 56, 60). This play more bitterly

5 Catholic Rulers and Downfallen Protestant Prisoners

and directly criticizes Catholicism and Spain, and more directly supports Protestantism than the Robin Hood plays. Such words as "England(s)" or "English" resound nineteen times throughout the play, while "Spaine," "Spaniard(s)," or "Spanish" occur twenty times, and the antagonism between the two countries is clearly presented.

Before rising against Mary, Wyatt, questioning Philip's foreign nationality, disputes with the Queen over her marriage. Wyatt reproaches Mary for seeking a husband from abroad and views her as base, remarking, "Is shee a beggar, a forsaken Maide, / That she hath neede of grace from forraine princes?" (3.1.81-82). Wyatt is worried that Philip will govern England, though Mary Claims their countries will be ruled by Mary and Philip respectively. Moreover, Wyatt does not want a half-Spanish heir to rule England. Wyatt criticizes her facile decision: "*Spaine* is too farre for *England* to inherit, / But *England* neare enough for *Spaine* to woe" (128-29). To defend herself, Mary asks Wyatt, "Has not the Kinges of *England* (good Sir *Thomas*) / Espous'd the Daughters of our Neighbour Kinges?" (130-31). Wyatt answers:

> I graunt, your predecessors oft haue sought
> Their Queene from *France*, and sometimes to from *Spaine*.
> But neuer could I heare that *England* yet
> Has bin so base, to seeke a King from either: (132-35)

Wyatt clearly shows his antagonism against to the two Catholic countries, as Guilford's father, the Duke of Northumberland, observes:

> I rather ioy
> To thinke vpon our ancient victories
> Against the French and Spaniard, whose high pride
> We leueld with the waues of [B]rittish shore,
> Dying the hauen of *Brit.* with guiltie blood,
> Till all the Harbor seem'd a sanguine pooles: (1.4.11-17)

Wyatt attempts one final argument, claiming "King *Henries* last will…

does prohibit Spaniards from the Land" (3.1.141-43), but Mary threatens him, "Vnto the Crowne of *England* and to vs, / Thy ouer-boldnesse should bee payde with death" (147-48). Mary, a Catholic, thus ignores her father's will and wants to marry Philip, or "a Spaniard, a proud Nation, / Whome naturally our Countrie men abhorre" (161-62), according to Wyatt. As a Catholic, Mary would be seen as a "base" tyrant by the Elizabethan audience as well.

Wyatt's uprising represents Protestantism and patriotism, as do the prison scenes in this work. Being anxious that Englishmen will suffer slavery under Philip's control, Wyatt cries, "Hee that loues freedome and his Countrie, crie / A *Wyat*" (4.1.23-24), and the soldiers cry, "A *Wyat*, a *Wyat*, a *Wyat*" (26). On the other hand, the comical Captain Bret is ordered by the lords of Arundel and Norfolk to suppress Wyatt's rising, but on the way he meets a clown, and they criticize the Spaniards together. They compare the Spanish with "a Dundego," namely "a kinde of Spanish Stockfish, or poore Iohn" (4.2.53), which humorously reminds us of King John, and they worry that if the fish come into England, "they will make vs all smell abhominably" (59). Continuing in his dialogue with the clown to criticize the Spanish, Bret decides to join Wyatt's army, and his soldiers cry Wyatt's name.

(c) *Sir Thomas Wyatt* and the Stuart Succession

In the context of Elizabeth's last years, Mary's accession and marriage to the Spanish King in *Sir Thomas Wyatt* may be identified with James's succession and foreign policy. As discussed above, James was the most likely potential candidate to become Elizabeth's successor, but his mother, another Mary, was Catholic, though James had converted to Protestantism. Mary Tudor of England may have brought to mind Mary Stuart of Scotland, considering the topicality of the succession question. In fact, James reconciled with the Spanish King, Philip III, in 1604, though this rapprochement was not favored by most English people. On the other hand, such

5 Catholic Rulers and Downfallen Protestant Prisoners

militant Protestants as James's son, Prince Henry, adopted an anti-Catholic and anti-Spain policy; such playwrights as Heywood and Dekker among others showed the same attitude and criticized James's pacifism in their works, though Daniel and Jonson devotedly produced court masques praising James for his pacifism.[13] Heywood was such an ardent supporter of the prince's policy that he wrote *A Funeral Elegy upon the Death of Prince Henry* (1613; STC 13323), while writing the two parts of *If You Know Not Me You Know Nobody* which dramatizes Elizabeth's reign, including her imprisonment as a princess, Dr. Parry's plot (1585), and the Armada. Similarly, Dekker described the Armada in *The Whore of Babylon*, including Elizabeth's patriotic speeches at Tilbury. Chettle, prior to these works, criticized Mary Tudor and the Catholic intrigues including that of Dr. Parry, and praised the victory over the Armada and Elizabeth at Tilbury in *England's Mourning Garment* (95, 105). These three writers thus denounced James by glorifying Elizabeth, and their anti-Catholic and anti-Spanish attitudes had been constant since *Lady Jane*, or *Sir Thomas Wyatt*.[14]

Furthermore, as many critics point out, Wyatt may be seen as representing the second Earl of Essex (Bevington 292; Gasper 44-61; McLuskie 40-41; Heinemann, "Political Drama" 197). Essex was a noble Protestant soldier like Wyatt; he rose against the Queen and marched through London, but failed and was executed as a traitor. Although Essex committed capital treason, many people deplored his death. His popularity lasted even into the Jacobean period, and he was glorified and consecrated in many plays (Heinemann, "Political Drama" 188-89). The situation of Wyatt rising against a monarch is, thus, very similar to Essex's, though Wyatt's riot seems to be more religious and patriotic.

The succession question leading to the conflict between the Catholics and Protestants is the most significant theme of the play, and the prison scenes, which occur in the latter part of the play, serve to reinforce the evil of the Catholics and the innocence of the Protestants. Bevington observes it is debatable whether the play objects to the succession of such foreign princes as James, but that the Spanish succession is primarily questioned (292). The Spanish succession alludes to the possibility of the Spanish Infanta, a daughter of Philip II, could succeed Elizabeth; she was supported by Parsons and William Cecil among others, though the Essex faction publicly rejected this claim. However, by late 1602 when the play was produced, the possibility of the Spanish Infanta's succession was most likely superseded by a more likely candidate, James, as Elizabeth's godson Sir John Harrington of Kelston urged James's succession (P. Williams, *The Later Tudors* 384-85).

Chettle expressed his negative feelings against Catholicism and James in *England's Mourning Garment*. In the first half of the first part of this pamphlet, Chettle looks back on the early Elizabethan period, and criticizes Catholics, particularly Mary Tudor and Spain; he recounts the intrigues against Elizabeth by Spanish Catholics and Irish rebellions supported by Spain (86-91). Chettle observes that Elizabeth was actually "much pittied" by people shortly after her accession because "that busie slander and respectlesse enuy had not long before brought her into the disfauour of her royall Sister *Mary*" (86). These criticisms imply Chettle's hostility to Catholicism.

This hostility is also expressed in the latter half of the first part. Chettle asserts that Elizabeth "established the true Catholicke and Apostolicall Religion in this Land," and criticizes Roman Catholics, who "condemned her sacred gouernement for Antichristian, when, to the amazement of superstitious Romanes, & selfe-praysing Sectuaries, God approued hir faith by his loue towards her" (100). Furthermore, Chettle claims through the voice of Collin, "I was borne and brought vp in the Religion profest by that most Christian Princesse *Elizabeth*" (100). Thus, Chettle opposes the Catholic and the Puritan separatists ("Sectuaries") and displays his Anglican feelings strongly.

James's unpopularity, as described by Heywood, Dekker and others, already became evident in the late Elizabethan period. Chettle expressed his skepticism toward James as early as his accession in *England's Mourn-*

5 Catholic Rulers and Downfallen Protestant Prisoners

ing Garment. A militant Protestant, Chettle, hopes James will follow Elizabeth's foreign policy, particularly toward Spain. Chettle praises her "[a]ct of Charitie extended to her neighbours: whom shee hath by her bountie deliuered from the tyrannie of oppression" (93), and refers to her support for "the low Countries" (94). After criticizing Roman Catholics, Chettle praises Elizabeth's charity again:

> As I first mentioned touching her Charitie, which was still so tempered, not withstanding, her great charge in aiding her distressed neighbours, that she was euer truly liberall, and no way prodigall: as I trust his Royall Maiestie shall by the treasure finde. (103)

Similarly, he wants James to follow Elizabeth's support for a strong navy:

> For such tenants made she many buildings, exceeding any Emperors Nauy in the earth, whose seruice I doubt not will be acceptable to her most worthy Successor, our dread Soueraigne Lord and King. (104)

The Spanish marriage described in the play alludes to the reconciliation between England and Spain, as peace was frequently expressed in the form of marriage in Jacobean court masques. James actually called for and carried out this reconciliation. Such militant Protestants as Chettle feared the reconciliation between England and Spain and also the spread of Catholicism into England, since it could lead to a repetition of the persecution of Protestants, that "Bloody" Mary Tudor had instigated: whether or not this became reality depended on the monarch.

*

The prisons in *Downfall, Death*, and *Sir Thomas Wyatt* are, thus, symbols of religious and political repression and also places for detention before execution, or graves, as Earle and Mynshul remarked, rather than places for correction. These prisons saw the unjust death of the innocent characters or martyrs, from the point of view of Protestantism. The lengthy, poetic depiction of the noble martyrs, as given by Young Bruce and Guilford Dudley, reinforced their innocence and misfortune and probably evoked strong emotional responses from the audience. On the other hand, the plays criticize the tyrannous monarchs, closely tied with Catholicism, for imprisoning innocent people mercilessly.

Although Matilda is not actually imprisoned, her escape to the abbey may be considered another form of imprisonment because she can no longer live in the outside world, and the abbey with the corrupt clergy as the jailer finally becomes her grave. The three history plays, thus, criticize Catholicism through representations of the vicious King or Queen and mirror the people's anxiety over social upheaval in the reign of the next monarch, who will probably be James. As the Huguenot civil war in France, which ended in 1598, became a warning example, Elizabethans anticipated such a civil war involving Catholics and also the persecution of Protestants. James was brought up a Protestant, but the monarch's religion could be temporary, as the example of French King Henri IV showed.

In the three plays, as in *Hoffman*, the question of the succession is the significant concern. Indeed, the succession had been questioned in such plays as Thomas Sackville and Thomas Norton's *Gorboduc* when it was at stake, particularly in the 1560s when Elizabeth contracted smallpox, while Mary, Queen of Scotland, married Darnley in 1565, and gave birth to James in the following year (Axton 38-60). The three history plays—*Downfall, Death,* and *Sir Thomas Wyatt*—are patriotic plays reflecting anxiety about a potential Catholic monarch like James among the Protestants and also the reconciliation between England and Spain. In 1602 the issue was so urgent and critical that *Sir Thomas Wyatt* more directly than the Robin Hood plays reflected the common anxiety over the succession, through Mary's marriage to Philip II and persecution of Protestants. In these plays, the prisons are described as symbols of political and religious power, and the sympathetic portrayal of the innocent prisoners emphasizes the evil of the monarchs

5 Catholic Rulers and Downfallen Protestant Prisoners

linked to Catholic powers.

As discussed at the end of Chapter 4 "Power Struggles in *The Tragedy of Hoffman* and Elizabethan Social Upheavals," Chettle's attitude toward Elizabeth is ambivalent. As far as *England's Mourning Garment* is considered, Chettle seems to praise Elizabeth, but at the same time he sympathetically describes Essex-like characters, such as Robert and Wyatt. However, it is certain that Chettle preferred Elizabeth to the foreign King, James. Through his experience as a printer in his early career, Chettle could perceive the tide of the times easily and know the feelings of ordinary people. In a short, he wrote plays for money rather than his political and religious creed, as did his contemporaries. The three works were more low-brow and less poetic than Shakespeare's plays, and reveal to us more explicitly some parts of the social fabric of the late Elizabethan period.

Notes

1 The quotation follows Harold Osborne's edition.
2 For a summary of the literary and historical background of Robin Hood, see Oakley-Brown 113-14. For details, see Holt and Knight.
3 The full title-page of *Death* refers to the legend of Matilda: "THE DEATH OF ROBERT, EARL OF HVNTINGTON. OTHERWISE CALLED Robin Hood of merrie Sherwodde: with the lamentable Tragedie of chaste MATILDA, his faire maid MARIAN, poysoned at Dunmowe by King IOHN."
4 See below, "(iii) *Sir Thomas Wyatt*" in this chapter.
5 See Chapter 1, "(ii) Chettle and John Danter," "(c) Literary Influence from Danter's Publications between 1591 and 1598."
6 Hamilton sees Munday as a hidden Catholic, but the idea does not seem persuasive, considering the Protestantism shown in his works (xv-xix).
7 For further discussion on Chettle's anti-Catholic and anti-Stuart attitudes, see Chapter 4, "(iii) Succession," "(b) *Hoffman* and the Stuart Succession."
8 The title of the Robin Hood plays "*Robert, Earl of Huntingdon*" seems to echo Peele's poetry work, *An Eclogue...to...Robert Earl of Essex* (1589), which Chettle probably read, and based on the date of the production of the plays, Essex seems to be more closely associated to Robert than Huntington, though there is no definite evidence.

[9] Chettle implicitly alludes to James and his succession as a foreign king in *Hoffman*. See Chapter 6, "(iii) Succession," "(b) *Hoffman* and the Stuart Succession."
[10] For Elizabethan nationalism, see McEachern and Baker.
[11] For the popularity of Robin Hood in Elizabethan England, see Laroque 37-41.
[12] All quotations from *Sir Thomas Wyatt* follow Bower's edition, *The Dramatic Works of Thomas Dekker*, vol.1.
[13] For the details of the pacifism of James and Jacobean drama, see Honda 1-17.
[14] Jacobean playwrights often honored Elizabeth as a means to disregard James. See C. Hill, *Writing* 57; P. Williams, *Later Tudors* 388.

Part III Society: Soldiers, Pirates, Beggars

6 *Hoffman* and Elizabethan Military Culture

(i) Elizabethan Military Background

Throughout the reign of Elizabeth, England struggled with military matters, in particular, conflict with Catholic powers. After Mary, Queen of Scotland, was executed in 1587 on suspicion of conspiracy against Elizabeth, the conflict between England and Spain grew intense. In 1581, the Netherlands declared their independence from the rule of the Spanish Hapsburg family (Oath of Abjuration or *Plakkaat van Verlatinghe*), and in 1585 Antwerp was invaded by the Spanish army. In the same year, Elizabeth decided to support the Netherlands and dispatched 4,000 troops to relieve Antwerp from the threat of a Spanish invasion. Also, she promised to provide £126,000 a year, until the end of the war, to maintain the English force (P. Williams, *The Later Tudors* 305-06). In 1588, the Spanish Armada attacked England for its support of the Dutch independence, but failed. In the following decades, England strived to suppress the Irish rebellion led by Hugh O'Neill, the Second Earl of Tyrone, who was a magnate supported by the Spaniards. The conflict between England and Spain, thus, did not end until the Treaty of London was signed in 1604 between James I and Philip III of Spain.

The victory over the Spanish Armada in 1588 eventually led England to prosperity, but the prospect of open war with Spain did not dissipate until the accession of James. People were still afraid of a Spanish counterattack and rumors about Spanish invasions frequently spread. In February 1593, another Spanish invasion was "credibly advertised," and in 1595,

Henry Chettle's Careers: A Study of an Elizabethan Printer, Pamphleteer, Playwright

Camden stated that "rumors were now abroad, and those not slight or uncertain, but unanimously brought from all parts of *Europe*, that the *Spaniards* were ready to set Sail with a stronger and better appointed Armada than before for the Conquest of *England*" (*Acts of the Privy Council of England* 1: 53; Camden 496-97).

In the 1590s, the continuing military problems with Spain, the Low Countries, and particularly Ireland required an increasing number of common soldiers. All healthy men between sixteen and sixty were to be recruited for military service and they were to be dispatched to fight in foreign as well as domestic conflicts (Cruickshank 23).

People's consciousness of an urgent need to be prepared for warfare is reflected in the large number of military books printed at the time. Elizabethan military books were originally based on the classics to provide instruction on the art of war by veterans, who had served on the Continent. The large number of such titles recorded in Cockle's *A Bibliography of Military Books up to 1642* suggests how conscious people were of war issues.

Most of these were educational books, dealing with the art of war to prepare for a Spanish invasion, written by returning soldiers from the Continental front: for example, Riche, Thomas Digges, Sir Roger Williams, Sir John Smythe, Humphrey Barwick, and Matthew Sutcliffe, all of whom were veterans of the wars in Holland and France.

In discussing the art of war, writers proposed various practical measures; for example, on weapons, Williams and Barwick insisted on the efficacy of guns, while Smythe argued for a reliance on longbows, as did Henry Knyvett, both a soldier and a member of parliament. The debate had continued since the 1540s, as part of a "military revolution" in England, and subsequently the supremacy of gunnery had been accepted by the beginning of the 1600s.[1]

The Elizabethan Age witnessed foreign wars in Spain, France, and the Low Countries as well as domestic ones in Ireland, while the church and some humanists criticized war and the military for actions against the laws of God. In the early Christian church, there had been a pacifist tradition, and war was condemned for killing people; however, Saint Augustine had defined the doctrine of a just war, in which war was to be accepted when the cause was "just." This idea was followed by Renaissance churchmen. For example, in *A Treatise* (1549), Bullinger declared that "all though it be lawfull for the Magistrates to kepe warr for iust and necessary causes, yet is warre a most daungerous thig [thing] and bringeth with it hepes of infinite troubles" (STC 4079; A8v). In *The Trumpet of War* (1598), Stephen Gosson claimed, "As warre must have a just title to make it lawful, so it must also be undertaken by lawfull authoritie" (STC 12099; B8r).

The theory of war became increasingly secularized, however, under the influence of Machiavelli, and a division emerged among humanist writings on war in the Renaissance period: Erasmus, Sir Thomas More, and Castiglione insisted on pacifism, whereas Caxton, Machiavelli, and Guicciardini supported the just war theory.[2] For example, Erasmus claimed Christian kings should be pacifists in *The Complaint of Peace* (1559; STC 10466): "Yf we shuld principally wyshe vnto a good prince...he must nedes detest warre, where outeflo with the pumpe of all impietie" (F1r). Machiavelli, on the other hand, insisted the prince should be a soldier and the subject must obey his command in *The Art of War* (1562; STC 17164): "the menne, which are conducted to warfarre, by commaundement of their Prince, they ought to come, neither altogether forced, nor altogether willingly" (D1r).

On the other hand, many from the nobility, such as Sidney and Essex, inspired by chivalric Protestantism, proclaimed the necessity of the war to defend their nation and religion, particularly against their great enemy Spain, and warned that peace corrupts the state. Essex asserted in *An Apology of the Earl of Essex* (1603; STC 6788): "Now it is no time to make peace with the chiefe enemie [Spain] of our Religion, when a conspiracy is in hand against al the professors of it" (F1v-2r). He also emphasized the danger of peaceful conditions, stating that "our nation growen generally vnwarlike; in loue with the name, and bewitched with the delights of peace:

and the Spaniardes corage recouered, together with his strength; which is the naturall roote of all true confidence" (F3r).

Military veterans held similar opinions. Riche argued in *Alarm to England* (1578; STC 20979): "although that peace be chiefly to be desired, yet many times by entring into warres it is the more safely & quietly maintayned" (A3v). In *The Defense of Military Profession* (1579; STC 11684), Gates regarded "peace" as a situation in which people "may wax rotten in idlenesse, and become of dulle wittes, slowe of courage, weake hanged, and feeble kneede," and warned his nation not to delight in peace (20). On the other hand, King James I and William Cecil were pacifists, believing that God would punish the enemy, and that war would only lead to ruin. As a consequence of James's pacifist policy, England and Spain reconciled with the Treaty of London in 1604.

In the Jacobean Age, some defended the necessity of wars against the pacifism of King James. On his accession, Sir Walter Raleigh recommended James to maintain British hostility against Spain, while in *Four Paradoxes* (1604; STC 6872), Thomas and Dudley Digges claimed, "warre sometimes lesse hurtfull, and more to be wisht in a well gouernd State than peace" in *Four Paradoxes* (96).[3] On the other hand, Sir Henry Nevil claimed "the Kingdom generally wishes this peace broken, but *Jacobus Pacificus* [James] I believe will scarce incline to that side" (Nichols 2: 50).

It appears that the pro-war view was dominant at this time, and a large number of military books suggest this general concern. Moreover, the popular consciousness of war is also reflected in late Tudor and early Stuart plays, especially in the genres of history. War is the main theme in Marlowe's *Tamburlaine the Great*, Shakespeare's *Henry V*, which is the most patriotic among his other English history plays and notable for its allusions to the campaigns of Essex in Ireland, Chapman's *Caesar and Pompey* and *The Conspiracy and the Tragedy of Charles Duke of Byron*.[4] Tragedies, including revenge tragedies such as *Hoffman*, also deal with warfare; for example, *The Spanish Tragedy*, *The Jew of Malta*, *Antonio's Revenge*, *Titus Andronicus*, *Julius*

Caesar, *Hamlet*, and *Othello*, a play which contains a great deal of reference to the arts of war, and the role of soldiers.

Specific campaigns are frequently alluded to in these dramas. The triumph of the Battle of Agincourt, which occurred in 1415, was described in the anonymous *The Famous Victories of Henry the Fifth*, *The Shoemaker's Holiday* written by Dekker, *The Life of Sir John Oldcastle* by Munday, Drayton, Richard Hathway, and Robert Wilson, Shakespeare's *Henry V* and the anonymous *Trial of Chivalry*. The victory of Sir Francis Vere at Turnhout in 1598 was dramatized in the anonymous *A Larum for London* and the anonymous lost play *Turnholt*.

The French Wars of Religion also provided topics for drama. These civil wars had started in 1562 and ended in 1598 with the Edict of Nantes between the Catholics supported by Spain and the Huguenots supported by England. English people were so interested in the French wars of Religion that the wars were dramatized on London stages. The most terrible single event, the St. Bartholomew's Day Massacre (1572), was represented in *The Massacre at Paris*.

On the other hand, the danger of peace and the need to be ready for war, as advocated by such military writers as Riche and Gates, were suggested in Wilson's *The Cobbler's Prophecy*, printed in 1594 by Danter, and the anonymous *A Larum for London*.[5]

The subject of war has not been adequately discussed in criticism of Renaissance drama, even though, as I have shown briefly, many plays deal with military issues. People's concerns about war can be thought to be reflected in such a large number of military books and plays. Moreover, as I will now go on to discuss, the problems of soldiers as described in *Hoffman* are also referred to in several of these prose and dramatic works.

(ii) Problems of Soldiers

(a) Captain's Exploitation and Poverty of Common Soldiers

"Poor soldiers" are mentioned twice in *Hoffman*, as discussed below, and familiar figures in contemporary plays. The words, including variants such as "pore souldier" or "poore souldiers," are mentioned thirty times in twenty-five other Elizabethan and Jacobean plays ioncluding the anonymous *The Contention between Liberalty and Prodigality*, *The Life of Sir John Oldcastle* by Munday, Drayton, Richard Hathway, and Robert Wilson, *Bussy D'Ambois* and *The Widow's Tears* by Chapman, *The Royal King, and Loyal Subject* by Heywood, *The Roaring Girl* by Middleton and Dekker, *Henry V* and *Cymbeline* by Shakespeare. For instance, in *The Contention between Liberalty and Prodigality* (1602; STC 5593), when a suitor entreats Liberality, a steward of Virtue, for money, he calls himself "a poore souldier."

> 3 SUITOR. Now, good my Lord, vouchsafe of your charitie,
> To cast here aside your pittifull eye,
> Upon a poore souldier, naked and needy,
> That in the Queenes warres was maimed, as you see.
> LIBERALITY. Where haue you serued?
> 3 SUITOR. In Fraunce, in Flaunders, but in Ireland most. (F2v)

The suitor has served as a soldier, mainly in Ireland, which suggests a reference to the Irish conflicts in the Elizabethan period (Somogyi 18), and he is now poor, unclothed, and lame, which was true of many veterans in Elizabethan society. His petition is accepted, and he is finally given money.

To take another example, in *The Life of Sir John Oldcastle*, "foure poore people, some soldiers, some old men" come to an outer court before the house of Sir John Oldcastle, Lord Cobham. One of them complains about a lack of almshouses:

> God helpe, God helpe, there's law for punishing,

> But there's no law for our necessity:
> There be more stockes to set poore soldiers in,
> Than there be houses to releeue them at. (B3v)

Each of them insists on their miserable state; poor, lame, and starving. Lord Cobham finally accepts their petitions and helps them in the court.

These descriptions of poor soldiers can be thought to reflect social situation. According to *The Description of England* by the historian and topographer, William Harrison, there were three sorts of poor people in those days; first, such helpless people as fatherless children, or aged, blind, lame, and diseased persons; second, such people suffering from casualties as wounded soldiers; third, such idle people as vagabonds, rogues and strumpets. The first and second, namely the aged, and the sick and wounded soldiers were regarded as the true poor, while the third were counted as false. Wounded soldiers included "[r]ufflers," who pretended to be lame and begged for money, but mostly such poor soldiers really suffered from poverty, and also they were in fact ill-treated by captains or the socially privileged (Book II, Ch. X, 213, 218).[6]

According to A. L. Beier, sailors and soldiers were the occupational groups showing the largest increase in vagrancy during the period from 1560 to 1640. Before 1580, the number of soldiers and sailors who became vagrant was 1.5%, but from 1620 to 1640, this figure grew to 12% (Beier 93, 224). Most of the wounded soldiers returning from war found no job, and thus they were forced to beg. Although there were three statutes of relief for returning veterans and maimed soldiers (1593, 1597, 1601), these measures did not work efficiently because of their rudimentary nature.[7] Many veterans complained about their status. For example, in the early 1590s, Matthew Sutcliffe, an old soldier claimed in *The Practice, Proceedings, and Laws of Arms* (1593; STC 23468): "Warres in our times being ended ... are the beginning of beggarrie and calamitie to many poore souldiers" (298-99). On the other hand, in the mid 1590s, Thomas Churchyard, the writer and soldier, complained in *A Pleasant Discourse of Court and Wars* (1596; 5249) about the neglect of veterans who had once been rewarded: in former times, "Kings gaue them [soldiers] grace, and honor great, / Fame sounded trumpet in their praise, / World placst them in the highest seate, / So that like gods they raigned those daies," but these days, "When Kings forget to giue good turns / For good desarts: then soldier shrinks, / The lampe of loue, but dimly burns" (B3v-4r).

Moreover, these veterans are described in late Elizabethan and early Stuart plays, which show their continual miserable status despite the three acts of relief for maimed and old soldiers, and the accession of the pacifist King James (Somogyi 12-13). Maimed soldiers are familiar figures, and they appear, as we have seen, in *The Contention between Liberality and Prodigality* and *The Life of Sir John Oldcastle*. Other examples appear in Shakespeare's histories, *Edward I*, *A Larum for London*, *The Trial of Chivalry*, *The Cobbler's Prophecy*, *The Shoemaker's Holiday*, and *If This Be Not a Good Play, the Devil Is in It* among others.

The economic plight of veterans is often suggested in these plays. Falstaff himself plans to gain a pension, asserting that "'Tis no matter if I do halt; I have the wars for my colour, and my pension shall seem the more reasonable" (*2 Henry IV*, 1.2.247-48), while he predicts the fates of survivors of his company after war, stating that "there's not three of my hundred and fifty left alive, and they are for the town's end, to beg during life" (*1 Henry IV*, 5.3.36-38).

Exploitation of soldiers by captains was another reason for the increase of poverty amongst veterans. Smythe criticized captains in *Certain Discourses* (1590; STC 22883). He says, regarding their apparel, "Captaines themselues verie gallant in apparel, and their purses full of gold; that their Soldiers should be in such poore and miserable estate;" food, "some of our such men of warre vpon their occasions of marches and enterprises, haue prouided plentie of victuall onlie for themselues and their followers, suffering their bands & regiments to straggle, & spoyle the people of the Countrie of tentimes to their own mischiefe, & in the rest to take starue, their aduentures and sometimes to starue, or at least to be driuen to great exremitie of hunger;" weaponry "for powder, shot, and ouerplus of weapons, they haue prouided no more than that which their soldiers haue carried about them, which haue been with great scarcity; which doth argue their small care of the health & safetie of their soldiers, & their little intention to doo any great hurt to the ememie, and there withal a great ignorance in the Art and Science Militarie" (iii, 1).

Thus, captains were rich and self-interested, while soldiers were vulnerable, "naked and needy" (*The Contention between Liberality and Prodigality*, F2 v). Also, with regard to monetary payment, the behavior of captains was even worse. Soldiers were supposed to receive half of their payment per week and the other half every six months from the captains. Their weekly wages were too low to buy food, clothes, gunpowder, and other things, as Smythe points out. Captains not only exploited their men financially, but also killed or sent off soldiers to dangerous areas in order to rob them of payment: this payment for dead soldiers was called "dead pay."

Smythe also discusses "dead pay": captains were supposed to "preserue by all meanes possible the liues of their soldiers"; nevertheless, they sent their soldiers to "manie daungerous and vaine exploites and seruices, without any reason Militarie, hauing sure regard to their owne safetiness; as though they desired and hoped to haue more gaine and profite by the dead paies of their souldiers slaine, than encrease of reputation by the atchieuing and preuailing in anie such enterprises."[8]

This pervasive and notorious corruption of captains is also alluded to by Shakespeare in *2 King Henry VI*. York suspects that Gloucester has received bribes and robbed soldiers of their payment, saying "'Tis thought, my lord, that you took bribes of France, / And, being Protector, stayed the soldier's pay, / By means whereof his highness hath lost France" (3.1.104-06).

Many people sympathized with these poor soldiers. In *Faults Faults, and Nothing Else But Faults.* (1606; STC 20983), Riche pitied "a poore man" who "hath spent his bloud in the defence of his Country," and who "being returned home, hurt, maimed, lamed, dismembered and should be suffered to crouch, to creepe, to begge, and to intreate for a peece of bread, and almost no body giue it him." Riche, therefore, hoped that these people would be relieved (M4r). Cecil emphasized the importance of relief for wounded soldiers, stating "I have seen soldiers deceived by their captains," and "A captain is a man of note, and able to keep himself; but a soldier is not" (Townshend 307).

The problems of these poor soldiers sometimes resulted in mutiny, riot and social unrest. Such violent unrest was usually due to lack of payment (Cruikshank 168; Beier 94; Philips 329). For instance, in 1589, a band of 500 veterans, who had returned from the expedition to Portugal, threatened to loot Bartholomew Fair (Judges xvii-xviii). The government suppressed this mutiny, but similar events occasionally re-occurred until 1604 (Beier 94).

In Dublin in 1590, a mutiny over pay arrears took place; the soldiers "made no submission nor show of their ordinary duty," and one of them threatened the Lord Deputy, Sir William Fizwilliam, with his musket. Subsequently, the mutiny was resolved, and the Deputy was moved by "the pitiful complaints of the poor unclothed soldiers, footmen" (*Calendar of the State Papers, Ireland* 4: 51).

Sir John Norris, an able soldier, reported the miserable conditions and complaints of soldiers in Ireland to Cecil by mail in 1595:

> there cometh daily such pitiful complaints from the borders of the misery of the soldiers, who have neither money, victuals, nor clothes, as no man but hath compassion thereof, and the fruit will be the overthrow of the services; for the soldier growth into desperate terms, and spare not to say their officers, that they will run away and steal rather than famish (*Calendar of State Papers, Ireland* 5: 356-57).

Such military problems were particularly serious in the late-Tudor period, when English armies were fighting in Ireland, the Netherlands, and France among other countries. After the Armada, England achieved a degree of naval supremacy, but their prosperity did not last; and war expenditure helped to contribute to the economic plight of unemployment and inflation. Thus, war gave jobs to people, but once the campaign was over, returning wounded, they could not find jobs and many wandered in the street as beggars.

(b) Veterans in Chettle's Works

The main plot of *Hoffman* is the revenge of the protagonist, Hoffman for his father, who has been executed for piracy before the play begins, as discussed in Chapter 4 "Power struggles in *The Tragedy of Hoffman* and Elizabethan Social Upheavals" and other chapters. The poor status of Hoffman is described in contrast with the aristocrats, but the poverty of soldiers in general seems to be emphasized even more strongly in this play.

The term "poor soldiers" appears twice in *Hoffman*. It is first mentioned by the protagonist Hoffman, when he praises the feats of his deceased father as admiral, complaining that he was banished for debt in spite of having gained and offered spoils to his rulers, and "payd poore souldiors from his treasury" (1.1.160). Hoffman here complains about arbitrary and ungrateful rulers, who have used his father, and at the same time he refers to social inequalities and injustice: the poor status of soldiers and the wealth of cunning monarchs. Such poverty was one of the most pressing problems of the Elizabethan period, as enactments of Poor Relief suggest, and most returning soldiers were poor because they could not find employment, as discussed above. Their poor conditions were well-known and pitiable.

The term recurs in the stage direction of Act III Scene ii, where a rebellion is instigated against a Duke by citizen soldiers: "*Enter Stilt, a rabble of poore souldiers: old Stilt his father, with his scarfe like a Captaine. A scuruy march.*" An idiot prince, Jerome, rebels against his father, the Duke of Prussia, because Prussia has disinherited him for his foolishness and adopted his favorite nephew, Otho, in reality, the disguised Hoffman, as his successor. Jerome's uprising involves civil soldiers supporting him as the true heir and evolves into civil war.

Stilt is a servant of Jerome, who is regarded by the common people as the most suitable heir and who has rebelled against their Duke. As quoted in Chapter 4, "(iii) Succession," Stilt asserts that "wee' l / haue a Prince of our owne chusing, *Prince Ierome*," and his father and "noble, ancient Captaine *Stilt*" (1156) counsels Prussia, "let your owne flesh and blood bee inherited of your Dukedome, and a stranger displac'd in his retority [territory]." In contrast with this rabble, Prussia with his magnificent army arrives to suppress them; the stage direction declares "*Enter with Drum, and Colours, Duke Ferdinand [Prussia], Hoffman [,] Lorrique, Captaiue [sic] to leade the drum, the souldiers march and make a stand; All on Ierome side cast up their caps and cry a Ierome*" (1185-89). The rebels make a poor impression militarily, while the Duke's army makes a rich impression with drum and military standards. The Duke scorns the common traitors and orders his "valiant gentlemen" to attack them, in a discriminatory and arrogant speech;

> Vpon those traytors valiant gentlemen:
> Let not that beast the multitude confront,
> With garlicke-breath and their confnsed [confused] cries
> The Maiesty of me their awfull Duke,
> Strike their Typhoean body downe to fire
> That dare 'gainst vs, their soueraigne conspire. (1189-94)

According to Jowett, the editor of a modern-spelling edition, "garlicke" (1191) was a food for poor people in the Elizabethan Age (36); therefore, the lines "Let not that beast the multitude confront, / With garlicke-breath and their confnsed [confused] cries" (1190-91) indicate that the Duke sneers at the poor living conditions of the common soldier. Moreover, Prussia calls himself loftily "maiesty of me their awfull Duke"(1193) and "vs, their soueraigne" (1194) and disdains "that beast the multitude" (1190). The class distinction in these lines seems to increase the emphasis on the poor conditions of commoners.

In the same scene, the character of Old Stilt, a sixty-seven year-old military veteran, is noteworthy. Fibs, the citizen soldier, calls Old Stilt "noble, ancient Captaine" (1156) and praises him, stating:

> ye haue remou'd mens hearts I haue heard that of my father (God rest his soule,) when yee were but one of the common all souldiers that seru'd old *Sarloys* [Hoffman's father] in Norway. (1156-59)

Old Stilt served Hoffman's father and he seems to have been a good soldier, but the times have changed, and he is now a captain of a poor army in rebellion against his monarch, supporting the idiot son's claim as being the true heir. He is one of the poor multitudes who eat "garlicke" (1191). His miserable circumstances can be thought to reflect the problem of veterans: he is poor and has complaints about the Duke, and then finally rebels against him, which reminds us of the mutinies caused by veterans in the real Elizabethan world.

Furthermore, though the term as such is not used, Hoffman's dying words seem to remind us of poor soldiers again. He criticizes those who "wring the poore, and eate the people vp" (5.2.2614) and "haue rob'd souldiers of / Reward" (2617-18); in other words, he attacks those at the top of the social hierarchy who exploit soldiers and those beneath them. Hoffman criticizes those like the Dukes, who extort and exploit the common people, and who have deprived the ordinary soldiers of their pay and other benefits. These phrases seem to suggest the complaint of the author against magistrates and officers, who take personal advantage from their service, as Brucher asserts (220).

Officers are again attacked as cunning intermediary agents in *England's Mourning Garment*, where Chettle criticizes them through the voice of Collin, a shepherd and a narrator in this work:

> ...base Ministers, and vnder officers, curtall [curtail] the liberalities of great and potent masters. Some haue in her [Elizabeth's] time beene taken with the man-

ner, and, besides bodily punishment and fines, displaced.... (93)

According to Chettle, some ministers and officers wronged their subjects against the wills of their masters. When such wrongs were revealed, they were punished with forfeit or dismissal, and "[m]any such false ones she [Elizabeth] hath punished with death" (93).

Chettle, thus, clearly describes poor soldiers with considerable sympathy in *Hoffman*. In the reign of Elizabeth, poverty was a general problem of great concern. The complaints of the poor are described in such contemporary literature as pamphlets by Greene and Dekker, and Shakespeare's plays, including *2 Henry VI*, *King Lear*, and *The Winter's Tale*.[9]

Chettle also seems to have been very conscious personally of poverty, since he had often been imprisoned for debt and his close friends, Greene and Nashe, both suffered from poverty. Chettle dealt with money matters in other works, especially in such pamphlets as *Kind-Heart's Dream* and *Piers Plainness*, both of which attacked money-lenders. *Henslowe's Diary* includes numerous records of his debts in marginal spaces, which implies the close relationship between the two, and there are also some records of his imprisonment. On 17 January, 1599, Henslowe records: "Lent vnto Thomas downton the xvii of Janeway 1598 to lend vnto harey chettell to paye his charges in the marshallsey the some of" "xxx" shillings (103). A little later he was again imprisoned for debt and again helped by Henslowe, who says: "Lent Thomas dickers & harey chettell the 2 of maye 1599 to descarge harey chettell of his A Reste from Ingrome the some of twentyshellyngs in Redy money I saye lent" (119).

In his descriptions of the poor, Chettle seems to have been most sympathetic toward soldiers. For example, in *England's Mourning Garment*, Chettle praises Elizabeth for her charity in giving money to sick and aged persons and building almshouses, and admires her generosity toward poor soldiers and pleaders:

6 *Hoffman* and Elizabethan Military Culture

> As for the poore and decrepit with age, her Royall Maiestie had this charitable care; so for soldiers, and suters, she was very prouident ... For souldiers, and men of seruice, her decrees of prouision are extant: besides, it is most cleare, no Prince in the world, to land- or Sea-men, was more bountifull or willing, than her Highness.... (92-93)

"Soldiers" in this reference may be thought to be casualties of war or veteran soldiers like Old Stilt in *Hoffman*. According to William Harrison's description quoted above, there were three sorts of poor in those days, and the second "the wounded soldiers" were probably true of poor soldiers like the veteran, Old Stilt, in *Hoffman*.

Chettle, thus, strongly shows his sympathy toward soldiers in this play, though his concern about war generally seems more clearly expressed in other works, such as *England's Mourning Garment* and *Blind Beggar*.[10] For example, in *England's Mourning Garment*, as we have seen, Chettle praised Elizabeth for aiding poor soldiers. In *Blind Beggar*, the protagonist, General Momford sympathizes with a poor soldier, giving him a "chain" (1: 163), remarking:

> Thou are not impudent, thou canst not begg,
> Thou art a Souldier, and thy wound-plow'd face
> Hath every furrow fill'd with failing tears,
> That arms and honour should be thus disdain'd.
> Have no gold to give thee, but this chains,
> I pray thee take it friend, thou griev's at me
> And I griev'd thy want and wounds to see. (159-65)

The word "furrow" (161) indicates that "Souldier" (160) with a "wound-plow'd face" (160) is an aged veteran. Here Momford feels compassion for his poor status, as he imagines the man's past glory and honour as a soldier, which reminds us of the veteran's plight in the Elizabethan times.

Proclaimed an outlaw, Momford disguises himself as an aged soldier and a blind beggar to keep living in England: "I am exil'd, Yet I will *Eng-*

land see, / And live in *England* 'spight of infamy. / In some disguise I'll live, perhaps I'll turn / A Beggar" (256-59), "But first I'll like an aged Souldier" (261). When Momford comes across his daughter, she shows her compassion for him, as she does not notice his disguise, and believes him to be an aged and poor soldier:

> Thon [Thou] seem'st a maymed Souldier, wo is me!
> I have a little Gold, good Father take it,
> And here's a Diamond do not forsake it;
> My father was a Souldier maym'd like thee,
> Thou in thy limbs, he by vil'd infamy. (641-45)

Her compassion for the two faces of Momford, as a disguised soldier and her father, is interesting. The real poor soldier, who is given a chain by Momford, and Momford, who disguises himself as a lame aged poor soldier, represent the figures of the maimed veterans, which must have been common in those days.

(iii) Chettle's Political Views on Peace/War Debate

The reason why Chettle was so interested in soldiers, especially in *Hoffman*, may lie in his political views about Elizabethan military policy. Chettle was anti-Catholic and also anti-James, as discussed in Chapter 5 "Catholic Rulers and Downfallen Protestant Prisoners." The debate over peace and war was of great interest and topical concern in the period. Shakespeare, also, was conscious of these issues as a pacifist, according to critics such as Steven Marx and Theodor Meron (Marx 49-95; Meron 16-46). Marx claims that Shakespeare described soldiers heroically in history plays like *Henry VI*, but that he came to criticize the futility of war in later plays, especially in *Troilus and Cressida*, which was written around the time of the accession of the peacemaker, James.

Like many Elizabethan people, Chettle must have supported the wars between England and the Catholic leagues led by Spain, when considering the description of soldiers in *Hoffman*. This idea is also suggested in his criticism of Spain in *England's Mourning Garment*. In addition, he insists on the justification for war in the Low Countries, where the Dutch fought against the Spanish over their independence with the aid of England:

> if she would cease to defend the low Countries, restore the goods taken by reprisall from the Spaniards, build vp the Religious houses diuerted in her Fathers time, and let the Romane Religion be receiued through her Land; why then she might haue peace...(94).

Therefore, Chettle can be thought to have regarded the wars against Spain as just and right.

The figure of the soldier seems not only to have been a metonymy of warfare, but also that of patriotism and nostalgia for the Elizabethan Golden Age, when the English navy defeated the Spanish Armada, and when such chivalric icons as Sidney and Essex gave energy to people, evoking their patriotism and anti-Catholicism.

Through these sympathetic descriptions of poor soldiers, Chettle, thus, implicitly contrasts the previous merry Elizabethan period with the current dark, corrupt society and shows his anxiety for the coming reign of James; his wistfulness for the past suggests criticism of the current society (Marinelli 16). It was the very turn of the century and a time when people's ideas about religion, politics, economics, and science were changing (C. Hill, *People* 21-64, 94-122, 274-96; Barton 710-11). Some were conservative, and others were radical. Chettle, in his early forties, can be thought to have still admired the soldiers and described them in the figures of Hoffman's father and Old Stilt, while such pacific courtiers as Cecil, who took the side of the potential King of England, James, began to rise to power. *Hoffman* is, thus, a fully political drama written in a time of great social change.

(iv) Pirates in *Hoffman* and the Elizabethan Government

The theme of pirates in Elizabethan and Jacobean literature has been neglected until recently, but in fact they can be seen widely.[11] Pirates were occasionally described in classical literature, but in the Renaissance, they seem to have drawn greater attention from the reader and audience, perhaps as a consequence of the expansion of overseas commerce and colonialism. As mentioned above, Drake and Raleigh were heroic and patriotic pirates at the time, and their legalized piracy is now called privateering. They were, in a sense, soldiers, who defeated their enemies including the Spanish navy.

Chettle described pirates in *Hoffman* and *England's Mourning Garment*, though only to a small extent. Hoffman's father has been executed for piracy before the play begins; however, his image haunts the other characters throughout the play; they frequently mention him. Pirates were occasionally viewed as dangerous destroyers and causes of social disorder, though in such plays as *Hamlet*, they were described as savage but kind, as discussed below. Piracy without license was forbidden and punished by hanging.

As Brucher observes, the play *Hoffman* obviously emphasizes the outlaw status of Hoffman's father, who has turned to piracy from being an admiral (211). Prince Otho asserts to Hoffman, "Thy father dyed for piracy" (1.1.219), which has legally justifies his execution. Lorrique calls Hoffman's father "a terrible pirate" (128) and "a damn'd pirate, a mayd rauisher" (350-51), which are typical images for pirates in the Elizabethan period, in front of his ex-master Otho and his uncle the Duke Ferdinand. On the other hand, his bravery is well remembered by Hoffman and Martha. Hoffman believes he is "my most warlike father" (5.2.2609), while Martha pities him as "that sad man / Lord of Burtholme some time Admirall" (4.2.1837-38).

The savage images of pirates are also seen in *England's Mourning Garment*.

In this work, a shepherd narrator, Collin, relates a brutal but silly episode concerning two pirates to praise Elizabeth's virtuous command of justice. The pirates, imprisoned for piracy, are nearly saved from execution by the mercy of Elizabeth; however, in the prison, they boast of their courage to each other, and one day the older pirate cuts off his flesh with a knife and asks the younger if he could do the same thing. Soon the younger does so, and they repeat it two or three times. In the end, the act is exposed to Elizabeth, and they are executed for their brutality (96).

Pirates are portrayed sympathetically as well as villainously in Renaissance drama. For example, Shakespeare describes them as marginal characters. In *The Twelfth Night* Antonio, who is called by Orsino "[n]otable pirate" and "salt-water thief" (5.1.65), saves Sebastian and takes care of him. Hamlet meets pirates on his voyage to England, thanks them as "good fellows" (4.6.25), noting, "They have dealt with me like thieves of mercy" in his letter to Horatio (19-20). Moreover, Heywood and Rowley depict the execution of two historical pirates, Clinton and Purser, as being heroic and patriotic, as is further discussed below. On the other hand, in *Pericles*, Lorrique's image of pirates, "a mayd rauisher," is echoed when Marina is found and seen by three pirates as "a prize" (Sc.15: 142), that is, an object of their lust. Nevertheless, they save her when she is nearly killed by Leonine, and subsequently they take her to a brothel where she experiences another kind of danger (Slights and Woloshyn 262-63). Likewise, in *2 Henry VI* York points out the mercantilism of pirates: "Pirates may make cheap pennyworths of their pillage, / And purchase friends, and give to courtesans, / Still revelling like lords till all be gone" (1.1.222-24); however, the pirates, who came across banished Suffolk, butcher him rather than take his ransom, as is discussed below. Pirates were thus fascinating figures associated with patriotism and rebellion against injustice as well as savagery.

The ambiguous description of pirates can be ascribed to Elizabethan governmental policy. Pirates were treated both well and ill by the authorities. With the growth of cartography and navigation, "[p]eople of all sorts, from the Queen and her councilors to common soldiers and seamen, contributed to the Elizabethan expansion" (Helgerson 171), and such adventurers or pirates as Sir John Hawkins, Drake, and Raleigh became national heroes because of their Protestantism and contribution to mercantilism. In this naval political background, pirate characters are seen to have appealed to the theater audience.

Piracy, however, was forbidden by law, while those pirates who had authorized royal licenses were exempted from punishment. Today the latter sort of pirates are called privateers, but the term did not exist until the mid-seventeenth century, with the first usage dating from 1641, according to the *OED*. This fact suggests there was no clear distinction between pirates and privateers. Hawkins and Drake were officially licensed privateers, and Elizabeth was their sponsor. Drake's great voyage around the world from 1577 to 1580 provided the state with a great profit of £700,000; therefore, the nation needed him, and in a sense piracy was thought of as a patriotic act, especially in the conflict with Spain. In this maritime fever, more and more amateur young gentlemen and unemployed men also started on similar enterprise, or gamble. King James forbade privateering/piracy, but piracy remained popular until 1615 (Andrews 3-31, 61-80; Potter 124-40; Jowitt, "Piracy and Politics" 216-32; Senior 7-11, 145).

Thus, the act of plundering at sea might be called illegal or legitimate depending on the situation (Fuchs 46). This was a suitable system for authorities, who wanted to rob foreign countries, especially Spain, of their treasures, and these acts were seen as patriotic, because the perpetrators sacrificed themselves to attack their opponents, as did soldiers. K. R. Andrews summarizes this ambivalent policy: "ordinary indiscriminate piracy remained a serious social evil and the government's attempts to suppress it were unavailing. But in times of crisis pirates could be useful, provided they concentrated on the right prey" (13-14).

On the other hand, pirates had their own democratic rule and anti-hierarchical perspectives. Peter Linebaugh and Marcus Rediker claim pirates were "class conscious and justice-seeking" and "egalitarian in a hierarchical age," distributing booty evenly (162-63). Lois Potter and Chris Fitter share this view. According to Potter, the pirates' justice was "a kind of justice that cannot be accepted in civilized society" (124) and points out the execution of Suffolk by pirates in *2 Henry VI* as an example. In Act IV Scene i, a pirate Walter Whitmore shows his grudge against Suffolk: "I lost mine eye in laying the prize aboard / And therefore to revenge it shalt thou die" (4.1.26-27). Moreover, another pirate bitterly criticizes Suffolk for the corruption of England: "reproach and beggary / Is crept into the palace of King, / And all by thee" (101-03). Potter claims the killing of Suffolk by the pirates "is clearly meant to be rough justice" (125). Fitter extends this analysis and sees the confrontation between Suffolk and the pirates as "one of raging class-conflict" (136). Thomas Cartelli makes the point that Holinshed's *Chronicle*, Shakespeare's source, does not use the term "pirates" for Suffolk's captors, and similarly claims that "their [the pirates'] actions operate in direct resistance to the kind of corrupt and corruption-inducing authority which, if allowed to flourish, would constitute a direct threat to the well-being of subject and citizen alike" (333-34, 340).

Brucher interprets the involvement of Hoffman's father in piracy and Hoffman's revenge as being a "political rebellion," and observes that they have "leveling sentiments" (211, 215, 220). Whether the piracy can be described as rebellion is uncertain because the text does not demonstrate it in detail, but the younger Hoffman is obviously subversive, killing the self-interested and corrupt ruling class. In this sense, the younger Hoffman resembles the pirates in *2 Henry VI*, though he himself is not a pirate; they are seen as horrible outlaws by other characters; they kill the immoral authorities. In short, they are villains in the eyes of the law, but morally contentious.

The justification for acts of piracy is seen in the act of Hoffman's father, who "[f]ill'd all treasures" of the Dukes of Prussia and Austria "with fomens spoyles, / And payd poore souldiors from his treasury" (1.1.159-60). Young Hoffman, believing the validity of his father's acts, implies the trial for his piracy had not been done fairly and criticizes the arbitrary rulers for having exploited his bravery at sea (Brucher 212). Although this play is set in Germany, the legal system and situation highly resemble that of the Elizabethan society, where piracy was illegal and hanging was required as its punishment, and thus the lives of pirates depended on the whims of the authority.

Potter observes that the theme of piracy was topical in Elizabethan and Jacobean plays. In the Elizabethan period, the 1583 execution of nine pirates, among whom Clinton and Purser were well-known, was of popular interest. The event was dealt with in two lost ballads, *Clinton's Lamentation* (1583) and *The Confessions of 9 Rovers, Clinton and Purser Being Chief* (1586), and in one extant pamphlet, Atkinson Clinton's *Clinton, Purser and Arnold*, printed by Wolfe for Wright (1583; STC 5432). In the extant text, the three pirates express their last repentance for their offenses. Mark Netzoloff observes:

> The ballads claims the pirates' obedience to queen and country: Purser pleads repeatedly that 'ever wisht my Queene and country well,' a point reinforced by Arnold's assurance that 'lives he not that can in conscience say, Purser or Arnold made one English praye' ... The ballads enables state power to speak through the pirates, representing the captains as endorsing *Clinton, Purser and Arnold*, position of the state that condemns them. (66)

Claire Jowitt, on the other hand, doubts this perspective and suggests this work criticizes authority implicitly:

> All three pirates' speeches make clear that there are mitigating circumstances which might perhaps undermine the wisdom of their execution, and imply that rival European nations have either caused, or will benefit from, the pirates' fall from grace. Even as he acknowledged his guilt in his lament at the scaffold, Purser emphasizes that he was highly serviceable to the English state. (156-57)

Furthermore, Jowitt remarks, Clinton "describes his position as arch-pirate in explicitly monarchical terms: 'Who raigned more then I that ruld coast?'" (158). For high-born Arnold, Jowitt reveals he was, in fact, pardoned and not executed and sees his lament as an "ironical gesture" (160). Consequently, Jowitt concludes:

> This pamphlet should be seen as hesitant in its support of the state power that condemns the pirates. There is no explicit attack on the Queen, or her representatives, but, perhaps, implicitly the three laments imply criticism of the regime that is incapable of accommodating such patriotic men, especially in times of national emergency against European enemies and rivals. (159)

Jowitt's view can be applied to the situation of Hoffman's father. Hoffman's speech about his father who served the Dukes resembles the utterances of the pirates, particularly "Who raigned more then I that ruld coast?" Interestingly, Jowitt suggests Clinton's situation may allude to that of Edward Fiennes de Clinton, Lord Admiral of England, and interprets his lines as a warning to the lord. That is the lord could be used and executed like Clinton. Although the lord, in fact, remained at court and as a member of the Privy Council till his death, the lord in *Hoffman* was executed for piracy. The text on the execution of the historical pirates thus suggests that *Hoffman* deals with and criticizes the topical political situation of rulers using and killing pirates capriciously.

Similarly, Heywood dealt with Clinton and Pursey in the play, *Fortune by Land and Sea* (c.1607-1609; pub. 1655; Wing, H1783) in collaboration with William Rowley, and also the pamphlet, *A True Relation of...Purser and Clinton* (1639; STC 20512). Regarding *Fortune by Land and Sea*, Jowitt claims that "the play seems intended to appeal to nostalgia for an age of simpler values." Both Potter and Jowitt quote Purser's last speech and see it as patriotic and worthy for sympathy:

> But now our Sun is setting, night comes on, the watery wildeness ore which we raign'd, proves in our ruins peaceful, [Merchants] trade fearless abroad as in the rivers mouth, and free as in a harbor, then fair *Thames*, through us, whose double tides must o'rflow our bodies, and being dead, may thy clear waves our scandals wash away, but keep our valours living. (F3r)

Jowitt remarks, "they [the pirates] represent themselves as monarchs of a seaborne empire here subservient solely to the 'Queen' Thames," while "in Drayton's *Poly-Olbion*, 'Thames' eulogizes Elizabeth's military glory during the river's catalogue of previous monarchs," and nostalgia for Elizabeth can be seen (229-30). Similarly, Netzloff observes that the execution of pirates reveals the inconsistency and hypocrisy of state policies toward lower-class mariners (71).

Purser and Clinton can be seen to have been popular and perceived as subversive figures even in the Jacobean period. *Hoffman* includes their implicit criticism of the ruling class and emphasizes their acts of piracy as being patriotic; also, the execution of the pirates would have drawn the audience's sympathy. The ambiguity of the pirates ultimately becomes a reproach against the arbitrary monarch who exploits them. In *Measure for Measure*, Isabella's brother and prisoner, Claudio is supposed to be hanged, and his head is to be sent to Angelo, but Provost suggests using the head of a pirate, who has died on that morning when Claudio is to be executed:

> Here in the prison, father,
> There died this morning of a cruel fever
> One Ragusine, a most notorious pirate,
> A man of Claudio's years; his beard and head
> Just of his colour. What if we do omit
> This reprobate till he were well inclined,
> And satisfy the deputy with the visage
> Of Ragusine, more like to Claudio? (4.3.66-73)

The Duke in disguise as a friar agrees with this, and Claudio is saved. Using the head of the dead villainous pirate, who is probably a native of Ragusa, instead of Claudio's seemingly makes sense, but some members of the audience may have felt that the authority uses a pirate simply for their convenience.

While *Hoffman* criticizes the ruling class implicitly through the pirate who

6 *Hoffman* and Elizabethan Military Culture

has lost position as Admiral, *England's Mourning Garment* seems to condemn the savagery of the pirates; at a glance, this episode shows the generosity of Elizabeth; however, as in the case of the ballad, the elegy can be seen to criticize implicitly the Queen through the execution of the pirates. Although their acts of piracy had been pardoned by Elizabeth, as in the case of the historical Arnold, their brutal games drove Elizabeth to execute them. This seems to reinforce Elizabeth's absolute power and control over the lives of her subjects. In short, their fate depends on her whim. In the tract, there is ambivalence in the way Elizabeth is depicted, though Chettle seemingly respects and admires her, and he certainly preferred her to James.

*

I have discussed the relations between the "poor soldiers" in *Hoffman* and those in the late Elizabethan society with a focus on Chettle's military concerns, the topical war/peace debate, and the problems of veterans and pirates. Chettle was strongly conscious of these concerns, and sympathetic to "poor soldiers," who had money neither for food nor clothes, who could not disobey their corrupt captains and superiors. He described these soldiers sympathetically, through the characters of Old Stilt and Hoffman's downfallen father, and criticized such exploiters as the Dukes.

Chettle felt clear antipathy toward Catholics, particularly the Spanish, and also seems to have been suspicious of James, at least in *England's Mourning Garment*. With respect to the peace/war debate, he was apparently pro-war against Spain, regarding an attack on the country as a "Just War." At the end of the Elizabethan Age, Chettle, like many others, must have been very anxious about the political future of England. This worry and nostalgia for the Elizabethan Golden Age is expressed in *Hoffman*.

Nostalgia for the Elizabethan period may be seen also in Chettle's other plays, such as *Death, Downfall, Blind Beggar*, and *Sir Thomas Wyatt*. In these works, Englishness and Protestantism are underlined. Also, Chettle praises all Tudor princes including Elizabeth in *England's Mourning Garment*, and describes England's prosperity under the reign of Elizabeth with such illustrations as the successful attack on the Armada.[12]

Chettle, thus, cautiously observed society and politics in the late-Tudor period, and in particular, the military background is described in both his pamphlets and dramas. He dealt with this topical war theme in *Hoffman* from a pro-war, in other words an anti-Catholic and anti-James, viewpoint.

The plight of the common soldiers appealed to the audiences, because, as Nashe observed in *Pierce Penniless*, large numbers of them were soldiers, whether captains or common soldiers (212). Chettle described them in this play to evoke patriotism as well as to gain popularity. In the description of the former glory of Hoffman's father and Old Stilt, Chettle probably attempted to reflect military heroes like Sidney and Essex, who also flourished in the Elizabethan Golden Age, and at the same time, he implicitly criticized current society.

The piracy of Hoffman's father is repeatedly mentioned in the play, and different characters exhibit different attitudes. The arrogant Prince Otho and villainous Lorrique insist on a savage image of Hoffman's father, but the virtuous Duchess Martha pities his misfortune. The Elizabethan government misused pirates; they favored Hawkins and Drake as patriots defeating their enemy, particularly the Spanish navy, while executing Clinton and Purser. The fate of Elizabethan pirates depended on the will of the authorities. Piratical characters in Renaissance drama seem to reflect this double-edged attitude. The historical pirates, Purser and Clinton, in *Fortune by Land and Sea* are central characters, and their execution is described with pity. Shakespeare's pirates are minor characters, but their speech and acts add some impressive qualities to the plays. In particular, the pirates in *2 Henry VI*, who murder Suffolk, suggest a kind of outlaw justice and the consequent corruption of the authorities, while Ragusine in *Measure for Measure*, the scapegoat for Claudio, implies the ruling class's misuse of pirates in order to display their power.

Like these plays, *Hoffman* questions the misuse of power by corrupt and capricious authorities, but unlike other plays, the pirate, Hoffman's father, does not appear on stage: he has already been executed when the play opens. However, his image as an Admiral/pirate haunts the other characters, and they frequently talk about him. In short, he is almost a legend in the play, and his miserable life influences all the characters. Such an outlawed noble figure is developed in Momford, who is banished from England and turns into a beggar, in *Blind Beggar*.

During the last years of Elizabeth, common soldiers were neglected, and exploiters feathered their nests, as we have seen. Chettle suggested this situation in *Hoffman* with the heroic episodes of Hoffman's father and Old Stilt, since the yearning for a Golden Age implies criticism against the present society. Chettle's attitude toward Elizabeth is ambivalent, but *Hoffman* clearly warns against the reign of James, her most potential successor and pacifist, through the way it deals with topical Elizabethan military issues.

Notes

1. For military revolutions, see Duffy; Parker; Eltis; Anglo 564-72.
2. For the details, see Hale 39-42, Marx 49-58, Meron 16-46, Somogyi 18-22.
3. Raleigh claims the necessity of war with Spain and independence of the Low Countries in a small tract, *A Discourse Touching a War with Spain, and of the Protecting of the Netherlands*. See Beer 18, n.1.
4. For further analysis of each of these plays, see Taunton 58-69; 79-91.
5. For the influence of *The Cobbler's Prophecy* on Chettle, see Chapter 1, "(ii) Chettle and John Danter," "(c) Literary Influence from Danter's Publications between 1591 and 1598."
6. For a definition of "ruffler," see Awdley 3 and Harman 29-31.
7. For the details, see Somogyi 142-43, Beier 95, P. Williams, *The Tudor Regime* 212-13, Nolan 416, N. Jones 35.
8. For further discussion of "dead pay," see *Acts of the Privy Council of England* 26: 336; Cruickshank 143, 153-58, and *passim*; Edelman 327.
9. For Greene and Dekker, see Clark 125-28; for Shakespeare, see Carroll, "Language, Politics, and Poverty in Shakespearian Drama" 142-54.
10. Perhaps Chettle's two lost collaborative plays with Dekker, *Troilus and Cressida* (1599)

and *Agamemnon, or Orestes Furious* (1599) dealt with the the theme of war, particularly the Trojan War, which was also depicted in Shakespeare's *Troilus and Cressida* and Heywood's *The Iron Age*. The plot of Chettle and Dekker's *Troilus and Cressida* is extant as a fragmentary manuscript in British Museum Ms. Additional 10449. See Chambers 2: 158-59, also Greg, *Dramatic Documents*, vol. 1, which contains it as a facsimile and its notes in vol. 2, 138-43.

[11] For example, a conference on pirates was held in Wales in 2005, and some of the papers are included in *Pirates? The Politics of Plunder, 1550-1650*, ed. by Claire Jowitt.

[12] For Tudor monarchs excluding Elizabeth, see Ingleby's edition, 83-84.

7 Beggars in *The Pleasant Comedy of Patient Grissil* and *The Blind Beggar of Bethnal Green*, and the Elizabethan Money Based Economy

(i) Background of Elizabethan Poverty

In the Elizabethan period, there was an excess of beggars or vagrants in England, especially in London. This increase dated back to the Wars of the Roses (1455-85), according to Gamini Salgado. After the wars, most professional soldiers became unemployed. They could handle weapons very well and robbed ordinary people of money in gangs. Henry VIII's dissolution of the monasteries added more people to these military vagrants; such workers as gardeners, cooks, and laundrymen at the monasteries lost their jobs and became unemployed, though monks received pensions. Moreover, many farmers came to be included among the vagrants due to the expansion of enclosures at the beginning of the Tudor period. Agriculture was replaced by the wool industry which required enclosures. As a result, farmers could no longer make a living, and many of them went to London. The population of the city exploded, and the number of vagrants rose sharply. In the Elizabethan period, inflation, bad harvests, and wars constantly contributed to producing more of these poor people (Salgado 117-20; Beier 3-7).

Before the Reformation, all Christian people had to carry out the following seven tasks as a form of religious duty in accordance with the teaching of Jesus (Matthew Ch. 25): feed the hungry, give drink to the thirsty, welcome a stranger, clothe the naked, visit the sick, visit the prisoner, and bury the dead. However, after the Reformation and the establishment of the Church of England, these values changed, and a law for relief was needed to protect the poor people. Moreover, the authorities feared that the increase of vagrants would lead to crime and social disorder, and it was necessary to regulate them strictly by law called the Poor Law (P. Williams, *The Later Tudors* 222-24; Briggs 34-35).

Despite this system, vagrants did not disappear; rather their numbers rose rapidly between 1560 and 1640. Beier estimated the number of the Elizabethan vagrants to be over 15,000—though William Harrison in the sixteenth century counted the number to be as 10,000—while estimating that of the Caroline period to be 25,000. On the other hand, following Carl Bridenbaugh, Fiona McNeill claims that in 1602 London had 30,000 idle men or masterless men, of whom at least 17,000 were likely to have been women and accounted for almost 12% of the city's population, 200,000 (Beier 14-16; Harrison, Book II, Ch. X, 218; Bridenbaugh 167; McNeill 150).

Although in the medieval period, poverty had been idealized by Christianity, after about 1300, some began to condemn the poor as being idle and objected to aiding them. After the Reformation, such advocates of poverty as St. Francis were defamed, and his ideology was replaced by St. Paul's dictum that good Christians should reject beggars and work hard without dependency (Beier 4-5). Consequently, beggars were generally criticized as being idle and a cause of social disorder in Elizabethan society, but the people's attitudes seem to be ambiguous. As Beier points out, the Puritan pamphleteer Philip Stubbes criticized vagrants as evil in *The Anatomy of Abuses*, and a diplomat, Richard Morison, associated them with criminals in *A Remedy for Sedition*; also, the authors of a set of homilies, published in 1596, stated the Franciscan idea of poverty; Beier quotes Morison's remark: "We are all God's beggars; that God therefore may acknowledge his beggars, let us not despise ours" (Beier 4-7, 109).

The number of the poor was substantial in Elizabethan society, and also their image fascinated contemporary writers and readers in what is called "rogue literature;" for example, Awdeley's *Fraternity of Vagabonds*; Harman's

7 Beggars in *The Pleasant Comedy of Patient Grissil* and *The Blind Beggar of Bethnal Green*, and the Elizabethan Money Based Economy

A Caveat; Greene's cony-catching series including Greene's *A Notable Discovery of Cozenage* (1591), *The Second Part of Cony-Catching* (1591), *The Third and Last Part of Cony-Catching* (1592), *A Disputation between a He Cony-Catcher, and a She Cony-Catcher* (1592), *The Black Book's Messenger*, and *The Defense of Cony-Catching*. (1592); the anonymous *Mihil Mumchance*; Dekker's The *Belman of London* (1608), *Lantern and Candlelight* (1608), *O Per Se O* (1612), *Villainies Discovered* (1616), *English Villainies* (1632); Rowlands's *Greene's Ghost Haunting Cony-Catchers*.

As discussed in Chapter 1, "(ii) Chettle and John Danter," Chettle's printing partner, Danter, issued three cony-catching pamphlets: *The Groundwork of Cony-Catching, The Black Book's Messenger*, and *Mihil Mumchance*. These and other such works may have affected Chettle's views of the poor. Rogue literature describes the undeserving poor, or the able-bodied vagrants, who make money by fraud in the underground economy, and this kind of pamphlet was very popular with the Elizabethan reading public.

On stage, the figure of the beggar frequently appeared, whether as a nobleman in disguise like Edgar in *King Lear* or one forced into such a state. They are usually described sympathetically rather than fearfully. More importantly, they make the audience aware of the social gap between the rich and poor, especially with the contrast of their clothing, and as victims of the hypocrisy and vice of the ruling class. For example, Lear says:

> Through tattered clothes great vices do appear;
> Robes and furred gowns hide all. Plate sin with gold,
> And the strong lance of justice hurtless breaks;
> Arm it in rags, a pygmy's straw does pierce it. (4.4.160-64)

Shabby clothes are similarly praised in *The Taming of the Shrew* when Petruchio tells Katherine:

> Our purses shall be proud, our garments poor,
> For 'tis the mind that makes the body rich,

And as the sun breaks through the darkest clouds,
So honour peereth in the meanest habit. (4.3.169-72)

William S. Carroll analyzes these beggar characters in Shakespeare and concludes that Shakespeare raises questions about poverty, class, and gender, though with less knowledge of the underworld, than other playwrights including Dekker, Chettle, and Chapman among others (*Fat King* 215); other writers, at least Chettle, seem to question social class and injustice through the portrayal of beggars more straightforwardly than Shakespeare.

(ii) *Patient Grissil*
(a) Representation of Beggars in *Patient Grissil*

Patient Grissil was written by Chettle, Dekker, and Haughton in December, 1599 (Henslowe 65, 128, 129). According to the title-page the play "hath beene sundrie times lately plaid by the right honorable the Earle of Nottingham (Lord high Admirall) his seruants," and "Imprinted for Henry Rocket" in "1603." Noticeably, Greg identifies the printer as Edward Allde from the ornaments and notes, "Rocket had no apparent right to the copy, but it is perhaps significant that he had been Burby's apprentice before taking up his freedom on 31 January 1602" (*A Bibliography* 315). Edward Allde was the son of John Allde, Munday's printing master, and partly printed the bad quarto of *Romeo and Juliet* for Danter in 1597, as discussed in Chapter 3 "Chettle as Dramatic Repairman." Burby frequently worked with Danter; remarkably, *2 Primaleon of Greece* was printed by Danter for Burby in 1596, and Chettle wrote an epistle "To his good Friend M. *Anthony Mundy*," as also discussed in Chapter 1 "Chettle as Printer." Chettle's personal connections with these printers and stationers apparently still continued even after he turned into a playwright. Although *Patient Grissil* was entered for Burby in 1600, it was not printed before 1603 (Arber 3: 158). For the payment, *Henslowe's Diary* holds some records, but the matter is quite complicated, as Jenkins observes. The three authors were first paid three pounds on 19 December 1599 with a receipt written by Chettle and including each of their signatures; and seven days later they received six pounds for the play (65, 128, 129). Chettle's writing parts are not exactly known, but Jenkins suggests Chettle composed the main plot of Griselda, and that Dekker wrote the parts about Glenthyan and Sir Owen's taming of the shrew plot, while Haughton worked on the minor plot of Gwalter's sister, Julia and her suitors (169-78).

This play is a dramatization of the Griselda story which was popular in Europe in the early modern period. The story originated from French folklore, and it became well known through its being the last story in Giovanni Boccaccio's *The Decameron* and its appearing in the "Clerk's Tale" in Geoffrey Chaucer's *Canterbury Tales*. Around 1559, John Phillip composed an English dramatic version of the Griselda story, which was partly followed by Chettle, Dekker, and Haughton, though the play sounds medieval with such allegorical names as "diligence" and "vice" for the courtier characters. In these tales, a beautiful and virtuous maid named Griselda/Grissil marries Gwalter, the Marquess of Saluzzo. Gwalter cruelly tests Grissil's obedience in various ways; he treats her as his hand-maid, takes two babies from her, banishes her from the court, and attempts to make her attend his new bride, who is actually their daughter, at his second wedding. Finally, Gwalter reveals the trial to everyone and resumes living with Grissil.[1]

Chettle's *Grissil* basically follows Boccaccio and others but with some alterations; the largest change is the introduction of new characters including Babulo (a fool serving to Grissil's father), Laureo (Grissil's pedantic brother), the Marquess of Pavia (Gwalter's brother), Mario and Lepido (Gwalter's courtiers), Gwenthyan (Gwalter's cousin), her husband Sir Owen (the Welsh Knight), and Julia (Gwalter's sister). Babulo and Laureo oppose Grissil's marriage to Gwalter, displaying skepticism about Gwalter; Babulo is particularly important as a social commentator in the play. Similarly, the Marquess of Pavia, Mario, and Lepido are against the marriage, despising Grissil's family by calling them "beggars." The introduction of these characters seems to enlarge the perceptual gap between the rich and poor.

Grissil's marriage and Gwalter's trial comprise the main plot, while there are two sub-plots; the couple of Gwenthyan and Sir Owen figure in a comical sub-plot with Welsh accents, parodying Grissil and Gwalter; Sir Owen struggles and finally succeeds in taming the shrewish Gwenthyan like Petruchio in *The Taming of the Shrew*, a play in which Kate mentions Grissil. As discussed in Chapter 1, "(iii) Chettle and Publications by Printers Other Than East and Danter," "(b) Literary Influence from Publications by Printers Other Than East and Danter," Chettle may have read the corrupt texts of *The Taming of the Shrew* (1594, 1596), issued by Short.

Patient Grissil describes real beggars as marginal characters in the sub-plot, while Grissil and her family, despite being basket-makers, are called "beggars" metaphorically by the higher class characters. The real beggars are invited by Gwenthyan, Gwalter's cousin, to spoil a feast and thus to torment her husband. The Gwenthyan-Sir Owen plot newly introduced in the play parallels the Grissil-Gwalter plot. Sir Owen is taught how to tame his shrew wife by Gwalter but always fails. One day Sir Owen invites Gwalter and some courtiers to dinner, but before their arrival, Gwenthyan gives all the food and wine to a group of beggars. These beggars are probably classified as "Palliard," "Washman," or "Clapperdogens," who travel around to beg, ragged with sticks in a group of two or three among other different kinds of beggars, as further discussed below (Awdley 4, 5; Harman 44). They are described as nice and polite. One of them asks Gwenthyan, "shall we scramble or eate mannerly?" (4.3.18-19), and they wait to eat after her prayers. The roles of these beggars are so small, but there seems to be some significance in presenting the contrast between the real beggars and the metaphorical ones (Grissil's family), because this scene is also new to this version of the story. This contrast probably emphasizes that Grissil's family is poor but not real beggars, and that they are noble in spirit.

(b) Conflicts between the Rich and Poor

Such critics as McLuskie and Edward Pechter argue that the theme of this play is marriage dictated by patriarchy, or the shift from arranged marriage to marriage based on love. On the other hand, Comensoli and Bronfman see sovereignty in marriage as the principal theme. Truly, Grissil's trial in her marital life is indeed pivotal in the play, but I will focus on the hierarchical and mercenary problems accompanying the marriage between the different ranks with reference to the Elizabethan changing economical system.

In early medieval England, birth and social rank separated people from each other, but in the late Middle Ages and the Renaissance, with the emergence of the money based economy and rise of the gentry class, the marriage market cut across class borders, as Fulton remarks:

> Griselda's marriage to the marquis provides a classic example of the upward movement of a humble family into the ranks of the nobility by means of marriage and the production of children who inherit their father's noble status. (30)

In the marriage market, however, such poor ladies as Grissil circulated as "base currency" without good status and dowry, and most of them remained single, though some of them had babies, and earned their living by sewing and spinning, according to McNeill (79).[2] In fact, Chettle's Grissil fully acknowledges this idea herself and refuses Gwalter's courtship, remarking, "None is so fond to fancie pouertie" (1.2.204) and "Oh my gracious Lord, / Humble not your high state to my low birth, / Who am not worthy to be held your slaue, / Much less your wife" (239-42). Moreover, Grissil's family and the courtiers furiously reject the marriage because of their difference in status. Nevertheless, eventually, Gwalter marries Grissil, and her status becomes higher. As a result, her father and brother rise to the position of courtiers, though their positions momentarily fall in the course of Gwalter's trial. Like his contemporaries, Chettle was interested in such social mobility, particularly the downfall of great men, as discussed in

Chapter 4, "(ii) Downfall," and in the play he describes the rise, downfall, and restoration of the status of Grissil and her family through the course of her marriage.

In the earlier works, Grissil is a weaver, a job, in which poor women engaged in Renaissance England, according to McNeill (28-34); her father seems to be a poor peasant, though this is not mentioned clearly. In Chettle's play, by contrast, she is a daughter of a basket-making father, Janicola, and her brother, Laureo, who is a newly invented character, returns from university for lack of money and begins basket-making. Another new character Babulo also makes baskets as Janicola's servant and fool. Basket-making, thus, seems to be a family business. These alterations and additions underscore the low status of Grissil's family. Moreover, Janicola and Laureo may have reminded the Elizabethan audience of the economic hardship and the position of poor craftsmen, and particularly Laureo is a realistic character, as Tom Rutter compares him with Jonson, who was unable to complete university for poverty. As Lee Bliss points out, "Under the economically hard-pressed 1590s," Laureo was a typical figure, "frustrated upward mobility, sixteenth-century style, as well as downtrodden intellectual merit" (301-43).

Furthermore, the play frequently employs such word as "rich" and "poor" to contrast the wealthy and impecunious characters; "rich" occurs twenty-one times, while "poor(e)," is repeated twenty-nine times. Overall, the poor (Grissil and Janicola) are described as more honest and obedient, while the rich (Gwalter and his courtiers) are depicted as more wicked to the extent that Gwalter, in the disguise of a basket-maker, calls himself a "tyrant" (4.2.170). They confront each other three times in the play: Gwalter's wooing; the banishment of Janicola, Grissil's father, and Laureo, her brother, from the court; and the banishment of Grissil. In the wooing scene, the courtiers are opposed to the marriage between Gwalter and Grissil. A courtier says, "This meane choice, will disdaine your noblenes" (1.2.275). Another follows, "shee's poore and base" (277). Gwalter's brother, the Marquess of Pavia, is more conscious of the people's attitudes: "What will the world say when the trump of fame / Shall sound your high birth with a beggers name" (279-80). Noticeably, the term "a beggers name" is used for Grissil and her family. Although they are not exactly beggars, but basket-makers, they are despised as beggars metaphorically throughout the play. According to the *OED*, "beggar" was used as "a term of contempt," that is, "Mean or low fellow" as early as the fourteenth century, and this metaphorical usage was common in Elizabethan plays (6. a.). There are several other examples in the play: to try Grissil's patience, Gwalter maliciously calls their baby "the base issue of thy begger wombe" (2.2.57) and orders his courtiers to "call her [Grissil] beggers brat" (159). Moreover, a courtier, Mario, shows antagonism against Grissil's family, who are raised to the position of courtiers through Grissil's marriage: "Hedlong I had rather fall to miserie, / Then see a begger rais'd to dignitie" (176-77). The phrase "beggers brat" used by Gwalter can also be seen in a ballad around 1600 from the Huth Collection at British Library and Phillip's play as well, though it refers to Grissil's children, not Grissil, in Phillip's (Jenkins 163). In the ballad, it is included in the opposition to the marriage, "Some did call her beggers brat" (l. 30); in the play, Politic Persuasion remarks, "I could finde in my hart to plucke out the beggers brats eyes" and goes on to say, "Is shee anie more then a Beggers brat" (ll. 911, 923). Moreover, Politic Pursuation shows further hostility against Grissil, calling her "a beggerlye Grissill" (892).[3] As discussed earlier, in the Renaissance Griselda stories, she is not accepted by the community due to her poor status; therefore, her poverty needs to be emphasized by the word "beggar" to show the gap in social rank and reinforce the hierarchical and mercantile aspects of marriage. Chettle's play seems to highlight not only their difference in status, but also the arrogance and wickedness of the upper classes with their repetitive use of the term beggar for the submissive poor.

In this play, the rich people also are not the only ones opposed to the marriage. Asked his opinion by Gwalter, Laureo, Grissil's brother, implies his objection in terms of class distinction: "If equall thoughts durst both your states conferre, / Her's is to lowe, and you to high for her" (1.2.262-63). Babulo shows his antagonism against the upper class more blatantly. He has already suggested it before Gwalter visits them: "I should be a rich man by right, for they neuer doe good deedes" (16-17), while Janicola offhandedly reveals his skepticism of Gwalter in warning Grissil to be careful of him (53-56). When Gwalter attempts to curry Babulo's favor and asserts, "we are al thy friends" (303), Babulo gives him a bitter response, "Its hard sir for this motley Ierkin, to find friendship with this fine doublet" (304-05). The metaphor, or rather metonymy, of clothes is repeatedly seen in this play, which thus seems to reflect Elizabethan commodity culture, as discussed below. Gwalter promises to make Babulo a courtier, but Babulo says "I haue a better trade sir, basketmaking" (311). Gwalter goes on to say "I will make her rich" (316), but Babulo believes "I am a fitter husband for her" (315), and that "beggers are fit for beggers, gentlefolkes for gentlefolkes; I am afraid that this wonder of the rich louing the poor, wil last but nine daies" (317-19).

Babulo's prediction is realized; Grissil's family becomes courtiers for a brief period as promised by Gwalter, but they are turned out of the court in order for him to test Grissil's patience. The courtiers, who had expressed opposition to the marriage in the former scene, are pleased to see them banished, or downfallen, though they know that this is a part of Gwalter's trial. Lepido, a courtier, says to Gwalter, "Your subiects doe repine at nothing more, / Then to beholde *Ianicola* her Father, / And her base brother lifted vp so high" (2.2.168-70). Mario, another courtier, laughs and says the afore quoted lines: "Hedlong I had rather fall to miserie, / Then see a begger rais'd to dignitie" (176-77).

In other versions, Grissil's father remains at his cottage even after the marriage, while this play makes him a courtier along with the new characters, Laureo and Babulo, which raises the issue of the socially upward movement through marriage, as was becoming widespread in the Elizabethan period. However, more importantly, the alterations seem to underline the villainy and vanity of the court and the peacefulness and warmness of the country, though no critic has picked up on this point. The conflict arising from different ranks extends to problem of difference in value; rich versus poor; court/city versus country; anxiety versus peace; cold heart versus warm heart.[4]

When Janicola leaves the court, Grissil comforts him, praising country life in front of the courtiers:

> To leaue the Court and care be patient,
> In your olde cottage you shall finde content.
> Mourne not because these silkes are tane away,
> You'le seeme more rich in a course gowne of gray. (3.1.46-49)

The happiness of country life is resonant in contrast with the coldness of the court surrounded by flattery. Before the wooing scene, Babulo sings a song for the rich and poor starting with "*Are thou poore yet hast thou golden Slumbers: / Oh sweet content! / Art thou rich yet is thy minde perplexed? / Oh punishment*" (1.2.94-97). This song anticipates "the Court and care" (3.1.46) which they will face later. Moreover, Janicola welcomes his son, who has returned from a university, "thogh I am poore / My loue shall not be so" (1.2.151-52), and prepare fish and bread for him. Such warmness or love of the poor seems a crucial point when juxtaposed with the coldness of the court in this play. Grissil has already mentioned the superiority of the gray gown, which, as well as a pitcher, indicates her status metonymically, as further discussed below. In the course of the trial, Gwalter mentions that Grissil is proud of her gorgeous attire, but she rejects this:

> Ile cast this gaynesse of, and be content
> To weare this russet brauerie of my owne,
> For that's more warme then this, I shall looke olde,
> No sooner in course freeze then cloth of golde. (2.2.73-76)

This speech well illustrates the contrast between richness and poverty in clothing, cynically refers to the shabby gown as "warme" (75), and questions the warmness and coldness of the mind. The "russet" (74) indicates the color of her gown, which Gwalter has mentioned sarcastically. According to Ann Rosalind Jones and Peter Stallybrass, "russet" indicated a "gray or another neutral color," though it was sometimes "reddish-brown" (229).

Furthermore, the banished Janicola is content to resume his old lifestyle as a basket-maker, remarking, "This labor is a comfort to my age" (4.2.3); he goes on to say, "The *Marquesse* hath to me been mercifull, / In sending me from Courtly delicates, / To taste the quiet of this country life" (4-6). When Grissil is banished from the court and arrives home, Janicola says, "*Grissill* is welcome home to pouerty" (32), and she joins him: "It is the pleasure of my princely Lord, / Who taking some offence, to me vnknowne, / Hath banisht me from care to quietnes" (37-39). This paradoxical pleasure of banishment is also found in Chettle's part of *Sir Thomas More*, where More laments his sentence to his wife, complaining about the court, but at the same time, gladly accepting his fate:

> Perchance the King,
> Seeing the court is full of vanity,
> Has pity lest our souls should be misled
> And sends us to a life contemplative.
> O, happy banishment from worldly pride,
> When souls by private life are sanctified! (Sc.13: 78-83)

More, like Janicola, is grateful for his banishment away from "vanity" and "pride," which is almost equal to what Janicola calls "care."

The final conflicts between the rich and poor occur during Grissil's banishment. Having given birth to twins, Grissil is proclaimed to be banished along with her babies by Gwalter, who continues to subject her to trials by pretending to believe that the children are not his. Unlike Laureo and

Babulo, Grissil has not protested against Gwalter until this moment, even though there have been some indications of her vexation. She challenges him for the first time by leaving the court. In short, this is "Grissil's rebellion" (Comensoli 208). When Gwalter urges Grissil to go, saying "Away with her I say," she responses sarcastically, "Away, away? / Nothing but that colde comfort? / wee'll obay, / Heauen smile vpon my Lord with gratious eye" (4.1.187-89). She goes on to say, "Thus tyranny oppresseth innocence, / Thy lookes seeme heauy, but thy heart is light, / For villaines laugh when wrong oppresseth right" (191-93). Grissil now sees Gwalter as a tyrant and calls him and his courtiers villains. Indeed, when Janicola and Laureo had been banished in the former scene, the two courtiers, Lepido and Mario, laughed at their downfall.

Having returned home, Grissil restarts her country life merrily, but Gwalter orders his courtier to take the babies away from her. To her children, she hopelessly cries: "Your father sendes and I must part from you, / I must oh God I must, must is for Kings, / And loe obedience, for loe vnderlings" (4.2.141-43). Grissil claims she never wants to separate from her babies, but she must do so because the socially inferior must obey the socially superior. This is the principle that the play takes issue with, and which also holds true for *Blind Beggar*.

(c) Different Values in *Patient Grissil* and the Elizabethan Money Based Economy

At first glance, Grissil's status seems to be raised by marriage, but she never forgets her low status and continues to feel the class distinction. The wall between the rich and the commoner is never ruptured. Although the happy ending suggests Grissil's patience has saved her marriage from the problems that exist between different social classes, Gwalter's tyrannical behavior, though it is a pretence, can hardly be wiped completely from the audience's mind. Moreover, his sister Julia remains single till the end, continuing to believe that marriage is a war even after being wooed by many suitors: "to be married is to liue in a kinde of hell" (2.1.259). This might imply that in Renaissance England such marital problems as result from hierarchy were difficult to resolve. In the real Elizabethan society, as Babulo has stated, "this wonder of the rich louing the poor, wil last but nine daies" (1.2.318-19); the distinction between the aristocrats and commoners, or the rich and poor may seldom have disappeared even through marriage.

Remarkably, such conflicts seem to question newly emerging values in Elizabethan society, based on the importance of money. In those days, lifestyles differed between the court/city and country. In literary works, the court/city is generally condemned as a place where desire for power and money is dominant, while the country is described as a Utopia full of nature (Worden 34; R. Williams; Tricomi).

In the Griselda stories, as Margaret Rose Jaster points out, there are three moments in which apparel carries considerable significance; Griselda's metamorphosis from a peasant girl to noble lady by marriage; her banishment from Gwalter's court; and the final denouement of Gwalter's explaining his actions (95); this play seems to underscore her changing social status through clothes much more than previous versions, particularly considering Gwalter's obsession with luxury.[5]

> Ile gild that pouertie, and make it shine,
> With beames of dignitie: this base attire,
> These Ladies shall teare of, and decke thy beautie
> In robes of honour, that the world may say,
> Vertues and beautie was my bride to day. (1.2.270-74)

Gwalter perceives "pouertie" (270), "dignitie" (271), "beautie" (272, 274), "honour" (273), "Vertues" (274) as being personified and Grissil as being his valuable commodity rather than his wife. He, thus, decides to buy Grissil's expensive merits by marrying her and asserts to Babulo, "I wil make her rich" (316). Gwalter believes gorgeous goods are valuable, and that Grissil will be happier through marriage. In contrast, for Grissil and Janicola, luxury signifies nothing because they prefer a poor country life full of love.

Gwalter's materialistic viewpoint is also found in the course of the trial he puts Grissil through, which begins shortly after their marriage. Gwalter mockingly calls her grey gown, pitcher, and hat "thine auncestrie" (2.2.63) and "[t]he monuments of thy nobilitie" (64), and hangs them on the wall. Shortly after this, Janicola and Laureo are turned out of the court. Gwalter complains to them that people are talking about their rise, Grissil's birth and dowry. Janicola tells Gwalter that he had already known of Grissil's poverty, and Gwalter argues that he gave Grissil "all precious robes" (3.1.81) from his "wardrop" (81) to make her "shine in beautie like the Sunne" (82). He goes on to say, "in exchange, I hung this russet gowne, / And this poore pitcher for a monument, / Amongst costliest Iemmes" (83-83).[6] Furthermore, he reminds Grissil of her former status; he claims, "You haue forgot these rags, this water pot" (89), and goes on to say, "you are proude of these your rich attyres" (92). After a while, the time comes when "the monuments," or Grissil's hat, pitcher, and gown are taken down, and Grissil is banished from the court. Gwalter orders his courtiers:

> Disrobe her of these rich abiliments,
> Take downe her hat, her pitcher and her gowne,
> And as she came to me in beggerie,
> So driue her to her fathers. (4.1.169-72)

The repeated image of poor Grissil, associated with the hat, pitcher, and gown, suggests Gwalter's obsession with material objects, and that these things represent her through metonymy, while rich attire suggests Gwalter's wealth and power. As he can move Grissil's belongings up and down, so he can change the status of Grissil and her family and banish them arbitrarily. He treats them as beggars, as do the courtiers. However, according to Janicola, Grissil's "portion / Is but an honest name" (1.2.49-48), and they prefer "quietnes" (4.2.39) in the country to "care" (39) in the court, or spiritual to material wealth.

As society changed from being agricultural to industrial, and more people moved to London, for the most part, ideology changed from being feudalistic to capitalistic, and a money based economy developed. This rapid growth of population and wealth in the Elizabethan and Jacobean periods gave cause for many dramatists to write about London and the aspects of life in massive urban areas in their plays, particularly city comedies.[7] Jonson, for one, satirizes the relation between wealth and power in foreign cities as well as London; the opening speech of *Volpone*, "Good morning to the day; and next my gold" suggests "a blasphemous violation of a 'natural' order, demonstrating that money is not only the root of all evil but of all power," as Michael Hattaway notes (104). However, of the contemporary dramatists Middleton had the greatest interest in London, writing the Lord Mayor's pageants and entertainments and focusing on middle-class city life—"profitable business deals, advantageous marriage bargains, inheriting a relative's wealth or alternatively being cheted and losing out," as Julia Briggs states (43-44). The image of the city in the Renaissance is thus generally closely associated with money, as Frederick, the Duke of Wirtemberg, who visited there in 1592, remarked: "London is a large, excellent, and mighty city of business...most of the inhabitants are employed in buying and selling merchandize, and trading in almost every corner of the world" (7).[8]

Chettle described historical Londoners in *Kind-Heart's Dream* and a beggar living in a suburb of London in *Blind Beggar*, while Dekker portrayed citizens living in London in *The Shoemaker's Holiday* and other works. Haughton's first known play, *Englishmen for My Money*, depicts a Portuguese usurer living in London, who wants to marry his daughters to foreigners, and it was "the first of the immensely popular genre of London city comedies," as David Kathman notes (838). This play has recently drawn the attention of critics, and it is included in *Three Renaissance Usury Plays* edited by Lloyd

7 Beggars in *The Pleasant Comedy of Patient Grissil* and *The Blind Beggar of Bethnal Green*, and the Elizabethan Money Based Economy

Edward Kermode as well as *The Three Ladies of London* and *The Hog Hath Lost His Pearl* by Robert Tailor.[9]

Dekker, Chettle, and Haughton were certainly conscious of the city life including its advantages and disadvantages, and particularly of the money based economy because all of them were imprisoned for debt. Chettle was imprisoned for debt in Marshalsea Prison in 1599 (Henslowe 103, 119; Jenkins 24-25). Dekker was imprisoned in the King's Bench Prison on a debt of forty pounds to the father of John Webster and remained there for seven years, as John Twyning remarks (700). He described this experience in the debtor's prison in a number of pamphlets, such as *Villanies Discovered* (1616; STC 6488) and *Dekker His Dream* (1619; STC 6497). Haughton was released from the Clink prison by Henslowe on 10 March 1600, though it is unknown for what reason he was imprisoned, according to *Henslowe's Diary* (131).[10] In the Elizabethan period, the Clink, close to the Rose in Southwark, was used for Catholic recusants and also thieves, prostitutes, and rogues, because of its locality and then became a debtor's prison by the mid-seventeenth century (Burford 9-12; Salgado 178).

Considering this social background, *Patient Grissil* can be thought to be condemning the materialism of the city, especially London, where money and luxurious commodities were worshipped, though the play itself is located in medieval Italy, following *The Decameron*. The play describes the conflicts between the rich and poor, and notably emphasizes Gwalter's obsession with commodity while depicting the poor sympathetically. This confrontation reflects divisions in the contemporary world, such as the court/city versus the country and the material versus the spiritual, and these are unique to this version. Gwalter believes money and power can resolve all, while Grissil and Janicola prefer poverty in the country to luxury at the court. Gwalter's empty wealth is symbolized in his rich attire, while Grissil's shabby gown is paradoxically "more warme" (2.2.75) and "more rich" (3.1.49) to her. This paradox of the poor being rich while the rich are poor seems a vital point of this play. The Griselda story has originally the moralistic message of the importance of virtue, but this play rather seems to question hierarchy, marriage, and money in Elizabethan society, especially London. The paradoxical idea of the poor being rich is taken up and expanded in *Blind Beggar*.

(iii) *Blind Beggar*

(a) Representation of Beggars in *Blind Beggar*

Blind Beggar is believed to have been written by Chettle and John Day, the playwright, around 1600 from the record for a payment of ten pounds five shillings to them on 25 May 1600 in *Henslowe's Diary* (135). However, the published play was not issued before 1659. According to the title-page, it was acted by the Prince's Servants; E. K. Chambers indicates the company was the later Prince Charles's Men (1631-41) and the ultimate successors of the Admiral's Men (2: 285). Jenkins believes the play must have been acted between 1631 and 1647, after when the theaters were reopened, and sees it as a revival of the earlier play acted by the Admiral's Men in 1600. The original *Blind Beggar* apparently had three parts, according to *Henslowe's Diary*, though only the first part is extant: the second part was written by Day and Haughton from January to May 1601; the third part was written by the same two from May to July 1601. Therefore, the series was popular at the end of the Elizabethan period. Moreover, Haughton's participation in the second and last part is interesting, and this may explain the similarity between *Blind Beggar* and *Patient Grissil*. Both plays deal with poor and wealthy people living in the city.

This play has been little studied, still less performed, possibly because of the corrupt texts and complex plots. As mentioned in the Introduction, there have so far been only three editions including one in facsimile; Bullen's edition (1881); Bang's edition (1902); and Farmer's facsimile of 1914; also, there is Will Sharpe's unpublished critical edition (2009). The play is composed of a main plot—the protagonist Momford's banishment, his disguise as a wounded soldier, blind beggar, and the beggar's brother, and the restoration of his status in the final scene—and two sub-plots: the hostility between Gloucester and Bewford and also the roguery plot of two cony catchers, Canby and Hadland, and the yeoman, Tom Strowd, who is robbed of his coat by Canby and Hadland, and who becomes a cony-catcher. Moreover, not only Momford, but also the marginal characters disguise themselves as serving men, gypsies, and a door keeper. This story seems very concerned with the contemporary social condition, especially beggars and the underworld and also appeals to the taste of the popular audience more clearly than *Patient Grissil*.

The plot of *Blind Beggar* opens with the downfall of the protagonist General Momford, as shown in Chapter 4, "(ii) Downfall." He has been a noble soldier, but is trapped by his brother, Sir Robert Westford; he is suspected of being a spy, and banished from London. However, he is worried about his daughter and decides to stay, disguised as a blind beggar to watch over her. She is deprived of her property and driven out of her uncle Westford's house. She comes across the blind beggar without knowing his true identity, feels sympathy for him, and starts to live in Bethnal Green to take care of him. The story involves complicated sub-plots and ends with the restoration of Momford's status by the King. In this play, Momford is described as a virtuous, loyal, and honest poor person, whereas his enemy, who belongs to the nobility, is depicted as wicked, greedy, and cold blooded; they confront with each other, as do the characters in *Patient Grissil*.

To some degree this play is based on the ballad of "The Beggar's Daughter of Bednall-Green." There are several extant versions, but all of them belong to the later seventeenth century, though Jenkins suggests the possibility of an earlier ballad in the Tudor period, pointing out that Act I Scene ii of *The Return from Parnassus* mentions the ballad (193). One extant example is the ballad in Thomas Percy's *Reliques of Ancient English Poetry* (2: 30-40), based on the legend or folklore in Bethnal Green. The model of the blind beggar is Henry de Montford, who was the son of Simon de Montford, and wealthy enough to inherit the mansion called Montford House. He became wounded and blinded at the Battle of Evesham in 1265. A baroness helped him, and they had a daughter called Besse after his recovery (*Reliques* 31). The story seems to have been popular for a long time during the eighteenth and nineteenth century. There is a chapbook in a small quarto form, "Begger of Bednal-Green," printed for T. Norris around 1715. The song was used in Robert Dodsley's light opera, *Blind Beggar*, and the chapbook, printed by William Smith in 1741, notes: "The songs and duetto, in The blind beggar of Bethnal Green; as perform'd by Mr. Lowe, and Mrs. Clive, at the Theatre-Royal, in Drury-Lane." In 1834, *The Beggar of Bethnal Green, A Comedy in Three Acts* by J. S. Knowles was published.

The play follows some key points of the ballad; the names of the blind beggar and beautiful daughter; the daughter's marriage; the beggar's showing coins to prove the wealth and nobility of his daughter. However, it also has three large alterations. The most important difference is the main plot. In the ballad, the focus is the chivalric romance; several suitors woo fair Bess, but they give up after realizing she is a beggar's daughter. However, a true knight continues to love her and finally marries her with the consent of her father who drops gold to show his wealth and prove her birth. On the other hand, in the play, the main theme is Momford's banishment and the restoration of his status due to the intrigue between his brother, Sir Robert Westford, and his daughter's fiancé, Young Playnsey, who are new characters. Bess marries Momford's loyal friend Captain Westford in the last scene, but this is a result of their chivalric friendship rather than love between them. In other words, this plot is political rather than romantic.

The other alterations are the two sub-plots involving the newly adapted marginal characters. First, there is the antagonism between the Duke of Gloucester and the Bishop of Winchester, Cardinal Bewford, over their love for Ellanor (Act I) and their reconciliation (Act V), which is pseudo-historical, based on Holinshed's *Chronicles* and Stow's *Survey of London*; the reconciliation occurred on 12 March 1426 (Bang vii-viii). Secondly, there is the comical underworld story in London among the "real" vagrants, Canby and Hadland, who dupe Young Strowd, a dull yeoman, into cony-catching. All these rogues are the creation of the authors. The former episode is a trivial pseudo-historical incident in the play and only happens in Act I. The latter serves to give a spice of hilariousness to the play, contrasting with the vicious intrigues by the upper class characters, as well as reminding the audience of the vagabonds in their own society.

There has not been conclusive evidence to prove which parts of the play Chettle wrote, but the intrigue plot seems to be Chettle's work as well as the comical sub-plot of Canby and Hadland. On the other hand, Young Strowd seems to be Day's work; Young Strowd's Norfolk accent can, in particular, be linked with Day's birth in Norfolk (Jenkins 202; Parr 587). Momford's downfall is reminiscent of that of Robert's fate in *Downfall*, which had been performed two years earlier, and the two plays share many points. Both protagonists are noble and fall into a trap laid by their greedy and wicked brother or uncle. Moreover, they disguise themselves as familiar characters from English legends and ballads, that is, the beggar in Bethnal Green and Robin Hood. Furthermore, the plot device whereby the disguised Momford lives with his daughter, who does not know his identity and their meeting again dramatically in the end is similar to the heartwarming reunion between Robert's fiancée Matilda, who has disguised herself as Marian, and her banished noble father, Fitzwalter.

In Elizabethan society, as discussed above, vagrants were generally condemned as idle men or feared by the authorities for their potential for disorder, and the Poor Law was established to control them. However, the number of these people increased due to inflation, bad harvests, and war. Some people were genuinely poor, while others were the sturdy poor, pretending to be real beggars with passports to show their status and permission to beg because begging was an easy way to make money.

The popularity of rogue literature describing rascals living by fraud or robbery in London, by writers such as Awdeley, Harman, and Greene, added to these official attitudes toward beggars. According to Awdeley and Harman, the underworld of the vagrants was well organized; they formed groups of robbers, who were ranked from the top as "an upright man" (head of the hierarchy of the vagrants), "a ruffler" (able-bodied rogue claiming to be an ex-soldier), "a rogue" (vagrant with forged papers), "a palliard" (vagrant in a patched cloak, often with sham sores), "a mort" (female vagrant), and "a doxy" (sexually initiated female vagrant). To be the upright man, a rogue had to serve a one year probation. The upright man went to a cottager's door and demanded money rather than begged under the pretext that he served their country as a soldier, asked all beggars he met on the street if they were formally registered in the organization, and also had the right to share or usurp the possessions and doxies, or female vagrants, of other inferior beggars. The ruffler had weapons and robbed "wayfaring poor men and market women" rather than beg (Awdeley 3-6; Harman 29-31, 33-35, 36-41, 44, 67-75; Salgado 121-22).[11]

There were also beggars who made the claim of being sick, whether it was mental or physical. According to Awdeley, "[a]n Abram man" claimed he was just released from Bedlam Asylum "bare armed, and bare legged," feigning madness and calling himself "poore Tom" like Edgar in *King Lear* (Awdeley 3). On the other hand, vagrants feigning handicap and begging in patched cloaks were called "Palliard," "Washman," or "Clapperdogens," (Awdeley 4, 5; Harman 44). Of the "Washman," Awdeley notes, "He vseth to lye in the hye way with lame or sore legs or arms to begge in the highway with lame or sore legs or arms to beg…They be bitten with Spickworts [spearwort], & sometime with rats bane" (5). Rogue literature described them as sturdy beggars, but there were also real disabled deserving poor. Diseases and also disasters allowed them to have licenses to beg, and parish records noted a great number of the deaf, dumb, blind, crippled, mad, epileptic, shipwrecked, and fire victims (Beier 112). With such a social background, Momford's disguise would make him appear as a real disabled beggar to other characters, especially Bess, who pities his blindness and old age.

There also seems to be a stage-convention of the adoption of the disguise of beggary by noble characters, and this is very different from the practice in rogue literature, which only depicts the evils of vagrants comically. According to Carroll, "most 'beggars' on the English Renaissance stage are not beggars at all, but gentry or noblemen in disguise" (*Fat King* 208). Edgar in *King Lear* is a typical example. He disguises himself as "Poor Tom," or a madman, due to his banishment, and afterwards he takes care of his father, who has become blind. Momford's situation is quite similar to that of Edgar, though he pretends to be a blind man, and he is taken care of by his daughter. Chapman's *The Blind Beggar of Alexandria* had been performed by the Admiral's Men and possibly had some influence on *Blind Beggar*, which was performed by the same theater company, but the plots are totally different.[12] In the former play, Duke Cleanthes has been banished for offering love to the Queen of Egypt and disguises himself as a blind beggar, Irus. In Francis Beaumont and John Fletcher's *The Captain*, Lelia's father disguises himself as a beggar and triumphs over all in the end. In Flethcer and Massinger's *Beggars' Bush*, Gerrard, a nobleman of Flanders, and two other noblemen disguise themselves as beggars, join a group of real beggars, and sing a merry song praising the freedom of vagrancy. At last, they reveal themselves, and Gerrard attempts to help the real beggars, but they refuse for fear of being sent to a house of correction like the Bridewell. In Jonson's *The Staple of News*, Frank disguises himself as a beggar and finally reunites with his prodigal son after his repentance. In the same writer's *The New Inn*, Lord Frampul disguises himself as the Host of the Inn and indulges in his fascination with villainous people living in the underworld.

Carroll claims "one difference between Edgar and the others is the signal lack of suffering on the part of the non-Shakespeare exemplars and, even, in some cases, the presence of a positive merriment" and goes on to say that only Shakespeare questions the class confrontations between the nobility and poor (*Fat King* 208, 215). However, some beggars in non-Shakespearean plays, including Momford, seem to deal with the conflicts more clearly and deeply. The "positive merriment," or the praise of a beggar's life can be thought to criticize the real hierarchical world where the aristocrat enjoys his power and wealth, while the poor are humiliated and controlled by the upper class. Momford seems to show explicitly his positive attitude toward beggars well as criticism against the nobility.

Despite the sentence of banishment from England, Momford decides to stay in disguise to watch over his daughter and Sir Robert Westford, to whom he has left Bess's property and house:

> I am exil'd, Yet I will *England* see,
> And live in *England* 'spight of infamy.
> In some disguise I'll live, perhaps I'll turn
> A Beggar, for a Beggars life is best,
> His Dyet is in each mans Kitchin drest…. (1: 256-60)

Momford asserts "a Beggars life is best," showing a touch of his soldierly nationalism with the word "*England*." His idealization of beggary seems to be in conflict with the Elizabethan public campaign to control vagrants because they are idle and vicious. Momford's idea is closer to St Francis's medieval idea that a beggar is holy, as discussed above.

This idealization of beggars is found in the plays above, but there was a literary tradition of beggars that could be traced back to the late fifteenth century (Carroll, *Fat King* 63). For example, *The Regiment of Poverty* (1572; STC 11759), written by Andreas Hyperius and translated by Henry Tripp, notes "a spare and sober supper, is yet a supper: and the poore mans parsimonye or frugalitie is much more healthfull, than the riche mans excesses" (70). In *The Honest Whore, Part 1*, Dekker observes that "although their bodies beg, their soules are kings" (5.2.504-05).[13] John Taylor more clearly idealizes beggars in *The Praise, Antiquity, and Commodity of Beggary, Beggars, and Begging* (1621; STC 23786). Taylor sees kings and beggars equally given

7 Beggars in *The Pleasant Comedy of Patient Grissil* and *The Blind Beggar of Bethnal Green*, and the Elizabethan Money Based Economy

such four elements as air, fire, earth, and water; he despises money and praises honest poverty.

> 'Mongst all estates most equally is giuen.
> Giu'n, not to be ingrost, or bought, not sold,
> For gifts and bribes, or base corrupting gold.
> These things nor poore or rich, can sell nor buy,
> Free for all liuing creatures, till they dye.
> ....
> Thus all degrees and states, what o're they are,
> With beggers happinesse cannot compare. (B1r-v)

Momford seems to follow these kinds of ideas, and his words anticipate the subsequent immoral behavior of the rich (Sir Robert Westford and Young Playnsey) and the good deeds of the beggars (Momford and Bess).

Similarly, Bess is satisfied with her destitution. In a later scene, after she has come to know that Momford is her father, Young Strowd proposes marriage to Bess, promising, "I'll make thee a wealthy Norfolk Yeomans wife." He does not know her identity. However, as a beggar's daughter, she rejects the offer for the sake of her father: "though our State be poor, / We live content and that's a good mans store" (4: 2071-72). The sublimity of honest poverty suggested by St. Francis can be seen in Bess as well as Momford.

Momford not only praises beggars, but also defends them. In the latter half of the play, Sir Robert Westford and Young Playnsey plot to kill the blind beggar (Momford in disguise), his brother (Momford in disguise, who has knocked down Young Playnsey in the former scene), and Bess, not realizing Momford's true identity. They hire Canby, Hadland, and Young Strowd; however, Young Strowd consequently spoils the plan, falling in love with Bess and exposing it to her. When the villains except Young Strowd, who has lured Bess out of the hut, knock on the door violently, Momford as a beggar complains about the "Englishmen," who go as far as to subject beggars to violence: "What means this out-rage at a Blind mans door? /

Are *Englishmen* become so inhumane / That Beggars cannot scape their violence?" (4: 2155-58).

A similar violence against a beggar, or Momford is mentioned by Sir Robert Westford when he visits the disguised Momford. In the earlier scene, Momford has found the wounded body of Sir Robert Westford and helped him, and Sir Robert Westford reveals his plots against Momford from a sense of guilt, believing Momford is a beggar. A few days later, Sir Robert Westford comes to Momford to take back his confession as a lie and threatens him not to let it out:

> I'le send the now and then a peny,
> But if thou tittle tattle tales of me,
> I'le clap thee by the heels, and whip thy Daughter,
> Turn thee to the wide world, and let thee starve. (3: 1557-60)

This is only a threat, and Sir Robert Westford never harms them physically, because the beggar is actually Momford himself and does not need to expose it; however, these lines are noteworthy in suggesting possible violence against the Elizabethan beggars by clapping, whipping, depriving of homes, and starving.

The Elizabethan period seems not to have seen casual violence against beggars, but the destruction of the shelters of beggars in the London suburbs and also such punishment as whipping to regulate the vagrants did indeed involve a level of violence. *The Acts of the Privy Council* in 1596-97 notes:

> [T]he great abuses that grow by the multitude of base tenements and howses of unlawfull and disorderly resort erected in the suburbs and owt places of the city of London, so have wee…given direction by our letters to divers men whom wee appointed for that purpose to stay or suppress such buildings as in their judgement they thought inconvenient and serving to such disorders. (25: 230)

7 Beggars in *The Pleasant Comedy of Patient Grissil* and *The Blind Beggar of Bethnal Green*, and the Elizabethan Money Based Economy

The authorities were, thus, afraid of disorderly houses which included "poor cottages and habitacions of beggars and people without trade, stables, ins, alehowses, taverns, garden howses converted to dwellings, ordinaries, dicying howses, bowling allies and brothel howses" (25: 230). Beggars were, thus, seen as being dangerous as whores, and their shabby houses in the suburbs like Bethnal Green, though the record does not specify the location, were destroyed by force.[14]

Another violent threat to beggars was the penalties for vagrancy, which can be categorized into two types; corporal punishment, which was more frequently exercised between the fourteenth and seventeenth centuries, and restriction of freedom, or imprisonment in such workhouses as Bridewell. Whipping was the most common punishment, though there were also stocking, forced labor, branding, and incarceration. The Poor Law of 1531 stated that vagrants without passports must be whipped, stripped naked, and drawn by trolleys until their bodies became bloody. Beier claims these punishments enhanced the animosity between the classes, and also strengthened authoritarianism; for example, whipping occasionally turned into murder by the authorities (10, 158-69). As in the case of prisoners and pirates, the authorities displayed their power over beggars with such cruel and violent behavior.

In *Kind-Heart's Dream*, Chettle also complains through the voice of Kind-hart about contemporary society showing no charity for beggars who endure bad food, clothes, and jobs: in "the hart of the Cittie [London]… extreame crueltie causeth much beggerie…Selfe loue hath exiled charitie… among the men, the great oppresse the meaner, they againe the meanest: for whom hard fare, colde lodging, thinne cloathes, and sore labour is onely allotted" (46).

Moreover, in *Piers Plainness*, Chettle shows his sympathy for poor London apprentices through Piers, an apprentice. Piers goes to one master after another in the city, and finally becomes a shepherd and finds peace and happiness in country life. Piers often experiences hunger; for instance,

– 257 –

when he serves Ulpian, the usurer, he has no breakfast, and "At dinner my allowaunce was two Anchoues, sheere water my drinke: and at night drie ryce (or rather rye bread) my best repast" (158). Apprentices, usually young people between their late teens and early twenties in London, were seen as marginal in "the city company hierarchy;" "they were dependents without fixed wages and were treated as children within their employers' households" (Burnett, "Henry Chettle's *Piers Plainness*" 172). Chettle's own experience is, more or less, possibly reflected in Piers's hunger and poverty.

Similarly, Hoffman curses those noblemen who exploit the poor, as discussed in Chapter 5, "(ii) Problems of Soldiers:" "But Hell the hope of all dispayring men, / That wring the poore, and eate the people vp, / As greedy beasts the haruest of their spring" (5.2.2613-15). Furthermore, as discussed in Chapter 3 "Chettle as Dramatic Repairman," *John of Bordeaux*, probably written by Greene, describes a noble lady who turns beggar alongside her children because her husband is wrongly banished. Writing twelve lines for the play, Chettle may have been influenced by the plot. In fact, an imprisoned noble lady in *Death* starves to death with her child in the dungeon, as previously discussed.

The reason why Chettle champions beggars may be attributed to his personal experience of destitution. Chettle might have suffered from poverty in his apprenticeship period, and later he was imprisoned for debt twice. As is often the case, many Elizabethan writers suffered from poverty. In fact, Greene died in poverty. Most of Chettle's colleagues including Dekker, Haughton, Day, Munday, Henry Porter, and Chettle himself owed money to Henslowe. As discussed above, Chettle, Dekker, and Haughton were imprisoned for debt. All the authors involved in depicting poor people in *Patient Grissil* and *Blind Beggar*, thus, had themselves experienced destitution.

(b) Conflicts between the Rich and Poor
The conflict between wealthy and destitute people is a more central is-

sue than the representation of beggars in this play. The conflict is caused by the marriage between a rich man and poor girl, and those with wealth are described as evil, while those without are portrayed as honest and patient.

The villains, Sir Robert Westford and Young Playnsey, commit a number of wicked deeds against Momford and Bess. These intrigues originate from Sir Robert Westford's private enmity against his brother Momford. The reason is never stated in the play, but Momford's property is a particularly important motive. They conspire to have Momford banished, cancel the engagement between Bess and Young Playnsey, and turn her out of her house, which is left in Sir Robert Westford's care by Momford, in order to take away from her "[a]bove ten thousand Marks, besides the Lands" (3: 1108). Sir Robert Westford, in fact, suggests to Young Playnsey:

> You marry with my daughter, shee's my heir,
> Still Mr. *Playnsey* there is land for you;
> I'll turn out *Momfords* daughter forth of doors,
> Seise all her goods and lands by a device;
> Still Mr. *Playnsey* there is Land for you. (1: 219-23)

With Momford's banishment, Bess's marriage, involving as it does such pecuniary problems, invokes class confrontation between the higher (Sir Robert Westford and Young Playnsey) and the lower (Momford and Bess). Sir Robert Westford attempts to make his daughter Kate, Bess's cousin, marry Young Playnsey in front of Bess and other relatives at her house. Chaste Kate, who knows the relation between Young Playnsey and Bess, rejects this marriage: "Oh it's impious match! I'll rather have / Than such a mariage-bed, a dismal grave" (2: 535-36); however, Sir Robert Westford regards Bess as "Your Cosen-Beggar, Child unto a Traytor" (541). At this point, Bess still has her property, but he sees her as a beggar because her father has been banished. Young Playnsey is contemptuous of Bess: "my mind therein is chang'd, / Her Father is disgraced and exil'd / And therefore *Playnseys* Son doth scorn his Child" (599-601). Like Grissil, Bess is metaphorically called a beggar; neither characters actually ever beg to earn money, but they are called such because the rich people want to disdain them and wish to avoid marriages between different classes.

On the other hand, such bystanders as Old Playnsey and Old Strowd are opposed to the marriage between Young Playnsey and Kate as well. Old Strowd comforts Bess, "'Tis more than Injury, but Lady grieve not you" (630), but she replies, "No Sir I am patient" (631). The word "patient" reminds us of Grissil, and is another reason why the authorship of this scene is probably attributed to Chettle. As in *Patient Grissil*, the pathetic description of the virtuous poor woman seems to emphasize the maliciousness of rich men, and anticipates the helplessness of the socially inferior against the socially superior.

Subsequently, Bess leaves her house, but shortly before this, Momford, who has watched the incident, comes in begging in the disguise of a wounded aged soldier. Sir Robert Westford disdains Momford as a "Rogue" (652), when he is given money by Old Strowd. Momford retorts, "I am a Souldier Sir, the name of Rogue / Ill fits a man of your respect to give / To a poor Gentleman, though in distress" (653-55). Here, he seems to play the role of a spokesman for wounded Elizabethan soldiers in their destitution, as opposed to immoral vagrants pretending to have been wounded in battle. Sir Robert Westford is disgusted to hear this, but Bess pities him and gives him diamonds. Watching this, Sir Robert Westford observes them to be "Beggar with Beggar" (694) and turns Bess out. This line is reminiscent of Babulo's words in *Patient Grissil*, "beggers are fit for beggers, gentlefolkes for gentlefolkes" (1.2.317). These phrases clearly show the strong disparity between the social ranks in the Elizabethan period and help place the proposed marriage in context.

Young Playnsey has, thus, forsaken Bess and marries her cousin; nevertheless, he attempts to attain Bess as his mistress, still believing she is a beggar's daughter. Young Playnsey gives Bess "a mark in gold" (3: 1524), but she rejects it: "I am wretched, mortal, miserable, poor, / But howsoever base, I'le be no whore" (1531-32). For this, Young Playnsey suggests, "Wilt thou be then my wife, for she is dead" (1533), but, as Bess points out, this is a lie. Bess, once refused by him, cynically attacks his contradictory attitude with the same theory used by himself in an earlier scene, that is, the disparity between the social positions: "It's much unlike, / A Gentleman of your worth will vouchsafe, / A Beggars Daughter to your Bridal bed" (1534-36).

The villains leave the stage after Sir Robert Westford has promised them money to keep quiet: "I'le send the now and then a peny" (1557). However, soon after that, Young Playnsey comes to Momford's hut alone to woo Bess again. The struggles due to the evil and lust of Young Playnsey are shown more vividly than in earlier scenes. Young Playnsey complains about his wife Kate and states that she will die soon, though giving no reason. Furthermore, he threatens to torment Bess violently if she refuses him:

> Deny me and I'll turn a *Tereus*
> Murder thy Father, then cut out thy tongue,
> Deform thy beauty with the hand of wrath,
> Lastly makes spoyl of thy Virginity,
> Then leave thee wretched. (4: 1802-06)

A virgin in danger was a common theme in the early modern plays, as seen in Shakespeare's *Measure for Measure*, *All's Well that Ends Well*, and *Pericles* among others. Particularly the myth of Tereus, widely known through Ovid's *Metamorphoses* (Book 6) and Seneca's *Thyestes*, fascinated contemporary writers and audience, as the popularity of *Titus Andronicus* suggests. As mentioned in Chapter 1, "(ii) Chettle and John Danter," the translation of *Metamorphoses* was so popular that it was issued seven times between 1567 and 1612; Danter printed it in 1593, and Chettle certainly read it along with *Titus Andronicus*, issued by Danter in 1594. As mentioned in Chapter 1, Chettle was probably allowed a chance to read *Thyestes* included in Seneca's *Ten Tragedies* edited by Newton and printed by Marsh in 1581 because Newton's book called *A View of Valyaunce* was printed by East in 1580. Chettle favored this theme and myth: in *Piers Plainness*, the lustful Duke Rhegius attempts to rape his beautiful and chaste neiece, Queen of Crete, but fails, while in the earlier scene, there is a foreshadowing description, "In this wood Tereus ravish and wrongd Philomele" (130); in *Death*, as described above, John's lust drives the virtuous Matilda to suicide; in *Hoffman*, Hoffman's accomplice, Lorrique, proposes that Hoffman should rape Martha, the Duchess of Prussia, "Shut her perpetuall prisoner in that den; / Make her a Philomel, proue Tereus" (5.2.2386-87).

On the other hand, Young Playnsey tempts Momford with money to persuade Bess, saying, "I'll make thee rich, and one day mary her" (4: 1822). Momford pretends to acquiesce to him to put him off his guard, remarking, "Fear nothing Child, but use him gently, / And I will fit his hot lust presently" (1823-24), while Bess observes that "I'd rather dye" (1819) than yield to "his abhorrid and intemperate lust" (1763). After this dialogue, Momford leaves the stage and soon reappears in disguise as a brother of the beggar to knock down Young Playnsey when Bess is nearly raped by him.

In these three scenes, marriage between different social positions is problematized. The problem of marriage and money is an important theme in this play, as it also is in *Patient Grissil*. The immoral gentleman, Young Playnsey, believes money and power can resolve all and attempts to obtain Bess through financial means. His perspective has been already displayed in the first act when he sees the Duke of Gloster, who wants to get married with Ellanor, offer Old Playnsey, her protector, "six thousand pound" to help him (1: 505). Young Playnsey comments that "Here's a good world when ev'ry Duke is King; / Thus I see power can master any thing" (511-12). These lines suggest that a powerful duke can control people like a king, and his "power" includes money and property.

Young Playnsey, thus, witnesses the behavior of nobler individuals and recognizes the value of power, and more significantly, following the example of the Duke of Glouster, uses it in an effort to obtain a woman. Cardinal Bewford also gives gold to the rogues, Canby and Hadland, to get married with Ellanor; therefore, the use of money in courtship by the Duke and Cardinal is paralleled, or rather parodied by their inferior, Young Playnsey, and this abuse of power by higher ranking people seems to be criticized in these scenes and in Momford's words.

The beggar, Momford, criticizes from the standpoint of one among the lowest ranks. After Sir Robert Westford and Young Playnsey have visited Momford to offer him a bribe and Young Playnsey has first wooed Bess, Momford and Bess pity themselves. Notably, Momford exclaims, "Oh times corrupt by men for want of truth!" (3.1570). He thus attributes his misfortune to social corruption and goes on to criticize the authorities:

> Now he [Sir Robert Westford] denies a deed as clear as day,
> Threatens poor want, and low-trod poverty
> Must not resist men in authority;
> Come lead me in, I would my daies were done,
> Since vice layes baits which virtue cannot shun. (3: 1589-93)

This passage may represent the complaints of Elizabethan poor people who must obey authority. In this context, "vice" points to Robert and Young Playnsey while "low-trod poverty" and "virtue" suggests Momford and Bess. The personnified images of "vice" and "virtue" fight each other as in morality plays, and "vice" defeats "virtue." This is paraphrased in Momford's exclamation, "Oh times corrupt by men for want of truth!" (1570).

In Young Playnsey's second wooing scene, Momford pretends to accept the former's offer to make him rich if he can persuade Bess give in, and in revealing his helplessness to Young Playnsey, emphasizes the distinction of their social status: "Sir I commit my Daughter to your hands…for what can I do more? / You're rich and strong, and I am weak and poor" (4: 1826-30). Hearing this, Young Playnsey gives Momford gold to comfort him, and Momford expresses his weakness and helplessness as a beggar; Momford notes, "For mony [money] few men now shun infamy" (1832), and goes on to say, "I a while I do, / But Playnsey I'll anon be even with you" (1834-35). These lines suggest the harms of the spreading money based economy. People used to value loyalty according to the chivalric code, as Momford suggests, but their thoughts were changing, and some started to weigh everything including honor and military service in terms of commercialism.

(c) Different Values in *Blind Beggars* and the Elizabethan Money Based Economy

The play, thus, describes the conflict between the rich and poor, and criticizes such vicious gentlemen as Sir Robert Westford and Young Playnsey, as well as the Duke of Gloucester and Cardinal Bewford, who value money, and who believe money can resolve all. On the other hand, it praises such "beggars" as Momford and Bess, who are satisfied with their destitution and endure the malicious behaviors of the socially superior patiently. Momford disguises himself as a beggar and regains his noble status in the end. Being a beggar is simply a disguise, and it is not his true identity. However, the disguise allows Momford to give voice to thoughts subversive to the Elizabethan society, such as "low-trod poverty / Must not resist men in authority" (3: 1590-91), "You are rich and strong, and I am weak and poor" (4: 1830), and "But Playnsey I'll anon be even with you" (1834-35). A character in disguise, who directs criticism against the authorities of a character in disguise, recalls Hoffman. Unlike Momford, Hoffman's status ascends though his disguise as the Prince of Luningberg, Otho. Villanous Hoffman kills the ruling class for revenge and also power, and eventually dies. Hoffman's rebellious behavior and speeches seem to be undermined by his death, which restores social order, while Momford's disguise makes it possible for him to complain about the society more safely. Since disguise obscures one's identity, it can be used to manipulate other characters and the audience, and also to carry out subversive acts including attacks on the authorities.

In the final scene of *Blind Beggar*, the gentlemen are ruined, while the beggar, though in disguise, succeeds. Momford's innocence is proved, and he is promoted to Lord High-Treasurer for his military achievements by King Henry VI. Bess marries Captain Westford, Momford's loyal friend. Moreover, Captain Westford is made General by the King. By contrast, Sir Robert Westford and Young Playnsey are to undergo trial for their plots to drive Momford from the court and kill Momford and Bess. Overall, the play expresses disapproval of a society which was introducing and valuing a money system. Traditional or old-fashioned values of loyalty and honor, embodied by Momford, are respected and cherished in this play. This idea, which is linked to nationalism based on militarism, is suggested in the numerous references to "England;" for example, "England," "English," and "Britany [Britain]" are repeated eighteen times, while the enemy, "French" and "France" are mentioned twenty-four times. *Blind Beggar* is a complicated comedy that interweaves three plots, but it can also be called a chronicle and patriotic play, though the events are pseudo-historical.

The play is set during a historical moment in England when Henry VI fought with Charles VII to claim his succession and expand his territory in France, that is, as part of the Hundred Years' War. Such a setting seems to enhance ideas of nationalism, though most of the events are pseudo-historical and subordinate to the main plot of Momford and Bess. The wars at Guines and Calais, historically England's territories at the time, are mentioned in Act I; Young Playnsey is willingly caught by the enemy in Amiens to gain intelligence of the French army and unjustly accuses Momford of selling Guines, his garrison, and Calais to the French by hiring a Swiss soldier as an accomplice.

England at war is emphasized at the end of Act V. At the beginning of the act, Henry VI's uncle, the Duke of Gloucester, and the Bishop of Winchester, Cardinal Bewford, reconcile with each other in front of the King. Their animosity comes from their love for Ellanor, who is possibly the Lady Elinor Cobham, according to Jenkins (192), as depicted in Act I, but historically, their confrontation arose when Henry VI was an infant under the protection of the Duke, and the cause was political. After Momford's innocence is proved, the marriage between Bess and Captain Westford is made official, and Momford reveals his true identity, taking off his "patch'd Gown" (5: 2511). The King makes Momford Lord High-Treasurer and Captain Westford "General / Of all our forces muster'd up 'gainst *France*" (2638-39). From this moment till the last, enmity against France is shown by the King more clearly.

> Thus our disjointed Kingdom being made strong,
> Each Member seated in his proper seat,
> Let's in to praise his name, whose powerfull hand
> Protects the safety of our peacefull land. (2640-44)

The speech first echoes the ending of such typical history plays as Shakespeare's, but in the context, "strong" suggests military power, while "powerfull hand" indicates strong armaments, and the necessity of militarism to uphold the order seems to be highlighted more obviously than in Shakespeare. The idea expressed in the last sentence is shown in military pamphlets, as we have already seen in earlier chapters, that war, especially with Spain, is necessary to keep peace in England.

Another example of nationalism is when rogues visit Momford's hut and beat on his door to kill him: "What means this out-rage at a Blind mans door? / Are *Englishmen* become so inhumane / That Beggars cannot scape their violence?" (4: 2155-57). These words suggest Momford's criticism against the Elizabethan governmental policy, which is cold and ruthless to beggars, as discussed above, but also recollects the good old days in England, when people were kind to the poor. In short, Momford expresses a feudal chivalric ideology, as Meron suggests, namely the importance of "justice, loyalty, courage, honour, mercy" (4).

On the other hand, Sir Robert Westford and Young Playnsey are obsessed with money and thus follow the rising capitalist ideology. They be-

7 Beggars in *The Pleasant Comedy of Patient Grissil* and *The Blind Beggar of Bethnal Green*, and the Elizabethan Money Based Economy

lieve their dreams will come true so long as they have money, and they can do anything with it. Young Playnsey actually sells Guines, a part of the English territory in France, to the French army and attributes this crime to Momford to please Sir Robert Westford, from whom Young Playnsey hopes to be rewarded. Although Momford as a beggar opposes Sir Robert Westford and Young Playnsey as gentlemen in terms of morality throughout the play, their values are also at odds: old-fashioned chivalry versus new capitalist ideologies. In addition, though the Duke of Gloucester and Cardinal Bewford appear less frequently, they also believe money will make their hopes come true, as they attempt to pursue Ellanor. Therefore, in the world, Momford is an outsider, not only as a beggar, but also as an old man with old-fashioned ideas.

In Renaissance England, people such as merchants were interested in commerce and trade as a result of the development of navigation, while others, such as soldiers, still believed in honor and loyalty to the nation through military service. Between these two positions, there seems to have been open conflict over the question of peace with their chief enemy, Spain. The merchants wanted to make peace with the Spanish to further trade, but the soldiers rejected such policies, particularly because Spain was their religious enemy. Several military veterans wrote on this conflict. For example, in *Four Paradoxes* (1604), Digges explains the two positions: "if you bee such a Merchant as hateth a Souldier, thinke it no victorie to picke matter of aduantage out of my weake handling of their good cause" ("To the Reader," π2r; STC 6872). In *An Apology of the Earl of Essex* (1603), Essex defended the necessity of war and showed his contempt for merchants: "But if we consider howe greedie our merchantes will be of such a trade at first, and how easie it will be for a faith breaking enemie to confiscate all our countrimens goodes, and to embarg and vse English shipping against England, wee would not bragge to much of this aduantage" (19; STC 6788). Moreover, "T. B. To the Reader" in William Segar's *Honor, Military, and Civil* (1602), dedicated to Elizabeth, states that commoners should be engaged in gaining profit, whereas nobles should perform military service for honor (π2r; STC 22164).

Thus, in his descriptions of Momford and Young Playnsey, Chettle seems to criticize the rising money based economy, which leads individuals to pursue profits, and champion nationalism based on chivalric military views, which was supposed to protect the state, as Henry VI's final speech suggests.

*

This chapter has discussed the representation of the beggar (or beggar-like) characters in *Patient Grissil* and *Blind Beggar*, focusing on conflicts between the evil rich and honest poor, and also the changing values which reflected the social transition in Elizabethan times. Grissil and her family are actually basket-makers, but mockingly called beggars by the upper classes. Their status rises with her marriage, but the courtiers are jealous of them, and Gwalter banishes them to try her patience. They resume a poor country life, but they enjoy it because they are freed from the cares of the court to the serenity of the country. Gwalter thinks material richness is all and is obsessed with gorgeous robes, but Grissil and Janicola paradoxically claim that to be poor is to be rich and prefer love and warmth in destitution to coldness and anxiety in the wealthy court. Although this play ends with Gwalter's exposition of how he had been testing his wife and the reconciliation between the courtiers and Grissil's family, their peace seems doubtful, because Gwalter's repeated tyrannical behavior cannot be wiped out from the minds of the audience, and also since Gwalter's sister, Julia, who remains single, believes marriage is war to very end.

Blind Beggar more directly and clearly praises the life of the poor, and criticizes the noblemen who are obsessed with power and money. Momford and his daughter Bess are content with their poor life, while such villains as Sir Robert Westford and Young Playnsey make various efforts to torment and kill them. As a beggar, Momford recognizes the helplessness of his state, saying the lower orders must obey the higher. He also criticizes the current relentless and violent attitudes of the upper classes toward beggars, as if he were a spokesman for Elizabethan vagrants, who were completely controlled by the authorities under the Poor Law. In addition, as a chivalric and patriotic soldier, he is obsessed with Englishness and laments the changing society, in which people are becoming colder.

Grissil cannot attack Gwalter and his courtiers so much because she has been brought up in a poor family, though her status rises through marriage. By contrast, Momford and Bess can criticize the evil gentry much more strongly because they remain noble, though Momford is banished and their social standing is momentarily in crisis through the intrigue of villains. Just as Grissil's status rises through marriage, Momford's position falls as he adopts his disguise, but their minds remain noble till the end. Through the descriptions of the poor, Chettle directs attention to the problems of Elizabethan society, social injustice, and the change from feudalistic to capitalist values. Chettle observed the city of London, where money or material goods had begun to replace loyalty and love, and felt sympathy for the poor, believing they were abused by the authorities. Indeed, poverty was something he understood all too well. Dekker, Haughton, and Chettle were imprisoned for debt, and Day owed money to Henslowe, while his friend, Greene died in poverty. Chettle obviously needed to represent the hardships of himself and these people, and criticized the spreading money-based values in the two plays.

Notes

[1] For the origin of the Griselda story and its adaptation in English plays, see Griffith, Jenkins 156-65, Bronfman.

[2] For general discussion of Elizabethan marriage, see Stone, Ingram, Cressy, and Sokol.

[3] All quotations from *Patient Grissil* are from Bowers's edition, *The Dramatic Works of Thomas Dekker*, vol. 1.

4 For a general analysis of the binary opposition between the city and country in literary tradition, see R. Williams 46-54.
5 Cf. Chettle's effective use of rich garments in *Hoffman*. Hoffman disguises himself as Otho, who has been killed by Hoffman, by wearing Otho's gorgeous robes, but mad Lucibella happens to find them and appears in them in front of Otho's mother and relatives, which leads to the exposure of Hoffman's identity and wrongs, and his death.
6 This description is reminiscent of Hoffman's hanging Prince Otho's skeleton next to his father's on the tree, saying that his father is now superior to Otho unlike before: "father this youth scorn'd…would he could see, / How the case alters, you [Hoffman's father] shall hang by him [Otho], / And hang afore him to, for all his pride" (1.3.400-04).
7 For the details of city comedy, see Gibbons, *Jacobean City Comedy*, Griswold 14-54, Leinwand, Howard, and Easterling.
8 For London in Elizabethan and Jacobean literature and culture, see Merritt, Dillon, Mehl et al., Smith et. al, Manley, Howard 29-161, and Grantley 51-140. For economic and social relations in London, see Bruster and Agnew.
9 Also, see a recent article, Crystal Bartolovich's "London's the Thing," which discusses London locations, markets, and Englishness among other things.
10 For the connection between Henslowe and the Clink, see Cerasano 342.
11 For further analysis of Elizabethan beggars, see Aydelotte, Fuller, Dionne and Mentz, as well as Salgado.
12 Peter Hyland pays attention to the disguised characters in four plays, including *Blind Beggar*, performed by the Admiral's Men at the Rose between 1594 and 1600, and suggests the four protagonist (John a Kent in *John a Kent and John a Cumber*, Irus in *Blind Beggar of Alexandria*, Skinke in *Look About You*, and Momford) were played by their star player, probably Alleyn, though he was well-known as a tragic actor (27).
13 The quotation is from Bowers's edition, *The Dramatic Works of Thomas Dekker*, vol. 2.
14 It is uncertain what Bethnal Green was like in those days. However, it was probably "adjacent to London," as Darryll Gratley states, and was seen as the outskirts of London or the City (52). Considering the suburban location of Bethnal Green, we can call it the countryside, but the superiority and peacefulness of rural life are not expressed so much in *Blind Beggar* as in *Patient Grissil*.

Conclusion

The aim of this book has not been to produce a critical biography of Chettle, as Jenkins's study remains the key work of that kind, but rather to construct a historical and cultural study of Chettle's work that discusses his roles and activities in printing, literary, and theatrical circles. The goal has been, thus, to provide a wider and deeper understanding of Elizabethan culture than Jenkins's narrower investigation of Chettle's life and works.

Chettle played an important and leading role in the Elizabethan printing, literary, and theatrical world. Starting his career as a printing apprentice, Chettle worked across the boundaries of printing, pamphleteering, and the theater. In particular, it is noticeable how greatly Chettle's career was determined by the network of contacts he built up during his printing and pamphleteering activities. In the later Elizabethan period, personal relationships were crucial for him to advance in the literary world, which suggests there existed an extensive community of writers, printers, and revisers. The Greene-Nashe-Chettle group, which several other writers including Dekker and Gabriel Harvey have noted, seems to have formed a notable part of this community, as it developed in the final decade of the sixteenth century. On the other hand, writers outside of Chettle's immediate network seem to have been regarded with suspicion and hostility, as in the case of Jonson, and with some degree of ambivalence, Shakespeare. Chettle took advantage of these personal relationships both in the printing and theatrical worlds and obtained various jobs from printing books to writing pamphlets, plays, prologues, and epilogues among other activities.

Chettle's own literary works, particularly his plays, demonstrate his insight into social issues and problems of the period. By invoking and questioning such political issues as power, class, the downfall of great men, and monarchical succession, the religious conflicts between the Protestant and Catholic, as well as such social problems as the increasing number of war veterans, piracy, and beggary, Chettle adopts a resolutely Protestant and satirical standpoint. In these works, Chettle takes the side of the poor whom he often depicts as the victims of a malicious, capricious, and self-interested ruling class. Since Chettle could not write directly about the hierarchical conflicts between the upper and lower class, he used such characters as outlaws and beggars to express an anti-hierarchical perspective.

The experience of printing and writing pamphlets probably increased Chettle's awareness of social problems, since pamphlets typically deal with such issues while pandering to popular taste. Like other pamphleteers and playwrights, he was required to produce timely and provocative texts to make a livelihood and entertain his readership and audience, but, at the same time, he expressed personal views about politics, religion, and social problems through the voices of his main characters. Clearly, he displayed a strong sense of professionalism as an author as well as a printer, which perhaps derived from his pride in his craftsmanship. Thus, there may be deeper meanings to the social positions taken in Chettle's works, which may be indicative of the tensions and ideologies of the skilled artisans and professional writing and printing community.

This book has covered the significant points of Chettle studies. However, there remain several issues to consider. It has been beyond the scope of the research to go into the still emerging and controversial field of statistical computer analyses of authorship in order to look more closely at the three poems written by "H. C.," which are considered to be Chettle's earliest literary works. Moreover, Chettle's relationships with printers and publishers, and also the process of publishing and advertising a book have considerable bearing on book history, and may be used toward a better understanding of early modern print culture. Also, the relation between performance and the

Conclusion

theatrical and printed text requires clarification in a way that does not lose sight of seventeenth century practice in the printing of plays; in particular, the reason why the first editions of *Hoffman* (1631) and *Blind Beggar* (1659) were published such a long time after the first performances around 1600 awaits a satisfactory explanation. Furthermore, the theme of disguise, especially in *Hoffman* and *Blind Beggar*, needs to be investigated further, especially in connection to Chettle's forgery, as seen in Groatsworth and the epistle by "T. N.;" disguise is employed by characters in Chettle's works to hide some intention from other characters, and usually the status of the character is turned upside down; similarly, Chettle seems to engage in forgery in order to mask his identity and also to hide his real intentions.

Moreover, further analysis of Chettle's activities will shed light on certain contradictory aspects of Elizabethan popular culture. Ironically, Chettle wrote pamphlets and plays which denounce money, in order to make money, as did his contemporaries including Nashe and Haughton. Chettle attacks usury in *Kind-Heart's Dream* and *Pierce Plainness*, while criticizing rich people in *Hoffman*, *Patient Grissil*, and *Blind Beggar*. Similarly, Nashe rejects usury and the evil of money in *Pierce Penniless*; and Haughton does so in *Englishmen for My Money*. This contradiction can also be seen in the attitudes and texts of other contemporary playwrights. The study of Chettle's careers can, thus, be developed into an examination of contemporary attitudes toward commercialism, and is significant in achieving a deeper understanding of Elizabethan popular culture.

Furthermore, the relationship between Chettle and Shakespeare remains to be explored. In other words, a tangential point that deserves further study is to determine the similarities or differences between Chettle and Shakespeare, another figure who was a Jack of all trades, is from Chettle. Henslowe's playwrights—including Chettle, Munday, Dekker, Haughton, Day, and Heywood—were certainly typical figures of the time; their subject materials are generally similar and entertaining. However, Shakespeare seems to have kept a distance from Chettle and his fellows, though

Munday and Chettle wrote *Sir Thomas More* in collaboration with Shakespeare. Whether or not Shakespeare was a typical playwright, who catered to popular tastes to make money, remains uncertain, and a comparison with Chettle's careers and writings could be helpful in illuminating the elusive figure of Shakespeare.

Chettle moved flexibly among printing, pamphleteering, and playwriting. In the Elizabethan period, even though the printing industry and theatrical world were closely connected, Chettle, because of his personal relationships with Danter, Henslowe, and other printers and playwrights, served as a bridge between the two worlds and linked them tightly. Chettle probably wrote stage directions and a couple of passages for Q1 *Romeo and Juliet* to help Danter publish it; also, in *Kind Heart's Dream*, Chettle shows the closeness of the printing and theatrical worlds, describing the Nashe-Harvey debate and Tarlton's defense of plays among other issues. Chettle was, thus, at the center of the literary world and a mirror of the period. In recent critical approaches to Renaissance literature, the printing process of plays has increasingly become significant. It is hoped that this study of Henry Chettle will draw more critical attention to his works and the man himself as an important central figure within this scholarly trend.

Appendices

Appendix I: Chettle's Plays[1]
Table 1: Plays for the Admiral's Men (1598-1603)

Date	Author	Title
Feb.-Mar. 1598 and Nov. 1598	Chettle and Anthony Munday	1, 2 Robin Hood [Downfall and Death]
Mar. 1598	Chettle, Thomas Dekker, and Michael Drayton	Famous Wars of Henry I and the Prince of Wales
Mar.-Jun. 1598	Chettle, Dekker, Drayton, and Robert Wilson	1, 2 Earl Goodwin and His Three Sons
Apr. 1598	Chettle, Dekker, Drayton, and Wilson	Pierce of Exton
May-Jul. 1598	Part 1: Chettle, Dekker, Drayton, and Wilson; Part 2: Chettle and Wilson	1, 2 Black Batman of the North
Jun. 1598	Chettle, Drayton, Munday, and Wilson	The Funeral of Richard Coeur de Lion
Jul. 1598	Chettle	A Woman's Tragedy
Aug. 1598	Chettle, Ben Jonson, and Henry Porter	Hot Anger Soon Cold
Aug. 1598	Chettle or Dekker, Drayton, Munday, Wilson	Chance Medley
Aug. 1598	Chettle and Wilson	Castiline's Conspiracy
Aug. 1598	Chettle	Vayvode
Sep.-Oct. 1598	Chettle	2 Brute
Nov. 1598	Chettle	'Tis no Deceit to Deceiver
Feb. 1599	Chettle	Polyphemus, or Troy's Revenge
Mar. 1599	Chettle and Porter	The Spencers
Apr. 1599	Chettle and Dekker	Troilus and Cressida[2]
May 1599	Chettle and Dekker	Agamemnon, or Orestes Furious
Aug.-Oct. 1599	Chettle and Dekker	The Stepmother's Tragedy
Sept. 1599	Chettle, Dekker, Jonson, and John Marston	Robert II, or The Scot's Tragedy
Oct.-Dec. 1599	Chettle, Dekker, and William Haughton	Patient Grissil
Nov. 1599- Sep. 1601	Chettle	The Orphan's Tragedy
Dec. 1599	Chettle and Haughton	The Arcadian Virgin
Feb.-May 1600	Chettle	Damon and Pythias
Mar. 1600	Chettle, John Day, Dekker, and Haughton	The Seven Wise Masters

Appendices

Apr.-May 1600	Chettle, Day, and Dekker	*The Golden Ass, and Cupid and Psyche*
May 1600	Chettle	*The Wooing of Death*
May 1600	Chettle and Day	*1 Blind Beggar*
Mar.-Apr. 1601	Chettle	*All Is Not Gold That Glisters*
Apr.-May 1601	Chettle and Dekker	*King Sebastian of Portugal*
June-Aug. 1601	Chettle	*The Life of Cardinal Wolsey*
Aug.-Nov. 1601	Chettle, Drayton, Munday, and Wentworth Smith	*The Rising of Cardinal Wolsey*
Nov. 1601-Jan. 1602	Chettle, Michael Hathway, and Smith	*Too Good to Be True*
Jan. 1602	Day and Haughton (1601) Chettle mended it (Jan. 1602)	*Friar Rush and the Proud Women of Antwerp*
May 1602	Chettle and Smith	*Love Parts Friendship*
May-Jun. 1602	Chettle	*Tobias*
Jul.-Dec. 1602	Chettle	*Hoffman*
Sept. 1602	Chettle and Robinson	*Felmelanco*
Dec. 1602-Jan. 1603	Part 1: Chettle and Thomas Heywood; Part 2: Chettle	*1, 2 The London Florentine*

Table 2: Plays for Worcester's Men (1602-1603)

Date	Author	Title
Aug. 1602	Chettle	Unnamed play
Oct. 1602	Chettle, Dekker, Heywood, Smith, and John Webster	*1 Lady Jane, or The Overthrow of Rebels*
Nov. 1602	Chettle, Dekker, Heywood, and Webster	*Christmas Comes but Once a Year*
Jan. 1603	Chettle and Heywood	Unnamed play
May 1603	Chettle and Day	*Shore*

Appendix II: Publications of Thomas East
Table 1: Chettle's Apprenticeship period (1577-1584)

Author	Title	Printer	Publisher	Year	STC Number	Genre and Notes
Caldwell, John.	*A Sermon Preached before the Right Honorable Earl of Darby*	East, Thomas.		1577	4367	Religion; Sermons
Dethick, Henry.	*Feriæ Sacræ Octo Libris Compensæ*	East, Thomas.		1577	6787	Religion; Church of England
Church of England	*Articles* [on Bishop John Aylmer]	East, Thomas.	Seres, William.	1577	10251	Law; Orders and Regulations
Hyperius, Andreas.	*The Practice of Preaching*	East, Thomas.		1577	11758	Religion; Preaching
Hyperius, Andreas.	*The Practice of Preaching*	East, Thomas.		1577	11758.5	Religion; Preaching
Hemmingsen, Niels.	*A Learned and Fruitful Commentary upon the Epistle of James the Apostle*	East, Thomas.	Woodcocke, Thomas, and Gregorie Seton.	1577	13060	Religion; Trans. from Latin by W. Gace.
Sarcerius, Erasmus.	*Common Places of Scripture*	East, Thomas.		1577	21756	Religion; Theology
Malory, Thomas, Sir.	*Le Morte d'Artur*	East, Thomas.		1578	805	Literature
Johnson, Laurence.	*Cometographia*	East, Thomas.	Walley, Robertus.	1578	1416	Astronomy; Comets
Brasbridge, Thomas.	*The Poor Man's Jewel*	East, Thomas.	George Bishop	1578	3549	Medicine

Author	Title	Printer	Publisher	Year	STC	Notes
Brooke, John [trans.].	A Christian Discourse upon Certain Points of Religion	East, Thomas.		1578	5158	Religion; Wars of the Huguenots; Anonymous Work in French
Gibutius, Tusanus.	Examen Theologicum	East, Thomas.	Man, Thomas, and Edward Aggas.	1578	11844	Religion; Theology
Lyly, John.	Euphues: The Anatomy of Wit	East, Thomas.	Cawood, Gabriel.	1578	17051	Literature
Ortúñez de Calahorra, Diego.	The Mirror of Princely Deeds and Knighthood [Part 1]	East, Thomas.		1578	18859	Literature; Trans. from Spanish by Margaret Tyler
Chauliac, Guy de.	Guydos Questions	East, Thomas.		1579	12469	Medicine; Galen; Trans. from Latin by George Baker.
Lyly, John.	Euphues: The Anatomy of Wit	East, Thomas.	Cawood, Gabriel.	1579	17053	Literature
Melanchthon, Philip.	Of the Wonderful Popish Monsters	East, Thomas.		1579	17797	Religion; Martin Luther; Trans. from French by John Brooke.
Marconville, Jean de.	The Praise and Dispraise of Women	East, Thomas.	Ponsonby, William.	1579	20182a.5	Literature; Essay; Trans. from French by John Alday
Viret, Pierre.	The Christian Disputations	East, Thomas.		1579	24776	Religion; Trans. from French by John Brooke
B., R.	An Epitaph upon the Death of the Worshipful Master Benedict Spinola	East, Thomas.		1580	1057	History; Memorial Writings; Benedict Spinola [Merchant of Genoa]

Bale, John.	The Image of Both Churches	East, Thomas.		1580	1301	Religion; Bible [New Testament]
Batman, Stephen.	The New Arrival of the Three Gracis	East, Thomas.	Norton, William, and Stephen Batman.	1580	1584	Ethics
Beroaldus, Phillippus.	A Contention between Three Brethren	East, Thomas.	Gosson, Thomas.	1580	1968.3	Literature; Vice; Trans. from Latin by Thomas Salter
Bird, Samuel.	A Friendly Communication	East, Thomas.	Harrison, John, the Younger.	1580	3086	Conduct of Life
Bourne, William.	A Regiment for the Sea	East, Thomas.		1580	3425	Navigation
Brasbridge, Thomas.	The Poor Man's Jewel	East, Thomas.	George Bishop	1580	3551.5	Medicine
Calvin, Jean.	The Commentary of M. John Calvin upon the First Epistle of Saint John	Kyngstone, John and Thomas East.	Harrison, John, the Younger.	1580	4404	Religion
Elyot, Thomas, Sir.	The Book, Named the Governor Devised by Sir Thomas Elyot	East, Thomas.		1580	7642	Politics [Education of Prince]
Fioravanti, Leonardo.	A Short Discourse of the Excellent Doctor and Knight	East, Thomas.		1580	10881	Medicine; Trans. from Italian by John Hester
Anon.	A Plain Pathway to the French Tongue	East, Thomas.		1580	11376.3	Language [French Grammar]
Hemmingsen, Niels.	The Epistle of the Blessed Apostle Saint Paul	East, Thomas.		1580	13057.8	Religion; Bible [New Testament]

Corporation of London	The Decree for Tithes to Be Paid in London	East, Thomas.	Cawood, Gabriel.	1580	16702	Law; Orders and Regulations
Corporation of London	Orders Taken and Enacted for Orphans and Their Portions	East, Thomas.	Cawood, Gabriel.	1580	16708	Law; Orders and Regulations
Lyly, John.	Euphues: The Anatomy of Wit	East, Thomas.	Cawood, Gabriel.	1580	17053.5	Literature
Lyly, John.	Euphues: The Anatomy of Wit	East, Thomas.	Cawood, Gabriel.	1580	17054	Literature
Lyly, John.	Euphues and His England	East, Thomas.	Cawood, Gabriel.	1580	17068	Literature
Lyly, John.	Euphues and His England	East, Thomas.	Cawood, Gabriel.	1580	17069	Literature
Lyly, John.	Euphues and His England	East, Thomas.	Cawood, Gabriel.	1580	17070	Literature
Ochino, Bernardino.	Certain Godly and Very Profitable Sermons	East, Thomas.		1580	18769	Religion; Sermons; Trans. from Italian by William Phiston
Ortúñez de Calahorra, Diego.	The First Part of the Mirror of Princely Deeds and Knighthood	East, Thomas.		1580	18860	Literature; Trans. from Spanish by Margaret Tyler
Newton, Thomas.	A View of Valyaunce	East, Thomas.		1580	21469	Spanish History
Rogers, Thomas.	A Pattern of a Passionate Mind	East, Thomas.		1580	24905.3	Ethics; Morality
Boaistuau, Pierre.	Theatrum Mundi	East, Thomas.	Wight, John.	1581	3170	Humanity; Trans. from French and Latin by John Alday

Cartigny, Jean de.	The Voyage of the Wandering Knight	East, Thomas.		1581	4700	Literature; Trans. from French by William Goodyear; Ed. by Robert Norman
Hemmingsen, Niels.	The Epistle of the Blessed Apostle Saint Paul	East, Thomas.		1581	13058	Religion; Bible
Lyly, John.	Euphues: The Anatomy of Wit	East, Thomas.	Cawood, Gabriel.	1581	17055	Literature
Lyly, John.	Euphues: The Anatomy of Wit	East, Thomas.	Cawood, Gabriel.	1581	17055.5	Literature
Lyly, John.	Euphues and His England	East, Thomas.	Cawood, Gabriel.	1581	17071	Literature
Merbecke, John.	A Book of Notes and Common Places	East, Thomas.		1581	17299	Literature; Commonplace Books
Spenser, Edmund.	The Shepheardes Calender	East, Thomas.	Harrison, John, the Younger.	1581	23090	Literature
Styward, Thomas.	The Pathway to Martial Discipline	East, Thomas.	Jennings, Myles.	1581	23413	Military
Styward, Thomas.	The Pathway to Martial Discipline	East, Thomas.	Jennings, Myles.	1581	23413.5	Military
Apuleius, Lucius.	The XI Books of the Golden Ass	East, Thomas.	Veale, Abraham.	1582	719a	Literature; Trans. from Latin by W. Adlington.
Apuleius, Lucius.	The XI Books of the Golden Ass	East, Thomas.	Veale, Abraham.	1582	719a.5	Literature; Trans. from Latin by W. Adlington.
Malory, Thomas, Sir.	Arthur of Little Britain	East, Thomas.		1582	808	Literature; Trans. from French by John Bourchier

Appendices

Author	Title	Printer	Publisher	Year	STC	Subject
Bartholomaeus, Anglicus.	*Batman upon Bartholomew*	East, Thomas.		1582	1538	Language; Trans. from Latin by John Trevisa
Gifford, George.	*A Godly, Zealous, and Profitable Sermon*	East, Thomas.	Cooke, Tobie.	1582	11860	Religion; Sermons
Gifford, George.	*A Sermon on the Parable of the Sower*	East, Thomas.	Cooke, Tobie.	1582	11863	Religion; Sower; Parable; Sermons
Gutierrez de la Vega, Luis.	*A Compendious Treatise Entitled De Re Militari*[3]	East, Thomas.		1582	12538	Military; Trans. from Spanish by Nicholas Lichefield
Lopes de Castanheda, Fernam.	*The First Book of the History of the Discovery and Conquest of the East Indies*	East, Thomas.		1582	16806	History; Trans. from Portuguese by Nicholas Lichefield
Lyly, John.	*Euphues and His England*	East, Thomas.	Cawood, Gabriel.	1582	17072	Literature
Mandeville, Sir John.	*The Voyage and Travel of Sir John Mandeville*	East, Thomas.		1582	17251	Travel
Merbecke, John.	*Examples Drawn out of Holy Scripture*	East, Thomas.		1582	17301	Religion; Catholic Church; Controversial Literature
Styward, Thomas.	*The Pathway to Martial Discipline*	East, Thomas, John Kingston, William How, and John Charlewood	Jennings, Myles.	1582	23414	Military

Nicholas, Thomas.	*A Pleasant Description of the Fortunate Islands, Called the Islands of Canary*	East, Thomas.		1583	4557	Navigation
Jones, Richard.	*A Brief and Necessary Catechism*	East, Thomas.		1583	14729	Religion; Catechism
La Roche de Chandieu, Antoine.	*A Treatise Touching the Word of God*	East, Thomas.	Harison, John, the Younger.	1583	15257	Religion; Catholic Church; Trans from Latin by John Coxe
Ortúñez de Calahorra, Diego.	*The Second Part of the Mirror of Princely Deeds and Knighthood* [Part 4 and 5]	East, Thomas.		1583	18866	Literature; Trans. from Spanish by Margaret Tyler
Powlter, Richard.	*The Fountain of Flowing Felicity*	East, Thomas.		1583	20173	? [The text is missing.]
Baldwin, William.	*A Treatise of Moral Philosophy*	East, Thomas.		1584	1261	Ethics
Bourne, William.	*A Regiment for the Sea*	East, Thomas.		1584	3425.5	Navigation
Cartigny, Jean de.	*The Voyage of the Wandering Knight*	East, Thomas.		1584	4700.5	Literature; Trans. from French by William Goodyear
Curio, Cælius Secundus.	*Pasquin in a Trance*	East, Thomas.		1584	6131	Religion; Catholic Church; Trans from Italian by W. P.
Greene, Robert [trans.].	*Gwydonius*	East, Thomas.	Ponsonby, William.	1584	12262	French Literature; Louise Labé's *Debat*
Lodge, Thomas.	*An Alarum against Usurers*	East, Thomas.	Clerke, Sampson.	1584	16653	Literature

Lyly, John.	*Euphues and His England*	East, Thomas.	Cawood, Gabriel.	1584	17072.5	Literature
Merbecke, John.	*A Dialogue between Youth and Old Age*	East, Thomas.		1584	17300.5	Age
Ursinus, Zacharias.	*A Very Profitable and Necessary Discourse*	East, Thomas.	Harrison, John, the Younger.	1584	24528	Religion; Trans. from Latin by John Stockwood

Table 2: Chettle's Blank Period (1585-1590)

Author	Title	Printer	Publisher	Year	STC Number	Genre and Notes
Pater, Erra [pseud.].	A Prognostication Forever	East, Thomas.		1585	439.17	Astronomy
Anon.	Sir Bevis of Hampton	East, Thomas.		1585	1990	Literature; Chanson de Geste
Clifford, Christopher.	The School of Horsemanship	East, Thomas.	Cadman, Thomas.	1585	5415	Horsemanship
Clowes, William.	A Brief and Necessary Treatise	East, Thomas.	Cadman, Thomas.	1585	5448	Medicine
John XXI, Pope.	The Treasury of Health	East, Thomas.		1585	14654	Medicine
Lyly, John.	Euphues: The Anatomy of Wit	East, Thomas.	Cawood, Gabriel.	1585	17056	Literature
Ortúñez de Calahorra, Diego.	The Second Part of the First Book of the Mirror of Princely Deeds and Knighthood	East, Thomas.		1585	18862	Literature; Trans. from Spanish by Margaret Tyler
Ortúñez de Calahorra, Diego.	The Second Part of the First Book of the Mirror of Princely Deeds and Knighthood	East, Thomas.		1585	18862.5	Literature; Trans. from Spanish by Margaret Tyler
Norman, Robert.	The [New Attractive]	East, Thomas.	Ballard, Richard.	1585	18648	Navigation; Magnetic Dip
Roberts, Henry.	A Most Friendly Farewell... to the Right Worshipful Sir Francis Drake	East, Thomas.		1585	21084	History; Memorial Writings; Sir Francis Drake
Gale, Thomas.	Certain Works of Surgery	East, Thomas.		1586	11529a	Medicine; Compilation of Galen

Galen.	Certain Works of Galen	East, Thomas.		1586	11531	Medicine; Trans. from Latin by Thomas Gale
Guazzo, Stefano.	The Civil Conversation of M. Stephen Guazzo	East, Thomas.		1586	12423	Etiquette; Trans. from Italian by George Peltie and Bartholomew Yong
Guevara, Antonio de.	The Golden Book of Marcus Aurelius, Emperor and Eloquent Orator	East, Thomas.		1586	12447	History; Trans. by John Bourchier Berners
Lyly, John.	Euphues and His England	East, Thomas.	Cawood, Gabriel.	1586	17073	Literature
Ortúñez de Calahorra, Diego.	The Third Part of the First Book, of the Mirror of Knighthood	East, Thomas.		1586	18864	Literature; Trans. from Spanish by R. P. [Robert Parry or Robert Parke]
Spenser, Edmund.	The Shepherd's Calendar	Wolfe, John and Thomas East.	Harrison, John, the Younger.	1586	23091	Literature
Da Vigo, Giovanni.	The Whole Work of That Famous Surgeon	East, Thomas.	Gale, Thomas.	1586	24723	Medicine; Trans. from Latin by Bartholomew Traheron
Borde, Andrew.	The Breviary of Health	East, Thomas.		1587	3377	Medicine
Bourne, William.	A Regiment for the Sea	East, Thomas.		1587	3426	Navigation
Bullinger, Heinrich.	Fifty Godly and Learned Sermons	Middleton, Henry, Eliot's Court Press, and Thomas East.	Newberie, Ralph.	1587	4058	Religion; Trans. from Latin by H. I.

Anon.	Certain Sermons	Charlewood, John and Thomas East.		1587	13657	Religion; Sermons; Church of England
Anon.	The Second Tome of Homilies	Charlewood, John and Thomas East.		1587	13673	Religion; Sermons; Church of England
Lyly, John.	Euphues: The Anatomy of Wit	East, Thomas.	Cawood, Gabriel.	1587	17057	Literature
Gonzales de Mendoza, Juan.	New Mexico	East, Thomas.	Cadman, Thomas.	1587	18487	Navigation; Trans. from Spanish by Francesco Avanzi
Polemon, John.	The Second Part of the Book of Battles Fought in Our Age	East, Thomas.	Cawood, Gabriel.	1587	20090	Military
Rogers, Thomas.	The English Creed [Part 2]	Day, John, and Thomas East.		1587	21227	Religion; Catholic Church
Arcaeus, Franciscus.	A Most Excellent and Compendious Method of Curing Wounds	East, Thomas.	Cadman, Thomas.	1588	723	Medicine; Trans. from Latin by John Read
Byrd, William.	Psalms, Sonnets, and Songs	East, Thomas.	Byrd, William.	1588	4253	Music
Byrd, William.	Psalms, Sonnets, and Songs	East, Thomas.	Byrd, William.	1588	4253.3	Music
Byrd, William.	Psalms, Sonnets, and Songs	East, Thomas.	Byrd, William.	1588	4253.7	Music

Appendices

Cataneo, Girolamo.	*Most Brief Tables*	East, Thomas.	Wight, John.	1588	4791	Military (Part 3 is mainly based on *The Art of War*); Trans. from Italian by H. G. (Henry Grantham?)
Edrichus or Etherege, George.	*In Libros Aliquot Pauli Aeginetæ*	East, Thomas.		1588	7498	Medicine
Lyly, John.	*Euphues and His England*	East, Thomas.	Cawood, Gabriel.	1588	17074	Literature
Lyster, John.	*A Rule How to Bring up Children*	East, Thomas.		1588	17122	Christian Life
Machiavelli, Niccolo.	*The Art of War*	East, Thomas.	Wight, John.	1588	17166	Military; Trans. from Italian by Peter Whitehorne
Terentius, Publius.	*Andria: The First Comedy of Terence in English*	East, Thomas.	Woodcocke, Thomas.	1588	23895	Literature; Trans. from Latin by Maurice Kyffin
Yonge, Nicholas.	*Musica Transalpina*	East, Thomas.	Byrd, William.	1588	26094	Music
Yonge, Nicholas.	*Musica Transalpina*	East, Thomas.	Byrd, William.	1588	26094.5	Music
Byrd, William.	*A Gratification unto Master John Case*	East, Thomas.	Byrd, William.	1589	4246	Music
Byrd, William.	*Superius [Cantiones Sacrae I]*	East, Thomas.	Byrd, William.	1589	4247	Music
Byrd, William.	*Superius*	East, Thomas.	Byrd, William.	1589	4256	Music
Byrd, William.	*Superius*	East, Thomas.	Byrd, William.	1589	4256.5	Music
Chaderton, Laurence.	*A Fruitful Sermon*	East, Thomas.	Waldegrave, Robert.	1589	4928	Religion; Sermons

Babington, Gervase.	*A Brief Conference betwixt Man's Frailty and Faith*	East, Thomas.	Chard, Thomas.	1590	1083	Christian Life; Faith
Caesar, Caius Julius.	*The Eight Books of Caius Julius Caesar Containing His Martial Exploits in Gallia*	East, Thomas.		1590	4336	Military; Trans. from Latin by Arthur Golding
Anon.	*The Discoverer of France to the Parisians*	East, Thomas.	Aggas, Edward.	1590	11272	French History; Trans. from French by Edward Aggas
Mascall, Leonard.	*A Book of the Art and Manner*	East, Thomas.		1590	17577	Gardening; Grafting; Partly Trans. of Davy Brossard's *L'Art et Maniere de Semer, et Faire Pepinieres des Sauvageaux*
Watson, Thomas.	*Superius*	East, Thomas.	Byrd, William.	1590	25119	Music
Whythorne, Tomas.	*Cantus*	East, Thomas.	Byrd, William.	1590	25583	Music

Appendices

Appendix III:
Publications of William Hoskins, Henry Chettle, and John Danter (1591)

Author	Title	Printer	Publisher	Year	STC Number	Genre and Notes
Anon.	*Fair Em*	Danter, John.	Newman, Thomas, and John Winnington.	1591	7675	Literature; Drama
Lodge, Thomas.	*Catharos.*	Hoskins, William, and John Danter.	Busby, John.	1591	16654	Literature; Morality
Sidney, Philip, Sir.	*Astrophil and Stella*	Danter, John.	Newman, Thomas.	1591	22537	Literature; Poetry
Smith, Henry.	*The Affinity of Faithfull*	Hoskins, William, John Danter, and Henry Chettle.	Ling, Nicholas.	1591	22656	Religion
Smith, Henry.	*The Affinity of Faithfull*	Hoskins, William, and John Danter.	Ling, Nicholas. and John Busby.	1591	22656.5	Religion
Smith, Henry.	*A Fruitful Sermon*	Hoskins, William, Henry Chettle, and John Danter.	Ling, Nicholas.	1591	22664	Religion
Smith, Henry.	*A Fruitful Sermon*	Hoskins, William, Henry Chettle, and John Danter.	Widow Broome	1591	22665	Religion

Appendix IV: Publications of John Danter (1592-98)

Author	Title	Printer	Publisher	Year	STC Number	Genre and Notes
Calvin, Jean.	Sermons... on the History of Melchisedech	Windet, John, and John Danter.	Maunsell, Andrew.	1592	4440	Religion; Sermons; Trans. from French by Thomas Stocker
Learned Physician	Present Remedies against the Plague	Danter, John.	Barley, William.	1592	5871.4	Medicine
Des Pèriers, Bonaventure.	The Mirror of Mirth and Pleasant Conceit	Danter, John.		1592	6784.7	Fiction; Trans. from French by Thomas Deloney
Greene, Robert.	The Black Book's Messenger	Danter, John.	Nelson, Thomas.	1592	12223	Literature; Cony-Catching
Greene, Robert, and Henry Chettle.	Greene's Groatsworth of Wit	Wolfe, John, and John Danter.	Wright, William.	1592	12245	Literature
Greene, Robert.	The Repentance of Robert Greene	Danter, John.	Burby, Cuthbert.	1592	12306	Literature
Gyer, Nicholas.	The English Phlebotomy	Hoskins, William, and John Danter.		1592	12561	Medicine: Bloodletting
Harman, Thomas.	The Groundwork of Cony-Catching	Danter, John.	Barley, William.	1592	12789	Literature; Cony-Catching
Harman, Thomas.	The Groundwork of Cony-Catching	Danter, John.	Barley, William.	1592	12789.5	Literature; Cony-Catching
Holme, John.	The Burden of the Ministry	Danter, John.	Winnington, John.	1592	13601	Christian Life
Nashe, Thomas.	Strange News	Danter, John.		1592	18377	Literature

Nashe, Thomas.	Strange News	Danter, John.		1592	18377a	Literature
Plato	Axiochus. A Most Excellent Dialogue, Written in Greek by Plato the Philosopher	Charlewood, John, and John Danter.	Burby, Cuthbert.	1592	19974.6	Literature; Philosophy; Trans. by Spenser or Munday
Smith, Henry.	Jurisprudentiæ Medicinæ et Theologiæ	Danter, John.	Man, Thomas.	1592	22678	Religion; Sermons
Smith, Henry.	Thirteen Sermons upon Several Texts of Scripture	Scarlet, Thomas, and John Danter.	Man, Thomas.	1592	22717	Religion; Sermons
Vives, Juan Luis.	The Instruction of a Christian Woman	Danter, John.		1592	24863	Education of Women; Trans. from Latin by Richard Hyrde
Wilson, Robert.	The Three Ladies in London	Danter, John.		1592	25785	Literature; Drama
Chettle, Henry.	Kind-Heart's Dream	Wolfe, John, and John Danter.	Wright, William.	1593	5123	Literature
Nashe, Thomas.	Strange News	Danter, John.		1593	18377b	Literature
Nashe, Thomas.	Strange News	Danter, John.		1593	18377b.5	Literature
Nashe, Thomas	Apology of Pierce Penniless	Danter, John.		1593	18378	Literature
Nashe, Thomas	Apology of Pierce Penniless	Danter, John.	Barley, William.	1593	18378a	Literature
Ovid	The XV. Books of P. Ovidius Naso: Entitled Metamorphoses	Danter, John.		1593	18960	Literature; Trans. from Latin by Arthur Golding

Smith, Henry.	*God's Arrow against Atheists*	Danter, John.	Barley, William.	1593	22666	Religion; Sermons
Anon.	*The Life and Death of Jack Straw*	Danter, John.	Barley, William.	1593-94	23356	Literature; Drama
Anon.	*The Most Strange and Admirable Discovery of Three Witches of Warboys*	Windet, John, John Danter, Richard Filed, and Others.	Man, Thomas, and John Winning.	1593	25018.5	News; Witches
W., T.	*The Tears of Fancy. Or, Love Disdained.*	Danter, John.	Barley, William.	1593	25122	Literature
Barnfield, Richard.	*The Affectionate Shepherd*	Danter, John.	Gubbin, Thomas, and E. Newman.	1594	1480	Literature: Poetry
Barnfied, Richard.	*Greene's Funerals. By R. B. Gent.*	Danter, John.		1594	1487	Literature: Poetry
Learned Physician.	*Present Remedies against the Plague*	Danter, John.	Barley, William.	1594	5871.5	Medicine
Church of England.	*Articles*	Danter, John.		1594	10314	Religion
Greene, Robert.	*Orlando Furioso*	Danter, John, and Thomas Scarlet.	Burby, Cuthbert.	1594	12265	Literature; Drama
Lodge, Thomas.	*The Wounds of Civil War*	Danter, John.	Kitson, Abraham or Richard Bankworth.	1594	16678	Literature; Drama

Nashe, Thomas.	*The Terrors of the Night or, a Discourse of Apparition*	Danter, John.	Jones, William.	1594	18379	Literature
Nashe, Thomas.	*Unfortunate Traveler*	Scarlet, Thomas, and John Danter.	Burby, Cuthbert.	1594	18381	Literature
Phillips, John.	*A Commemoration of the Life and Death of the Right Worshipful and Virtuous Lady; Dame Helen Branch*	Danter, John.		1594	19863.7	History; Memorial Writings
Anon.	*Strange Signs Seen in the Air, Strange Monsters*	Danter, John.	Barley, William.	1594	21321	News; Monster
Shakespeare, William and George Peele.	*Titus Andronicus*	Danter, John.	White, Edward, and Thomas Millington.	1594	22328	Literature; Drama
Baptista, Mantuanus.	*The Eclogues of the Poet B. Mantuanus Carmelitanus*	Danter, John.	Barley, William.	1594	22991.5	Literature; Trans. from Latin by George Turberuile
Wilson, Robert.	*The Cobbler's Prophesy*	Danter, John, and Thomas Scarlet.	Burby, Cuthbert.	1594	25781	Literature; Drama
Andrewes, Bartimaeus.	*Certain Very Worthy, Godly and Profitable Sermons*	Danter, John.	Man, Thomas.	1595	585a	Religion; Sermons; Bible (Old Testament)

Henry Chettle's Careers: A Study of an Elizabethan Printer, Pamphleteer, Playwright

Borget, Juvenall [pseud.].	The Devil's Legend	Danter, John.	Gosson, Thomas.	1595	3388	Literature
Breton, Nicholas.	Mary Magdalene's Love	Danter, John.	Barley, William.	1595	3665	Religion; Sermons
Chardon, John.	Fulfordo et Fulfordæ	Danter, John.	Barley, William.	1595	5000	Religion; Sermons
Chettle, Henry.	Piers Plainness' Seven Years' Prenticeship	Danter, John.	Gosson, Thomas.	1595	5124	Literature
Fiston, William [trans.].	The School of Good Manners.	Danter, John.	Jones, William.	1595	10922.5	Etiquette; Trans. from French by William Fiston
Greenham, Richard.	A Most Sweet and Assured Comfort	Danter, John.	Jones, William.	1595	12321	Religion; Spiritual Life
Johnson, Thomas.	Cornucopiæ, or Divers Secrets	Danter, John.	Barley, William.	1595	14707	Natural History
La., R.	Worship in England	Danter, John.	Gosson, Thomas.	1595	15115.5	News
Anon.	A Most Horrible and Detestable Murder	Danter, John.	Barley, William.	1595	17748	News; Murder
Peele, George.	The Old Wife's Tale	Danter, John.	Hancocle, Raph, and John Hardie.	1595	19545	Literature; Drama
Perry, Henry.	Eglvryn Phraethineb	Danter, John.		1595	19775	Literature; Welsh Treatise on Rhetoric
Playfere, Thomas.	A Most Excellent and Heavenly Sermon	Danter, John.	Wise, Andrew.	1595	20014.3	Religion

Appendices

Playfere, Thomas.	*A Most Excellent and Heavenly Sermon*	Danter, John.	Wise, Andrew.	1595	20014.5	Religion
Munday, Anthony [trans.].	*The First Book of Primaleon of Greece*	Danter, John.	Burby, Cuthbert.	1595	20366	Anonymous Spanish Literature; Trans. from French and Italian
Robinson, Clement.	*A Handful of Pleasant Delights*	Danter, John.	Jones, Richard.	1595	21105.5	Literature
Anon.	*News from Rome, Venice, and Vienna*	Danter, John.	Gosson, Thomas.	1595	21294	News
Smith, Henry.	*The Lawyer's Question.*	Danter, John.	Gosson, Thomas.	1595	22679	Religion
Barley, William.	*A New Book of Tablature*	Danter, John.	Barley, William.	1596	1433	Music
Giotti, Giovanni Battista.	*A Book of Curious and Strange Inventions, Called the First Part of Needleworks*	Danter, John.		1596	5323a.8	Domestic Science; Needlework
Copley, Anthony.	*A Fig for Fortune*	Jones, Richard, and John Danter.	C., A. [Copley, Anthony?]	1596	5737	Literature
Anon.	*A Merry Pleasant and Delectable History, between King Edward the Fourth, and a Tanner of Tam*	Danter, John.		1596	7503	Literature
Anon [Richard Whitford?].	*Jesus Psalter*	Danter, John.		1596	14567	Religion; Catholic Church; Ed. and Trans. by George Flinton

Henry Chettle's Careers: A Study of an Elizabethan Printer, Pamphleteer, Playwright

Johnson, Richard.	*The Most Famous History of Seven Champions of Christendom*	Danter, John.	Burby, Cuthbert.	1596	14677	Literature
Johnson, Thomas.	*Cornucopiæ, or Divers Secrets*	Danter, John.	Barley, William.	1596	14708	Natural History
Nashe, Thomas.	*Have with You to Saffron Walden*	Danter, John.		1596	18369	Literature
Partridge, John.	*The Treasury of Hidden Secrets*	Danter, John.	Jones, Richard.	1596	19429.5	Domestic Science
Anon.	*The Pathway to Music*	Danter, John.	Barley, William.	1596	19464	Music
Phillips, John.	*The April of the Church*	Danter, John.		1596	19856.3	Religion
Munday, Anthony [trans.].	*The Second Book of Primaleon of Greece*	Danter, John.	Burby, Cuthbert.	1596	20366a	Anonymous Spanish Literature; Trans. from French and Italian
Middleton, Christopher.	*The Famous History of Chinon of England*	Danter, John.	Burby, Cuthbert.	1597	17866	Literature; Arthurian Romance
Anon.	*Mihil Mumchance*	Danter, John.		1597	17916	Literature; Cony-Catching
Shakespeare, William.	*Romeo and Juliet*	Danter, John, and Edward Allde.		1597	22322	Literature; Drama
Johnson, Richard.	*The Pilgrimage of Man*	Danter, John.		1598	14691.1	Conduct of Life

Appendix V: Addition, Amendments, and Changes for Henslowe by Chettle and Other Contemporary Writers[4]

Author	Date	Work	Payment
Chettle	18 Nov. 1598	"mendynge of the firste pt of Robart hoode" (101)	10 shillings
Chettle	25 Nov. 1598	"mendinge of Roben hood.for the corte" (102)	10 shillings
Chettle	28 Jun. 1601	"altrynge of the boocke of carnowlle wollsey" (175)	20 shillings
Chettle	21 Jan.1602	"mendinge of the Boocke called the prowde womon" (198)	10 shillings
Chettle	15 May 1602	"the mendynge of the fyrste pte of carnowle wollsey" (200)	20 shillings
Chettle	29 Dec. 1602	"a prologe & a epyloge for the corte" (207)	5 shllings
Day, John	5 Nov. 1602	"mery as may be for the cort" (206)	40 shillings
Day, Wentworth Smith, Michael Hathway, and ?	21 Feb. 1603	"adicyones for the 2 pte of the blacke dog" (224)	10 shillings
Day, Smith, Hathway, and ?	24 Feb. 1603	"adycyons in the 2 pte of the blacke doge" (224)	10 shillings
Day, Smith, Hathway, and ?	26 Feb. 1603	"adycyones for the 2 pte of the blacke doge" (224)	20 shillings
Dekker, Thomas.	12 Dec. 1599	"the eande of fortewnatus for the corte" (128)	40 shllings
Dekker	14 Dec. 1600	"faye^e ton…for the corte" (137)	10 shllings
Dekker	22 Dec. 1600	"alterynge of fayton for the corte" (137)	30 shllings
Dekker	12 Jan. 1602	"A prologe & a epiloge for the playe of ponescioues pillet" (187)	10 shllings
Dekker	16 Jan. 1602	"alterynge of tasso" (187)	20 shllings
Dekker	17 Aug. 1602	"new A dicyons in owldcastelle" (213)	40 shllings
Dekker	7 Sep. 1602	"adicions in owld castell" (216)	10 shllings

Dekker	3 Nov. 1602	"mendinge of the playe of tasso" (206)	40 shillings
Heywood, Thomas.	20 Sep. 1602	"new a dicyons cvttyng dicke" (216)	20 shillings
Jonson, Ben.	25 Sep. 1601	"adicians in geronymo" (182)	40 shillings
Jonson	22 Jun. 1602	"Richard crock backe & for new adicyons for Jeronymo" (203)	10 pounds
Middleton, Thomas.	14 Dec. 1602	"a prologe & A epeloge for the playe of bacon for the cort" (207)	5 shillings

Notes

[1] The list is based on Chambers (3: 265-67).

[2] This is a lost play, but its plot is extant as a fragmentary manuscript in the British Museum Ms. Additional 10449. See Chambers 2: 158-59, also Greg, *Dramatic Documents*, vol. 1, which contains it as a facsimile and its notes in vol. 2, 138-43.

[3] This was also issued as the second part of Thomas Styward's *The Pathway to Martial Discipline* (1582).

[4] The date is based on *Henslowe's Diary*, ed. Foakes (2nd ed.).

Bibliography

Primary Sources

Acts of the Privy Council of England. New Ser. Ed. John Roche Dasent. 32 vols. London: H. M. Stationery Office, 1890-1964.

The Antient, True, and Admirable History of Patient Grisel. London, 1619.

Arber, Edward, ed. *A Transcript of the Registers of the Company of Stationers of London 1554-1640*. 5 vols. London, 1875-94.

Awdeley, John. *Fraternity of Vagabonds. The Rogues and Vagabonds of Shakespeare's Youth*. Ed. Edward Viles and F. J. Furnivall. London: N. Trübner, 1880. 1-16.

Bacon, Francis. *The Essays*. Ed. John Pitcher. Harmondsworth: Penguin Books, 1985.

Barwick, Humfrey. *A Brief Discourse Concerning the Force and Effect of all Manual Weapons of Fire*. London, 1591.

Beaumont, Francis and John Fletcher. *The Captain*. London, 1647. 2009.

Boccaccio, Giovanni. *The Decameron*. Trans. J. M. Rigg. 1930. New York, 1973.

———. *De Casibus Virorum Illustrium. Lydgate's Fall of Princes*. Ed. Henry Bargain. 4 vols. London: Oxford UP, 1967.

Bodin, Jean. *The Six Books of a Commonweale*. Ed. Kenneth Douglas McRae. Cambridge, Mass: Harvard UP, 1962.

Bullinger, Henry. *A Treatise or Sermon of Henry Bullinger*. London, 1549.

Caesar, Julius. *The Eight Books of Caius Julius Caesar*. Trans. Arthur Golding. London, 1590.

Calendar of Assize Records: Hertfordshire Indictments, James I. Ed. J. S. Cockburn. London, 1975.

Calendar of Assize Records: Surrey Indictments, Elizabeth I. Ed. J. S. Cockburn. London, 1980.

Calendar of Assize Records: Sussex Indictments, James I. Ed. J. S. Cockburn. London, 1975.

Calendar of the State Papers Relating to Ireland. Ed. H.C. Hamilton. Vol. 4. Nendeln: Kraus, 1974.

Camden, William. *The History of the Most Renowned and Victorious Princess Elizabeth*. London. 1635.

C., H [Chettle, Henry?]. *A Doleful Ditty, or Sorowful Sonnet of the Lord Dar[n]ly*. London,

1579.

———. *The Forrest of Fancy.* London, 1579.

———. *The Popes Pitiful Lamentation.* London, 1579.

Chapman, George. *Blind Beggar of Alexandria.* London, 1598.

———. *Bussy d'Ambois.* Ed. Nicholas Brooke. 1964. Manchester: Manchester UP, 1979.

———. *Caesar and Pompey.* London, 1631.

———. *The Conspiracy and Tragedy of Charles, Duke of Byron.* Ed. John Margeson. Manchester: Manchester UP, 1988.

———. *The Revenge of Bussy d'Ambois.* Ed. Katherine Eisaman Maus. *Four Revenge Tragedies.* Oxford: Oxford UP, 1995. 175-248.

Chaucer, Geoffrey. *The Canterbury Tales.* Ed. David Wright. Oxford: Oxford UP, 1998.

Chettle, Henry. *England's Mourning Garment.* Ed. C. M. Ingleby. *Shakespeare Allusion-Books.* Part I. The New Shakespeare Society. London: N. Trübner, 1874. 77-108.

———. *Kind-Hart's Dream.* Ed. G. B. Harrison. New York: Barnes and Noble, 1966. 5-65.

———. *Kind-Hart's Dream.* Ed. Edward F. Rimbault. London: The Percy Society, 1841.

———. *Piers Plainness's Seven Year's Prentiship.* Ed. James Winny. *The Descent of Euphues: Three Elizabethan Romance Stories: Euphues, Pandosto, Piers Plainness.* Cambridge: Cambridge UP, 1957. 122-74.

———. *The Tragedy of Hoffman.* Ed. Richard Ackermann. Bamberg: Kommissionsverlag von H. Uhlenhuth, 1894.

———. *The Tragedy of Hoffman.* Ed. Harold Jenkins. Oxford: Oxford UP, 1951.

———. *The Tragedy of Hoffman.* Ed. John Jowett. Diss. U of Liverpool. Nottingham: Nottingham UP, 1983.

———. *The Tragedy of Hoffman.* Ed. H. B. L[ennard]. London, 1852.

———. *The Tragedy of Hoffman. The Tragedy of Hoffman by Henry Chettle: A Critical Edition with Textual Commentaries and Notes, Edited from the 1631 Quarto.* Ed. E. J. Schlochauer. Diss. Princeton U. 1948. Ann Arbor: UMI, 2003.

———. *The Tragedy of Hoffman.* Ed. Emma Smith. *Five Revenge Tragedies: Kyd, Shakespeare, Marston, Chettle, Middleton.* London: Penguin Books, 2012. 243-324.

Chettle, Henry, and John Day. *The Blind Beggar of Bethnal Green.* Ed. A. H. Bullen. Day's Work. London, 1881.

———. *The Blind Beggar of Bethnal Green.* Ed. Willy Bang. Louvan: Uystruyst, 1902.

———. *The Blind Beggar of Bethnal Green.* Ed. J. S. Falmer. Amersham: Tudor Facsimile Texts, 1914.

———. *The Blind Beggar of Bethnal Green.* "A Critical Edition of *The Blind Beggar of Bethnal Green* by John Day and Henry Chettle (1600)." Ed. Will Sharpe. Diss. U of Birmingham, 2009.

Bibliography

Chettle, Henry, and Anthony Munday. *The Death of Robert, Earl of Huntington.* Ed. J. C. Meagher. Oxford: Oxford UP, 1967.
———. *The Death of Robert, Earl of Huntington. The Huntingdon Plays: A Critical Edition of The Downfall and the Death of Robert, Earl of Huntingdon.* Ed. J. C. Meagher. New York. Garland, 1980. 284-461.
———. *The Downfall of Robert, Earl of Huntington.* Ed. J. C. Meagher. Oxford: Oxford UP, 1964.
———. *The Downfall of Robert, Earl of Huntington. The Huntingdon Plays: A Critical Edition of The Downfall and the Death of Robert, Earl of Huntingdon.* Ed. J. C. Meagher. New York. Garland, 1980. 119-283.
Chettle, Henry, Thomas Dekker, and William Haughton. *The Pleasant Comedy of Patient Grissill. The Dramatic Works of Thomas Dekker.* Vol. 1. Ed. Fredson Bowers. Cambridge: Cambridge UP. 1953. 207-98.
Chettle, Henry, Thomas Dekker, Thomas Haywood, Wentworth Smith, and John Webster. *Sir Thomas Wyatt. The Dramatic Works of Thomas Dekker.* Ed. Fredson Bowers. Vol.1. Cambridge: Cambridge UP, 1953. 397-469.
Churchyard, Thomas. *A Pleasant Discourse of Court and Wars.* London, 1596.
Clarke, John. *The Trumpet of Apollo.* London, 1602.
Clinton, Atkins. *Clinton, Purser and Arnold.* London, 1583.
The Contention between Liberality and Prodigality. London, 1602.
Danuel, Samuel. *Philotas.* London, 1607.
Davies, John. *Scourge of Folly.* London, 1611.
Dekker, Thomas. *The Belman of London.* London, 1608.
———. *Dekker His Dream.* London, 1616.
———. *English Villainies.* London, 1632.
———. *The Honest Whore, Part 1. The Dramatic Works of Thomas Dekker.* Ed. Fredson Bowers. Vol. 1. Cambridge: Cambridge UP, 1953. 20-109.
———. *A Knights Conjuring.* London, 1607.
———. *Lantern and Candlelight.* London, 1608.
———. *O Per Se O.* London, 1612.
———. *The Shoemakers' Holiday. The Dramatic Works of Thomas Dekker.* Ed. Fredson Bowers. Vol. 1. Cambridge: Cambridge UP, 1953. 18-89.
———. *Villainies Discovered.* London, 1616.
———. *The Whore of Babylon. The Dramatic Works of Thomas Dekker.* Ed. Fredson Bowers. Vol. 1. Cambridge: Cambridge UP, 1953. 491-584.
———. *The Wonderful Year. 1603.* Ed. G. B. Harrison. New York: Barnes, 1966.
Dekker, Thomas, and Thomas Middleton. *The Roaring Girl.* Ed. Paul A. Mulholland. Manchester: Manchester UP, 1987.

Devereux, Robert, the Second Earl of Essex. *An Apology of the Earl of Essex*. London, Digges, Thomas. *Four Paradoxes, or Politic Discourses*. London, 1604.

———. *Stratioticos*. London, 1579.

Dodsley, Robert. *Blind Beggar of Bethnal Green*. London, 1741.

Doleman, D. [Robert Parsons]. *A Conference about the Next Succession to the Crown of England*. Antwerp, 1594.

Drayton, Michael. *Matilda*. *The Works of Michael Drayton*. Ed. William Hebel. Vol. 1. Oxford: Shakespeare Head, 1931. 214-15.

———. *England's Heroical Epistles*. London, 1597.

Earle, John. *Microcosmographie*. Ed. Harold Osborne. London: University Tutorial P, 1933.

Erasmus, Desiderius. *The Complaint of Peace*. Trans. Thomas Paynell. London, 1559.

Fair Em. Fair Em: A Critical Edition. Ed. Standish Henning. New York: Garland, 1980.

The Famous Victories of Henry the Fifth. London, 1595.

Fletcher, John, and Philip Massinger. *Beggars' Bush*. London, 1647.

Foxe, John. *The Acts and Monuments of These Latter and Perilous Days*. London, 1563.

Frederick, Duke of Wirtemberg. "A True and Faith Narrative (1602)." *England as Seen by Foreigners*. Ed. William Brenchy Rye. London: John Russell Smith, 1865.

Gates, Geoffrey. *The Defense of Military Profession*. London, 1579.

George a Green. London, 1599.

Gosson, Stephen. *The Trumpet of War*. London, 1598.

Grafton, Richard. A *Chronicle at Large and Meer History of the Affairs of England and Kings of the Same*. London, 1569.

Greene, Robert. *Arbasto*. London, 1589.

———. *The Black Book's Messenger*. London, 1592.

———. *Ciceronis Amor*. London, 1589.

———. *The Defence of Cony-Catching*. London, 1592.

———. *A Disputation between a He Cony-Catchier, and a She Cony-Catcher*. London, 1592.

———. *Friar Bacon Friar Bungay*. Ed. John Johnson. Oxford: Oxford UP, 1926.

———. *Groatsworth of Wit*. "A Critical Edition of Robert Greene's *Groatsworth of Wit*." Ed. Thomas William Cobb. Diss. Yale U, 1977.

———. *Gwydonius*. London, 1587.

———. *The History of Orlando Furioso*. Ed. Horace Hart. 1907; Oxford: Oxford UP, 1963.

———. *Mamillia. Part 1*. London, 1583.

———. *Mamillia. Part 2*. London, 1593.

———. *Menaphon*. London, 1589.

———. *Morando*. London, 1584.

Bibliography

———. *A Notable Discovery of Cosenage*. London, 1591.
———. *Pandosto*. London, 1588.
———. *The Scottish History of James the Fourth*. London, 1598.
———. *The Second Part of Cony-Catching*. London, 1591.
———. *The Third and Last Part of Cony-Catching*. London, 1592.
Greene, Robert, and Henry Chettle. *Greene's Groatsworth of Wit: Bought with a Million of Repentance (1592)*. Ed. D. Allen Carroll. Binghamton: Medieval and Renaissance Texts and Studies. 1994.
Greene, Robert, and Thomas Lodge. *A Looking Glass for London and England*. Ed. John Johnson. Oxford: Oxford UP, 1932.
Harman, Thomas. *A Caveat. The Rogues and Vagabonds of Shakespeare's Youth*. Ed. Edward Viles and F. J. Furnivall. London: N. Trübner, 1880. 17-91.
Harrison, William. *Description of England. Harrison's Description of England in Shakespeare's Youth*. Ed. F. J. Furnivall. Part 1. The New Shaksepeare Society. London: N. Trübner, 1877.
Haughton, William. *Englishmen for My Money. Three Renaissance Usury Plays*. Ed. Lloyd Edward Kermode. Manchester: Manchester UP, 2009. 164-274.
Henslowe, Philip. *Henslowe's Diary*. Ed. R. A. Foakes. 2nd ed. Cambridge: Cambridge UP, 2002.
———. *Henslowe's Diary*. Ed. W. W. Greg. 2 vols. London: A. H. Bullen, 1904-08.
Heywood, Thomas. *A Funeral Elegy upon the Death of Prince Henry*. London, 1613.
———. *If You Know Not Me You Know Nobody, Part 1*. Ed. Madeleine Doran. Oxford: Oxford UP, 1935.
———. *If You Know Not Me You Know Nobody, Part 2*. Ed. Madeleine Doran. Oxford: Oxford UP, 1935.
———. *The Royal King, and the Loyal Subject*. London, 1637.
———. *A True Relation of the Lives and Deaths of the Two Most Famous English Pirates, Purser and Clinton*. London, 1639.
Heywood, Thomas, and William Rowley. *Fortune by Land and Sea*. London, 1655.
Holinshed, Raphael. *The Chronicles of England, Scotland and Ireland. Holinshed's Chronicles—England, Scotland, and Ireland*. Ed. Vernon F. Snow. 6 vols. New York: AMS, 1976.
Hyperius, Andreas. *The Regiment of the Poverty*. Trans. Henry Tripp. London, 1572.
James I. *Basilikon Doron*. Edinburgh, 1599.
———. *True Law of Free Monarchies*. Edinburgh, 1598.
John of Bordeaux: or The Second Part of Friar Bacon. Ed. W. L. Renwick. Oxford: Oxford UP, 1936.
Jonson, Ben. *The New Inn*. Ed. Michael Hattaway. Manchester: Manchester UP, 1984.

———. *Sejanus*. Ed. Philip J. Ayres. Manchester: Manchester UP, 1999.

———. *The Staple of News*. Ed. Anthony Parr. Manchester: Manchester UP, 1988.

———. *Volpone, or The Fox*. Ed. Brian Parker. Manchester: Manchester UP, 1999.

Knowles, J. S. *The Beggar of Bethnal Green, A Comedy in Three Acts*. London, 1834.

Kyd, Thomas. *The Spanish Tragedy*. Ed. J. R. Mulryne. London: Methuen.

A Larum for London. London, 1602.

The Life and Death of Jack Straw. London, 1593-94.

Lodge, Thomas. *Rosalind*. London, 1590.

———. *An Alarum against Usurers*. 1584.

———. *The Wounds of Civil War*. Ed. John Dover Wilson. 1910. Oxford: Oxford UP, 1965.

Lodge, Thomas, trans. *A Treatise of the Plague*. By François Valleriole. London, 1603.

Lyly, John. *Euphues: Anatomy of Wit*. London, 1578.

———. *Eupheus and His England*. London, 1580.

Machiavelli, Niccolò. *The Art of War*. Trans. Peter Withorne. Book 1. London, 1562.

Marlowe, Christopher. *The Jew of Malta and the Massacre at Paris*. Ed. H. S. Bennett. New York: Gordian, 1931.

Marston, John. *Antonio's Revenge*. Ed. Reavley Gair. Manchester: Manchester UP, 1978.

Maus, Katharine Eisaman, ed. *Four Revenge Tragedies*. Oxford: Oxford UP, 1995.

Mendoza, Diego Hurtado de. *The Pleasant History of Lazarillo de Tormes*. Trans. David Rowland. London, 1586.

Mihil Mumchance. London, 1597.

Munday, Anthony. *A Brief Discourse of the Taking of Edmund Campion*. London, 1581.

———. *The Book of Sir Thomas More*. Ed. W. W. Greg. 1911. Oxford: Oxford UP, 1961.

———. *A Discovery of Edmund Campion and His Confederates*. London, 1582.

———. *The English Roman Life*. London, 1582.

———. *The Mirror of Mutability*. London, 1579.

———. *A Watch-Word to England to Beware of Traytors*. London, 1582.

———. *Zelauto*. London, 1580.

Munday, Anthony, trans. *Gerileon of England, Part 2*. By Etienne de Maisonneuve. London, 1592.

———. *The Second Book of Primaleon of Greece*. By Anon. London, 1596.

Munday, Anthony, and Henry Chettle with revision and additions by Thomas Dekker, William Shakespeare and Thomas Heywood. *Sir Thomas More*. *William Shakespeare: The Complete Works*. Ed. John Jowett, William Montgomery, Gary Taylor, and Stanley Wells. 2nd ed. Oxford: Clarendon, 2005. 813-42.

Munday, Anthony, Michael Drayton, Richard Hathway, and Robert Wilson. *The Life of Sir John Oldcastle*. London, 1600.

Bibliography

Munday, Anthony, and Others. *Sir Thomas More*. Ed. Vittorio Gabrieli and Giorgio Melchiori. Manchester: Manchester UP, 1990.
Mynshul, Geoffrey. *Essays and Characters of a Prison and Prisoners*. London, 1618.
Nashe, Thomas. *The Anatomy of Absurdity*. London, 1589.
———. *Have with You to Saffron Walden. The Works of Thomas Nashe*. Ed. Ronald B. McKerrow. Vol. 3. London: Sidgwick and Jackson, 1910. 1-139.
———. *Pierce Penniless His Supplication to the Devil. The Works of Thomas Nashe*. Ed. Ronald B. McKerrow. Vol. 1. London: Sidgwick and Jackson, 1910. 137-245.
———. *Strange News. The Works of Thomas Nashe*. Ed. Ronald B. McKerrow. Vol. 1. London: Sidgwick and Jackson, 1910. 253-335.
———. *Unfortunate Traveller. The Works of Thomas Nash*. Ed. Ronald B. McKerrow. Vol. 2. London: Sidgwick and Jackson, 1910. 187-328.
Nichols, John, ed. *The Progress and Public Processions of Queen Elizabeth*. 2 vols. London, 1823.
———. *The Progresses, Processions, and Magnificent Festivities of King James the First*. London, 1828.
Norton, Thomas and Thomas Sackville. *Ferrex and Porrex: Or, Gorboduc*. 1908; New York: AMS, 1970.
Ovid. *Metamorphoses*. Ed. E. J. Kenny. Trans. A. D. Melville. Oxford: Oxford UP, 2009.
Peele, George. *The Battle of Alcazar*. Ed. Frank Sidgwick. 1907. Oxford: Oxford UP, 1963.
———. *An Eclogue...to...Robert Earl of Essex*. London, 1589.
———. *The Famous Chronicle of King Edward the First*. London, 1593.
———. *A Farewell...to...Sir J. Norris and Sir F. Drake*. London, 1589.
Plato. *The Axiochus. The Axiochus of Plato*. Ed. Frederick M. Padelford. 1934. Baltimore: Johns Hopkins UP, 1934.
Pollard, Alfred W., and G. R. Redgrave, eds. *A Short-Title Catalogue of Books Printed in England, Scotland, and Ireland and of English Books Printed Abroad 1475-1640*. Rev. W. A Jackson, F. S. Ferguson, and Katherine F. Pantzer. 2nd ed. 3 vols. London: The Bibliographical Society, 1976-91.
Polemon, John. *The Second Part of the Book of Battles Fought in Our Age*. London, 1587.
Raleigh, Sir Walter. *A Discourse Touching a War with Spain, and of the Protecting of the Netherlands. The Works of Sir Walter Raleigh, Kt*. Vol. 3. New York: Burt Franklin. 299-316.
Records of the Court of the Stationers' Company: 1576 to 1602, from Register B. Ed. W. W. Greg and Eleanore Boswell. London: Bibliographical Society, 1930.
The Return from Parnassus. London, 1606.
Riche, Barnaby. *Alarm to England*. London, 1578.

———. *Faults Faults, and Nothing Else But Faults.* London, 1606.
———. *Greene's News Both from Heaven and Hell.* London, 1593.
Ritson, Joseph. *Bibliographia Poetica.* London, 1802.
Rowlands, Samuel. *Greene's Ghost in Haunting Cony-Catchers.* London, 1602.
Shakespeare, William. *Cymbeline. William Shakespeare: The Complete Works.* Ed. John Jowett, William Montgomery, Gary Taylor, and Stanley Wells. 2nd ed. Oxford: Clarendon, 2005. 1185-1219.
———. *An Excellent Conceited Tragedy of Romeo and Juliet.* Ed. Cedric Watts. London: Prentice Hall, 1995.
———. *The First Part of the Contetion (2 Henry VI). William Shakespeare: The Complete Works.* Ed. John Jowett, William Montgomery, Gary Taylor, and Stanley Wells. 2nd ed. Oxford: Clarendon, 2005. 55-90.
———. *The First Quarto of Romeo and Juliet.* Ed. Lukas Erne. Cambridge: Cambridge UP, 2007.
———. *Hamlet.* Ed. Harold Jenkins. London: Methuen, 1982.
———. *Henry IV, Part One.* Ed. David Bevington. Oxford: Oxford UP, 1987.
———. *Henry V.* Ed. Gary Taylor. Oxford: Oxford UP, 1984.
———. *Julius Carsar.* Ed. David Daniell. Walton-on-Thames; Thomas Nelson, 1998.
———. *King John. William Shakespeare The Complete Works.* Ed. John Jowett, William Montgomery, Gary Taylor, and Stanley Wells. 2nd ed. Oxford: Clarendon, 2005. 425-52.
———. *Measure for Measure. William Shakespeare The Complete Works.* Ed. John Jowett, William Montgomery, Gary Taylor, and Stanley Wells. 2nd ed. Oxford: Clarendon, 2005. 843-71.
———. *Richard Duke of York (3 Henry VI). William Shakespeare: The Complete Works.* Ed. John Jowett, William Montgomery, Gary Taylor, and Stanley Wells. 2nd ed. Oxford: Clarendon, 2005. 91-124.
———. *Richard III.* Ed. James R. Siemon. London: Arden Shakespeare, 2009.
———. *Romeo and Juliet.* London, 1597.
———. *Romeo and Juliet.* London, 1599.
———. *Romeo and Juliet.* Ed. Brian Gibbons. London: Methuen, 1980.
———. *Romeo and Juliet.* Eds. Jill Levenson and Barry Gaines. Oxford: Oxford UP, 2000.
———. *Romeo and Juliet.* Ed. Cedric Watts. London: Prentice Hall, 1995.
———. *The Taming of the Shrew. William Shakespeare The Complete Works.* Ed. John Jowett, William Montgomery, Gary Taylor, and Stanley Wells. 2nd ed. Oxford: Clarendon, 2005. 25-53.
———. *The Tragedy of King Lear: The Folio Text. William Shakespeare The Complete Works.*

Bibliography

———. Ed. John Jowett, William Montgomery, Gary Taylor, and Stanley Wells. 2nd ed. Oxford: Clarendon, 2005. 1153-84.

———. *Twelfth Night*. *William Shakespeare The Complete Works*. Ed. John Jowett, William Montgomery, Gary Taylor, and Stanley Wells. 2nd ed. Oxford: Clarendon, 2005. 719-42.

———. *The Winter's Tale*. *William Shakespeare The Complete Works*. Ed. John Jowett, William Montgomery, Gary Taylor, and Stanley Wells. 2nd ed. Oxford: Clarendon, 2005. 1123-54.

Shakespeare, William, and George Peele. *Titus Andronicus*. *William Shakespeare The Complete Works*. Ed. John Jowett, William Montgomery, Gary Taylor, and Stanley Wells. 2nd ed. Oxford: Clarendon, 2005. 155-82.

Shakespeare. William, and George Wilkins. *Pericles: A Reconstructed Text*. *William Shakespeare: The Complete Works*. Ed. John Jowett, William Montgomery, Gary Taylor, and Stanley Wells. 2nd ed. Oxford: Clarendon, 2005. 1059-86.

Smythe, Sir John. *Certain Discourses*. London, 1590.

Spenser, Edmund. *The Shepheardes Calender*. *Edmund Spenser's Poetry*. Ed. Hugh Maclean. 2nd ed. New York: W. W. Norton, 1968.

Stow, John. *Annals of England*. London, 1592.

———. *A Survey of London*. London, 1598.

Stubbes, Philip. *The Anatomy of Abuses*. London, 1583.

Sutcliffe, Matthew. *The Practice, Proceedings, and Laws of Arms*. London, 1593.

Tarlton's Jests. London, 1613.

Tarlton's News out of Purgatory. London, 1590.

Taylor, John. *Tom Nash His Ghost*. London, 1643.

———. *The Praise, Antiquity, and Commodity of Beggary, Beggars, and Begging*. London, 1621.

Townshend, Hayward. *Historical Collections*. London, 1680.

The Tragedy of Locrine. London, 1595. Ed. Vivian Ridler. Oxford: Oxford UP, 1908.

The Trial of Chivalry. London, 1605.

The Troublesome Raigne of King John. London, 1591.

Two Most Strange and Notable Examples. London, 1591.

Warner, William. *Albion's England*. London, 1586.

Wilde, Oscar. *The Picture of Dorian Gray*. 1891. Harmondsworth: Penguin Books, 1949.

Williams, Roger, Sir. *A Brief Discourse of War*. London, 1590.

Wilson, Thomas. *The State of England, Anno Dom. 1600*. *Camden Miscellany* 16. Ed. F. J. Fisher. London: Offices of the Society, 1936.

Wilson, Robert. *The Cobbler's Prophecy*. London, 1594.

———. *The Three Ladies of London*. *Three Renaissance Usury Plays*. Ed. Lloyd Edward Kermode. Manchester: Manchester UP, 2009. 79-163.

Wing, Donald, ed. *Short-Title Catalogue of Books Printed in England, Scotland, Ireland, Wales, and British America, and of English Books Printed in Other Countries, 1641-1700.* 2nd ed. 4 vols. New York: Index Committee of the Modern Language Association of America, 1972-1998.

Wotton, Sir Henry. *A Parallel between Robert Late Earl of Essex and George Late Duke of Buckingham.* London, 1641.

Secondary Sources

Achinstein, Sharon. "Audience and Authors: Ballads and the Making of English Renaissance Literary Culture." *Journal of Medieval and Renaissance Studies* 22 (1992): 311-26.

Agnew, Jean-Christophe. *Worlds Apart Market and the Theater in Anglo-American Thought 1550-1750.* Cambridge: Cambridge UP, 1986.

Al-Ghamdi, A. A. "The Protagonist as Playwright and Stage Manager in Two Elizabethan Revenge Tragedies." *Journal of King Saud University Arts* 6 (1994): 21-32.

Andes, H. R. D. *Shakespeare's Books: A Dissertation on Shakespeare's Reading and the Immediate Sources of His Works.* New York: AMS, 1965.

Andrews, K. R. *Elizabethan Privateering: English Privateering During the Spanish War, 1585-1603.* Cambridge: Cambridge UP, 1964.

Anglo, Sydney. *Machiavelli—The First Century: Studies in Enthusiasm, Hostility, and Irrelevance.* Oxford: Oxford UP, 2005.

Ardolino, Frank. "The Protestant Context of George Peele's 'Pleasant Conceited' *Old Wives Tale.*" *Medieval and Renaissance Drama in England* 18 (2005): 146-65.

Austin, Warren B. *A Computer-Aided Technique for Stylistic Discrimination: The Authorship of "Greene's Groatsworth of Wit."* Washington, D.C.: U.S. Department of Health, Education, and Welfare, 1969.

Axton, Mary. *The Queen's Two Bodies: Drama and the Elizabethan Succession.* London: Royal Historical Society, 1977.

Aydelotte, Frank. *Elizabethan Rogues and Vagabonds.* London: Frank Cass, 1967.

Baker, Christopher. *Religion in the Age of Shakespeare.* Westport: Greenwood, 2007.

Bartolovich, Crystal. "London's the Thing: Alienation, the Market, and *Englishmen for My Money.*" *The Huntington Library Quarterly* 71 (2008): 137-56.

Barton, Anne. "Harking Back to Elizabeth: Ben Jonson and Caroline Nostalgia." *ELH* 48 (1981): 706-31.

Bate, Jonathan. "In the Script Factory." *Times Literary Supplement.* 18 April 2003: 3-4.

Beer, Anna. *Sir Walter Raleigh and His Readers in the Seventeenth Century: Speaking to the People.* Houndmills: Macmillan, 1997.

Beier, A. L. *Masterless Men: The Vagrancy Problem in England, 1560-1640.* London: Methuen,

Bibliography

1985.

Bennett, H. S. *English Books and Readers 1558 to 1603: Being a Study in the History of the Book Trade in the Reign of Elizabeth I*. Cambridge: Cambridge UP, 1965.

Berek, Peter. "'Follow the Money': Sex, Murder, Print and Domestic Tragedy." *Medieval and Renaissance Drama in England* 21 (2008): 170-88.

Bergeron, David M. "Anthony Munday." *DNB*. Ed. H. C. G. Matthew and Brian Harrison. 3rd ed. Vol. 39. Oxford: Oxford UP, 2004. 739-46.

Bevan, Bryan. *King James VI of Scotland and I of England*. London: Rubicon, 1996.

Bevington, David. *Tudor Drama and Politics: A Critical Approach to Topical Meaning*. Cambridge, MA: Harvard UP, 1968.

Bingham, Caroline. *James I of England*. London: Weidenfeld and Nicolson, 1981.

Blayney, Peter W. M. "*The Booke of Sir Thomas Moore* Re-Examined." *SP* 69 (1972): 167-91.

Bowers, Fredson. *Elizabethan Revenge Tragedy 1587-1642*. Princeton: Princeton UP, 1940.

Boyer, C. V. *The Villain as Hero in Elizabethan Tragedy*. 1914. New York: Russell and Russell, 1964.

Bret, Philip. *William Byrd and His Contemporaries: Essays and a Monograph*. Berkley: U of California P, 2007. Bridenbaugh, Carl. *Vexed and Troubled Englishmen, 1590-1642*. New York: Oxford UP, 1968.

Briggs, Julia. *This Stage-Play World: English Literature and Its Background 1580-1625*. Rev. ed. Oxford: Oxford UP, 1997.

Bronfman, Judith. "Griselda, Renaissance Woman." *The Renaissance English Woman in Print*. Ed. A. M. Haselkorn and B. S. Travitsky. Amherst: U of Massachusetts P, 1990: 211-23.

Broude, Ronald. "Revenge and Revenge Tragedy." *RQ* 28 (1975): 38-58.

Browne, Paul. "A source for the 'Burning Crown' in Henry Chettle's *The Tragedy of Hoffman*." *NQ* 51 (2004): 297-99.

Brucher, Richard. "Piracy and Parody in Chettle's *Hoffman*." *Ben Jonson Journal* 6 (1999): 209-22.

Bruster, Douglas. *Drama and Market in the Age of Shakespeare*. Cambridge: Cambridge UP, 1992.

Budra, Paul Vincent. *A Mirror for Magistrates and the De Casibius Tradition*. Toronto: U of Toronto P, 2000.

Burford, E. J. *A Short History of Clink Prison*. London: Clink Prison Museum, 1989.

Burnett, Mark Thornton. "Apprentice Literature and the 'Crisis' of the 1590s." *The Yearbook of English Studies* 21 (1991): 27-38.

———. "Henry Chettle's *Piers Plainness Seven Years' Prenticeship*: Contexts and Consumers." *Framing Elizabethan Fictions*. Ed. C. C. Relian. Kent: Kent State UP, 1994.

169-86.

Bullen, A. H. "Henry Chettle." *DNB*. Ed. Leslie Stephen. Vol. 10. London, 1887. 207-10.

Byrne, M. St. C. "Bibliographical Clues in Collaborate Plays." *The Library* 13 (1933): 21-48.

Campbell, L. B. *Tudor Conceptions of History and Tragedy in "A Mirror for Magistrates."* Berkley: U of California P, 1936.

Carroll, William C. "Language, Politics, and Poverty in Shakespearian Drama." *Shakespeare and Politics*. Ed. Catherine M. S. Alexander. Cambridge: Cambridge UP, 2004. 142-54.

———. *Fat King, Lean Beggar: Representations of Poverty in the Age of Shakespeare*. Ithaca: Cornell UP, 1996.

Cartelli, Thomas "Suffolk and the Pirates: Discovered Relations in Shakespeare's *2 Henry VI*." *A Companion to Shakespeare's Works: The Histories*. Ed. Richard Dutton and Jean E. Howard. Vol. 2. Malden, MA: Blackwell, 2003. 325-43.

Cerasano, S. P. "The Geography of Henslowe's Diary." *SQ* 56 (2005): 328-53.

Chambers, E. K. *The Elizabethan Stage*. 4 vols. Oxford: Clarendon, 1923.

Chillington, Carol. "Playwrights at Work: Henslowe's Not Shakespeare's *Book of Sir Thomas More*." *English Literary Renaissance* 10 (1980): 439-79.

Clare, Janet. *"Art Made Tongue-tied by Authority": Elizabethan and Jacobean Dramatic Censorship*. Manchester: Manchester UP, 1990.

Clark, Sandra. *The Elizabethan Pamphleteers: Popular Moralistic Pamphlets 1580-1640*. London: Athlone, 1983.

Clarke, Bob. *From Grub Street to Fleet Street: An Illustrated History of English Newspaper to 1899*. Aldershot: Ashgate, 2004.

Cockle, Maurice J. O. *A Bibliography of Military Books up to 1642*. 2nd ed. London: Holland, 1957.

Collier, J. P. *The History of English Dramatic Poetry*. George Bell and Sons. London, 1831.

Collinson, Patrick, Arnold Hunt, and Alexandra Walsham. "Religious Publishing in England 1557-1640." *The Cambridge History of Book in Britain*. Vol. 4. Cambridge: Cambridge UP, 2002. 29-66.

Comensoli, Viviana. "Refashioning the Marriage Code: The *Patient Grissil* of Dekker, Chettle and Haughton." *Renaissance and Reformation / Renaissance et Réforme* 25 (1989): 199-214.

Cooper, Helen. *Pastoral: Medieval into Renaissance*. Ipswich: P. S. Brewer, 1977.

Cressy, David. *Birth, Marriage and Death: Ritual, Religion and the Life-Cycle in Tudor and Stuart England*. Oxford: Oxford UP, 1997.

Cruickshank, C. G. *Elizabeth's Army*. Oxford: Clarendon, 1966.

Bibliography

Crupi, Charles. *Robert Greene*. Boston: Twayne Publishers, 1986.

Daugherty, Leo. "The Question of Topical Allusion in Richard Barnfield's Pastoral Verse." *The Affectionate Shepherd: Celebrating Richard Barnfield*. Ed. Kenneth Borris and George Klawitter. Selinsgrove: Susquehanna UP, 2001. 45-61.

Dean, Paul. "Forms of Times: Some Elizabethan Two-Part History Plays." *RS* 4 (1990): 410-30.

Delius, N. "Chettle's Hoffman und Shakespeare's Hamlet," *Jahrbuch der Deutschen Shakespeare-Gesellschaft* 9 (1874): 166-94.

A Dictionary of Anonymous and Pseudonymous Publications in the English Language. Ed. Samuel Halkett and John Laing. 3rd ed. Harlow: Longman, 1980.

Digges, Leonard, and Thomas Digges. *Stratioticos*. London, 1579.

Digges, Thomas, and Dudley Digges. *Four Paradoxes, or Politique Discourses*. London, 1604.

Dillon, Janette. *Theatre, Court and City 1596-1610: Drama and the Social Space in London*. Cambridge: Cambridge UP, 2000.

Dionne, Craig, and Steve Mentz, eds. *Rogues and Early Modern English Culture*. Ann Arbor: U of Michigan P, 2004.

Dobb, Clifford. "London's Prisons." *Shakespeare in His Own Age*. Ed. Allardyce Nicoll. Cambridge: Cambridge UP, 1965. 87-100.

Dollimore, Jonathan. *Radical Tragedy: Religion, Ideology and Power in the Drama of Shakespeare and His Contemporaries*. Brighton: Harvester, 1984.

Doran, Madeleine. *Endeavors of Art: A Study of Form in Elizabethan Drama*. Madison: U of Wisconsin P, 1954.

Duffy, Michael, ed. *The Military Revolution and the State 1500-1800*. Exeter: U of Exeter P, 1980.

Duncan-Jones, Katherine. "Who Was Marlowe's 'Brocher of Atheisme'?." *NQ* (2006): 449-52.

Dunworth, Felicity. "A 'Bosom Burnt up with Desires': The Trials of Patient Griselda on the Elizabethan Stage." *Paragraph: A Journal of Modern Critical Theory* 21(1998): 330-53.

Edelman, Charles. "Peele's *The Battle of Alcazar*." *The Explicator* 61 (2003): 196-97.

Eltis, David. *The Military Revolution in Sixteenth-Century Europe*. London: Tauris Academic Studies, 1995.

Farley-Hills, David. "The 'Bad' quarto of *Romeo and Juliet*." *SS* 49 (1996): 27-44.

Farnham, William. *The Medieval Heritage of Elizabethan Tragedy*. Oxford: Blackwell, 1956.

Fellowes, Edmund H. *William Byrd*. London: Oxford UP, 1936.

Ferguson, W. Craig. "Valentine Simmes." *DLB* 170. Ed. James K. Bracken and Joel Silver. Detroit: Gale Research, 1996. 44-48.

Fisher, Keely. "The Crying of ane Playe; Robin Hood and Maying in Sixteenth-Century Scotland." *Medieval and Renaissance Drama in England* 12 (1999): 19-58.

Fitter, Chris. "Emergent Shakespeare and the Politics of Protest: *2 Henry VI* in Historical Contexts." *ELH* 67 (2000): 45-69.

Foucault, Michel. *Discipline and Punish: The Birth of the Prison*. Trans. Alan Sheridan. 1977. New York: Vintage Books, 1979.

Fox, Alistair. "The Complaint of Poetry for the Death of Liberality: the Decline of Literary Patronage in the 1590s." *The Reign of Elizabeth I: Court and Culture in the Last Decade*. Ed. John Guy. Cambridge: Cambridge UP, 1995.

Freyd, Bernard. "Spenser or Anthony Munday?" *PMLA* 50 (1935): 903-08.

Fuchs, Barbara. "Faithless Empires: Pirates, Renegadoes, and the English Nation." *ELH* 67 (2000): 45-69.

Fuller, Ronals. *The Beggar's Brotherhood*. London: George Allen and Unwin, 1936.

Fulton, Helen. "The Performance of Social Class: Domestic Violence in the Griselda Story." *Journal of the Australasian Universities Modern Language Association* 106 (2006): 25-42.

Gaskell, Philip. *A New Introduction to Bibliography*. Oxford: Clarendon. 1972.

Gasper, Julia. *The Dragon and the Dove: The Plays of Thomas Dekker*. Oxford: Clarendon, 1990.

Gibbons, Brian. *Jacobean City Comedy*. 2nd ed. London: Methuen, 1980.

Glady, S. J. "Revenge as Double Standard in *The Tragedy of Hoffman*." *Discoveries* 18 (2001): 3-4.

Grantley, Darryll. *London in Early Modern English Drama: Representing the Built Environment*. New York: Palgrave Macmillan, 2008.

Green, D. M. "The Welsh Characters in *Patient Grissil*." *Boston University Studies in English* 4 (1960): 171-80.

Greg, W. W. *A Bibliography of the English Printed Drama to the Restoration*. 4 vols. London: Oxford UP, 1939-59.

———. *Dramatic Documents from the Elizabethan Playhouses: Stage Plots: Actor's Parts: Prompt Books*. 2 vols. Oxford: Clarendon, 1931.

———. *English Literary Autographs, 1550-1650*. 4 vols. Nendeln, Liechtenstein: Kraus, 1968.

———. *The Shakespeare First Folio: Its Bibliographical and Textual History*. Oxford: Oxford UP, 1955.

Griffith, Dudley David. *The Origin of the Griselda Story*. Seattle: U of Washington P, 1931.

Griswold, Wendy. *Renaissance Revivals*. Chicago: U of Chicago, 1986.

Gurr, Andrew. *Shakespeare's Opposites: The Admiral's Company 1594-1625*. Cambridge: Cambridge UP, 2009.

———. *The Shakespearean Stage, 1574-1642*. Cambridge: Cambridge UP, 1970.

Bibliography

Hadfield, Andrew. "Thomas Lodge and Elizabethan Republicanism." *Nordic Journal of English Studies* 4 (2005): 89-105.

Halasz, Alexandra. "Paper Monsters: Pamphlets, Writers, and Printing in England at the End of the Sixteenth-Century." Diss. John Hoskins U, 1991.

Hale, John. "Shakespeare and Warfare," *William Shakespeare: His World, His Work, His Influence*. Ed. J. F. Andrews. New York: Scribner, 1985. 85-98.

Halstead, W. L. "Collaboration on *The Patient Grissill*." *PQ* 18 (1939): 381-94.

Hamilton, Donna. *Anthony Munday and the Catholics, 1560-1633*. Aldershot: Ashgate, 2005.

Hammer, Paul E. J. *The Polarisation of Elizabethan Politics: The Political Career of Robert Devereux, 2nd Earl of Essex, 1585-1597*. Cambridge: Cambridge UP, 1999.

———. "Robert Devreux." *DNB*. Ed. H. C. G. Matthew and Brian Harrison. 3rd ed. Vol. 15. Oxford: Oxford UP, 2004. 945-60.

Hanabusa, Chiaki. "Edward Allde's Types in Sheets E-K of *Romeo and Juliet* Q1 (1597)." *PBSA* 91 (1997): 423-28.

———. "Insatsu-Gyosha, Shokunin, Eijento [Printer, Craftman, Agent]." *Shakespeare to Sonojidai wo Yomu [Reading Shakespeare and His Time]*. 25-49.

———. "John Danter's Play-Quartos: A Bibliographical and Textual Analysis." 2 vols. Diss. U of Birmingham. 2000.

———. "Notes on the Second Edition of Thomas Nashe's *The Unfortunate Traveller*." *NQ* 56 (2009): 556-59.

———. "Shared Printing in Robert Wilson's *The Cobbler's Prophecy* (1594)." *PBSA* 97 (2003): 333-49.

———. "The Printer of Sheet G in Robert Greene's *Orlando Furioso* Q1." *The Library* 19 (1997): 145-50.

Harbage, Alfred, ed. *Annals of English Drama 975-1700*. Rev. ed. London: Routledge, 1964.

Harley, John. *The World of William Byrd: Musicians, Merchants and Magnates*. Farnham: Ashgate, 2010.

Hattaway, Michael. "Drama and Society." *The Cambridge Companion to English Renaissance Drama*. Ed. A. R. Braunmuller and Michael Hattaway. Cambridge: Cambridge UP. 1990. 91-126.

Heinemann, Margot. "Political Drama." *The Cambridge Companion to English Renaissance Drama*. Ed. A. R. Braunmuller and Michael Hattaway. Cambridge: Cambridge UP. 1990. 161-205.

———. *Puritanism and Theatre: Thomas Middleton and Opposition Drama under the Early Stuarts*. Cambridge: Cambridge UP, 1980.

Helgerson, Richard. "Writing Empire and Nation." *The Cambridge Companion to English*

Literature 1500-1600. Ed. Arthur F. Kinney. Cambridge: Cambridge UP, 2000. 310-29.

Henning, Standish. "The Printer of *Romeo and Juliet*, Q1." *PBSA* 60 (1966): 363-64.

Hill, Christopher. *The Collected Essays of Christopher Hill: People and Ideas in 17th Century England*. Vol. 3. Brighton: Harvester, 1986.

———. *The Collected Essays of Christopher Hill: Writing and Revolution in Seventeenth Century England*. Vol. 1. Brighton: Harvester, 1985.

Hill, Tracey. *Anthony Munday and Civic Culture: Theatre, History and Power in Early Modern London 1580-1633*. Manchester: Manchester UP, 2004.

Holt, J. C. *Robin Hood*. London: Thames and Hudson, 1985.

Honda, Marie. "Pacifism and Patronage of King James I in Court Masque and Popular Drama." *Horaizun* 46. Tokyo: Waseda-Daigaku Eibei-Bungakukai, 2014. 1-21.

Hoppe, Harry H. *The Bad Quarto of "Romeo and Juliet:" A Bibliographical and Textual Study*. Ithaca: Cornell UP, 1948.

———. "*John of Bordeaux*: A Bad Quarto That Never Reached Print." *Studies in Honor of A. H. R. Fairchild*. Ed. Charles T. Prouty. Columbia: U of Missouiri P, 1946. 119-32.

Howard, Jean E. *Theater of a City: The Places of London Comedy, 1598-1642*. Philadelphia: U of Pennsylvania P, 2006.

Hoy, C. H. *Introductions, Notes, and Commentaries to Texts in The Dramatic Works of Thomas Dekker*. Ed. Fredson Bowers. Cambridge: Cambridge UP, 1980.

Hunt, M. H. *Thomas Dekker*. New York: Columbia UP, 1911.

Hunter, Lynette. "Adaptation and/or Revision in Early Quartos of *Romeo and Juliet*." *PBSA* 101 (2007): 5-54.

Ingram, Martin. *Church Courts, Sex and Marriage in England, 1570-1640*. Cambridge: Cambridge UP, 1987.

Ioppolo, Grace. *Dramatists and Their Manuscripts in the Age of Shakespeare, Jonson, Middleton and Heywood: Authorship, Authority and the Playhouse*. London: Routledge, 2006.

Ishikawa, Naoko Komachiya. "The English Clown: Print in Performance and Performance in Print." Diss. U of Birmingham, 2012.

Jackson, MacDonald P. "The Date and Authorship of Hand D's Contribution to *Sir Thomas More*: Evidence from 'Literature Online.'" *SS* 59 (2006): 68-114.

Jaster, Margaret Rose. "Controlling Clothes, Manipulating Mates: Petruchio's Griselda." *SS* 29 (2001): 93-108.

Jenkins, Harold. *The Life and Work of Henry Chettle*. London: Sedgwick, 1934.

Johnson, Nora. *The Actor as Playwright in Early Modern Drama*. Cambridge: Cambridge UP, 2003.

Jones, F. L. "Henry Chettle: A Study of His Life and Works." Diss. Cornell U, 1925.

Bibliography

Jones, Norman. "Shakespeare's England." *A Companion to Shakespeare*. Oxford: Blackwell, 1999.

Jones, Rosalind Ann, and Peter Stallybrass. *Renaissance Clothing and the Materials of Memory*. Cambridge: Cambridge UP, 2000.

Jorgensen, Paul. *Shakespeare's Military World*. Berkley: U of California P, 1956.

Jowett, John. "Credulous to False Prints: Shakespeare, Chettle, Harvey, Wolfe." *Shakespeare Continuities: Essays in Honour of E. A. J. Honigman*. Basingstoke: Macmillan, 1997. 93-107.

———. "Henry Chettle." *DLB* 136. Ed. David A. Richardson. Detroit: Gale Research, 1994. 38-44.

———. "Henry Chettle and the First Quarto of *Romeo and Juliet*." *PBSA* 92 (1998): 53-74.

———. "Henry Chettle and the Original Text of *Sir Thomas More*." *Shakespeare and Sir Thomas More. Essays on the Play and Its Shakespearian Interest*. Ed. T. H. Howard-Hill. Cambridge: Cambridge UP, 1989. 131-49.

———. "*Henry Chettle*: 'Your Old Compositor.'" *TEXT* 15 (2002): 141-61.

———. "Johannes Factotum: Henry Chettle and *Greene's Groatsworth of Wit*." *PBSA* 87.4 (1993): 453-86.

———. "Notes on Henry Chettle." *RES* 45. 179, 180 (1994): 385-88; 516-22.

Jowitt, Claire. "Piracy and Politics in Heywood and Rowley's *Fortune by Land and Sea*." *RS* 16 (2002): 216-32.

———. ed. *Pirates? The Politics of Plunder, 1550–1650*. Basingstoke: Palgrave Macmillan, 2006.

Judges, A.V. *The Elizabethan Underworld*. London: G. Routledge, 1930.

Jusserand, J. J. *A Literary History of The English People—From the Origins to the Civil War*. Vol. 3. London: George Allen and Unwin, 1909.

Kahan, Jeffrey. "Henry Chettle and the Unreliable Romeo: A Reassessment." *Upstart Crow* 16 (1996): 92-100.

———. "Henry Chettle's *Romeo* Q1 and *The Death of Robert, Earl of Huntingdon*." *NQ* 43 (1996): 155-56.

Kathman, David. "William Haughton." *DNB*. Ed. H. C. G. Matthew and Brian Harrison. 3rd ed. Vol. 25. Oxford: Oxford UP, 2004. 838-39.

Kawai, Shoichiro. *Nazotoki Shakespeare [Solving the Shakespearean Enigma]*. Tokyo: Shinchosha, 2008.

Kelsey, Harry. *Sir Francis Drake: The Queen's Pirate*. New Haven: Yale UP, 1998.

Keyshian, Harry. "Griselda on the Elizabethan Stage: The *Patient Grissil* of Chettle, Dekker, and Haughton." *SEL* 16 (1976): 253-61.

Kinney, Arthur F., ed. *Rogues, Vagabonds, and Sturdy Beggars: A New Gallery of Tudor and Early*

Stuart Rogue Literature. Amherst: U of Massachusetts P, 1990.
Knecht, Robert J. *The French Civil Wars, 1562-1598.* Harlow: Longman, 2000.
Knight, Stephen. *Robin Hood: A Complete Study of the English Outlaw.* Oxford: Blackwell, 1994.
Kumaran, Arul. "Print, Patronage, and the Satiric Pamphlets: The Death of Robert Greene as a Defining Textual Moment." Diss. U of Saskatchewan, 2001.
———. "Robert Greene's Martinist Transformation in 1590." *SP* 103 (2006): 243-63.
Laroque, François. *Shakespeare's Festive World: Elizabethan Seasonal Entertainment and the Professional Stage.* Trans. Janet Lloyd. Cambridge: Cambridge UP, 1991.
Lever, J. W. *The Tragedy of State: A Study of Jacobean Drama.* London: Methuen, 1971.
Levin, Carole. "'Lust Being Lord, There is No Truth in Kings:' Passion, King John, and the Responsibilities of Kingship." *Sexuality and Politics in Renaissance Drama.* Ed. Carole Levin and Karen Robertson. New York: Mellen, 1991. 255-78.
Linebaugh, Peter, and Marcus Rediker. *The Many-Headed Hydra: Sailors, Slaves, Commoners, and the Hidden History of the Revolutionary Atlantic.* Boston: Beacon, 2000.
Logan, Terence P. and Denzell S. Smith, eds. *The Predecessors of Shakespeare: A Survey and Bibliography of Recent Studies in English Renaissance Drama.* Lincoln: U of Nebraska P, 1973.
Lopez, Jeremy. "Time and Talk in *Richard III* I. iv." *SEL* 45 (2005): 299-314.
Maguire, Laurie E. "(Mis)diagnosing Memorial Reconstruction in *John of Bordeaux*." *Medieval and Renaissance Drama in England* 11 (1999): 114-28.
Manley, Lawrence. *Literature and Culture in Early Modern London.* Cambridge: Cambridge UP, 1995.
Marcus, Leah S. "Jonson and the Court." *The Cambridge Companion to Ben Jonson.* Ed. Richard Harp and Stanley Stewart. Cambridge: Cambridge UP, 2000. 30-42.
Marinelli, P. V. *Pastoral.* London: Methuen, 1971.
Massai, Sonia. "Richard Barnfield." *DNB.* Ed. H. C. G. Matthew and Brian Harrison. 3rd ed. Vol. 4. Oxford: Oxford UP, 2004. 1-2.
Marx, Steven. "Shakespeare's Pacifism." *RQ* 45 (1992): 49-95.
McEachern, Claire. *The Poetics of English Nationhood, 1590-1612.* Cambridge: Cambridge UP, 1996.
McKenzie, D. F. "Apprenticeship in the Stationers' Company, 1555-1640." *The Library* 13 (1958): 292-99.
McKerrow, Ronald B., and H. G. Aldis, eds. *A Dictionary of Printers and Booksellers in England, Scotland and Ireland, and of Foreign Printers of English Books 1557-1640.* 1910. London: Bibliographical Society, 1968.
McLane, Paul. *The Shepheardes Calender: A Study in Elizabethan Allegory.* Notre Dame: U of Notre Dame P. 1961. 47-60.

Bibliography

McLuskie, Kathleen. *Dekker and Heywood: Professional Dramatists*. Houndmills: Macmillan, 1994.

McMillin, Scott, and Sally-Beth MacLean. *The Queen's Men and Their Plays*. Cambridge: Cambridge UP, 1998.

McNeill, Fiona. *Poor Women in Shakespeare*. Cambridge: Cambridge UP, 2007.

Meagher, J. C. "Hackwriting and the Huntingdon Plays." *Elizabethan Theatre*. Ed. J. R. Brown and Bernard Harris. *Stratford-Upon-Avon Studies* 9. New York: St. Martin's, 1967. 197-219.

Mehl, Dieter, Angela Stock, and Anne-Julia Zwierlein, eds. *Plotting Early Modern London*. Aldershot: Ashgate, 2004.

Meron, Theodor. *Bloody Constraint: War and Chivalry in Shakespeare*. New York: Oxford UP, 1998.

Merriam, Thomas. "Correspondences in *More* and *Hoffman*." *NQ* 50 (2003): 410-14.

———. "Influence Alone? More on the Authorship of *Titus Andronicus*." *NQ* 243: 304-08.

Merritt, Julia, ed. *Imagining Early Modern London: Perceptions and Portrayals of the City from Stow to Strype, 1598-1720*. Cambridge: Cambridge UP, 2001.

Mentz, Steve. "Forming Greene: Theorizing the Early Modern Author in the *Groatsworth of Wit*." *Writing Robert Greene: Essays on England's First Notorious Professional Writer*. Ed. Kirk Melnikoff and Edward Gieskes. Aldershot: Ashgate, 2008. 115-31.

Mets, G. Harold. "'Voice and Credyt;' the Scholars and *Sir Thomas More*." *Shakespeare and Sir Thomas More. Essays on the Play and Its Shakespearian Interest*. Ed. T. H. Howard-Hill. Cambridge: Cambridge UP, 1989. 11-56.

Monson, Craig. "William Byrd." *DNB*. Ed. H. C. G. Matthew and Brian Harrison. 3rd ed. Vol. 9. Oxford: Oxford UP, 2004. 325-29.

Moore, Helen. "Henry Roberts." *DNB*. Ed. H. C. G. Matthew and Brian Harrison. 3rd ed. Vol. 47. Oxford: Oxford UP, 2004. 166.

Morris, Norval. *The Oxford History of the Prison: The Practice of Punishment in Western Society*. Ed. Norval Morris and David J. Rothman. New York: Oxford UP, 1995.

Motoyama, Tetsuhito. "Shakespeare's and Peele's *Titus Andronicus*: A Critical Re-Examination of a Co-Authored Play." Diss. International Christian University, 2005.

Murphy, Donna. "Did Gabriel Harvey Write *Greene's Groatsworth of Wit*?" *NQ* 54 (2007): 249-53.

Nelson, M. A. "*The Earl of Huntington*: The Renaissance Plays." *Robin Hood: An Anthology of Scholarship and Criticism*. Ed. Stephen Knight. Cambridge: Brewer, 1999.

Netsloff, Mark. *England's Internal Colony: Class, Capital, and the Literature of Early Modern English Colonialism*. New York: Palgrave Macmillan, 2003.

Nicholl, Charles. *A Cup of News: The Life of Thomas Nashe*. London: Routledge and Kegan Paul, 1984.

———. "Thomas Nashe." *DNB*. Ed. H. C. G. Matthew and Brian Harrison. 3rd ed. Vol. 40. Oxford: Oxford UP, 2004. 237-43.

Nolan, J. S. "The Militarization of the Elizabethan State." *The Journal of Military History* 58 (1994): 391-420.

Oakley-Brown, Liz. "Framing Robin Hood: Textuality and Temporality in Anthony Munday's Huntington Plays." *Robin Hood: Medieval and Post-Medieval*. Ed. Helen Phillips. Dublin: Four Courts, 2005. 113-28.

Oliphant, E. H. C. "*Sir Thomas More*." *Journal of English and Germanic Philology* 18 (1919): 226-35.

Orgel, Stephen. *The Authentic Shakespeare and Other Problems of the Early Modern Stage*. New York: Routledge, 2002.

Parker, Geoffrey. *The Military Revolution: Military Innovation and the Rise of the West, 1500-1800*. Cambridge: Cambridge UP, 1988.

Parmenter, M. H. "Spenser's 'Twelve Aeglogues Proportionable to the Twelve Monethes.'" *Journal of English Literary History* 3 (1936): 190-217.

Parr, Anthony. "John Day." *DNB*. Ed. H. C. G. Matthew and Brian Harrison. 3rd ed. Vol. 15. Oxford: Oxford UP, 2004. 587-89.

Partridge, A. C. *Orthography in Shakespeare and Elizabethan Drama: A Study of Colloquial Contractions, Elision, Prosody, Punctuation*. London: Lincoln, 1964.

Patterson, Annabel. *Shakespeare and the Popular Voice*. Cambridge, MA: Basil Blackwell, 1989.

Paylor, W. J. "Thomas Dekker and the 'Overburian' Characters." *The Modern Language Review* 21 (1936): 155-60.

Pechter, Edward. "*Patient Grissil* and the Trials of Marriage." *The Elizabethan Theatre* 14. Ed. A. L. Magnusson and C. E. McGee. Tronto: Meany, 1998. 03-100.

Pelling, Margaret and Charles Webster. "Medical Practitioners." *Health, Medicine and Moralisty in the Sixteenth Century*. Ed. Charles Webster. Cambridge: Cambridge UP, 1979. 165-236.

Pendry, E. D. "Elizabethan Prisons and Prison Scenes." Diss. U of Birmingham, 1954.

Percy, Thomas. *Percy's Reliques of Ancient English Poetry*. Ed. Ernest Rhys. 2 vols. London: J. M. Dent, 1906.

Pesta, Duke. "Articulating Skeletons: Hamlet, Hoffman, and the Anatomical Graveyard." *Cahiers Elisabéthains* 69 (2006): 21-39.

Plant, Majorie. *The English Book Trade: An Economic History of the Making and Sale of Books*. London: George Allen and Unwin, 1939.

Plomer, Henry R. "Bishop Bankroft and a Catholic Press." *The Library* 8 (1907): 164-76.

———. "Thomas East, Printer." *The Library* 2 (1901): 298-310.

Bibliography

Potter, Lois. "Pirates and 'Turning Turk' in Renaissance Drama." *Travel and Drama in Shakespeare's Time*. Ed. Jean-Pierre Maquelot and Michele Willems. Cambridge: Cambridge UP, 1986. 124-40.

Price, G. R. *Thomas Dekker*. New York: Twayne Publishers, 1969.

Pritchard, R. E., ed. *Shakespeare's England: Life in Elizabethan and Jacobean Times*. Stroud: Sutton Publishing, 1999.

Raymond, Joad. *Pamphlets and Pamphleteering in Early Modern Britain*. Cambridge: Cambridge UP, 2003.

Reynolds, Bryan and Henry S. Turner. "From *Homo Academicus* to *Poeta Publicus*: Celebrity and Transversal Knowledge in Robert Greene's *Friar Bacon and Friar Bungay* (c. 1589)." *Writing Robert Greene: Essays on England's First Notorious Professional Writer*. Ed. Kirk Melnikoff and Edward Gieskes. Aldershot: Ashgate, 2008. 73-93.

Rice, Warner G. "A Principal Source of *The Battle of Alcazar*." *MLN* 58 (1943): 428-31.

Ritson, Joseph. *Bibliographia Poetica*. London, 1802.

Rogers, Judith K. "John Danter." *DLB* 170. Ed. James K. Bracken and Joel Silver. Detroit: Gale Research, 1996. 71-77.

Ruff, Lillian M., and D. Arnold Wilson. "Allusion to the Essex Downfall in Lute Song Lyrics." *Lute Society Journal* 12 (1970): 31-36.

———. "The Madrigal, the Lute Song and Elizabethan Politics." *Past and Present* 44 (1969): 3-51.

Rutter, Tom. "*Patient Grissil* and Jonsonian Satire." *SEL* 48 (2008): 283-303.

Salgado, Gamini. *The Elizabethan Underworld*. London: J. M. Dent, 1977.

Salingar, L. G. "Tourneur and the Tragedy of Revenge." Ed. Boris Ford. *The Age of Shakespeare*. Harmondsworth: Penguin, 1955. 334-54.

Sanders, C. E. "Robert Greene and His 'Editors.'" *PMLA* 48 (1933): 392-417.

Saunders, M. A. "*The Tragedy of Hoffman*: A Critical Analysis." Diss. Georgia State U, 1982. Ann Arbor: UMI, 1983.

Schillinger, Stephen. "Begging at the Gate: *Jack Straw* and the Acting Out of Popular Rebellion." *Medieval and Renaissance Drama in England* 21 (2008): 87-127.

Scott, Mary Augusta. *Elizabethan Translations from the Italian*. Boston: Houghton Miffin, 1916.

Senior, Clive. *A Nation of Pirates: English Piracy in Its Heyday*. London: David and Charles, 1976.

Shaaber, M. A. *Some Forerunners of the Newspaper in England 1476-1622*. Philadelphia: U of Pennsylvania P, 1929.

Shapiro, James. "*The Scot's Tragedy* and the Politics of Popular Drama." *English Literary Renaissance* 23 (1993): 428-49.

Sharpe, J. A. *Judicial Punishment in England*. London: Faber and Faber, 1990.
Shaw, Philip. "The Position of Thomas Dekker in Jacobean Literature." *PMLA* 62 (1947): 366-91.
Simpson, Percy. "The Theme of Revenge in Elizabethan Tragedy." *Proceedings of the British Academy* (1935): 101-36.
Singman, Jeffrey L. "Munday's Unruly Earl." *Playing Robin Hood: The Legend as Performance in Five Centuries*. Ed. Lois Potter. Newark: U of Delaware P, 1998. 63-76.
Skretkowicz, Vitor, Jr. "Greville and Sidney: Biographical Addenda." *NQ* 21 (1974): 408-10.
Slack, Paul. "Mirrors of Health and Treasures of Poor Men: The Uses of the Vernacular Medical Literature of Tudor England." *Health, Medicine, and Morality in the Sixteenth Century*. Ed. Charles Webster. Cambridge: Cambridge UP, 1979. 237-74.
———. *Poverty and Policy in Tudor and Stuart England*. London: Longman, 1988.
Slights, William W. E., and Shelly Woloshyn. "English Bess, English Pirates, English Drama: Feminism and Imperialism on the High Seas." *Explorations in Renaissance Culture* 33 (2007): 252-75.
Smith, David, Richard Strier, and David Bevington, eds. *The Theatrical City: Culture, Theatre and Politics in London 1576-1649*. Cambridge: Cambridge UP, 1995.
Smith, Emma. "Henry Chettle." *DNB*. Ed. H. C. G. Matthew and Brian Harrison. 3rd ed. Vol. 11. Oxford: Oxford UP, 2004. 355-56.
Smith, Jeremy L. *Thomas East and Music Publishing in Renaissance England*. Oxford: Oxford UP, 2003.
Smith, L. B. *Treason in Tudor England*. Princeton: Princeton UP, 1986.
Smuts, Malcolm. *Culture and Power in England, 1585-1685*. Houndmills: Macmillan, 1999.
Somogyi, Nick de. *Shakespeare's Theatre of War*. Aldershot: Ashgate, 1998.
Spierenburg, Pieter. "The Body and the State: Early Modern Europe." *The Oxford History of the Prison: Practice of Punishment in Western Society*. Ed. Norval Morris and David J. Rothman. Oxford: Oxford UP, 1995. 44-70.
Stephens, Michell. *A History of News*. 3rd ed. New York: Oxford UP, 2007.
Stoll, E. E. *John Webster*. Boston: Alfred Mudge and Son, 1905.
Stone, Lawrence. *The Family, Sex and Marriage in England 1500-1800*. London: Weidenfeld and Nicolson, 1977.
Swan, Marshall W. S. "The Sweet Speech and Spenser's (?) *Axiochus*." *ELH* 11 (1944): 161-81.
Tannenbaum, Samuel. *The Booke of Sir Thomas Moore: A Bibliotic Study*. New York: Tenny, 1927.
Taunton, Nina. *1590s Drama and Militarism: Portrayals of War in Marlowe, Chapman and*

Bibliography

Shakespeare's Henry V. Aldershot: Ashgate, 2001.
Taylor, Gary. "The Date and Auspices of the Additions to *Sir Thomas More*." *Shakespeare and Sir Thomas More. Essays on the Play and Its Shakespearian Interest*. Ed. T. H. Howard-Hill. Cambridge: Cambridge UP, 1989. 101-29.
Taylor, Gary, and Stanley Wells, ed. *William Shakespeare: A Textual Companion*. Oxford: Oxford UP, 1987.
Thaiss, Christopher J., and Frank Day. "Robert Greene." Ed. Frank N. Magill. *Critical Survey of Drama*. Vol. 3. Rev. ed. Pasadena: Salen, 1994. 1031-42.
Thomas, J. E. *House of Care: Prisons and Prisoners in England 1500-1800*. Longhborough: Echo, 1983.
Thomas, Sidney. "Henry Chettle and the First Quarto of *Romeo and Juliet*." *RES* 1 (1950): 8-16.
———. "The Printing of *Greenes Groatsworth of Witte* and *Kind-Harts Dreame*." *Studies in Bibliography* 19 (1966): 196-97.
Thorndike, A. H. "Hamlet and Contemporary Revenge Plays." *PMLA* 17 (1902): 125-220.
Turner, Celeste. *Anthony Munday: An Elizabethan Man of Letters*. Barkley: U of California P, 1928.
Twyning, John. "Thomas Dekker." *DNB*. Ed. H. C. G. Matthew and Brian Harrison. 3rd ed. Vol. 15. Oxford: Oxford UP, 2004. 697-700.
Ueno, Yoshiko. *Robin Hood Monogatari* [*The Story of Robin Hood*]. Tokyo: Iwanami Shoten, 1998.
———. "Robin Hood Plays and Pastoral: Two Huntington Plays and the Sad Shepherd." *SEL* 19 (1979): 19-36.
Vickers, Brian. *Shakespeare, Co-Author: A Historical Study of Five Collaborative Plays*. Oxford: Oxford UP, 2002.
Waldo, T. R. [Untitled Review of Austin's *A Computer-Aided Technique*.] *Computing and The Humanities* 7 (1972): 109-10.
Watkins, John. *Representing Elizabeth in Stuart England*. Cambridge: Cambridge UP, 2002.
Weatherby, Harold L. "*AXIOCHUS* and the Bower of Bliss: Some Fresh Light on Sources and Authorship." *Spenser Studies* 6 (1986): 95-113.
Webb, Henry J. *Elizabethan Military Science: The Books and the Practice*. Madison: U of Wisconsin P, 1965.
Wells, Stanley. *Shakespeare and Co.: Christopher Marlowe, Thomas Dekker, Ben Jonson, Thomas Middleton, John Fletcher and Other Players in His Story*. London: Penguin Books, 2006.
Westley, Richard. "Computing Error: Reassessing Austin's Study of *Groatsworth of Wit*." *Literary and Linguistic Computing* 21 (2006): 363-78.

Whitworth, Charles. "George Peele." *DLB* 172. Ed. David A. Richardson. Detroit: Gale Research, 1996. 165-70.

Widmann, R. L. [Untitled Review of Austin's *A Computer-Aided Technique*] *SQ* 23 (1972): 214-15.

Williams, Penry. *The Later Tudors: England, 1547-1603*. Oxford: Clarendon, 1995.

———. *The Tudor Regime*. Oxford: Oxford UP, 1979.

Williams, Raymond. *The Country and the City*. New York: Oxford UP, 1973.

Worden, Blair. "Shakespeare and Politics." *Shakespeare and Politics*. Ed. Catherine M. S. Alexander. Cambridge: Cambridge UP, 2004. 22-43.

Wright, C. T. *Anthony Munday: An Elizabethan Man of Letters*. Berkley: U of California P, 1928.

———. "Anthony Munday, 'Edward' Spenser, and E. K." *PMLA* 76 (1961): 34-39.

———. "Young Anthony Munday Again." *SP* 56 (1959): 150-68.

Wurzbach, Natusha. *The Rise of the English Street Ballad*. Cambridge: Cambridge UP, 1990.

Yamada, Akihiro. "Peter Short." *DLB* 170. Ed. James K. Bracken and Joel Silver. Detroit: Gale Research, 1996. 239-43.

———. "Thomas Creede." *DLB* 170. Ed. James K. Bracken and Joel Silver. Detroit: Gale Research, 1996. 65-70.

About the Author:

Marie HONDA is a Lecturer at Toyo University. She reccieved M.A. degrees from Waseda University and the Shakespeare Institute, the University of Birmingham, and her Ph.D. from Waseda University. Her current areas of interest are the relationship between people in the Elizabethan theatrical world and the printing industry, and also the relationship between Early Modern rogue literature and the rise of novel.

Henry Chettle's Careers:
A Study of an Elizabethan Printer, Pamphleteer, Playwright

2015年2月20日 印刷   2015年2月25日 発行

著者© 本 多 ま り え

発行者 佐 々 木 元

制作・発行所 株式会社 英 宝 社
〒101-0032 東京都千代田区岩本町2-7-7 第一井口ビル
☎ [03] (5833) 5870 Fax [03] (5833) 5872

ISBN978-4-269-72134-0 C3098
［製版：㈱マナ・コムレード／印刷：㈱マル・ビ／㈲井上製本所］

定価（本体4,600円＋税）

本書の一部または全部を、コピー、スキャン、デジタル化等での無断複写・複製は、著作権法上での例外を除き禁じられています。本書を代行業者等の第三者に依頼してのスキャンやデジタル化は、たとえ個人や家庭内での利用であっても著作権侵害となり、著作権法上一切認められておりません。